ENTWINED

Lynda La Plante was born in Liverpool in 1946. She trained for the stage at RADA, and work with the National Theatre and RSC led to a career as a television actress. She turned to writing - and made her breakthrough with the phenomenally successful TV series *Widows*. Her four subsequent novels, *The Legacy, Bella Mafia, Entwined* and *Cold Shoulder,* were all international best-sellers.

Her original script for the much acclaimed *Prime Suspect* won a BAFTA award, British Broadcasting award, Royal Television Society Writers award and the 1993 Edgar Allan Poe Writers award and the novelization of the series won the prestigious Prix du Roman d'Aventure award. Lynda La Plante also received the Contribution to the Media award by Women in Films, and most recently, a BAFTA award and an Emmy for the drama serial *Prime Suspect 3*.

The latest blockbuster novelization of her hit TV series, *She's Out,* the sequel to *Widows,* and the hard-hitting drama about prison life, *The Governor I* and *II,* and also published by Pan Books.

Entwined

LYNDA LA PLANTE

PAN BOOKS

First published 1992 by Sidgwick & Jackson

This edition published 1993 by Pan Books
an imprint of Macmillan Publishers Ltd
25 Eccleston Place, London SW1W 9NF
and Basingstoke

Associated companies throughout the world

ISBN 0 330 32327 X

12 14 16 18 19 17 15 13

A CIP catalogue record for this book is available from
the British Library.

Typeset by Cambridge Composing (UK) Limited, Cambridge
Printed and bound in Great Britain by
Mackays of Chatham PLC, Chatham Kent

La Plante dedicates *Entwined* to a wonderful mentor, a woman she worked closely with for many years, who died shortly after the editorials for *Entwined* were completed. Jeanne F. Bernkopf was a constant encouragement, a source of inspiration who will be sadly missed, a consummate professional whose advice and dedicated work will never be forgotten. Goodbye, dear Jeanne F. Bernkopf, and thank you.

AUTHOR'S NOTE

Of the estimated three thousand twins – most of them
young children – who passed through Mengele's
experimental laboratories at Auschwitz between 1943 and
1944, less than two hundred were known to have survived.
Their survival rate had been less than ten per cent. Theirs
was the untold story of the Holocaust.

CHAPTER ONE

HYLDA DIEKMANN moved silently across the sitting room of the exclusive hotel suite and paused to check her appearance in one of the floor-to-ceiling gilt mirrors. Her dress had seen better times – but, then, so had the hotel. It was not back to its original splendour, but it heralded the changing times. East Berlin was free; that nightmare Wall had come down.

Hylda stood by the sashed windows. She could see, way below in the street, the hotel porters in their new red and gold uniforms. She had not been told who booked the suite, and she waited with excitement. An adjoining smaller suite had also been reserved; there would be no other guests to disturb the penthouse occupants.

From the windows Hylda saw a black Mercedes limousine glide to the entrance and a tall man in a fur-collared coat step from the front passenger seat. He gestured to the porters for the luggage to be removed from the boot of the car as a second car drew up behind them carrying more luggage. A blonde woman, wearing a bright red coat, was assisted out of the rear of the Mercedes. She turned to speak to the fur-collared gentleman as a second woman, wearing a dark coat and hat, hurried from the second car. All three conferred, before bending to the remaining passenger, still seated in the Mercedes. Before Hylda could see who was about to leave the car, the double doors to the suite opened.

An array of matching fawn leather cases and trunks was wheeled in on a cart. Hylda directed the porter towards the master bedroom, then turned to see a second cart containing more leather travel bags. The suite was suddenly filled with movement: the porters removed the cases and placed them on luggage racks; champagne was brought in by a flustered waiter with a large silver ice bucket and tall fluted glasses, iced and ready for use, followed by a young waiter with caviar, finely chopped onions and egg whites, arranged on a scalloped crystal dish.

In swept the assistant manager, his face red from the rush up the stairs. He moved a champagne glass one inch, waved frantically for the porters to leave, then snapped instructions to the waiters. He came over to Hylda and told her that he was not sure if her services would be required: the Baroness appeared to have her own lady's maid.

Hylda could hear voices in the corridor speaking in French; the manager's stilted, heavy-accented replies were in English. 'You will be assured of the utmost privacy . . . please, this way.'

Baron Louis Maréchal, his fur-collared coat now hanging loosely on his shoulders, swept in. He was an exceptionally handsome man, grey-white wings at the side of his temples, his thick hair combed back from his high forehead. He wore a grey pin-striped suit and an oyster-grey tie with a diamond pin. The heavy gold ring on his left hand gleamed as he gestured to the suite.

The Baron turned as the woman in the red coat, carrying a square leather vanity case, was ushered in. The Baron again gestured to the rooms, as the manager directed them to the bedrooms. They remained at the doorway, turning to the corridor as a rather plain, drab young woman entered. She, too, carried a square leather vanity case, but paid no attention to the room, looking back down the corridor.

'Madame . . . please.'

Baroness Maréchal paused at the open doorway. It

2

seemed as if everyone held their breath in anticipation of her approval. She was very tall and so slim that her black mink stole appeared to weigh her down. Her gloved hands rested on the fur. She wore large dark black-rimmed glasses that hid most of her face. Her black hair was cut short, almost boyishly. She gave the impression of feather lightness, as if at any moment she would faint, or fall, or float. She moved like a dancer, quick light steps as she walked into the suite.

She let her wrap drop, and the young woman was at her side to retrieve it. The Baroness turned, almost spinning, and her voice was husky as she exclaimed: 'Champagne! Chandelier! Flowers! Caviar! Louis – it is divine!' She was everywhere in a rush of energy, touching and admiring, running like a girl to the bedroom suite, throwing wide the doors. As if by magic she brought the sun into the room . . . and yet her face, her eyes, her expression remained hidden.

Hylda blushed as the tall willowy figure rushed to her side. She was introduced to the Baroness Vebekka Maréchal, and there was a lovely gurgling laugh as the Baroness repeated: 'Lady's maid, lady's maid! My lady's maid – but how divine! Do I have you all to myself, Hylda? I do? Well, isn't that lovely! Louis! My very own lady's maid. I love this hotel – this hotel is the most divine hotel. Close your eyes, Louis, we have travelled back in time!' Hylda saw the look that passed between the Baroness's own maid and the woman in the red coat.

The room, as if by unspoken command from the Baron, had emptied. The Baroness didn't appear to notice as she continued in her light, dancer's steps from one side of the room to the next. Hylda asked the Baron if she was to unpack the Baroness's clothes. He turned, smiling, clicking his heels. 'Yes, Hylda, immediately.' The Baron spoke German quite well. He introduced Hylda to Anne Maria, the young woman, and then to the woman in red, Dr Helen Masters, a family friend, who would be using the adjoining suite.

Hylda's head was spinning – she felt so unsure of herself – but then the Baroness was at her side, cupping her chin in her hands. Her height meant that she had to look down into Hylda's startled face. 'Hylda, do you speak English? You do? Good. Then, Hylda, we shall be able to talk to each other. I don't speak German, I apologise, Hylda. Hylda, we shall become good friends.'

The Baroness jumped as her mink stole was slipped around her shoulders but the Baron gripped his wife's elbow, whispered something to her, and guided her out of the room. Hylda looked over the stacked trunks and was about to open one when Anne Maria returned. She pointed to three cases and asked for them to be taken to her quarters. Hylda nodded, and attempted her English. 'I hope to be of good service, if you need for me to do special, you ask me, yes? You are the Baroness's maid, yes?'

Anne Maria paused at the doorway. 'No, I am not the Baroness's maid. I am . . .' She hesitated, but said no more, closing the door behind her.

Hylda opened the first of the Baroness's standing trunks and began to put away the garments in the wardrobe. One trunk contained silk lingerie, the delicate silks and fine embroidery reminiscent of bygone days, many embroidered with the letter V. In all the trunks not one item appeared ever to have been worn; even the rows of shoes looked new and each pair had a small handwritten note tucked inside, giving details of the matching handbag and scarf, the colours all co-ordinated: muted soft fawns, palest oyster pinks and blues. Hylda read one designer label after another.

The large leather vanity case which the woman in red had carried was placed at the side of the bed. Hylda carried

4

it into the maid's room, and could not resist a peep inside. It was not, as she had expected, filled with jewels or make-up, but with bottles and bottles of pills.

Just then, the doors burst open. The Baroness hurried in and called out for Anne Maria to come to the bedroom. Hylda tapped on the bedroom door and the Baroness wheeled round to face her, startled. 'Hylda! I can't remember if I carried my jewel-box in with me. It's a square, dark blue leather box.'

Hylda looked around the room; she could not recall seeing it. The Baroness rushed to the dressing-table. A vanity case, smaller than the one Hylda had placed in Anne Maria's room, was stashed on a shelf beneath the mirrored top. The Baroness hugged it tightly. Hylda watched the Baroness take small silver-framed photographs from it and place them on her bedside table. She then gestured for Hylda to come to her side. 'My children, my two daughters, Sasha, Sophia, and my sons . . .'

Hylda studied the photographs of the smiling children, no more than toddlers . . .

The Baroness's hands fluttered constantly, touching her mouth, her hair . . . She was sure she had lost her make-up, her hair brushes. She began to rifle through the unpacked clothes, throwing garments to the floor. 'My make-up box, where is my make-up box?'

Anne Maria walked in and said rather sharply that there was no vanity case downstairs. The Baroness said she had found it but now she was looking for the navy-blue box, her make-up box. Hylda stood silently as if she were part of the furnishings: she was confused about the vanity cases, or boxes, or indeed how many there were.

'The photographs . . . you've unpacked the box, Baroness!'

The Baroness retorted that she had found her children, but now she could not find the other case. She was on her hands and knees, looking beneath the bed, when the Baron walked into the room, carrying yet another square case, placing it on the bed.

'I think, dearest, you should rest, it's been a long journey. Hylda, please run a bath for the Baroness.' He turned to his wife. 'Darling, do you want your jewels put into the hotel safe?'

'*No!* I want them with me!' She held tightly to the jewel-box. He raised his hands.

'All right, all right, but take care of them.' He turned to Hylda, his face set with anger. 'Run her bath – she needs to rest!'

The bath was filled with oils and perfumes and the towels were warming on the heated rails. Hylda tested the water. The Baroness, wrapped in a white towelling robe and still wearing her glasses, was singing at the top of her voice as she let the robe drop. She was skeleton-thin, her body white-skinned – the body of a young girl. She handed Hylda her dark glasses, and then stepped into the bath. 'Hylda, will you order some hot chocolate and biscuits – chocolate biscuits.'

The Baroness was not as young as Hylda had at first thought. The tell-tale signs of age showed beneath her chin, the skin a little loose, and around her mouth were fine lines, as also around her eyes, big dark amber eyes, very bright. Like a child she submerged herself in the soapy water, blowing at the bubbles; then she lay back and let the water cover her face, her dark hair fanning out. Hylda heard the soft low voice whispering . . . 'I am drowning . . . drowning . . .'

Unsure if she had heard correctly Hylda moved closer, but then stepped back as the Baroness submerged her head deeper. She was transfixed, as first the Baroness's hands

6

broke the surface of the water like a ballet dancer's, then her back arched, the nipples of her small breasts lifted, and lastly her face emerged, cheeks puffed out. Like a child at play she spurted a stream of water from her mouth.

Hylda gave a light, nervous laugh, but the Baroness seemed unaware of her presence. As she slowly submerged herself again, Hylda left the bathroom and didn't hear the low gurgled voice, distorted by the water, as the Baroness repeated again, 'Drowning . . . help me.'

The Baron was sipping a cocktail in the sitting room with Dr Masters. From the bedroom, Hylda could hear their voices, mingled with soft laughter. She busied herself putting away the array of cosmetics, perfumes and powders. The Baroness had tried on and discarded a number of shoes; she was still barefoot and the black crêpe gown she had chosen to wear to dinner was trailing the floor.

Hylda saw her cross to the wardrobe, then move back to the dressing-table. She repeated the movement twice but took nothing from the wardrobe, nor did she look at herself in the mirror. Then the Baroness quickened her pace and arched her back, her hands in front of her as if pushing something away. She caught Hylda's reflection in her dressing-table mirror, saw that she was being watched, and didn't like it: her lips pulled back over her teeth and her body arched again, like a cat's. Hylda was mesmerised.

The moment was broken as the Baron entered, took one look at his wife, ordered Hylda from the room and called out for Anne Maria, at the same time gripping his wife's wrists. Anne Maria entered the bedroom with the case of pills and slammed the door behind her. Hylda heard screams of terror mixed with a stream of abuse in French and English. Then there was silence.

When the Baron left the bedroom, he found Hylda still

7

waiting. 'My wife is very sick, she is in Berlin to get treatment. I would be grateful if you did not repeat what you have seen tonight.'

Hylda nodded, murmured that she was going home, but added, 'I will be here in the morning.'

'I think not, Anne Maria will take care of her needs.'

Helen Masters hurried into the bedroom and found him looking at the toothmarks in his hand, his head bowed. 'She bit me, like a dog! An animal.'

'She's quiet now . . . Do you want a brandy?'

He shook his head. 'I've seen this coming on all day. She gets excited, a rush of energy and then she explodes with this terrible rage, always against – it's against me.'

'I know, Louis. Here, drink this.'

He ignored her. 'It's as if she hates me, hates her children . . . She attacked Sasha. Sasha! I think she's going to kill someone – me probably!'

Helen stood by the mantelpiece, running her fingers along the cold marble carving. She felt uneasy, she had never spent time alone with the Baron, except for brief meetings when he came to collect Vebekka from her office. It had been her decision to travel to Berlin with them, taking two weeks' holiday break to do so, and now she realised how deeply she was becoming involved. She had suggested that they consult Dr Franks, her mentor and former teacher, because Vebekka was clearly beyond her help; this evening more than substantiated that. 'I have not seen her this bad, but that is all the more reason to take her to Dr Franks.'

She looked at the Baron, whose face was taut with anger. She chose her next words carefully. 'Dr Franks will have to ask you a lot of personal questions – he'll need to probe into the background of her illness, which means your background, your marriage.'

Louis drained his glass and sprang to his feet. 'Illness! Everyone she has been to has cloaked her madness with a name. Well? What do you think, now you've seen her in the midst of one of her furies?'

Helen coughed. 'She is obviously very distressed tonight—'

'Distressed? You tell me she has been like this with you?' he snapped.

'No, but I was aware the journey might upset her, and her behaviour was not unexpected. Now, if you'll excuse me, I'll go to my room.'

Louis gave a small disarming bow. 'I'm sorry, you must be tired, forgive me. Will you dine with me?'

Helen paused by the door, and half turned. 'You have nothing to be sorry for, I understand this must be a very emotional time for you.'

He gave a wonderful smile, all his previous anger melted, as if the trouble had not occurred. 'Can I order dinner?'

'Thank you, but no, I'll just have a sandwich in my room. Goodnight.'

He did not press the issue further. 'Goodnight, Helen.' As she left, he noticed that she had very shapely legs. He picked up his brandy glass, rolled the liquid around the bowl before taking a sip, then pursed his lips, reprimanding himself for allowing his mind to wonder what the neat Dr Masters would look like with her oh-so-neat chignon loosened to her shoulders.

Vebekka was unaware of whether it was day or night but she knew it had happened again, though she was beyond remembering what she had done, what she had said or who

9

she had hurt this time. The strange room, with its ceiling so far away . . . Why did they not understand? How many strange rooms had she been brought to over the years? She stared at the ornate chandelier above the bed, and wondered if, half hoped that, it would fall and crush her to death. Why had she agreed to come to this place? Why had she insisted they stay in East Berlin? *Had* she insisted? She could not remember. She could not remember why Louis had brought her to Berlin.

The tranquillisers made her thirsty; she slipped out of bed and stood by the adjoining room's partly open door. Louis was sleeping, one arm crooked over his face, the other spread across the empty space next to him. She had often watched him sleeping, sometimes for hours, fascinated by the contours of his handsome face. Vebekka moved silently around the bed, sniffing, closer and closer to him. She was close enough to touch him, wanted to lie in the crook of his arm, wanted to slip her hand into his, but she could see the dark red bruises, the toothmarks, and she crept out, knowing she had subjected him to yet more violence. She wanted to weep, but she had wept too many times for too many years. She knew she had alienated him – and even her children. It was a terrible thing to see the fear in their eyes if she laughed too loudly, called out too sharply; no matter what assurance she gave, the fear hung in the air. And, lately, she had no longer known when she was well. She could no longer fight it. It was just a matter of time before she was swallowed by the darkness.

The streets were empty but as she stared at the curtained window, someone called out down below, a disembodied voice, and made the panic swamp her. It was coming, it was beginning.

'Oh, please, dear God, no.'

She tried to draw back the dark green curtain, but her

hand pulled away. Something was crawling inside the curtain, she didn't want it to open. Her heart began to beat rapidly and she couldn't catch her breath. She was suffocating. She whispered, for someone, anyone, to help her, she didn't want the curtain to open.

She felt her hands tighten, the nails cut into her palm. Her right hand clenched into a fist and she began to make heavy downward punches. Deep, dark, blazing flashes burned across her eyes, and a red rage took hold. Now both hands clenched together in hammer blows. She knew she had to stop, had to turn the rage onto herself. The blows would not stop, could not stop. She picked up a heavy marble ashtray, began banging it against the table until it cracked and shattered, but the blood-red blaze was still there, still blinding her.

Anne Maria had heard the muffled sounds, the breaking glass, and quickly checking the Baroness's room, found the bed empty. Panicked, she ran into the adjoining bathroom where she found Vebekka, naked, curled up by the toilet. She had slashed her arm with a razor. The tiles and floor were covered with blood. She was weeping, saying over and over she wanted to leave Berlin. As Anne Maria touched her, she struggled and kicked out viciously. She wanted to be taken home, she wanted to die. Her voice rose to a screech as she cried out that it was here, it had come for her, it was here, it was taking over, and they should let her die.

Anne Maria woke Helen Masters, and the two women sedated Vebekka and together carried her to her bed. The struggle had exhausted her, and at last she seemed calm. They waited until she fell into a deep sleep.

It was a sleep of nightmare dreams, unknown terrors, a terror no one could understand. As the darkness swamped her, she was powerless to tell them to stop the demons, the devils in white coats who worked on her brain when she slept. She fought against the induced sleep, but she was helpless.

Anne Maria had left, and Helen Masters sat by Vebekka's bedside, her head throbbing; she inched open the shutters to get some fresh air, staring down into the dark street below. She was startled when the Baron opened the adjoining door and looked in. He was still half asleep, his hair unruly. 'What happened?'

She flushed, drawing her dressing-gown closer. 'Rather a lot, but she's quiet now. I'll stay with her.'

He crossed to the bed and leaned over Vebekka, gently brushed her hair from her brow and rested his hand against her cheek. 'My poor baby.' He saw her wrist was bandaged, lifted her hand, kissing the palm, and then tucked it beneath the duvet. As he returned to his bedroom, he said to Helen, 'I am glad you are here.' The door closed silently behind him, and Helen concentrated on her patient, sleeping deeply, her face, in repose, like an innocent child's.

At 10.30 a.m. Hylda was ushered into the suite. The Baron was dressed and taking a late breakfast in the restaurant with Dr Masters. Anne Maria whispered to Hylda that the Baroness had specifically asked for her lady's maid to assist her dressing, but that Hylda must make no mention of what had occurred the previous evening. The Baroness had been taken ill during the night, but she was calm now. 'Don't worry, she won't do anything, she's sedated, she may not even remember she asked for you.'

Hylda entered the bedroom, smiled and murmured, 'Good morning.' The Baroness's hair and make-up were immaculate, and she had painted her nails a dark crimson. Her eyes were expressionless, her voice low, husky. 'I apologise if I caused you any embarrassment yesterday.' She pushed her breakfast tray away. The glass of fresh orange juice was untouched, there was an almost full cup of black coffee. The bread, however, had been carefully rolled into balls: small grey pellets surrounded her place setting.

While Hylda helped the Baroness to dress, not a word was spoken. She spent a long time deciding what she would wear, touching the clothes, holding them against herself. She chain-smoked, taking no more than two or three puffs of the gold-tipped cigarettes before she stubbed them out. She carefully placed into a small black clutch bag a gold cigarette case, a lighter, a handkerchief and a gold compact. Nothing else, no wallet or cards.

The Baroness had tried on three hats before she was satisfied. She flipped open the jewel-box, her hand shaking badly as it hovered over the array. She removed an ornate brooch of a tiger's head and then seemed upset and let it fall back into the suede-lined box before she withdrew an exquisite sapphire and diamond bluebird clip. She held it to the light, smiling, whispering to herself, oblivious to Hylda.

The Baroness sat patiently by the drawing-room window and smoked while she waited for the Baron to come for her. She had eventually pinned the bluebird to the side of her hat; the bird's exquisite wings glittered as if about to take flight.

Hylda remained in the bedroom, but could see the Baroness clearly from the open doors. Anne Maria was watching from her own room, the door ajar. The seated, immaculate woman appeared unaware of their presence. Both saw the Baron come in and take his wife's arm,

13

watched her withdraw from him and his head bend to whisper to her that she must come. Finally she gave way to his quiet persistence.

Before leaving the apartment, the Baroness gave the sweetest of smiles to Hylda, then put on her dark glasses and bowed her head. But not before Hylda had seen the fear in the beautiful eyes.

After they had left, Hylda looked over the breakfast table. 'The Baroness did not eat anything,' she said with motherly concern.

Anne Maria nodded to the small balls of bread. 'She always does that, or hides food in her pocket.'

'She seemed very frightened.'

'She's always frightened, frightened of doctors, frightened of anyone in a white coat.' Anne Maria gave a soft smile. 'They are going to hypnotise her – she's always refused before.'

Hylda placed the blood-stained towels into a laundry bag. 'Have you worked for Baron Maréchal long?' she asked Anne Maria.

'Five years, I think I'm number thirteen . . . unlucky. Not many stay long: when she's nice, she's very very nice and those times, well, obviously I am not needed, but when she's bad, she's – she can be very dangerous. I was told not to tell you, but you should know, especially since she has taken quite a liking to you. Don't trust her, these violent moods seem to come on without reason, she just goes crazy, and she'll go for you like an animal, so be prepared.'

Hylda pursed her lips and continued to tidy the room. Anne Maria drew the curtains back from the window. 'I used to like her, she was the kindest, sweetest woman I had ever met. I also felt deeply sorry for her.' She turned to Hylda. 'She was exceptionally kind to me and my little daughter.' She let the curtains fall back. 'But she can be so hurtful, say such terrible things, things you cannot forget, or forgive. She is evil, and she is very strong. So be warned, when she turns, get out. Just run away from her – all the others did . . . but I need the money.' She sipped the orange juice, looking at the small pellets of bread.

'They brought her to Berlin to see some specialist. I doubt it'll help. We've been visiting doctors for years, but there's little that can be done with schizophrenia, apart from controlling it, and she won't take her pills. I've waited and watched her, sure she's swallowed them but then I find . . . she holds them under her tongue, you see, so I am not to be blamed, what happened last night was not my fault, she must have spat out the pills, and I get the blame.'

The Mercedes moved slowly through a group of jeering students. It was almost time for the yearly celebrations to begin marking the fall of the Wall. The students gathered by a café set up in an old barracks, the ominous sentry box, now swathed in ribbons. They shouted abuse, their shorn heads and leather jackets, their boots and jeers directed towards the sleek car. Their raised voices frightened Vebekka. She sat between Dr Masters and the Baron, her hands clasping and unclasping in her fine black leather gloves.

The Baron took a hand and held it tightly. 'It'll be all right, no one is going to hurt you.'

When she replied, her husky voice was almost inaudible. 'It's close, Louis, it's so close I can feel it. You should take me away from this place, please, I've never felt it so close to me before, I'm so scared.'

Helen Masters looked at the Baron, and then turned to stare out of the window. It took her by surprise: Vebekka's small gloved hand reaching for hers, holding on tightly. They both held a hand, as if she were a child, and they could both feel her body shaking.

CHAPTER TWO

DR FRANKS'S waiting room was comfortable, with deep sofas and coffee tables. The receptionist and secretary were kind and friendly, offering coffee or tea, trying to make the patients feel relaxed and at ease.

Franks had been told that the Baroness had a deep distrust of anyone wearing a white coat, so he strolled into the reception room in a sweater and shirt, his hands stuffed into his old cord trousers. He was sixty-nine years old. His craggy face and gnarled hands belied his sharp-eyed nature; he was a man who could smile warmly, but his eyes would bore into you.

The Baron shook the doctor's hand and Helen kissed him warmly. Without waiting to be introduced, Dr Franks moved to the sofa and sat beside Vebekka. He took her hand and kissed it. 'Baroness, there is nothing to be afraid of. I will spend most of my time today with your husband. You will chat with my nurse and my assistant . . . Maybe tomorrow you and I will spend some time together. Would you like coffee? Or tea?'

Vebekka kept her head down and withdrew her hand; she said nothing.

'Helen, will you stay here, or do you want to sit in on the sessions?' asked Franks.

Helen bent her head to try to meet Vebekka's eyes. 'Would you like me to stay with you? Vebekka?'

The Baroness looked up, and her wide amber eyes met Dr Franks's. 'I will stay here. I am quite capable of being left on my own, thank you, doctor.'

Dr Franks noticed the way she recoiled from Helen, as if she did not want her touch. He gestured towards Maja, his assistant, to indicate she should stay with his patient, but Vebekka paid no attention. Nor did she see Maja switch on a tape-recorder; she was too busy reaching forward to the coffee table as Dr Franks, the Baron and Helen Masters left the room.

A child's worn storybook lay on the table for younger patients; Vebekka slipped it beneath her coat. Maja pretended she saw nothing. She sat opposite Vebekka, as the elegant woman slowly began to inch the child's book into her handbag.

Maja waited patiently, watching as Vebekka looked around the room. Their conversation would be recorded so that Dr Franks could listen to it before he began a formal session with his patient.

'Will they be a long time?' the Baroness asked.

Maja smiled. 'Knowing Dr Franks, the answer is yes.'

The lovely throaty giggle took Maja by surprise. 'Oh, my husband won't like that, I'm supposed to be the crazy one.' Maja laughed, and Vebekka reached over and tapped her knee. 'I've forgotten your name!'

'Everything you can tell me will be of interest and importance.'

The Baron sat opposite Dr Franks, asked if he might smoke, and lit a cigar without waiting for a reply. Helen Masters had drawn up a chair, not too close to the doctor.

'Tell me everything you know of your wife's childhood, her relationship to her parents and family, how many brothers and sisters, etc. I see from the files there is very little recorded on her background.'

The Baron shrugged his shoulders. 'I know very little. I met Vebekka in Paris, 1961, when she was twenty-two

17

years old. We married two years later, but the year I met her, her mother died, and then in 1972 her father died. I never met either of them. They were originally from Canada, then emigrated to Philadelphia when Vebekka was still quite young. She is an only child, and I have never met any relative – she has said there is no one. All I know is that her parents were wealthy, and that on her father's death Vebekka was left a considerable amount of money. When I have questioned her about her childhood she has always said it was unexceptional, but very happy. She speaks fondly of her parents.'

Franks seemed to doodle on a notepad. 'So your wife is not French by birth?'

'No, Canadian, but she has always spoken fluent French. Doctor, I have questioned my wife over the years to determine if any other member of her family suffered a similar illness. After all, I have four children . . .'

'Has she made any mention of mental illness in her family?'

The Baron's lips tightened. 'No. She is adamant about that. She can recall no member of her immediate family ever being ill.'

'Does she speak about her family?'

The Baron hesitated, only a moment, then shook his head. 'No, she has never really discussed that part of her life with me. In fact when I offered to accompany her to her father's funeral, she refused. Perhaps I should mention that my own family were very much against my marriage. I was the heir, an only son, my family felt Vebekka was not a suitable match, I was only twenty-three years old myself.'

'Do you know if there is any possible way we can contact anyone who knew your wife in America?'

The Baron flicked his cigar ash. 'I know of no one, but if you think it is important, I can try to trace someone.'

'It is, believe me, of the utmost importance. I would

appreciate your trying to find any documents, medical or scholastic, schools, friends, anyone who knew your wife in her early childhood.'

The Baron nodded his agreement, and the doctor leaned back in his chair. 'So you met your wife in Paris . . .' He gestured for the Baron to continue.

'She was an in-house model for Dior. I was at a function with my mother. We met, I asked if Vebekka would dine with me, and she accepted. We were married two years later as I have said, my first son was born ten months after that, 1964 – he is twenty-seven – my second son was born eighteen months later and my first daughter after another eighteen months. My fourth child, Sasha, is only twelve years old.'

The doctor swivelled in his chair. 'Is your wife, or was she, a good mother?'

The Baron nodded, again flicking his cigar ash. 'Excellent, very loving but firm. They adored her. They are all well adjusted, normal children. However, of late her behaviour has greatly disturbed them.' The Baron stared into space and then looked down at his hands. 'My younger daughter has suffered the most. Perhaps it was unwise for us to have her. Vebekka's breakdowns had begun before Sasha was born.'

The doctor again motioned for the Baron to continue, but noted how agitated he was becoming.

'After the birth of each of my sons she was depressed and unstable, twice spending some time in a clinic.'

'So you think her illness is connected in some way to the children?' asked Dr Franks.

'No, no, I have always had nannies to oversee them – she never had any responsibility, nothing that would put pressure on her, I always made sure of that. I am in a financial position to make her life very comfortable. We have the family château outside Paris, a summer villa in

Cannes and two apartments – one in London and another in New York.'

Dr Franks interrupted him. 'Explain how she behaved during pregnancy, and after the births.'

The Baron began twisting his signet ring round and round. 'She had a fear the baby would be born deformed, which became obsessive. She insisted on visiting her doctors sometimes five times a week. Midway through a pregnancy the fear of producing a malformed child made her even consider an abortion even though her doctors insisted her pregnancy was normal. After the birth, after being told the baby was perfectly well, she seemed to sink into a terrible despair, a depression, not wanting to hold the baby, touch it. She seemed almost afraid of it, but then the depression would lift, and she would be exhilarated, checking the child out, inspecting every finger and toe, looking for any possible problems. I thank God there was none.'

'When, in your opinion, did you detect a severe behaviour pattern, or breakdown as you call it, not connected to her pregnancies?'

The Baron still twisted his signet ring round his finger as he answered, 'There have been so many, but the worst breakdown occurred – it was totally unexpected, it came out of the blue – after a lengthy period when she had been so well I believed our problems were all in the past. Then she became as obsessive about having another child – we had two sons by then – as she had been about them being born with some disease. She wanted a daughter, and so, when she did recover, I gave way, partly because she had been so well and stable . . .'

Dr Franks frowned and tapped his desk with his forefinger. 'But you have two daughters, so the same pattern continued some years later when your second daughter was born, er . . . Sasha, yes?'

The Baron nodded, and then gestured with his hands,

shrugging. 'Sasha was – how do you say? – not expected, and my wife's gynaecologist suggested terminating the pregnancy.' He paused, crossing his legs, and again he gave the slight shrugging gesture with his hands. 'It was unacceptable, the termination, on two counts. I am Catholic, and . . .'

Franks waited for him to continue, but the Baron seemed disinclined to embroider on the religious aspect.

'So now tell me, in your opinion, when did the problems begin that were not directly linked to the births of your children?'

The Baron sighed. 'The birth of Sasha was not as traumatic for my wife, in fact she recovered quite quickly. Sasha was doted upon, spoiled I suppose. She is the most delightful child, and the one most physically like my wife. I really felt the problems were over, but they began again. This time my wife said, or felt, that someone was taking over her body.'

'So that culminated in another breakdown?'

The Baron stubbed out his cigar and clenched his hands. 'Yes. We were in Monaco for the polo season and Vebekka took the children to a circus. During one of the acts, I don't recall which one, my wife began to behave strangely, she kept on getting out of her seat, she appeared to want to get into the circus ring herself. She became abusive when she was restrained by one of the ushers – she was screaming about the clown – it was a midget or a dwarf but she was screaming at him, totally hysterical. She somehow got into the ring from her seat, physically attacked the clown, and by the time I was called she had been taken, incoherent, to a hospital and sedated. That was the first time she had actually been violent, to my knowledge. Since that time, her violence and irrational behaviour have grown. She has attacked every member of the family, including myself. Sasha is very much afraid of her.'

'Are you saying she has physically attacked her own daughter?'

'No, no, not actually gone for her, but she has destroyed Sasha's possessions.'

'I don't understand, what do you mean?'

The Baron looked to Helen, and then back to Franks. 'The child's toys, her dolls, she . . . she breaks them, burns them, destroys them.'

Franks muttered, and then leaned back in his chair. 'Has she ever been self-abusive, hurt herself in any way?'

'Very often, she has tried to kill herself countless times, in fact she attempted to do so in the hotel last night. But surely you have her medical history?'

Dr Franks raised his bushy eyebrows. 'Of course, but I would like to hear first-hand. Please continue.' Again he noted the way the Baron looked to Helen Masters, as if for approval, or out of embarrassment, he couldn't surmise which.

'Dr Franks, this present attack has been coming on, or building, in my estimation, for weeks . . . It was Helen's suggestion that with a possible attack imminent, this would be the best time for you to see her. I think Vebekka agreed because of Sasha.'

'If I decide that I can help your wife, would you agree to her staying in my clinic even though I cannot tell how long she will need to be there?'

'Dr Franks, if you can help my wife, I will agree to anything you suggest. I cannot subject my children, myself, to any more torment. I have had enough.'

The silence in the room felt ominous, as if in some way accusing, and the doctor could see a small muscle twitching at the side of the Baron's mouth. 'Do you regret marrying your wife, Baron?'

The Baron pursed his lips. 'That is an impossible question. I have four beautiful children, of course I do not

22

regret marrying. But my sons, my daughters must know if this illness is hereditary. I need to know, that must be understandable – if my wife is to be institutionalised it will affect each and every one of us. You are my last hope, Dr Franks.'

Franks coughed. 'Tell me about the first time you noticed your wife behave in an irrational manner.'

The Baron leaned back and raised his eyes to the ceiling. 'You have all her records, doctor, is this really necessary?'

'Yes, yes, it is.'

The Baron remained silent for at least half a minute, then sighed. 'She was four months pregnant with my first son, she was very beautiful, and being pregnant even more so. She took great care of herself, she ate well, good healthy food, and seemed content and very happy, we both were. We were very much in love, exceptionally close, idyllically happy. One night I woke up, and she was not beside me. I searched for her, called out for her. I found her in the kitchen, food everywhere, eating, stuffing food into her mouth, she must have been doing it for some time because there was vomit on the floor, over the table, and . . . she was eating it, her own vomit. Her face was rigid, she was like a stranger. It was terrible.'

Franks interrupted, holding up his hand. They could hear laughter from the next room. Helen stood up, as if prepared to go into the reception area, but Franks waved his hand. 'Maja is with her – she is very adept at relaxing my patients . . . seems she has succeeded!'

Vebekka had been telling Maja, the doctor's assistant, about her days as a model: the behind-the-scenes gossip and back-biting. She was entertaining, witty, and the more she relaxed the more animated she became. She stood up to demonstrate how she had first been taught by the

Madame at Dior to cat-walk: arching her back at an angle, pushing forward her hips and parading up and down the small waiting room.

'You know how many models have back trouble? I mean, can you imagine any sane person walking in this way?' She swivelled on her heel, turning to demonstrate, and then she glided to the sofa and sat. 'The gowns were spectacular, and it was amusing for us to see which celebrity bought which design. Can you imagine the fun we had, seeing those superb works of art adorning the most frumpy, the most rotund women?'

Maja was entertained – it was difficult not to be – but she also detected a strange wariness. Vebekka's eyes constantly strayed to the closed door and she would fall silent, sometimes in mid-sentence, and then quickly recover and launch into a different story. Maja did not attempt to steer her into discussing how she felt, knowing it would either come out naturally or not at all. But, as adept as she was, she was still taken by surprise when suddenly, in one quick move, Vebekka gripped her wrist.

'What are they doing in there? Why are they taking so long?'

Maja made no move to withdraw her hand.

'He's talking about me, isn't he? Of course, stupid question, stupid question.' She released her hold, and her hand went to her hair, patting it in place.

'He may not speak with you today, but he needs to know so much about you,' Maja said kindly.

'Why doesn't he ask me?'

'He will, but your husband will probably speak more freely without your presence.'

Vebekka nodded. 'Yes, yes, that's true, poor Louis. I am all right though, now. This is a waste of time, you know.'

Maja looked at her watch. They had been there a long time. She got up and went towards a window panel between

24

the rooms. She was going to pull up the blind to see if one of the kitchen helpers was there to make some fresh coffee but, as her hand reached for the string, she froze—

'*Don't* – please don't. I don't want to see through the window.'

Maja let her hand fall and turned to Vebekka. The Baroness was hunched in her seat, staring ahead. Before Maja could say anything, the Baron came in, alone and grey with fatigue.

'I'm to take you home, darling,' he said flatly.

Maja watched Vebekka closely, saw the relief when she learned she would not have to see the doctor. She kissed Maja warmly as she left with her husband.

Dr Franks leaned on the kitchen sink, as Maja washed up. 'Well, what do you think?'

Maja slowly turned off the water tap. 'I think she is a very disturbed woman. She is very entertaining, very sharp and witty, but I think she is also—'

'Dangerous?' he enquired with his head tilted to one side. Maja touched her wrist, remembered how strong Vebekka's grip had been, and nodded her head. 'Yes. Very.'

Dr Franks returned to his study, where Helen was still waiting. He shut the door, and stuffed his hands into his pockets. 'Maja agrees with you.' He poured Helen a glass of sherry. 'Tell me about her violence. Have you witnessed it?'

'Yes, she becomes disorientated, very angry, verbally and physically. She is quite frightening, because although she appears to lose control and has no recall of what she has said or done, I think she has, and refuses to admit to it – or is unable to admit it. For example, she knows what she did to Sasha, her daughter; she knows, but denies it.'

Franks asked Helen to elaborate on the destruction of the dolls, and listened intently as she described what the Baron had told her Vebekka had done. Helen, chewing her

25

lips, looked directly at Franks. 'He said he had come in in response to Sasha's screams, had found to his horror that his wife had taken every doll belonging to the child, mutilated all of them, smashed their faces in, torn off their arms. She had stacked them, one on top of the other, and set light to them. The house could have caught fire, but she just stood watching the toys burning, forcing her daughter to watch with her. Sasha was terrified, tried to run, but Vebekka held her by her hair, forcing her to see the dolls melt. The Baron quoted her as saying, "Watch the babies, Sasha, watch the baby dolls!" He had had to pull his daughter from her grip.'

Franks interrupted. 'Did she give a reason for her actions?'

Helen shook her head. 'I spoke with Sasha, asked her to tell me about the incident, but she kept repeating that her mama looked strange. Oh, yes, I remember something else. Sasha said she screamed for her father, said she called out, "Papa", and this is interesting, Vebekka was still holding the child by the hair and she said, "He is my papa, not yours, my papa. Papa loves me." I asked the Baron about this, and he said that his wife did not allow any of the children to call him papa. When I asked her about it, she said only that she didn't like them using "Papa", and when I pressed her on why not, she had no answer.'

'The Baron said she attempted to take her own life last night. Is this true?'

Helen shrugged. 'She cut herself, self-abuse. I don't think she would have killed herself. She wants attention, screams for attention all the time. She is a great attention seeker.'

'What about the violence to her husband? I noticed he had a nasty bite mark on his right hand.'

Helen drained her sherry glass. 'She will attack anyone who is close to her when she is irrational. He happened to be there. I surmise that she mistrusts everyone when these periods occur – that includes her children. But I find it interesting that she did not actually attack her daughter, just her toys. Yet her daughter was close by . . .'

'What about the other children?'

Helen referred to her notes. 'Again, these attacks have occurred when they were close by her. When she was in her so-called irrational state, she would bite, kick, punch, but she has not to my knowledge taken a weapon, a knife or anything like that.'

'What does she say when she is in this condition?'

Helen flicked through her notes. 'Back in 1982 she was to be given the truth drug, sodium pentathol. I sent you the transcript.'

Franks opened his own file and leafed through.

Helen continued. 'She believes someone is taking over her mind, just as she believes that anyone in a white coat, doctor or nurse, is going to hurt her. She has a terror of injections, and refused the pentathol treatment. She was disorientated at the time, but still was able to refuse the injection just as she has refused shock treatment, and, until now, refused adamantly any form of hypnotherapy.'

'Why do you think she has changed her mind?'

'She knows she is getting more dangerous, has even told me she fears she will kill someone. I have gone as far as I know how. Can you help her? Do you think you can?'

Franks tapped her nose. 'My dear, I never give up hope. But first things first, sweet Helen, we must eat. I am starving and there's a nice little restaurant, close by. And you can give me more details of her obsession.'

Hylda had dressed Vebekka for dinner, and was delighted by her good spirits and exuberance. Louis, however, was tired and not in good spirits. He could hear his wife on the telephone to Sasha; Vebekka's resilience was astonishing, unnerving. He could hear her telling Sasha about Berlin, their plane journey, as if they were on holiday. The call completed, she danced over to the dinner table and began lifting the silver lids from the tureens with relish. But she ate little, just sat with her chin cupped in her hands watching his every mouthful. She reached over and stroked his hand gently. 'I'm sorry for all the trouble I cause you, my darling.'

He smiled, as she poured a glass of wine for him. She was forbidden any alcohol, but he took his glass and raised it to her. In the candlelight her amber eyes were as bright as a cat's. Looking at her now made him feel deeply, horribly sad. This was the Vebekka he had fallen in love with, the young girl he had showered with gifts and flowers until she had succumbed to his charms. She had been crazy, fun-loving, mad-cap and wilful. She was still all those things, but now, the craziness, the madness was a hideous constant torment.

'What are you thinking about, Louis?'

'How beautiful you look! You remind me of when we first met.'

The next moment she was on his knee, kissing him frantically. 'I'm still your favourite baby, I haven't changed. Please, please, take me to bed, carry me into the bedroom, the way you used to, please, Louis, let's pretend this is a honeymoon.'

He lifted her from his knee. 'Eat, finish your dinner.'

She pouted, then returned to her side of the table, but she continued to pick at the food, nibbling on the french beans as she watched him. She had a glass of lemonade, and she slurped it like a child, trying to amuse him with coy, sweet smiles, smiles that had won him over so many times. But Louis wondered how long it would be before she turned on him. He could no longer tell how long the bad

28

spells lasted, all he knew was that this sweet creature would turn, if not tonight, then a week, a month or a year later, into a vicious, violent bitch.

Her eyes narrowed, but she smiled. 'Take me home, Louis, please. I'm all right now, it's over. I know I have said this to you before, but this time I know it's over. The darkness is gone. I felt it go in the waiting room at Dr Franks's. And Sasha misses me, she needs me to be with her.'

He drained his wine glass, patted his lips with his napkin. She fetched a cigar, clipped the end for him, struck the match, like a puppy. 'Please, Louis, take me home, we can be together, a family. I am fine now, really . . .'

He grabbed her wrist and held it tightly. 'No, no, we stay here, we stay until Dr Franks has seen you. That's what we came for.' She made no attempt to free herself and he released his hold.

'Bekka, please don't do this to me, please don't. Maybe you feel fine now, but it could change – in the car, on the plane. Please give it a try, if not for yourself, if not for me, do it for Sasha.'

Vebekka wrapped him in her arms. 'I would never hurt my baby, please believe me. Just say you will take me home, I don't want to stay here.'

Louis pushed her away. 'Sasha is afraid of you.'

Vebekka recoiled as if he had slapped her. 'She is not, I just talked to her on the phone. She is not afraid of me.'

Louis spun round. 'You don't even know what you do to her! You will stay here, you will go to Dr Franks. I'll make you see this through.'

She cocked her head to one side and smirked. 'Then you will leave me? Yes? That's why I'm here, you want to get rid of me. I will never divorce you, Louis, not for any of your women. I will never release you, you are mine.'

29

The Baron ignored her, turning towards Anne Maria's room. 'I'm going to bed, I suggest you do the same. *Anne!* Anne!'

Anne Maria appeared from her room.

'The Baroness is retiring. Will you see to her needs?'

Vebekka swiped at the dishes on the table. 'I don't want any pills. I don't want that ugly little bitch near me. I won't be locked in my room.'

The Baron looked hard at his wife. Her act was dropping already. He walked into his room and slammed the door.

Vebekka turned on Anne Maria. 'I don't need anything, especially from you. Go to your room, you plain, ugly bitch! Go on, get out of my sight! Get those short squat legs moving. You smell – in fact you *stink* – your body is putrid!'

Anne Maria began to return to her room, but paused at the door to look back at the Baroness. 'At least my daughter isn't terrified of me.' She shut her door quietly.

The Baroness's bedroom was lit by one bedside light. Vebekka threw herself on to the bed, then sat up panic-stricken. Where was her jewel-box? Her make-up box? Finding them comforted her, soothed her. She carried them to the bed and spread the contents around her. Then, in a rapid mood change, she gleefully began to make up her face.

Louis's eyes were closed, but he was not asleep; he knew she was in the room. The bed moved on his right side, the covers lifted. He sighed, lifted his arm, and she nestled against him, curling round him. He slowly turned to look at her.

It took all his willpower not to push her away. Her face

was painted in hideous streaks and colours, like a clown's. He tried to keep his voice steady. 'What's that all over your face, Bekka? What are you doing?'

'I'm a clown for you, don't you remember? When we were in New York that time? How we laughed at the little midget, the little clown . . .' She slid off the bed and fell to her knees, bouncing up and down, pulling at her face grotesquely. He sat up, looked at the time, then back at his wife. She jumped up on the bed, rolled on top of him, giggling and tickling him, until he held her tightly.

'It's one o'clock in the morning, I'm exhausted, this is crazy.'

She pulled her mouth down. 'In the present circumstances I don't think that is a very funny thing to say.'

He sighed. It was horribly true. It was as if she were balanced on a delicate trapeze wire; if he said the wrong word, made the wrong action, she would fall, fall from his hands, from his care, a care he hated still to feel. He could contain himself no longer; his body shook as he wept. Vebekka held him as she would her children, soothed him, quieted him. Louis had taken a mistress within months of the birth of his first son, and he had continued a similar pattern throughout his entire marriage. He told himself that he had needed to do so because of the anguish Vebekka caused him, and yet she could still make him want her like no other woman he had ever known. She whimpered now, whispered for him to forgive her, then asked again if he loved her. He could feel himself giving way, too tired to argue. She rested her head against his shoulder, her lips touching the nape of his neck, inching upwards to touch his.

Her soft feather-light touches to his cheeks, his ears, his temples, began to arouse him. 'Don't do this, Bekka, please don't . . .'

'Let me make love to you, please, Louis, I can feel that you want me.' Her hands drew his pyjama top open, pulled it from his body. She began to kiss his nipples.

'Bekka, listen to me, it's over between us. I will always take care of you, I promise you, but . . .'

She slid open the cord of his pyjamas, easing them over his buttocks, caressing, never stopping her sucking, kissing, licking until she eased herself to her knees. He moaned as she began to masturbate him. 'You see, Louis, you do want me.'

Suddenly she sprang to her feet, and smiled at him. He made an unconscious move to draw up his pants, as if to hide his erection, and she laughed a soft, low, vicious laugh. 'You'll never get rid of me.' She twisted the handle on his door, and she was gone.

He felt wretched, sick to his stomach, but he didn't follow her. Not this time.

Helen Masters had covered her head with a pillow so as not to hear them, but even after Vebekka had left Louis – she had heard the door closing – she was still unable to sleep. She got up and went into the main suite to fetch a brandy. As she eased the stopper from the brandy decanter, her heart almost stopped. There was the Baroness, like a broken doll, hideous make-up smudged over her face, curled up by the window. Her eyes were staring blindly into the darkness beyond the cold windowpane.

Helen gently touched her shoulder. 'Come to bed, you'll catch cold. Come on, Vebekka.'

Helen tucked the quilt around her, and then sat on the edge of the bed. 'Do you want a hot drink?'

Vebekka slowly turned her head, as tears streamed down her face. She whispered, 'No, nothing, thank you, Helen.'

She was staring ahead, as if listening intently. 'There's something here. Can you feel it?'

'Feel what?' Helen asked.

'I don't know. I don't know, but it's here, it's taking me, Helen, it's taking me over.'

Helen felt Vebekka's brow: she was sweating. Her head felt sticky from the make-up, damp. 'Do you need Anne Maria to give you something to help you sleep?'

'No, I don't want her. Please, take me away from this place.'

'I can't . . . this is for your own good. It will all be all right, you'll see.'

The Baroness clung to Helen, her hands strong as she gripped her tightly. 'Something takes over me, Helen. I have to leave here. Please talk to Louis, tell him I must go home.'

Helen embraced Vebekka, rocked her in her arms. 'There's nothing here, try to sleep.'

Vebekka whispered, 'We have done something terrible tonight.'

Helen went rigid. Dear God, had the woman hurt Louis? She eased Vebekka from her arms, tucked her in, sat with her until she was quiet, and then ran to Louis's room. He was sleeping deeply. Make-up covered his pillows, clown's make-up, it was even on his face. She shut the door and leaned against it. The insanity was getting to each of them, dragging them all down.

Vebekka could not sleep. She could see by the bedside clock it was almost two-thirty. The dread slowly began to envelope her, the dread she was incapable of describing. A terrible weight began in her feet, trapped her legs. Like wet cement, the weight oozed slowly over and up her body. She could not call out, could not move as it trapped her arms, restricted her throat, a deadly white substance that left only her brain to fight the terror of the whiteness inching towards it. Only her willpower could keep the creeping mass away. It took all the energy she could conjure up to drive the substance back, replacing the whiteness with brilliant colours and forcing them to cut across her brain, bright flashing primal reds, greens and sky blue; like electric shocks, shaking her, swamping her with such an intense violence she became exhausted, had to give in, had to let the mass consume her. As it seeped over her nose she could no longer breathe, as it filled the sockets of her eyes she became blinded. And then it hardened: she was encased in cement and she could not move, as if she had been buried alive. Just as she felt she was dying she caught a glimpse of a girl in a white frilly dress, little white socks and black patent shoes, a child holding a doll in her arms. She was so far away, so distant. Then a white-gloved hand drew a dark curtain, hiding her, and the darkness oozed over her face and she heard the soft persuasive voice whispering for her to remember, remember the colours. The gloved hand began to draw back the heavy curtain again, inch by inch, but what lay hidden behind it filled her with such terror that she gave in to the darkness.

Hylda was the first person in the suite that morning – the first to see Vebekka. She was lying on the floor, her eyes unseeing, staring in horror, her limbs rigid, her body in a catatonic state. Spittle and vomit covered her white night-dress. Hylda called frantically, first for Anne Maria, then for the Baron and Dr Masters, who told her that she would not be needed further that day. But it was not until Hylda was on the bus heading for her apartment later on that what had occurred that morning took effect. She got off the bus a stop early in her confusion. The cool air calmed her, and she patted her face with a handkerchief, repeating over and over, 'Poor woman, poor woman.'

As she waited at the pavement edge for the next bus, she decided she would walk and prepared to cross to the opposite side of the street. Not until then did she see the brightly coloured poster pasted to a wall, about five yards to her right. Schmidt's Circus was appearing in West Berlin, the big brash poster announced. Hylda moved closer, and stared in disbelief. The central part of the poster was a massive male lion's head. Beneath the lion was the defiant face of a woman, a strong face with wild hair; a woman with wide, amber eyes that were daring, yet mocking.

THE WORLD'S MOST FAMOUS
FEMALE WILD ANIMAL TRAINER,
RUDA KELLERMAN – award-winning act
straight from Monte Carlo!

For a moment Hylda could have sworn that the woman in the poster was Baroness Vebekka Maréchal.

CHAPTER THREE

R UDA KELLERMAN stepped down from her trailer.
The weather was not good, the sky overcast, with rain
falling lightly. She drew her raincoat collar up and tightened her belt; her black boots barely showed beneath the
long trenchcoat. Ruda wore a man's old cloth cap and her
long hair was braided in a plait down her back. She carried
a small riding crop and was tapping it against her leg as
she strode towards the Grimaldi cages, their canvas covers
rolled up. There were sixteen tigers, four lionesses, five
lions and one black panther. The animals were three or
four to a cage, except for one lion, Mamon, who sat alone
in his own vast cage, and the panther, Wanton, who had a
small one to himself. Ruda had, as always, checked their
arrival and unloading from the circus train. Now she was
making her second inspection of the morning, noting each
animal with a piercing stare of her wide cat-coloured eyes.

The tigers were very vocal now; occasionally she stopped
as one or the other called to her. She pressed her face close
to the bars, blowing what appeared to be a kiss. It was a
welcome, a contact, a call of recognition from one animal
to another. She rubbed their noses, calling their names
softly, but she was never over-familiar; Ruda had always to
remain the dominant figure of authority.

The purring sound was so loud it was like a rumble, but
there was no purring from the smallest cage in the semi-
circle, Wanton's cage. Ruda called out to him, but kept at
arm's distance, as he sliced his paw through the bars, his
sharp claws always ready to lash out against anyone

passing close. Wanton was the smallest cat, but one of the most dangerous, and Ruda glanced upward to check that the tarpaulin over the top of his cage was well battened down. Her sharp eyes checked that there was no loose rope for Wanton to leap at, possibly hurting himself. Unlike the tigers, he paid no attention to Ruda's voice as he pawed and snarled at her. She laughed at him and, in a frenzy of anger, he lashed out again and then slunk to the back of his cage.

Ruda moved on to her babies, her lionesses. The rain was heavier and she snapped orders to two of her helpers to keep the tarpaulins on all the cages until it was time to move the cats into their sheltered quarters. Hearing her voice, the lionesses pressed their massive bodies to the bars, and each one received a rub on her nose. Ruda spoke softly, calming, soothing them, knowing they would be restless for some time, that they always were when they arrived at a new site. Any new location was greeted with suspicion, and it would be at least twenty-four hours before they settled down. Now they called to each other, acknowledged Ruda and paced their cages.

Ruda ran her crop along the bars of the next to last cage, and three of her prize babies, the fully grown male lions, loped to the bars, their massive heads bent low, their paws too large to reach through the bars. These lions with their full manes never ceased to touch a chord of wonder inside her; they were kings, magnificent killers, and she admired the sheer force and power of their muscular bodies. As they pressed their heads against the bars, she noted that their straw needed changing. She turned angrily to an assistant, snapping out the order to prepare the clean straw. The young man, Vernon, who had been with Ruda's team for only six months, muttered for her to give him a break, he had just arrived himself.

In two quick strides Ruda was at his side. 'Do it now!

And don't answer me back!' The rise in her voice made one of the lions snarl, then all three huddled together at the rear of their cage, watching her, ears flattened, eyes sharp.

The boy backed off, and hurried towards the store trailer, where four helpers were pitchforking the new hay and sawdust. Ruda made sure every bale was checked, lest they were damp in the centre, and each sack of sawdust tested for the tell-tale smell of poison, laid down to get rid of rats from farmers' barns, which could endanger her cats. All of it was always sifted by hand until she was satisfied.

The air was filled with the sound of animals calling out, the elephants trumpeting their arrival. Horses were led from trailers to the practice ring, dogs were barking, and a group of performers were greeting each other almost as loudly as the animals.

Ruda stood looking over the bales of sawdust, prodding one bale after another with her crop. 'Keep them out of the rain, don't let any damp sawdust get into the cages. I'll be with you in a moment to open up, get everything ready for me.' Turning back to her last cage, she quickened her step. She gave a soft whistle, and then leaned by the side of the cage, whistled again and peered around to the front bars. He was in solitary confinement, a state he seemed to prefer. Ruda often wondered if he misbehaved to ensure he was solo . . . and Mamon could misbehave like none of the others. But, then, even his name was unique. He had had it when Ruda purchased him. Mamon was moody, unco-operative, a bully, but he could also be playful and sweet-natured. Lions, on the whole, are family-orientated and like each other's company, but Mamon was very much a loner and he constantly tested her. Ruda liked that.

His unpredictability made him dangerous to handle, and he had been exceptionally difficult to train, but he was the sharpest, the most willing performer of all the Grimaldi cats. Mamon seemed genuinely to enjoy the crowd's adulation.

As if he knew his value, he behaved at times like a real star: his tantrums, however, were a lot more lethal. He swung his head towards Ruda as soon as he heard her soft whistle, then loped slowly to the side of the cage. When Ruda whistled for the second time, he squatted down on his haunches, his nose pressed to the bars, his massive black mane protruding through the rails. As Ruda peered round to him, his jaws opened and snapped shut. 'How you doing, eh? Want to say hello to your mama? Eh?'

Mamon rolled on to his back and Ruda reached through and tickled his underbelly, but she never stopped talking to him, soothing him, always aware that even in play he could slice off her arm.

The high-pitched voice that interrupted their play was like that of a young boy reaching puberty, slightly hoarse, half low, half falsetto. 'So you got what you wanted, after all . . .'

Mamon sprang to his feet, all four hundred and ten pounds of him, in one swift move, ready to attack. The cage rattled as he lunged at the bars. Ruda gripped the riding crop tighter. The voice was unmistakable. 'You got even taller, Ruda.'

Ruda turned and snapped. 'I wish I could say the same for you, Tommy. What piece of wood have you crawled from under?'

Tommy Kellerman gave a mirthless, twisted smile. 'You're doing all right for yourself. That's some trailer parked up front! How much does a trailer that size set you back, then?'

Ruda relaxed her grip on the riding crop, forced a smile. This was something, after all, that she had expected. She had known he would turn up one day. Ruda had to look down almost to her waist level to meet his eyes. Tommy Kellerman was very spruce: his grey suit and red shirt must have been made for him, as was his red and grey striped tie. She had seen the white trenchcoat before: he wore it as he had always done, slung round his shoulders; he also sported a leather trilby, a hat being about the only normal garment Tommy could buy outside a children's-wear department. Kellerman was a dwarf.

'That raincoat's had some wear!' She tried to sound casual, but her heart was hammering, and she gave a furtive look around to see if there was anyone she knew close by.

'We got to talk, Ruda.'

'I've got nothing to say to you, Tommy, and I'm busy right now.'

Kellerman inched his leather hat up a fraction. 'You didn't change your name. How come?'

'I paid enough to use it. Besides, I like it.'

Ruda walked a few steps to the side of the cage, out of sight of anyone passing. She leaned against it and beckoned for him to come to her. After a moment, Kellerman joined her. He was drenched in some sweet-smelling cologne which wafted up, mixing with the smell of the cats' urine.

'Like I said, Ruda, we need to talk. I just got in from Paris – I got a room reserved in the Hotel Berlin.' He had a small leather-sided bag which he dropped by his tiny feet. Then he took a stance against the wheel of the cage, his square hands stuffed into the small pockets, his polished child's shoes and red socks scuffed with mud.

'Have you been to my trailer? Asked for me there?'

He laughed his high-pitched laugh, and shook his head. 'No, I came straight from the station. I've been following you on quite a few venues – not in your league, of course, but I keep on seeing your posters, your face, star attraction. You got what you wanted, eh?'

'What do *you* want, Tommy?' Her voice was flat and emotionless.

He looked up at her, and inched his hat further up his

domed forehead, scratching his head. Then he removed the hat and ran his stubby fingers through thick curly hair flecked with grey. The last time Ruda had seen him, it had been coal black. It was the nicest thing about him, his curly hair. She noticed it was dirty now, sweaty from the hat.

'I said, what do you want, Tommy? You're not here for a job, are you? Not after what happened – they wouldn't touch you. I'm surprised you can still find circuses that'll employ you.'

Kellerman spat into the mud. 'Isn't there some place we can discuss this in comfort? It's raining, and I could do with a bite to eat . . .'

'I'm real busy, Tommy, it's feeding time any minute now. Maybe we can meet some place later.'

He stared up at her, and his eyes searched hers before he spoke. 'You owe me, Ruda: all I want is my fair share. I can't get work, good work. I'm broke, I've had to sell most of my props and, well, I reckon you can give me a cut.'

'Cut of what?'

'Well, there's a few ways to look at it. I'm still your legal husband, and I bet *any* dough your old man doesn't know that! Now you're rollin' in it, and you're on the number-one circuits, this must be one hell of a contract . . . and all I want is a part of it. You either get me in on the act—'

'They'd fucking eat you, Tommy, no way!'

One of the helpers passed the small alleyway between the cages. He paused. 'Excuse me, Mrs Grimaldi, but the freezers are open. You want to come over and sign for the meat?'

Ruda nodded. 'Be right with you, Mike.' She hid Tommy by standing in front of him, and remained there until Mike had gone.

'Ruda, I need money, I'm broke.'

She turned on him, snapping angrily. 'When have you not needed money, Tommy? If it moves, you'll slap a bet

41

on it. You owed me, remember? I paid you off years ago, I owe you nothing.'

Kellerman's face twisted with anger. 'You had nothin', not even a fucking passport, I got you out of Berlin, me! I put food in your mouth, clothes on your back. Don't give me this bullshit, you owe me a lot, Ruda, and if Grimaldi was to know you was still married, he'd hit the fuckin' roof. I keep my ears to the ground, bitch. I know you took over his act, and I know he's relegated to watchin' outside the ring like a prick! And I hear he hates it, he's still screwing everythin' in a skirt, so how do you think he'd feel if he knew you never got divorced? I reckon he'd be a happy man, Ruda. Now you tell me how much you owe me. I am your husband, and I got the marriage licence to prove it. You got the divorce papers? Huh? Well?'

Ruda scraped at the ground with the toe of her boot. 'Don't mess me around, Tommy. How much do you want?'

'Well, you got two options, sweetheart. Make me a part of the act, cut me in, or . . . I know what they pay top acts, so I don't think it's too much, just give me one hundred thousand dollars.'

'Are you crazy? I don't have that kind of money! Everything I earn goes into the act. I swear I don't have—'

Kellerman's short squat legs ran to the front of Mamon's cage. He pointed with his stubby finger. 'Well, sell this bastard. They're worth a lot of dough, aren't they? Or flog your trailer, I know how much that's worth, and I know Grimaldi must be set up. I need dough, I got to pay some heavy guy off, and I got no one else. What you want from me, want me to beg? Fuck you! *You owe me!*'

Ruda remained in the narrow alley between the cages. It took all her willpower to contain her anger. 'Tommy, don't stand in front of the cages, they don't like it, come round here. I'll get you as much as I can, but not dollars, not here.'

Kellerman leered back at her. 'That's not good enough, Ruda. You want me to go over and have a chat with Grimaldi? You can get the cash from the head cashier. You think I dunno how much dough you're getting paid per show – it was the talk of Paris, so don't give me any bullshit.'

Ruda reached out and drew him close. 'I'll see what I can do. I'll see what I can raise and I'll come to your hotel tonight after I fix their night feed. But only on condition you don't work here, you leave. I also want our marriage licence. Is it a deal?'

Kellerman looked at his watch, the big cheap clock face almost the entire size of his wrist. 'OK, I'll go grab a bite to eat. You get me the dough, I'll give you the licence. We got a deal, my love.'

'Then leave now, I don't want you yapping to anyone.'

Kellerman grinned. 'Eh! There's guys here that'd cut my throat if they saw me, so I'm gone . . . but you'd better turn up. You got until midnight.' He scrawled on a card the hotel and phone number and tucked it into her pocket, smiling. Then he perched his hat at a jaunty angle and departed.

Ruda watched the small squat figure scuttle away, watched him leave the perimeter of the trailer park. She was rigid, her face set with anger, but she forced Kellerman to the back of her mind, she had work to do. She strode over to the meat trailer that had arrived from the city and spent some time arranging the delivery, signing for the fresh carcasses and even haggling with the butcher until she had a good deal. She signed the delivery orders, then went over to her own freezer trailer.

Mike was already sorting out the midday feed. He used

a heavy-handled hatchet to slice the meat from the bone, and a carpenter's sledgehammer with a short handle to crack open the carcass. Ruda collected the large trays, carefully listed and tagged for each cat: the trays were clean, the freezer trailer immaculate. Between them, she and Mike weighed the feeds, placing the trays in readiness for the cages. By now Ruda had on a rubber apron, blood over her hands and arms. Like Mike she wielded the knives and hatchets professionally.

After they had washed off the blood, Ruda said, 'You can grab a coffee, Mike, I'll do the rest. What time have they allocated the arena for us?'

He handed her a carefully worked-out rehearsal schedule showing when the main rings would be available for her to rehearse the act. Ruda looked over it, frowning. 'Have the new plinths I ordered arrived yet?'

'I think so, but until everyone's settled, I can't get to the delivery trucks. They're all parked out at the rear.'

She swore under her breath, and snapped, 'Go and check, I'll need to rehearse with them tonight. We've no time to mess around.'

Ruda fed the cats herself, as she always did – no one else was allowed to; that way she had a constant check on whether any were off their food or had tooth problems. After the feed, she helped the boys clean out, sweeping and washing down the boards. By the time she had done the last cage, the first would be dry and ready for the clean straw. Not until each one was dry, straw and sawdust covering the floors, meat trays removed, was she satisfied to leave her animals, lazily snoozing, their bellies full.

The helpers were tired, it had been a long journey, and they retired to their trailers exhausted. None of them had ever been able to keep up with Ruda; she seemed to have unending energy and stamina. She was as strong as any

44

man, and her expectations were high: anyone not prepared to give one hundred per cent was fired on the spot.

Not until now did Ruda allow herself to concentrate on the Kellerman problem, and she was soon so engrossed in her own thoughts, desperately trying to think what she should do about her ex-husband, that she virtually moved on automatic pilot. She had been so anxious to leave him that she had never considered divorce, but she had always consoled herself that no one would ever know because when she married Grimaldi, Kellerman was in gaol. He wouldn't know, and Luis would have had no reason to suspect she wasn't divorced. Now she knew what a stupid mistake she had made. For Luis Grimaldi to find out now that they were not legally married would be very dangerous, especially since Ruda was poised to make her move and take over the act. Ruda and Grimaldi were partners, everything split fifty-fifty, but they were at loggerheads. The act alone tied Ruda to Grimaldi, the act that she had built up. Ruda was planning to draw up new contracts to alter her take to seventy per cent of the proceeds. After months of bitter quarrels, she felt she had Grimaldi ready to sign. But what if he now discovered they weren't legally married and she had no legal hold over him at all? The act was still in Grimaldi's name, every contract she signed was in his name. It didn't matter that everyone knew she had taken over – the act was still his.

Ruda dragged her boots over the iron grille outside the trailer, inched them off and stepped on to the portable steps in her stockinged feet, opening the door. Carefully she placed her boots just inside the door, and then hung up her raincoat. The trailer was spacious. Her large bedroom led off the central sitting room, her husband's was at the far end by the kitchen. Grimaldi had not travelled with the trains but had driven their trailer and hooked it up to the water system. Ruda showered and washed her hair. Wrapped in a robe with a towel around her head she went into the kitchen. The coffee pot was on: she tested it with her hand – it was still warm – and poured herself a cup of thick black coffee, then sat with the mug in her hands.

The walls of the trailer were hung with framed photographs of herself, Grimaldi and the various animals and circuits. Her eyes rested on the large central picture of herself. It was the new poster, the first time Ruda was the main attraction of a circus. The fame of Schmidt's was worldwide and she was at the pinnacle of her career, her life.

The coffee tasted good, bitter, and she clicked her tongue against her teeth. Her big, strong, mannish hands were red raw, the skin hard, the nails cut square. She wore no wedding ring, no jewellery. Slowly she removed the damp towel, and her hair uncoiled in a wet dark twist. When it was scraped back from her strong, heavy-boned face, strange deep red scars were evident on her temples: they looked like burn scars, as if someone had held a red-hot poker to either side of her head. Ruda often aggravated the scars, because she had a habit, when she was thinking, of rubbing her forefinger up and down them, as if the feel of the smooth scarred skin comforted her. She began to do that now, worrying about Kellerman, what she should do – what could she do? – all the while staring at the picture of herself. In the photograph, surrounded by her lions, she looked so powerful, so invincible. This was not just her career at stake, or her partnership, it was her life. And no one was going to take it from her. No one had a right to take it away.

Ruda rinsed her mug and placed it on the draining board by the small sink. Suddenly she realised she was not alone in the trailer. She moved silently towards Luis's bedroom;

a low orgasmic moan made her step back. Then she heard her husband gasping, his groan louder, louder, until he sighed deeply. Ruda remained standing by the bedroom door, wondering which of the young girls was being serviced – more often than not it was one of the eager starstruck grooms. Grimaldi earmarked these young girls virtually on arrival at the site. In his heyday he wouldn't have looked in their direction but now he fucked whoever he could still dazzle.

Ruda sat down on one of the comfortable cushioned seats and lit a cigarette. She inhaled deeply, letting the smoke drift into rings above her head. She heard a soft girlish laugh, and looked to the bedroom, wondering if they were about to start again, but the clink of glasses and the low voice of her husband asking for a refill made her think that she should move away as they could both be coming out. She half rose to her feet.

'I love you . . .' Ruda raised her eyebrow; poor little besotted tart. 'When will you tell her?'

Ruda sighed, the poor stupid little girl didn't know his wife was well aware of these affairs. She looked to the bedroom, and said to herself, 'Well? Answer her!'

'I'll discuss it tonight, after the show. She'll be too busy beforehand.' Ruda could tell by the slight slur in Luis's voice that he had been drinking.

The girl's voice rose to a whine. 'You said that days ago, you promised me. If she doesn't care about you, why wait? You promised me, Luis, you promised.'

'I'll discuss it tonight, sweetheart, I give you my word.'

Ruda decided she had heard enough. She was about to open the main door of the trailer and slam it hard, so they would know she was there, when she was stopped in her tracks.

'The baby won't wait. I want you to promise me you'll tell her tonight, ask for a divorce tonight, promise me?'

'Shit!' Ruda pursed her lips. The bloody tart was pregnant!

Grimaldi's voice grew a little louder. 'Come here, look at me, Tina, I promise you we'll talk tonight, OK? But it's feeding time now. I can't talk it over until tonight – she's gonna have to rehearse. It's not the right time.'

Ruda walked out of the trailer, her feet stuffed into her old boots. So what was another bloody Grimaldi brat? But could this one turn his head? He was over sixty. Could this one make his warped, drink-befuddled mind take some kind of responsible action? The timing could not have been worse. Jesus Christ, if Grimaldi was to discover he wasn't legally married, maybe he would, out of sheer perversity, think about marrying this tart.

Ruda's mind began to spin. Grimaldi was old, he was feeling bitter and jealous of her success, he had been relegated to nothing more than a watcher outside the ring. This child coming now could give Grimaldi some sense of power. Would this bitch of a girl give Ruda's husband the strength to confront her? With her shoulders hunched, Ruda sloshed through the mud, hands clenched into fists at her sides. The rage inside her made her whole body stiffen, and the cats picked it up. As soon as she reached the perimeter of their cages, they began to prowl, to growl, pacing up and down, heads low.

The cages had to be driven under cover. The rain was pelting down, and the big animal tent had been pitched; all the animal trailers were being moved into the covered arena, each having a delineated site within it. Ruda climbed aboard the tractor with the first caged wagon ready and Mike gave her the signal to drive it in. Ruda wheeled the tractor round, hitching and unhitching each cage, her arms straining; to her this was as much a part of the act as feeding, and she wanted to oversee every single stage. Not until all the cages were positioned and secured in their allocated space did she relax. The large heaters were on full blast to ensure that the tent and grounds were kept dry and warm. All the tarpaulins from the tops of the cages were removed, laid out flat, and rolled up in readiness for the next journey.

When she at last returned the tractor to the car park, she started checking the massive equipment trucks to make sure that all her props had arrived. Then she had to check out the show cages: each one weighed a ton, but they had to be carried and stacked. She worked along with her boys until the sweat ran down her face. Time was now pressing: she had to be ready for her rehearsal period. Each act had its specific rehearsal time, and if she was not ready she would lose hers. The new plinths and pedestals were still in their wrappers. Ruda helped the men heave them down from the truck and roll them into the practice ring, reinforced steel-framed leather-based seats or stools for the cats, ranging in height, and with reinforced interlocking frames; some were barrel-shaped, some used under the ends of the planks that connected them. Each section had to be stacked for easy access and fast erection. They ranged from three feet to forty feet high, and they were very heavy to take the weight of the cats.

She had stripped down to a T-shirt, and sweat glistened on her face and under her armpits as she drove herself to work harder than any man. Her boots were caked in mud, her big hands covered in old leather gloves as she used wire clippers to uncover the first plinth. Standing back to view it, she swore loudly, then ripped off the second and third covers. The plinths were correct in measurement, and exceptionally well made, but she swore and cursed even louder as she pointed to the leather seat base. She had paid in advance for the plinths and pedestals to be made for her in Berlin, and had stipulated the specific colours to be used:

red, green and blue. They were, as she had instructed, red, green and blue – but they were too bright, too primary, and the gold braid too yellow.

Ruda had just completed unwrapping the last one – stacking them side by side, all the covers and wires removed – and was standing, hands on hips, in a rage, when Grimaldi at last made his appearance. He stood over six feet tall, and had thick black curly hair, very black as he regularly dyed it. His once handsome face was bloated now from age and excessive drinking, his dark eyes red-rimmed, but he could still turn heads. He was wearing his high black polished boots over cords, and a Russian styled shirt, belted at the waist. He reeked of eau-de-Cologne. Ruda smelt him before she saw him.

'We got a problem?'

Ruda snapped that indeed they had, and it was all his fault. 'All you had to do, Luis, was give the colours for the plinths and you fouled that up – look at them, they're far too bright. I'm gonna have to use the old ones when I link up the pyramid formation. *Look* at the fucking colours. I want our old ones.'

Grimaldi shrugged. 'You can't have them. I sold them in Paris. These are OK – they'll get used to them. Give them more rehearsal time, they look fine to me. What's the panic? A few rehearsals, they'll get used to them.'

Ruda turned on him. 'It's not you in the ring with them, Luis, it's me. And I'm telling you, those colours are too fucking bright!' Her face was flushed red with fury. Luis knew, probably better than anyone else, the danger that new equipment always generated – even a different coloured shirt worn in the show could disturb the cats. They hated change of any kind. Although they accepted Ruda's old rehearsal clothes, they seemed to know instinctively if she wore a different stage costume and they could really play up. They always had to be given time to get to know the changes – and two days, Ruda knew, was not long enough.

Ruda glared at her husband. 'Get the old ones back, Luis, and get them by tonight!' she snapped.

His eyes became shifty; he hated to be spoken to in that way in front of the workers. 'I said I sold them. Just work through the act, they'll get used to them. No way can I get them back from Paris in time for the opening.'

Ruda kicked out at one of the plinths in fury. 'Just do what I ask. Jesus Christ! It was the only thing you had to do and you foul it up!'

Luis began to pick his teeth with a matchstick. 'I'll call around. What time do you rehearse?'

Ruda was walking out of the tent and shouted over her shoulder for him to check the schedule. Luis ambled across to the main noticeboard: they were not on until later that afternoon, so he joined a group of men going off to the canteen and restaurant provided for the performers.

Alone in the trailer, Ruda paced up and down like one of her cats. She opened the safe, counted the money kept for emergencies and noted that Luis must have been dipping into it. She slammed the door. There was about fifteen thousand dollars left. She checked her own bank balance: in her private account she had fifty-two thousand dollars of hard-earned money. She rubbed her scar until it was inflamed, then began to open drawers in her dressing-table, feeling under her clothes for small bundles of dollars she kept for day-to-day emergencies – like a squirrel she hid small stacks of notes in various currencies and denominations. But no matter how she searched and calculated, she did not have one hundred thousand, and the more she mentally added up the amount, the more her fury built. This was hers, every single hard-earned cent was hers, and that little bastard felt he had a right to it. Kellerman had no right to anything, least of all her money.

The cashiers said they could give Ruda an advance on her salary, but not until after lunch when they would go to the bank. They would require Grimaldi to sign the release form, but if she came back at three they would have the money in dollars as she had requested. Ruda smiled, and then shrugged, said not to bother, she'd changed her mind. She was smarting with the knowledge that she needed Grimaldi's signature for an advance on her own wages.

Ruda fixed herself a salad in the trailer, and then changed into her practice clothes. She was just about to leave when Luis returned. He shook his head, his hair soaked. 'It's really coming down, maybe going to be a storm. It's sticky, clammy weather, and the forecast isn't good.'

'Did you try to sort out the pedestals?'

Luis had totally forgotten. He nodded, and then lied that he was expecting a return call at the main box office. She watched him in moody silence as he unlocked the wooden bench seat and checked over his guns; he rarely had one when watching out for her, but it was a habit from the past when his own watchers had always been armed. He habitually checked that his rifles were intact, but never even took them out of the box.

'I'll need you in the arena. Can you get the boys ready? We're due to start in an hour.'

Luis sat on the bench, picked up the towel Ruda had used to dry her hair and rubbed his head. 'Ruda, we need to talk – maybe after rehearsal.'

Ruda was already at the trailer door. 'Which tart was it today?'

Luis laughed, tossing the sodden towel aside. 'It's been the same one for months and you know it – it's Tina, she's one of the bareback riders.'

'You'll be screwing them in their diapers soon, you old goat.'

Luis laughed again. He had a lovely rumbling laugh and it relieved her, maybe it wasn't as serious as she had thought. He said, 'See you in the ring, then! After, we can go out for dinner some place, you need a break.'

Ruda paused, still by the door. 'Maybe, but I've got a lot to do, we'll see . . .'

He gave a rueful smile. 'I'm sorry about the mix-up with the plinths. I'll get on to them and see you in the ring.'

Luis heard the door click shut after her, lifted his feet up on to the bench, his elbows behind his head, and stared at the photographs along the top of the wall. Some of them were going brown with age. They were of him in his prime, standing with his lions, smiling to the camera; there was such a powerful look to him, such youthfulness . . . Slowly his eyes drifted down, as he aged from one poster to the next; it was as if his entire life was pasted up in front of him. He stared at the central poster, Ruda's face where his had always been. The side wall was filled with Ruda. He eased his feet down and stood, slowly moving to the wall, to the pictures that showed he was past it, a has-been.

He opened a bottle of Scotch, drank heavily from it, and looked at a photograph, curling up with age. The Grimaldi family, the act passing from father to son. There was the old man, the grandfather, his own father, with Luis beside him no more than ten years old. Luis's father had taught him everything he knew, just as his father had before him, three generations of big-game trainers.

Luis downed more Scotch as he stripped to get showered and changed. He bent to look at himself in the bathroom mirror, staring at the scars across his arms – warrior scars his papa used to call them – scars from breaking up the tiger fights. But there was one, a deep jagged line from the nape of his neck to his groin. His fingers traced the deep jagged line, and he started to sweat, needing the Scotch more and more as his mouth dried up. He could never go back into the ring. She had done that to him. Ruda had made him inadequate, but it had been Mamon, her favourite baby, that had almost killed him. The cold water eased the feverish sweats, and he soaped his chest. He had been mauled so many times; how often he had stepped between two massive tigers, more afraid they would hurt themselves than him, but every one of those scars had been dismissed as part of the game. Only the terrible scar on his chest made the fear rise up from his belly.

Mamon had lunged at him, dragged him like a rag doll around the practice ring, toyed with him, dared Luis to dominate him, and Luis had been overcome with a terror of which he had not believed himself capable. It had frozen him. He had no memory of how he had been dragged from the arena, no memory of anything until he woke in the hospital, the wound already filling with poison, a wound that wouldn't heal, a nightmare wound that opened with pus every time he moved. The anguish and the pain had kept him in a state of fever for weeks. Nightmares had kept him afraid to sleep, because in dreams the scar opened and oozed and suffocated him. Luis Grimaldi had almost died. To be so physically incapacitated was hard enough for him to deal with, but harder still was the relentless fear. A fear that he could confess to no one. At first he had tried to hide it, making excuses – so many excuses – as to why, months after he was healed, he had still not been near his cats. It was during those months that Ruda had begun working solo with the cats. He had said that he wasn't fit enough, that he needed more time to regain his strength, but the relentless fear was still there, and Ruda knew he was afraid. Ruda had encouraged him, half-heartedly he realised now, because she didn't want him back in the ring. She wanted the act for herself and she had encouraged him to take his time.

The bottle was almost empty, and the more drunk he became the more embittered he felt. He did not consider the lengths to which Ruda had gone to salvage the act, how she had worked herself to exhaustion, keeping him and his cats at their winter quarters. Luis had forgotten that he never lifted a hand to help her, never queried how she had managed to finance them. All he could recall was the way she had humiliated him.

It was all Mamon's fault, he had decided. He could not get back into training with a cat that no longer respected him. Luis had entered the arena and a cold sweat had drenched his body. He felt it as if it were yesterday, the terrible fear as Mamon's cage was drawn closer to the gate. A number of people at the winter quarters had gathered to watch: they came in admiration, to watch the famous man face his attempted killer, and they stood in silence as the cage drew closer and closer.

Mamon was motionless, his head lowered, but his eyes held Grimaldi's. Ruda, standing close to the cage, had spoken calmly, softly, asking Grimaldi when she should release the cat . . . Grimaldi drank now, gulping the liquor from the bottle as the heat of his humiliation made him shake.

Alone in the arena, he had not been able to stop his legs shaking; his breath felt tight in his chest. He looked from Mamon to Ruda, he wanted more than anything to give her the signal. But he froze. She kept watching him, her eyes like the cat's, and she was smiling. It was her smile, mocking him, knowing he was afraid, that finished him. The great Grimaldi walked out of the arena and back to their quarters. That short moment finished his career, he knew it then.

He began to cry as he remembered the way she had held him close, wrapped him in her arms. He recalled every

55

word she had said. 'It's not the scars on your body, Luis, but the ones inside. They are always the worst, the unseen ones. I understand more than anyone else, I understand.'

Luis had pushed her away from him, shouted that she did not understand, there was nothing wrong in his mind, and he had pulled open his shirt to display the raw ragged line of the tear. Mamon, he said, was dangerous, he was a rogue lion, he should be shot. He had then tried to get his gun, pushing Ruda out of his way. Ruda's physical strength had stunned him, she had almost lifted him off his feet with a back-hander that sent him sprawling. Standing over him, her eyes as crazy as a wild cat's, she had virtually spat out the words. 'You touch Mamon, and I swear to God I'll kill you.'

Luis had dragged himself to his feet. 'You shoot him then, it's him or me, Ruda.'

Ruda had taken his own whip, the whip Luis's grandfather had used, and, for a second, he thought she was going to use it on him. Instead, she laughed in his face. 'Watch me! Just watch me, Luis.'

From the trailer window, Luis had seen her stride to the practice arena. He heard her shrill voice instruct the old hand who had been with Grimaldi's for thirty years, heard her give the order for Mamon to be released into the arena. She had wheeled the old, well-worn and well-used plinths into the centre of the ring, and then stood waiting, hands on her hips. The massive lion moved slowly and cautiously through the makeshift barrier tunnel from his open cage. Luis inched open the window to hear her. Her voice rang out, a high-pitched call: 'Mamawww, Mamawwwww *up*, *yup yup* . . . Mamon . . . come on, angel . . . good boy, Mama's angel.'

Mamon swung his massive black-maned head from side to side and then, to Luis's astonishment, reared up on to his hind legs and walked towards Ruda, his front paws swung towards her. He kept on walking towards her and then, as she called out to him, he turned, as if dancing for her. Her high-pitched voice called out something – Luis couldn't quite hear the command, a rolling 'rr' sound . . . '*Reh!* Rey, *reh* . . . *reh* . . .' and then Mamon jumped on to the red plinth. After steadying himself, he cautiously tested the plank, a thick wooden board balanced between the two plinths. Carefully, cautiously, front right paw patting the plank, still balancing himself as she now called: '*Huppp! Blue* . . . *blue* . . . Ma'angel!' The animal trod the narrow board towards the blue-based plinth. He eased himself into a sitting position, his thick tail trailing the ground as he perched. Ruda moved closer and closer to the blue plinth, until she was near enough to be within the lion's territory. Only another trainer would know that this was reasonably safe: the animal sitting on the plinth, needing all four paws to give him balance, is unlikely or unable to attack, his hindquarter overhanging due to the position of his tail. If he attacked from a seated position, he would automatically lose his balance.

Luis couldn't take his eyes off Ruda, as she moved in close and then audaciously turned – leaving her back within half a foot of the animal. She never stopped talking, whispering encouragement, as she knelt down on one knee, her head virtually beneath the massive cat's. She gave another high-pitched command, lifting her voice because she was facing away from Mamon: '*Up* . . . *up* . . . *greeee, greeee* . . .' The green-based plinth was five feet in front of her and she was encouraging the lion to leap from one pedestal to another, from the blue to the green.

Mamon lifted his front paws and balanced himself to stand on his hind legs on the pedestal. All his muscles strained as he made a flying jump, right over Ruda's head on to the green pedestal. She ran to him and gave him a titbit, rubbing his nose. She then looked to the trailer window, just a fleeting look, but there was a small, tight smile on her face. Finally she lifted both her arms, giving the final command for Mamon to head out of the arena, and bowed mockingly to the small group of onlookers, who applauded, as Luis slunk away from the trailer window.

The word spread fast that the great Luis Grimaldi had lost his nerve. They joked that his wife had taken it from him.

Now Grimaldi staggered slightly as he left the trailer. The rain had not ceased and the ground was mud. He made his way towards the rehearsal tent. The cashier who had talked with Ruda earlier that morning called out to him. He turned bleary-eyed towards her large brown umbrella. 'I can give you the advance, Mr Grimaldi, if you come over and sign for it.' Luis had not the slightest idea what she was talking about, and stumbled towards her. 'Your wife wanted an advance on her salary. If you need it, I've come back from the bank, I just require your signature.' Grimaldi mumbled incoherently, and she passed on, turning to see him slither and slide against one of the trailers. The cashier shrugged, disinterested; his drink problem was well known.

The big man mumbled to himself. Not content with taking over his act, Ruda was trying to steal his money. He was going to face her, and nothing was going to stop him.

Ruda had made the boys dismantle and re-erect the cage arena twice. She timed them to the last second, and even bolted and heaved two of the cage walls herself. She wanted it timed down to less than two minutes. This was tough going: the arena cage was very heavy and unwieldy, the caged tunnel sections even heavier. As they dismantled it all for the third time, they moaned and muttered to each other, making sure 'Madame Grimaldi' didn't overhear. She now checked the formation of the cages at the entrance tunnel. The cats were to be released on cue to head down the tunnel into the arena.

Mike asked if they were using the new pedestals, which were still stacked outside the ring. Ruda pursed her lips and then shook her head. 'No, I'll do that first thing in the morning when I'm fresh. Let's just run the easy routine for today, give them some exercise, and tomorrow we'll have a real crack at it . . . so for now it's the herd, then the leap, followed by the roller roll.'

She called up to the electrician. 'Can you give me a few spotlights, in the usual places, just to keep them on their toes, red, green and blue formation?'

A disembodied voice called down that it was rather her toes than his, and a few spots came on and off.

Ruda shaded her eyes, calling out to the electrician again. 'Most important one is directly after the leap, Joe. Last show it was a fraction late.'

She paced up and down, her head shaking from side to side as she relaxed her shoulders. The rehearsal would have no music, it was simply to warm up the act, get the cats used to the new location. It also kept them on their mettle after a long night's travelling and calmed their restlessness.

The cages were now lined up, ready to herd in the animals. Ruda gave a look around the ring and noticed that Luis had not turned up, but two of the boys had already placed chairs at either side of the arena, waiting to watch over the act should they be needed. They had no guns; they could, if needed, break up trouble by creating noise and yelling.

'Okay, Mike, let's go for it!' she shouted at the top of her voice to the tunnel and waiting cages some distance from the arena.

Ruda used the small trapdoor at the side of the main show cage and entered the arena, then turned back to head into the animals' entrance tunnel. When the act was live,

59

she always entered from the tunnel, straight into the ring, as if she was one of the cats herself. She double-checked that the sections were bolted, as she headed down the tunnel, bending her head slightly as the bars joined over the top. Midway she gave Mike the signal to release the cats on the count of ten: the exact time the opening music used. She tightened her thick leather gloves, her voice hissed slightly, one . . . two . . . three . . . As she reached nine, she spun around, running back down the tunnel into the wide caged arena. She carried only her short practice stick, and wore old trousers and a shirt knotted at the waist with her old worn black-leather knee-high boots, caked with mud and excreta – they had never seen a lick of polish since Luis gave them to her.

By now the cats had been released, any second they would be heading into the arena. Ruda paced herself, gave a bow to the empty auditorium: she always practised every move she would do in front of a live audience. Arms raised, adrenaline pumping, she could feel the ground shudder as the animals charged down the tunnel. She loved this moment, as the sixteen tigers hurtled into the main ring, as if frighteningly out of control. But the cats knew exactly which was their leader and which place each had. Ruda backed to the wall of the arena and picked up a heavy double-sided weighted ladder. The cats stormed round the arena, forming a wide circle around Ruda, as she stood nonchalantly next to a small ladder plinth. They were loping, moving fast . . . The circle tightened as she yelped a command. Her second command, hardly detectable, was a lift of her right hand to the lead tiger, her eyes never off him. Roja was the number one cat, and it was he who appeared to split up the circle, breaking to his right. Now the cats gathered into two factions, grouping either side of her. A third command, again to Roja, and the animals began to weave around each other. The circle became tighter, tighter, closing in around her. She became more vocal, calling each tiger by name, high-pitched calls. Then, on a signal to Roja, the cats touched, pressing their bodies hard against one another. Ruda, her back to the small ladder, slowly eased herself up it, step by step, as they kept up their circle, like a Catherine wheel turning, turning.

Ruda reached the top rung of the three-foot ladder. There was total silence in the big arena as off-duty circus performers watched the rehearsal. Luis entered the arena, lifting the flap aside, and stood for a moment before he began slowly to thread his way through the seats. Ruda gave Roja the command: 'Down . . . Rohja, down . . . ja ja ja down!'

Tigers are instinctive fighters; their close crossing of each other's body territory was dangerous, filled with snarls and teeth-baring. But one by one they began to lie down side by side, until sixteen tigers lay like a wondrous carpet. Twice, Ruda reprimanded two females for beginning a spat, banging her hand flat on the top rung of the ladder as a warning. The watchers were uneasy now, aware of how perilous a position Ruda was in – if one tiger accidentally knocked over the ladder, brushed too close, they could attack.

More and more performers had slipped in to watch. But Ruda saw nothing, no one, her attention riveted on the carpet of cats. Satisfied they were in position, she lifted both arms above her head, speaking all the time, never stopping talking to them . . . Then she gave the command: 'Upo . . . upahhh.' Sixteen tigers rose up, sixteen tigers in almost perfect formation, then lowered their heads. It was a magnificent sight, as the glorious carpet of gold and black stripes lifted and rose magically into the air.

Ruda called out again, made it on to the top rung of the ladder and then flung herself forwards, face down, to lie spreadeagled across the sixteen cats, balanced on their

61

backs. They began to move, carrying her round in a terrifying wheel. She then dropped to her feet, arms above her head in the centre of the seething mass. She flicked Roja with her stick and he broke the circle and spread wide at a run; the others followed, spreading wider, running around her as she gave a low bow. She held the bow as rehearsed for three long beats, then turned back towards the tigers. As if by no command at all, they formed two lines facing her. She yelped out an order, her voice cutting through the air, high-pitched, and up they reared to sit on their hind quarters. They clawed the air, Helga and Roja in a snarling match; Ruda quickly pushed Helga aside and flicked her hand at Roja, stepping back. Facing them she spread her arms wide, giving a small signal to Sasha, one of her females, leading the second section of the line-up. They were ready, and she gave the command. '*Up* . . . *upppp.*' Now they all reared up from squatting to stand on their hind legs, their growls and swiping paws showing their dislike of the position. They were poised perfectly to attack, for tigers always attack from the front, never the rear. Shouting, she urged them back like a chorus line.

Grimaldi wanted to weep. She was spectacular, he had never attained such perfection even at the zenith of his career. Her face shone, her eyes were brilliant in the spotlight, as if the risk to her life was exhilarating. There was a radiance to her that humbled him and, drunk as he was, he bowed his head, trying to steady himself on the seat in front of him. The seats had not been battened down, and the chair was loose; it fell forwards, Luis with it, into the second row of seats. The bang was as loud as a shot.

Ruda turned and saw him and, at the same time, Sasha and Roja lost concentration, came down on to all fours. Ruda gave the command to move out, signalled for the watchers to open the trapdoor – fast. One of the boys watching for Ruda hurried to Grimaldi's side, helped him to his feet.

Ruda turned all her attention on Roja, dominated him, knowing that if he was in the tunnel the others would follow. She never took her eyes off him, as he hesitated, then wheeled round to head back down the tunnel, followed after a moment by the others. Ruda clamped the trapdoor, shouting for Mike to hold the rest of the act. She moved like lightning, but she didn't go for Grimaldi. Instead, she strode to the boy who had helped him to his feet and grabbed him by the scruff of his neck. 'What the fuck do you think you're doing? You watch out for *me*. If this place goes up like an inferno, *you watch out for me!*' She swiped him a back-hander, so hard he fell to his knees.

Still ignoring Grimaldi, Ruda turned to the watcher on her left, and snapped for him to put the next part of the act on hold. '*Now! Do it right now*, get to Mike, tell him to keep the cages shut!' The two boys ran, leaving the drunken man standing alone, his face flushed a deep red.

Then Ruda slowly removed her thick leather gloves, and spoke to her husband, her voice kept low. 'Get out of here, Luis. Get out before I have you thrown out.'

Grimaldi held his own; swaying slightly, he glared at her.

'I'm sorry, I fell, you know I'd never—'

Ruda flicked his face with the glove. 'Get out of my sight, you drunken bum!'

Luis touched his cheek. 'I want a divorce, you hear me, bitch? I want a divorce. *I want you out of my life.*'

The show continued for those performers still hanging around. Ruda gripped her husband by his shirt and hauled him to the exit of the tent. She pushed Grimaldi out; he fell face down in the mud. She said nothing, but turned on her heels and strode back into the tent. She saw a cleaner standing with his wide long-handled broom, and told him to sweep out the drunk, and not to let him near the arena until she was through.

By the time Ruda had finished the rehearsal, got the cats back into their cages and fed, it was after six. She hoped Luis had passed out so she wouldn't have to confront him, but when she walked back into the trailer he was remarkably sober – and obviously waiting for her. A pot of steaming black coffee made the trailer windows thick with condensation. She switched on the air-conditioner without saying a word. Luis poured coffee and handed her a mug. 'I'm sorry, I should never have done that, I was drunk. I am ashamed, I'm sorry.'

Ruda threw her coat on to the heater and began to unbutton her shirt. 'You know how dangerous it was, you don't need me to tell you that, dangerous and stupid, and from you of all people.'

Grimaldi nodded glumly and held out his hand, but Ruda didn't take it. She unzipped her trousers, kicking them off. He picked them up, and fetched her shirt from where she threw it, took them to the laundry basket. She wore a silk one-piece with dark green stains under the armpits. But she didn't strip completely. After all the years they had been together, Ruda was still self-conscious about her body. She fetched an old worn robe, wrapping it around herself before she took a sip of the coffee. She uncoiled her hair, the nape of her neck still damp from the workout.

'Did you mean it, Luis? About the divorce?'

Grimaldi looked at her sheepishly and sat down, his big hands held between his knees. 'I guess so, I've been meaning to talk to you about it for a while now, but . . .'

'But what?'

'Well, why not? We don't have a marriage, we haven't ever really had one – you know that . . . and she's – Tina's going to have a baby.'

64

'You've got kids all over Europe, what's one more? Anyway, knowing that little tart, how could you be sure it's yours?'

Grimaldi cocked his head to one side. 'It's mine – I may be worn out and past it, but my dick can still work. It's about the only thing that never lets me down.'

'What about the act?' She tried to keep her voice nonchalant, but she was shaking. He still wouldn't look at her. 'Luis, what about the act . . . if we divorce. We're partners, do you still want me to run the act?'

He turned to her then. 'You can do what you like with it, it's not mine anyway, but I'll still retain fifty per cent. I mean, half the animals are mine.'

Ruda felt drained. 'I see. So my money, all the money I've earned and poured into the act, everything, all the new cats that I've trained, my cats, it's all split fifty-fifty, is that right?'

Luis nodded. 'That's only fair, you had nothing when we met, everything you have is from me. I mean, if you want you can pay me what you think the act is worth, what the animals are worth, and then, do whatever you want, but you can't use my name – not any more.'

Ruda snatched the poster off the wall. 'Look at it, Luis, it's not your name, it's mine! I've not used your name for the past two years, I don't want your name!'

'Just my act! You think nobody knows? My name is still a crowd-puller, may not be on the fucking headlines, but it's the Grimaldi Cats.'

'It's not your act any more.'

Grimaldi shook his head and half smiled. 'All I want is my fair share, my cut. Anyone can take over an act. I can work in someone else.'

'You can what? *What did you say?*'

'I said I can work in someone else. If you want to take the act as it stands, then pay me – it's as simple as that.'

Grimaldi opened the trailer door. 'Where are you going?' she snapped at him.

'I'm going out, OK? And while I'm gone, Ruda, just sit down and remember, remember where you came from, what you were before you met me. Sit on what you made your living on an' *tell me how much you fucking owe me*!'

The trailer rocked as he slammed the door. She buried her head in her hands, gripping her head in a rage, wanting to rip out her hair. What did he know about pain? What could he know? Almost in confirmation she felt the burning sensation in her head. He couldn't stand up to pain, but she could. She kicked out at the trailer wall, punched out at the doors, the walls, with all her strength until she had to heave for breath. It was then that she shouted, 'I was tested, he tested me, I was Papa's favourite!'

She began to pace the confined space of the trailer, her hands clenching and unclenching. First Kellerman, now Luis, both wanting to take from her everything she had fought to get. She wouldn't let them, either of them. As she showered and changed, she talked down the blinding fury which boiled up inside her, forcing herself to think what she had to do.

Ruda did a last check of the cats, staying a moment longer with Mamon than the others. He was restless, as if he felt her own unease, and pressed close to the bars, then lay down totally submissive; she reached through to touch him, let his rough tongue lick her hand. She whispered to him. 'You know, you know, I won't be kicked, I won't take it, nobody kicks me, yes? *Yes?*' She loved this creature more than any other living being. It was Mamon, her angel, who had drawn from Ruda a love she had believed herself incapable of feeling.

She clung on to his bars. 'I'm ready for him, I can deal with him, I am strong, I am strong.' The bars felt cold to her brow, she pressed closer, closer. The voice whispered to her, soft, persuasive: 'You can do it, fight through the pain with your mind . . . that's my little girl, that's Papa's girl, you can do it, pain is sweet, pain is beautiful, come on, Ruda, give your papa what he wants. You love me, prove it!'

She was ready, ready to face out Kellerman, ready to go into East Berlin. She pushed herself away from Mamon. 'I'll be back.'

Ruda passed by her trailer and, through the lit window, saw Luis unwrapping a fresh bottle of brandy. She walked on, caught the bus into the city centre, went first to the taxi rank, and then changed her mind. She waited for another bus, to take her into East Berlin.

It was a strange experience crossing through the shabby Kreuzberg district. In the old days it hugged the Wall, but now it was home to most of the Turkish population. From the window of the bus she was shocked to see racist slogans daubed on the walls of the rundown houses. '*Ausländer* – foreigners – *raus* . . . get out!' Bricks were thrown at the bus as it passed through the district. The passengers were mostly women and children, and they cowered back in their seats. Anti-Semitic slogans were smeared on the sites of former synagogues and Jewish schools. Ruda began to sweat as a group of young skinheads spat as the bus passed, their hands lifted, their voices screaming, '*Sieg Heil!*' Their yells made Ruda bow her head. She hissed under her breath, 'Bastards . . . bastards!' but kept her head lowered.

A woman seated in front of Ruda began shouting and shaking her fist at the skinheads. She turned to her companion, and they began talking to the rest of the occupants of the bus. 'If your skin is the wrong colour, if it isn't pale enough, if your hair is too dark, too curly, these pigs will attack. Something must be done! Why has this hatred been allowed to continue and fester? Turn the machine guns on them, the fascist pigs!'

By the time Ruda got off the bus she was engulfed in a strange fear. Not two yards from the bus stop, she faced a massive poster of herself. The incongruity made her gasp . . . but the poster calmed her, comforted her.

She took out her street map, looking for the right direction to Kellerman's hotel. She hesitated, checked his scrawled note and passed on, heading down a dimly lit street to a small bed and breakfast establishment that could not be described as a hotel. It was almost ten when she entered the dingy reception area. There was no one around, and Ruda turned the guest register, or what was deemed a guest register but was scrawled across with memos and messages, to read it. 'T. Kellerman' was listed, occupying room 40. She waited another moment before she headed to the elevator, and pressed for the fourth floor. She stood outside room 40 listening to the sound of a television set, the volume turned up loud. She tapped and waited, tapped louder and the door inched open.

'They should have called from reception,' he said petulantly, but he swung the door open wider. He was in his shirt, the tie loosened, and he had on wide, cut-down red braces. Ruda closed the door, and looked around the small single room, dominated by the television set.

'Jesus, Tommy, what made you choose this dump?'

'It's cheap, nobody asks questions, and nobody's likely to come looking for me – that answer enough?'

'Yeah, I suppose so, but I'm surprised you've not had a brick through your window, or a turd in your bed.'

'Got scared, did you?'

Ruda shrugged, then, after a moment, 'Sickened, more like.' She placed her large leather bag on the edge of the bed. As she turned, Kellerman suddenly clasped her tightly round the thighs, his head buried in her crotch. She didn't resist. 'Still working the same foreplay game, are we?' she asked sarcastically.

He chuckled, and stepped back. 'Lemme tell you, that's turned on more women than I can count, they love it, hot breath steaming through their panties. Just a taste of what is to come, because when I ease the skirt down, really get stuck in, no woman can resist me, not when I've got my tongue working overtime.'

Ruda laughed and unbuttoned her coat, tossing it over her bag. 'You disgusting little parasite, I'd have thought at your age you'd have grown up, but then I suppose it's tough – not ever growing, I mean.'

Kellerman hitched up his trousers and crossed to the courtesy fridge. 'Want a miniature drinkie? From your own miniature lover?' He peered at the rows of bottles in the fridge and chose a vodka for himself.

'I won't have anything.'

'Suit yourself,' Kellerman said as he opened a tonic, and fetched a glass. His squat hands could reach only half-way round the tumbler.

Ruda sat on the bed watching him as he fixed his drink, dragged a chair from the small writing desk by the fridge, moved it closer to the bed, then waddled back to collect his glass, handing it to her as he gripped the chair by the arms to haul himself into it. Sitting, his feet hung just over the edge of the chair, child's feet encased in red socks to match his braces, his scuffed shoes on the floor.

'Cheers!' Kellerman took the glass, drank almost half its contents, burped and wrinkled his nose. 'So! You came. I was half expecting you not to turn up.'

Ruda opened her handbag and took out her cigarettes. Kellerman delved into his pockets to bring out a Zippo lighter. 'Did you go to the cashier?' he asked, pointedly looking at the large leather bag.

'Yes.'

He flashed a cheeky grin. 'Good. I'm glad we understand each other. The licence, all our papers, are in that drawer over there. They still look good . . . guy was an artist!' He eased himself off the chair. 'You may not believe this, but I don't like asking for the money.'

Ruda laughed. 'Asking? Blackmailing is the word I would use.'

'You have to do what you have to do. I'm flat broke, and in debt to two guys in the US. It's been tough for me ever since you left.'

Ruda smiled. 'It was tough before I left. I'm surprised they employed you in Paris. Those folks worked hard for their dough. Way I heard it you were blacklisted – you'd steal from a kid's piggy bank. You've never given a shit for anyone but yourself. How long did you get?'

Kellerman shrugged. 'Five years. It was OK, I survived, the cons treated me OK. The screws were the worst, bastards every one of them, called me Monkey or Chimpy.'

'You must be used to nicknames by now.'

'Yeah, haw haw, sticks and stones may break my bones but—'

He leaned forward, a frown on his face. 'I'm shrinking, Ruda, did you notice? Prison doc said it was something to do with the curvature of my spine. I said to him, Jesus Christ, Doc, I can't get any smaller can I? I said to him, if this goes on I'll be the incredible shrinking man, and he said—' Kellerman shook his head as he chortled with laughter. 'He said, that was done with mirrors! They built giant chairs and tables, then . . . fuck it! How could he know, eh? How could he know?'

Kellerman was referring to his obsession, a fun-fair mirror he used to haul everywhere he went. The mirror distorted a normal human being, but it made Kellerman look tall and slender, normal. In a fit of rage one night he had smashed it to pieces, and wept like a child at his broken dream image. He turned now to peer at himself in the dressing-table mirror, his head just reaching the top of the table. The effect was comical, even funny, but Kellerman was not a clown. He was a man filled with self-hatred, and obsessed with the idea that if he had grown, he would have been as handsome as a movie star, a Robert Redford, a Clint Eastwood.

He cocked his head, grinning. 'You know they got drugs now to stop dwarfism? They detect it early enough, pump you full of steroids, and you grow. Ain't that something?'

Kellerman loathed his deformity; when drunk he was always ready to attack anyone he caught staring at him. The circus had been virtually his only employment, his short body rushing around the ring, being chased and thrown around, drenched in water. He opened another miniature and drank the vodka neat from the small bottle.

'Did you work with the Frazer brothers in Paris?' Ruda asked the question without really wanting a reply; her heart was hammering inside her chest. She had to get him into a good mood – she didn't have the money.

Kellerman nodded. 'Yeah, the Frazers bought my electric car just before I was sent down. So when I turned up and told them I just needed a few dollars they put me in the act. I timed it right, though. You know little Frankie Godfrey? He joined the Frazers about four years ago. Well he's been really sick, water on the brain maybe, I dunno. Some crazy woman, a few years back, got up from her seat and attacked him, just hurtled into the ring and began knocking him around. The audience thought it was all part of the act, but she was a fruit and nut case. Ever since the poor sod's had these blinding headaches. Still, it paved the way for me to earn a few bucks. Then the management found out about me, gave me my cards, or told the Frazers to get shot of me – cunts all of them.'

'Serves you right. If you steal from the only people who employ you, and virtually kill a cashier to get it, what else do you expect? I did that show – Monte Carlo, wasn't it?'

'I borrowed the dough, I was gonna pay it back. Yeah, Monte fuckin' Carlo, I only went there to date Princess Stephanie! Haw haw!'

Ruda laughed. 'Oh, yeah, where were you gonna find two hundred thousand dollars? From Prince Rainier?'

Kellerman chortled, and pointed to her handbag. 'I'm looking right at half that amount now. You know something? We made a good team, we could do it again. I'm good with animals.'

'Fuck off. You hate anything with four legs.'

He shrugged. 'No, I'm serious. You hear what that high-wire act got paid for a stint in Vegas? I mean, that's where the real dough is – cabaret. And there's a double act with big cats, you know, mix it with magic – they make their panthers disappear. I dunno how the fuck he does it, but it's got to be a con. You ever thought of trying the Vegas circuit? I got contacts there. I mean, maybe me in the act might not be a good thing but I could manage you. Grimaldi's washed up, or filled up with booze, so I hear, and you were shit hot with that magic stuff.'

'The day I need you to manage me, Tommy, *I'll* be washed up.'

Kellerman continued talking about acts he had managed, and she let him talk, only half listening. A long time ago now, Ruda had felt deeply sorry for him, because she had been in the same dark place. In retrospect she had made herself believe that their past experience was the reason she had married him – it united them. He was the only connection – now he was the reminder.

When they had first met, Kellerman was not as grotesque as he was now. He had seemed very boyish, innocent, his full-lipped mouth always ready to break into a wide smile, revealing white even teeth. But as he aged, the anguish inside him, his self-loathing, not only seemed to have deformed his body, but was etched on his face.

She was so engrossed in her own thoughts that Kellerman startled her when he suddenly hopped on to the bed beside her. 'You aren't listening to me!'

'I'm sorry, I was miles away.'

Kellerman rested his head against the pillows, his feet in their red socks pushed at her back, irritating her, so she got up and sat in the chair he had vacated. She was tense, her hands clenched, but the small voice in her head kept on telling her to be patient, be nice to him, she mustn't antagonise him.

'Strange coming back after all these years, isn't it?'

She made no reply. He tucked his short arms behind his head, and closed his eyes. 'You think it's all stored away, all hidden and then – back it comes. I've had a long time to think about the past, in prison, but being here, I dunno, it makes me uneasy, it's like a hidden drawer keeps inching open.'

Ruda began to assess how she should go about telling him there was no money, even trying to contemplate some kind of deal she could offer him. She was surprised by the softness, the sadness in his voice; he spoke so quietly she had to lean forwards to catch what he was saying.

'When my mama handed me over, there were these two women, skeleton women, I can remember them, their faces, almost as clearly as my mama. Maybe even clearer. One woman was wearing a strange green satin top, and a torn brown cloth skirt . . . filthy, she was filthy dirty, her head shaved, her face like a skull. She clawed at Mama, she hissed at her through toothless gums. "Tell them he's twelve years old, tell the guards he's twelve." My mama held on to me, almost hauling me off my feet, she was so confused. She said, "He's fourteen, he's fourteen but he's small, he's just small." The woman didn't hear because one of the guards hit her, and I saw her sprawled on to the station line, and I could see her shoes, she had one

73

broken red high-heeled shoe, and a wooden clog on her other foot.'

'I've heard all this before! Come on, why don't we go some place for a meal.' She had to get him out, stop him drinking, talk to him, reason with him.

Kellerman continued, ignoring her. 'The next moment Mama and me were pushed and shoved into a long line . . . Eva was crying, terrified, and then the second woman passed us. The second woman whispered to Mama, she said "Twins . . . say your children are twins."'

Ruda arched her back. 'Shut up!' She gripped her arms tightly around herself. Her heart began to beat rapidly, as if she was being dragged under water. Her nostrils flared, she felt the damp darkness, the stench and she clenched her teeth, not wanting to remember. 'Don't, Tommy. Stop. I don't want to hear!' But she could hear the voice: 'Twins . . . twins . . . *twins*,' and she got to her feet still hugging herself. She moved as far away from the bed as possible, to stand by the window. She could feel the hair on the nape of her neck stand up, her mouth was dry, and the terror came back . . . The rats scurrying across her, the ice cold water. In the gloom, the white faces of the frightened, the gaunt faces of the starving and the stinking sewer water which rose up, inch by inch, until they held her up by her coat collar. A blue woollen coat with a dark blue velvet collar: hers had been blue, her sister's had been red. 'Don't, Tommy, please don't . . .'

But he wasn't hearing her, he was too wrapped up in his own memories. He gave a soft, heartbreaking laugh. Eva, his little sister, was almost as tall as he, with the same curly black hair: she was only ten years old. Eva had always been so protective of him, so caring, how he had adored her. Ruda moved closer to the bed again determined to calm him, but it was as if he was unaware that she was in the room. He stared at the ceiling and began to cry.

74

'"My son is fourteen," Mama shouted, and all around us was mayhem, but all I did, all I could do, was keep staring at that second woman who had approached us. She had a pink see-through blouse, it was too small, the buttons didn't do up, you could see her breasts, her ribs, she was covered in sores, and she had a blue skirt . . . it had sequins on it, some of the sequins were hanging off by their threads, and the skirt must have been part of a ballgown, because it had a weird train. It was caught up and tied in a knot, a big knot between her legs. Like the other skinny woman, she had one high sling-backed gold evening shoe and what looked like a man's boot. I was so fascinated by these two skeleton women that I didn't really understand what was going on. But the next moment, this guard dragged Eva away, he kicked Mama, he kicked so hard she screamed in agony. She was screaming, her voice was screeching, like a bird. "He's fourteen, but he's a dwarf, he's a dwarf, please don't hurt him, he's strong, he can work, but don't hurt him, don't kick him in his back, please . . ."'

He sobbed. 'She said it, my mama said it, for the first time I heard her say what I was . . .'

Ruda sat on the bed, she reached out to touch Kellerman's foot, to stop him talking, but he withdrew his leg, curling up like a child. His voice was no longer a whimper, but deeply angry. 'He took me then, pointed with his white glove, first to me, and then to a line-up of children on the far side of the station yard. That was the first time I saw him, that was the first time. I've never told you that, have I?'

Ruda's nails dug into her arms. She was pushing shut her own memories with every inch of willpower she possessed. She forced herself to move closer to him. 'Stop it, Tommy, I won't hear. I won't listen to you.'

'Yes, you will,' he snapped. 'You will listen, because I want you to know, you more than anyone else. I want you to know.'

She wanted to slap him, but she kept tight hold of her mounting, blinding anger. 'I know, you've told me all this before, and we made a promise—'

He was like a child, his red-socked feet kicking at the bedspread. 'Well, fuck you! Won't keep the promise – I want you to know!' He clenched his hands, punching the bed. 'I was dragged away from Mama, and still she screamed, first for Eva and then for me, but no one took any notice, everyone was crying and shouting, but I heard Mama, I heard her clearly call out to me, "Wait for me at the station, I'll be at the station."'

Ruda snatched one of the pillows and held it over his face. 'Stop it! I know this, I don't want to hear any more!' She pressed the pillow down hard on his face, and he made no attempt to fend her off or push the pillow aside. After a moment she withdrew it and looked down into his face. His beautiful, haunted, pain-racked eyes looked up to her.

'No more, Tommy. Please.'

He nodded, and turned away, his cheek still red from the pressure of the pillow. 'Oh, Ruda, she never said which station. She never said which station.'

Ruda lay beside him, not touching, simply at his side. He was calmer now, and she heard him sigh, once, twice.

'You know, Ruda, no matter how many years pass, how long ago it was, I still hear her calling me. Every station, in every town I have ever been to, there is a moment – it comes and goes so fast – but no matter where I am, here or in America, in Europe, whatever station, I say to myself: "Which station, Mama, where did you wait for me? Did Eva find you? Why didn't you tell me which station?" It's strange, I know they're dead, long, long ago, but there is this hope that some day, some time I'll reach a station and my mama will be there, with Eva, walking the streets, and every corner I think maybe, just maybe I'll see Eva. I never give up hope – I *never* give up.'

Ruda whispered she was sorry, and he turned to face her. 'Is it the same for you?'

He searched her eyes, wanting and needing confirmation that he was not alone in his pitiful hope. The amber light in her eyes startled him — cruel eyes. With a bitter, half-smile she said, 'It is not the same for me. It never was.' With some satisfaction she felt the chains, the locks tighten on her secrets.

Kellerman leaned up on his elbow, touching her cheek with his index finger. 'I'll tell you something else my mama said. She said never tell a secret to anyone, a secret is a secret, and if you tell it, it is no longer a secret. You are the only person I have ever told what they made me do, and whatever I have done since — I mean, I admit I have stolen, I am a thief, I know I did wrong. I stole from the circus, from my people, but they are not me, they don't know who I am.'

Ruda sat up, took a sneaking glance at his small alarm clock. It was almost ten-thirty. She knew she had to discuss the money he wanted, and that she didn't have it.

'I'm not blackmailing you, Ruda. All I want is my fair share.'

It was as if he had read her mind. He rubbed the small of her back. 'You don't hate me, do you? You know I've no one else but you.'

His touch made her cringe inside. He rested his hands on her shoulders and stood up behind her, planting a wet kiss on the nape of her neck.

'If you do that again, I'll throw you off the bed.' She pushed him away. 'Get off me!'

Kellerman began to jump up and down as if the bed was a trampoline. 'Oh, you liked it once. You couldn't get enough of me once!'

The next moment he slipped his arms around her neck; she could feel his erect penis pressing into the small of her back. 'Let me have you one last time, please, Ruda, the way you liked it, let me do it.'

Ruda didn't even push him away this time. There was no anger in her voice, just revulsion. 'I never liked it. I loathed it to such an extent I used to be physically sick. Now, take your hands off me or I'll elbow you in the balls – they are about the only normal-sized thing about you, as I recall – and I will make your voice even higher.'

He released his hold, but remained standing behind her. 'Did you mean that? Did you mean what you just said?'

She sighed, angry with herself. She had to be nice, she had to be calm. 'Oh, come on, Tommy, we both know why I married you so why pretend otherwise? Sit down and have another drink.'

'Physically sick? I made you vomit?'

She couldn't stop herself as she snapped back, 'Yes, as in puke.' Again, she could have slapped herself. Never mind him, why was she getting into this? She could so easily have laughed it off, teased him into a good mood, but it was as if she was caught on a roller-coaster, and out it came, her face twisted in a vicious grimace. 'Sick, you made me sick! Have you any idea what it felt like? To have you clasped at my back, shoving your dick up my arse? It was like I had some animal clinging to me. All I did was grit my teeth and pray for you to get it over with. I hated it, hated every second you touched me with those squat square hands, pawing me like a dog, rough hands, hideous rough hands like dog's paws.'

Kellerman was stricken, backing from her on the bed, treading the mattress as if on water. Ruda glared. Her eyes frightened him because he almost knew what she was going to say next. 'But then you, Tommy, you must really know what it felt like, what it really felt like . . . because you know, don't you, Tommy?'

His small hands clenched into fists. 'You fucking bitch,

whatever I have done, you, for you to throw that in my face—'

'I warned you to shut up, but no – you kept on and on. I warned you.'

Kellerman slithered off the bed, and punched Ruda hard in the groin, then he reached for her bag, shouting at her. 'Give me my money, and get out, I never want to see you again, you whore, you two-faced bitch!'

Ruda snatched back her bag, hugging it tightly to her chest. He made a grab for the handle, and again she stepped back but he had it gripped in his hand and he tugged. Kellerman was very strong and they struggled between them. Suddenly he released his hold and Ruda fell backwards. 'You haven't got it, have you? You lied, you haven't got my money.'

Ruda was shaking, she fumbled with the bag, lying. 'Yes, I have, but I want our marriage licence before you get it.'

Kellerman crossed to the wardrobe and opened a drawer, his back to Ruda. He delved around, and then threw the envelope at her.

'Take it – and you owe me more than one hundred thousand. I saved your skin, I gave you a life, you bitch. If it wasn't for me you'd still be on the streets, you'd still be a whore, a cheap disease-riddled whore – taking it up the arse like a dog.'

She spat at him, and he spat back then kicked out at her again. 'Whore!'

She swung the bag and hit him in the face. He dived away from her and picked up the chair. 'Come on, lion tamer, try me, try and tame me, *come on.*' Kellerman pushed at her with the chair, she thrust it away, and he crashed it against her thigh. She stumbled against a coffee table, tripped and fell backwards. He came at her, the chair above his head. 'You can't fight me, Ruda, I'll fucking beat the living daylights out of you!'

She rolled to one side as the chair crashed down on to the table. The heavy green ashtray slid to the ground. Ruda grabbed it, and as Kellerman came forward to hit her again, she held one chair leg with her left hand, and with her right hit him with the ashtray.

Kellerman seemed stunned for a moment. He touched his temple, saw the blood on his hand. 'You asked for it now!' He started to shriek, jumping up and down like a chimpanzee, then threw the chair aside and grabbed the bright red candlewick bedspread from the bed, holding it up and out in front of him like a matador. 'Come on, come on, Ruda. Try – try to hit me!'

Ruda lunged at him, and he dodged aside, laughing, tossing the bedspread this way and that. The red blurred, like a red-hot fire in her brain. 'Stop it, Tommy, just stop it!'

'Oh, you never used to say that to me, you used to say, "More, more, I love it." That's what you used to say. You loved it from the dog in heat! Come on, bitch!'

The swirling bedspread swished this way and that, and the next minute she was on top of him, throwing it over his head, and the heavy ashtray came down, again and again. The bedspread swamped him, he struggled frantically. She heard him laughing, shrieking that she had missed him and it drove her into a frenzy. Ruda thudded her hand down, over and over again. She could feel his head, at one point held it firmly in her left hand, pressing it down as she hit him. She could feel the blows finding his face, over and over again.

She didn't know how many times she had struck him, but at last he was still and she sat back on her heels.

'Tommy? Tommy? Get up!'

He lay still, and she pulled at the coverlet, drew it away from his head. His face was a mass of blood, bloody bubbles frothed at his mouth and nose. She pushed herself away from him. 'Oh, God. Tommy, get up! *Get up!*'

He was motionless, his body swathed in the coverlet. She felt for his pulse, could find no heartbeat. She backed away, terrified, and leaned against the wall. She could feel every muscle tensing, then giving way as she slithered down the wall to sit like a rag doll, her legs stretched out in front of her.

'Oh, God, now what do I do? Tell me what to do.'

The television screen flickered, and she crawled over and turned up the volume, afraid someone would hear. Slowly, as the sound of the television cut through her senses, she began to think logically, talking herself calm. 'Get out fast, save yourself, Ruda. Get out, be careful, no one must know you came here. You never came here.'

She picked up the envelope and checked that the marriage licence was there. She took all his papers and stuffed them into her bag – his passport, diary, address book. She dragged him by his feet to the side of the bed then attempted to lift him, and it was then that the terrible realisation dawned. Cradled in her arms was the only link with her past. Only Kellerman knew, he was the only person she had ever told, and now she had killed him. She sobbed because she remembered what it had meant to be able to tell someone ... someone who had been in the darkness. She hugged him tightly, hard, dry, tearless sobs shaking her body as she recalled how, shortly after they had arrived in the United States, Tommy had tried to purge the past which clung unspoken to each of them. In their small trailer he had banged down two tumblers and opened a bottle of bourbon, hitching himself up on to a chair opposite Ruda. He had poured almost to the rim before he pushed the glass towards her. 'Right. You and me are gonna get loaded, and we're gonna let the ghosts

81

free, because I think we'll both go crazy if we don't. We got a new life. Now we open and close the old. So, cheers!'

It had been a long, memorable night as they tried to empty the terrors that haunted them both. The more they drank, the more fragmented horrors were whispered. They had cried, they had comforted, and they had promised to keep each other's terrible secrets.

Now Ruda rocked him gently back and forth. She had broken the pact, she had hurt him more than any living soul could have done. His anguished shame when he had told her what he had been forced to do she had thrown back in his face. She had done that to him. 'I'm sorry, Tommy, forgive me . . .' His blood stained her face, clung to her hair, but she held him close in a last embrace and eventually her gentle rocking stopped, because nobody knew now. Only Tommy had known that she had killed before; no one must know she had killed again.

She began to gasp with panic, unable to get her breath. She felt dizzy and had to fill the glass he had used at the sink. She gulped the water, her hands shaking uncontrollably. She saw her own reflection in the mirror, the bloodstains, her frightened eyes staring back at herself. 'It was always different for me, Tommy. For you, every station, every corner. For me, every mirror.' She put her hands over her ears as if to block out that voice, 'Twins . . . Twins . . . Twins.' Ruda shouted, 'I know she is alive. *I know, I know!*'

The fury seared up within her, the fury of betrayal which had kept her alive in the early years, a fury which now gave her an inner strength to survive. With a forced calmness, she began to clear all traces of her presence from the room.

Ruda packed all Kellerman's belongings in his own case, emptied every drawer, checked the bathroom and collected his shaving equipment. They would find out who he was soon enough, but they could also find out something else: Ruda held Kellerman's toilet bag in her hand and rifled through it, opened the razor, and looked back to his still figure. She hurried to his side, rolled up his left shirt-sleeve until she found what she was looking for.

The razor slit deep into his arm. She cut a square, and began to slice deep, cutting away the tattoo, but then fell back. As she sliced the artery his blood spurted over her face, her chest. Kellerman was not dead. Her rage went out of control.

She wanted to be sick, could feel the bile rising from her stomach. She picked up the ashtray and hit him again, and again, her teeth gritted as she used all her force. Then she waited, knew this time he had to be dead, and carried the heavy marble ashtray into the bathroom, washed it, dried it, left it wrapped in the stained bloody towel, sure it was clean of prints. Then she washed around the sink, the taps. Suddenly she caught sight of her reflection again. Her eyes were crazy, her face white, the blood splashes now running like tears over her face. She backed out of the bathroom, rubbing frantically at her skin.

She had to face Kellerman again. The force of the last blow had made his head jerk sideways: his teeth had fallen out, his top set of dentures. As she tried to drag and push his body under the bed, the heel of her boot ground the dentures into the carpet. Her breath came in short, sharp pants, but she kept on working. She cleaned the room, the door handles, anything she may have touched. Then she found Kellerman's hat, was about to tuck it into his case but changed her mind. She turned over the blood-soaked rug on which he had been lying and tucked the stained area beneath the bed. She then fetched the 'Do Not Disturb' notice, hung it on the door and, carrying Kellerman's belongings in his own case, wearing his hat, she slipped down the stairs, afraid to use the lift in case she was seen. There was still no one in reception; she grabbed the guest register, and tore out the page with Kellerman's name.

Ruda was back at her trailer by midnight but she could hear Luis snoring loudly, his door ajar. She slipped out as silently as she had crept in and went over to the freezer trailer. Knowing she couldn't sleep, Ruda needed to keep herself occupied and she began to prepare the morning's feed for the cats. She was so intent on her work that she didn't hear the door open. When Luis spoke she sprang back in shocked surprise.

'Jesus Christ, what are you doing? Do you know what time it is?'

Ruda returned to cutting the meat. 'I couldn't sleep.'

'I've only just woken up. I saw the lights on, I thought someone was breaking in. What are you doing? It's after midnight.'

Ruda continued cutting the meat. 'I couldn't sleep because your snoring drove me to distraction. You left your door open – I've told you to keep it shut.'

Luis grinned sheepishly, and offered to give her a hand. She refused, and he came to her side. 'I'm sorry, I know what I did this afternoon was unforgivable.' He backed away from her, her blouse was covered in bloodstains. 'Why haven't you got one of the rubber aprons on? Have you seen your shirt?'

Ruda looked at her hands, covered in blood from the meat, but her shirt was covered in Kellerman's blood. 'It doesn't matter, it was falling apart. I'll chuck it out in the morning. You go back to bed, I'll be a while yet.'

Again Luis offered to help her, but she ignored him, and after a moment he left. Ruda washed and scrubbed down the tables, scrubbed and cleaned the knives, hammer and hatchets before she washed her own arms, scrubbed them with a wooden scrubbing brush, paying particular attention to her nails. She stared at her own left wrist, and one more time the full impact of what she had done that night dawned on her, but she would not give in to it. She compressed it down further and further inside her, closing it tightly, locking it out of sight in her mind.

She took off her blouse, and stuffed it into Kellerman's case. She saw that the inside of her raincoat was stained and knew she would have to destroy it, along with all his belongings.

Ruda returned to her trailer, grabbed an old sweater, took off her stained trousers and pulled on an old pair of Luis's. She then carried Kellerman's suitcase, her raincoat, shirt and trousers to the big garbage barrels. She tossed his case into the huge bins waiting for the morning collection, dug deep into the filthy garbage and covered up the case. She then carried Kellerman's papers, and her marriage licence, to the main incinerators and eased back the burning hot lid. She stuffed the papers inside, one by one, making sure each caught fire. She watched the flames slowly lick and eat his treasured green passport, watched the black letters disintegrate. The flames, the heat, the charred black smoke, the smell made her so desperate to replace the lid that she didn't use the holder, but picked it up, red-hot, in her bare hand. Her skin hissed, but she didn't even feel the pain.

There was a low rumble of thunder and the rain became heavier. The ground was still muddy underfoot, and she slithered over the gangplanks in her haste to get inside. In the vast animals' arena, all were sleeping, stored under-cover for the night. The heaters were on full blast, and three night-lights made a warm, soft pink light. Ruda headed towards her cages as there was a second rumble. The animals loathed thunder, and lightning made it even

85

worse. She paused, head tilted to one side, but the storm was still too distant for any concern.

Ruda passed the tigers, huddled together; a few raised their heads in recognition of her smell, then returned to sleeping. Only Mamon was awake, his amber eyes bright. Ruda pressed close to the cage and called to him; he crawled on his belly closer to the bars. She pressed herself against his bars as he rubbed at them with his head. She stayed with Mamon for a while, comforted by him, soothed by him.

By the time she got into her bed she was exhausted. She drew her clean sheet closer to her naked body, tired but relieved it was over. Kellerman's passport, their marriage licence, the hotel guest register, all his papers were charred to a cinder, gone . . . all gone. It was over at last, and there was no witness, no one to threaten her new-found fame and security.

Ruda concentrated hard, just as she had as a child, waited until she felt the weight ease over her body, covering her like a gentle drowning, creeping upward from her toes, to her knees, to her heart, to her arms. She breathed deeply, making her mind lose consciousness. Gradually she allowed the weight to cover and spread, from her lungs, to her mouth. She slept in a deep, dreamless whiteness, protected, peaceful; no one could break through.

CHAPTER FOUR

THE NIGHT that Tommy Kellerman died was the night Baroness Maréchal experienced the horror of a living death, the terrible white weight she was powerless to control or stop. The attack had left her so exhausted she remained sedated for the next day. She had no memory of the visit by Dr Franks, or of how many people monitored her slow recovery to consciousness. She had no knowledge of the murder that had taken place, but felt a drugged relief. The violent rage that had gripped and twisted inside her was quietened.

Dr Franks had asked that Anne Maria be allowed time off to visit him at his office. He wanted, as well, another interview with the Baron and Helen Masters, to find clues to what lay behind Vebekka's mental disorder. It was finally agreed that Hylda be brought in to sit with the Baroness until Anne Maria returned.

Ruda Grimaldi felt refreshed, as if her deep dreamless state had revitalised and calmed her. She went over to the canteen and ordered a full breakfast. Hungry, she waited impatiently for the food. She sipped her hot chocolate smiling to herself; her hands were steady, not so much as a tremor. She felt rested, she felt in total control.

When Hylda reached the hotel suite, the Baroness was in a deep sleep. She sat down in a comfortable chair by the bed, and all that could be heard in the vast silent bedroom was the click-click of her knitting needles.

Vebekka slept peacefully, motionless, her hands folded on the starched white linen sheet. She was wearing a white frilly negligée, which did not disguise the sharp bones of her neck and shoulders, the thinness of her arms. Her face was drawn, deep dark circles beneath her closed eyes. The lines around her mouth, her eyes, gave a skeletal look to her face. Saline and glucose drips were still attached to her hands; the tubes and needles had left dark black bruises and a bandage was still wrapped around her left wrist. The room was filled with flowers and baskets of fruit, the air heavy with their perfume. Hylda would have liked to open the window, but it was a dark thundery day, with rain showers.

Half an hour after Hylda arrived, the Baroness stirred and turned her head to face the maid. 'Would you be so kind as to take the drips out of my hand? They hurt me.'

'I don't think I should do that, Baroness, and Anne Maria is not here, and the Baron and Miss Masters are also out.'

The Baroness sighed, as if in acceptance, and Hylda turned back to her knitting. In a second, her charge had pulled out the drip needles, ripped off the adhesive and tossed them aside. She smiled coyly at Hylda, drew her hands beneath the covers, and curled up on her side. Hylda could do nothing but pick up the adhesive from the floor and hang up the drips, switching off the lock.

'Hylda, will you call room service? I want some vanilla ice cream, with chocolate sauce, nuts, and those chocolate Oliver biscuits, plain chocolate, white biscuits – if they haven't got chocolate Oliver, I'll have any plain chocolate biscuits, plain black chocolate.'

Hylda obliged, and in due course a trolley was sent up

with an array of chocolate biscuits and ice creams. She helped the Baroness sit up, and watched in stunned amazement as she slowly began to eat, first a spoonful of ice cream, then a small bite of biscuit. Like a squirrel she nibbled and sucked at the spoon with such childish delight that Hylda felt even more motherly towards her; she tried to hint that perhaps eating so much sweet food was not good for her, but her pleas were ignored, and the entire tray of sweet food was, nibble by nibble, demolished.

The Baroness snuggled down, closer to Hylda, dark chocolate stains round her mouth, even some on her finger tips. The click-click of Hylda's knitting needles soothed her, and she slept again. When the roll of thunder came, she didn't seem to wake, but her hand slipped from the warmth of the covers to hold Hylda's, and the knitting was quietly put aside.

Anne Maria inched open the door, and crept into the room; she put her fingers to her lips, and looked at the dressing-table. She began to take all the medicine and pills visible on it and then rifled the vanity cases. With her arms full, she came to Hylda's side, and whispered, 'The doctor said she is to have no more medication, no more sedation, unless from him.'

Anne Maria hurried from the room and returned with a large packet, unwrapped it, and held it out to show Hylda. 'You know what this is?' Hylda shook her head, and put her fingers to her lips for Anne Maria to lower her voice. 'It's a straitjacket. I don't know about this great doctor – if you ask me he's yet another quack – so I got this just in case.' She put down the jacket and was about to leave when she saw that the drips were not attached. 'Who took those out?'

Hylda gripped the Baroness's hand and whispered, 'I did, they were causing her pain. Let her sleep, she's sleeping . . .'

Anne Maria pursed her lips. 'She needs glucose, she's got to keep up her strength, I'll have to re-do them.'

Hylda felt the Baroness's fingers grip her so tightly that it hurt. She was awake, listening, but Hylda didn't give her away.

'When she wakes, I'll call you, but she has just eaten, and I think it is better she sleeps.'

Anne Maria hesitated and then flounced to the door. 'But I have not seen them, and I will not take any responsibility.'

The grip relaxed, and Hylda gently patted the Baroness's hand. She straightened the bedcovers, leaning over, her face close to the Baroness's, and was touched when the sick woman slipped her arms around her neck and kissed her lips in gratitude.

'I have a terrible fear of needles – of things in my body – she knows, but she hates me. Thank you.'

Hylda smiled, returned to her chair. She picked up her knitting, and the Baroness laughed softly. 'Not knitting needles, though.'

Dr Franks tilted his chair, pulling at his hair. 'Your nurse, Anne Maria, says your wife has some kind of . . . not exactly an obsession, with boxes, vanity boxes. She always travels with three, sometimes four, yes?'

The Baron looked puzzled. 'Yes, they are part of her luggage, one is for her jewellery, one for make-up, one for medical and – I suppose it seems excessive, but not out of the ordinary. I can't understand why on earth the girl would even discuss my wife's travelling accessories with you.'

Franks leaned on his elbows. 'Because I asked. You and your wife travel extensively, yes? And these boxes always accompany her?'

'Yes, so do our cases and trunks. Perhaps you will find some ulterior motive in the fact I always have more—'

Franks interrupted. 'I am only interested in your wife at the moment, Baron. She always travels with an extensive wardrobe but rarely if ever wears three-quarters of the contents. According to Anne Maria, many items your wife insists on travelling with have *never* been worn, yes? What I am trying to determine is, does your wife appear, in your personal opinion, to have items of clothing in very different styles? Perhaps appear to you as different characters, or seem different to you at times?'

'That is the entire reason I am here. My wife has periods of sanity and insanity.'

Franks wandered around the room. 'Has anyone ever suggested to you that your wife may have a personality disorder? Could possibly be a multiple personality?'

The Baron shook his head and glared at Helen Masters.

Franks turned his attention to her. 'What do you think?'

'No, I don't think she is – or I didn't. But she said something that'll interest you. I wrote it down, actually . . .'

Helen opened her bag and took out a small notebook. 'Quote, when I found her last night, she said, "We have done something terrible." Not I, but we.'

The telephone rang and Franks snatched it up, but spoke only for a second before he handed it to the Baron. 'It's for you, long distance. If you wish to be in private, I am sure Dr Masters and I can—'

The Baron gestured with his hand for them to stay as he listened to the caller. He then covered the mouthpiece. 'It's all right, it's Françoise, my secretary, from Paris.'

The doctor handed him a pen and notepad.

The call went on for some time, the Baron saying little but making notes. Helen whispered to Franks, 'She is very particular about her clothes, they are in many cases designed for her, but I have never noticed a marked difference in styles – say little girl to tart – I would simply say that the Baroness has a wardrobe any woman would be envious of. However, she does seem obsessive about the vanity cases.'

She was interrupted as the Baron dropped the phone back on the hook, and sighed. 'Gerard, my man in New York, has been having great difficulty tracing my wife's family. He started at her old model agency. They had no record of Vebekka ever having been signed with them. They then passed him on to someone who had run the agency before them. He said he had represented a girl called Rebecca Lynsey; he recalled she later changed her name to Vebekka, using just her Christian name for work. He had no records on hand but would see if he could trace his ex-wife who ran the business with him. But one thing he was sure about – or as sure as he could be ...' the Baron was very disturbed as he continued, 'He said that my wife's maiden name, Lynsey, was not her real name either, but one used for modelling. He could not recall ever having heard her real surname. Why would she have lied to me? I don't understand it.'

Franks rubbed his head. 'But when her father died, didn't you see a name, something to indicate that Lynsey wasn't her family name?'

The Baron shook his head. 'Gerard'll call again as soon as he has anything else. He's going to Philadelphia tonight. I don't understand, I mean Lynsey was the name on her passport, I'm sure of it. I've asked him to fax any new developments to the hotel.'

Franks raised an eyebrow at Helen. 'Well, this is getting very interesting. Vebekka is really Rebecca, and you have never heard her mention this, never seen it on any document? She has never referred to herself as Rebecca?'

The Baron shook his head. 'No, never. I have always known her as Vebekka Lynsey.'

Franks patted the Baron's shoulder. 'When she was in New York, did she meet anyone there, have friends there?'

'No, we have mutual friends, or family friends, but I have never seen anyone walk up to her and call her Rebecca, if that is what you mean. Also I have never seen her birth certificate, there never seemed to be a reason before now – that is, if there is a valid reason now.'

Franks's eyes turned flinty as he said, 'I am simply trying to find clues to your wife's mental problems, because I want to begin my treatment as soon as she is physically capable of walking into this place unaided.'

Franks sat on his desk, his heel tapping. The Baron's antagonism infuriated him, but he could not let his irritation show. Pleasantly, he asked, 'You recalled yesterday – Baron? Are you listening to me? – you recalled the first time you witnessed your wife's mental instability, yes?'

The Baron nodded. Franks asked if he could remember any other instances.

The Baron sighed, crossing his legs, staring at his highly polished shoe. 'I mentioned the circus. Er, to be quite honest there have been so many, over so many years and . . .'

He paused, and Franks knew something had come to him: he could see it, feel it in the way the Baron frowned then hesitated, as if recalling the moment and then dismissing it. Franks leaned forward. 'Yes? What is it?'

The Baron shrugged. 'It was in the late seventies, and this one had no connection to any of the children. We were in New York. We were at my apartment, we were both reading the *New York Times*. She was reading the real-estate section, I had the rest of it. She suddenly snatched the paper from my hands; it fell on to the table, the coffee pot tipped over me. I don't think she intended to spill the coffee, though at the time I believed she had done it for some perverse reason – perhaps because I wasn't paying her any attention, I don't know, sometimes she is exceptionally childish. Anyway, I suppose I behaved childishly too, because I insisted she give me the paper back. She refused, there was an argument, not a very pleasant one, and—'

The Baron shrugged his shoulders again, as if he suddenly felt the episode not worth continuing. Franks, however, leaned forwards: 'Go on . . . she took the rest of the paper, and then what?'

'Well, as I recall, I went into my bathroom, showered, and was dressing when the maid – no, it was my butler – said there seemed to be a slight fracas in the foyer. The apartment was, still is, exceptionally well managed. The block has a foyer and a doorman. Directly next door to the building is a small news-stand. My wife, still in her dressing-gown, was, so I was told, in the foyer, her arms full of every conceivable newspaper, and when I went down I discovered her sitting on the floor ripping the newspapers apart, throwing pages aside. She was on her hands and knees, scouring each page, but to this day, I have no idea what for or why. All I know is that it was exceptionally embarrassing, and she took a great deal of cajoling and persuasion to return to the apartment.' Franks waited, expecting more, but the Baron clasped his hands together. 'That's it, really.'

'Did you ever ask her why she wanted the papers?'

'Of course.'

'Did she give you an explanation?'

'No, she didn't speak at all for over a week. She seemed elated, slightly hysterical, always smiling, but I couldn't get a word out of her as to why she was behaving in such a way, or what on earth had sparked the breakdown.'

'Breakdown?'

'Well, that is what the therapist called it, and Vebekka calmed down eventually, even seemed to forget the entire incident.'

'Did you ever check through the papers, find anything in them to give a reason for her behaviour?'

The Baron shook his head. 'I took it to be just another of her . . . problems.'

Franks remained silent for a moment before asking if the Baron could get his contact in the United States to check back to the exact date and obtain copies of the papers. The Baron looked to Helen Masters with an exasperated shrug of his immaculate shoulders, but agreed to try. Franks fell silent again, closing his eyes in concentration, and then asked, softly, whether when the Baron said his wife behaved childishly this meant her voice altered? That she sounded like a child?

'It was just a manner of speech, her act was childish. She didn't, as far as I can recall, speak in a childlike voice.'

Franks noted it again – the fleeting look of guilt or recall passing over the Baron's face. 'Yes? You've remembered something else?'

The Baron stared at the wall. 'She cried, in the night. I woke up, or was wakened by, her crying. I was confused because it sounded – dear God I've never thought of it before – but it was high-pitched, like a child. In fact, so much so, that for a moment, half asleep, I was confused and then I remembered the boys were in Paris.'

Franks said nothing, simply waited.

After a long pause the Baron continued. 'I went into her room and she was sitting up in bed. There was a shadow on the wall from the curtains, the lights from the streets. She was sobbing, pointing to the wall. She said, let me think, what was it now? . . . er . . . oh, yes, she said the curtains were a – no, they were a "Black Angel", then she said over and over, "It wasn't true! It wasn't true." I have no idea what she meant, but when I closed the curtains tightly and there was no more shadow she went back to sleep, but her voice . . .' The Baron looked this time to

Helen, helpless. 'I would describe it now, it was . . . it was like a little girl's, the way she shook her shoulders, and . . . how would you say, that hiccup, you know, the way children do? It was as if she was a child having a nightmare.'

Franks clapped his hands. 'Now we are getting somewhere, and I think some tea would go down well. For you, Baron? And you, Helen?'

Before either had time to reply Franks had scuttled out, barking to some unseen assistant that he wanted tea. He returned to the room, and produced a child's picture-book; he held it like a piece of evidence, as if in a court of law. 'Your wife removed, stole, slipped into her handbag, a similar child's book when she was waiting in reception yesterday. Interesting?'

'When did she do that?' asked Helen Masters.

'When she was here, sitting with Maja. Maja saw her do it. Odd, don't you think? Especially as it's in German. Do you know if this book is also published in Paris, or the United States?'

The Baron was standing with his back to the room, staring from the window, his hands deep in his trouser pockets. 'How would I know?'

'Has your wife stolen or ever been involved in shoplifting?'

The Baron snapped, 'No, never, my wife is not a thief!'

Helen accepted the tea-tray from Maja at the door and carried it to the desk. Franks joked that kleptomania was about the only thing not diagnosed in the Baroness. His humour did not strike the right chord, and Helen quickly passed round the teacups, then sat on a hard-backed chair.

Franks seemed unaware of the atmosphere in the small room. He munched one biscuit after another in rapid succession until the plate was cleared. 'Would you say your wife suffered from agoraphobia?'

The Baron replied curtly that his wife was neither agoraphobic nor claustrophobic, turning to Helen as if for confirmation. She wouldn't meet his eyes.

Franks brushed the biscuit crumbs from his cardigan. 'But she is obsessive. Tell me more about her obsessions.'

'What woman isn't!' the Baron retorted, and then he apologised. 'I'm sorry – that was a stupid reply, considering the situation. Forgive me, but I find this – this constant barrage of questions disturbing, perhaps because ... because I am searching for the correct answers and I am afraid that everything I say, when placed under the microscope, so to speak, makes me appear as if I have not been caring enough, when, I assure you, nothing could be further from the truth.'

The room was silent. The Baron had cupped his chin in his hands, his elbows resting on his knees. Helen Masters focused on a small brown flower-shaped stain on the wall directly in front of her. Franks looked from one to the other. 'Maybe we should take a break now.'

Helen picked up the files as Franks gave her a tiny wink. She went ahead to the waiting car and was about to step inside when the Baron announced that he had to return to the doctor's reception. 'I won't be a moment, wait for me here.'

Dr Franks looked up in surprise as the Baron tapped on his open door and entered, but did not ask if the Baron had forgotten something. He knew intuitively that the Baron wished to speak to him alone. Dr Franks cleared his throat. 'You know, if you would prefer to have these sessions with me alone, Helen is a very understanding woman, perhaps more than you realise. She is, after all, a very good doctor herself.'

'Yes, I know, of course I know, I have tremendous respect for her. I wanted to talk to you privately though.' The Baron could not meet Franks's eyes and turned his face away from him. 'I'd like to tell you something. It concerns my wife – obviously, I suppose.' He smiled, and Franks was struck anew by the man's perfect features, his strong aquiline nose, and deep dark blue eyes.

The Baron moved to the office window and stood with his back to the room. 'I have had many women, known many, I suppose you might call me a promiscuous man, but . . . I did love my wife. I say did, because over the years her behaviour, her illness, has gradually made me hate her. I have, may God forgive me, wished her dead more often than I care to admit, and yet, when she attempts to kill herself . . . my remorse, my dread of her dying and leaving me is very genuine, and my relief when she recovers, very real.' He rested his head against the glass. 'She was, doctor, the most beautiful creature. I wanted to possess her the moment I laid eyes on her. She simply took my breath away. She was sweetness itself, she was naïve, she was nervous, like an exquisite exotic bird, and her fragility made me almost afraid of her, as though if I held her too tightly, kissed her too deeply, she would be crushed. The more I got to know her, the more delightful she became, but in those days my fear of—' He hesitated as if searching for the right word, then turned to face Franks. 'I had a fear of breaking her, that I could break her, hurt her. She soon assured me I could not, and during our courtship she became more vibrant, even more outgoing. She was very amusing with a wicked sense of humour, a great tease. She was, doctor, everything I had ever dreamed. I married her against tremendous opposition from my family, especially my mother. Perhaps Mama had some insight into Vebekka, but I would hear none of it. I refused to listen. The first few months of marriage, I don't think I have ever known such happiness, such total commitment. I had never loved like that, or felt so loved, or been so satisfied.'

The Baron moved from the window, one, two paces, then

turned back. His voice was hardly audible. 'I had my first sexual encounter when I was fourteen. I had countless women, from society to brothel. I was a normal and healthy man, I was obviously eligible, and known to be wealthy. I had very rarely, if ever, had to court a woman. Perhaps that was why I wanted Vebekka so much, because she was, to begin with, unobtainable and completely uninterested in me. We did not sleep together until after we were married. I know it may sound laughable but I presumed she was a virgin.'

Franks leaned back in his chair, waiting, but eventually he had to ask as the Baron seemed wrapped in his own thoughts. 'Was she? A virgin?'

The Baron drew out a chair and sat down. 'No . . . no, she was not, she was very experienced. I was a little – no, more than a little – I was shocked. My bride was sexually aggressive, demanding, explicit, and insatiable, a state that I quickly rose to and, as I have said, the first few months with her – I have never known anything so totally consuming, I never experienced such peaks of emotion, such sexual gratification, and then . . . then she became pregnant.'

Franks threaded his hands together, making a cat's cradle with his fingers, waiting.

After a moment the Baron continued, but was obviously very uncomfortable, running his index finger around the collar of his shirt, as if it constricted him in some way. 'A few months after she fell pregnant, she changed. She would not allow me to touch her, allow me anywhere near her, she was terrified of losing the baby by having sex. And then this illness, whatever name we want to call it, began. I was broken, she broke my heart, doctor. It was as if I had never known her, she behaved as if she hated me, and even when I was told that it was because she was ill, all I felt was rejection. My wife had rejected me.'

Franks stared at the church tower he had made with his

fingers, then split his hands apart and placed them flat on the desk. 'But after the birth, she was herself again? Yes? Did you have your old sexual relationship again?'

'No, she continued to reject me as a husband for a long time, at least eight months. Then all of a sudden it was as if it had never happened. I returned home one evening and she was my Vebekka again. But I could not be turned on and off like a tap.'

'So you rejected her?'

The Baron laughed, it was a gentle, self-mocking laugh. 'My wife was a very persuasive woman. For two months it was like a second honeymoon, and then as quickly as it had begun, it was over – she was pregnant again.' The Baron explained that after his second son was born he had attempted to persuade his wife to use birth control, but she had adamantly refused. So the pattern had repeated itself yet again, but after that third time, when she had been ill for six months, he had no desire to be reunited, no desires left.

'So you stopped loving her, after your third child?'

'I realised she was sick, knew by then that she did not really know what she was doing during these periods. So I simply arranged my life around her.' His face flushed with guilt. He had not been at home as often as he should have been, he blamed himself. There was nothing of great importance in anything the Baron was discussing, but Franks waited patiently.

And then the guilty expression in the Baron's eyes was replaced by an icy coldness. When he spoke, his voice grew quieter, almost vicious. 'I knew my wife had taken to leaving the house late in the evening. She never took the car, always hired a taxi, and on many occasions did not return home until the following morning. I began to have her followed, for her own good, you understand?'

'Were you considering a divorce?'

The Baron dismissed the question with a shake of his head. He spoke quickly, not disguising his disgust. 'She was picking up men, truck drivers, cab drivers, wandering around the red-light districts. As soon as I discovered this, I faced her with it, and she denied she had ever left the house, but she continued her midnight crawls. Even when I was threatened with blackmail, she denied she was – virtually soliciting.'

'You mean, she was paying for sex?'

'Occasionally, or she was paid. It was a terrible time, and I was at my wits' end. I have never considered divorce. She is my wife and the mother of my children. We are a Catholic family. It was out of the question.'

'Was? Have you changed your mind?'

The Baron picked up his coat, gave a distant smile. 'Just a slip of the tongue.' His arrogance returned, he was remote, icy cold. 'If you can do nothing, then I am – and I assure you I have never considered this before – but I am prepared to have my wife certified.'

The control slipped again. The Baron leaned over the desk. 'I don't understand myself, you see, I just don't understand, after everything I have been through! I don't understand.'

Franks slowly stubbed out his cigar. 'Understand what exactly?'

'That I can . . . last night, I felt attracted to my wife. I did not believe myself capable of wanting her again. I must not allow her to manipulate me. I am tired, worn out by her. You are my last chance, perhaps hers. I ask you not just to help my wife, but me – help me!'

Franks nodded, it was time for dinner, his stomach rumbled. He hoped the Baron would leave.

At that moment, Maja tapped on the door and popped

her head in. 'I'm sorry to interrupt, but Dr Masters said to tell you the car's still waiting, but not to worry, she has taken a taxi back to the hotel.'

Franks gave Maja a pleading look.

'And you have another appointment in half an hour, doctor!' Maja closed the door.

Franks rose to his feet, and the Baron was already by the door, his hand on the handle. 'Thank you for your time, I appreciate it.'

Franks clasped the Baron's hand in a firm handshake. 'I thank you for your honesty, and let us hope we will gain some results.'

At last Franks was alone and he slumped into his chair, buzzing the intercom for Maja. She appeared almost immediately, and smiled. 'My, that was a long return visit! I hope it was beneficial.'

Franks laughed, and rubbed his belly. 'I need food. I am starving to death!'

Maja brought in a tray of sandwiches and coffee, plus the paper which Franks hadn't yet had time to read. He settled back, making himself comfortable, his eyes roaming over the headlines, and then he flipped the paper open to the second page, glancing over the ads for the forthcoming circus, paying no attention to the short news bulletins. One five-line article stated that the *Polizei* had discovered a body in a small East Berlin hotel the previous day.

CHAPTER FIVE

THE CHAMBERMAID had not changed the bed linen of room 40, because the 'Do Not Disturb' card was hanging from the door. It was not until later in the afternoon when she was vacuuming the corridor that she tapped on the closed door, waited for a reply and, receiving none, entered using her master set of keys. The curtains were drawn, the television set turned on. The room was neat, except for the unmade bed, its coverlet bunched on the floor under the bed.

The maid fetched clean towels, sheets and pillowcases, and went back into the room. She tossed the clean linen down on the chair and drew back the curtains. She went into the bathroom, collected the dirty towels and dropped them on to the floor. Two were bloodstained and she picked them up between finger and thumb distastefully. She then replaced the towels with fresh ones, and was washing down the sink and bath when a friend popped her head round the door to ask if she was nearly through for the day as it was after three.

Both women were due off at two-thirty and both had other jobs to do in the early evening. Together they began to clean the room, and one pulled the sheets back. 'It's not been slept in. Christ! It's freezing in here, they must have turned off the central heating, some people are weird.'

Both women bent down to the rolled bedcover and tugged it from beneath the bed. They felt it catch on one of the wire mattress springs, and pulled together. And screamed, virtually in unison.

Tommy Kellerman's body rolled free of the bedcover, the section covering his head dried hard with black blood.

Screaming at the tops of their voices the women ran down the corridor towards the elevators. Someone carrying a loaded tea-tray of dirty crockery was about to step out of the lift when they appeared, arms waving and shouting garbled half-screams as they pointed frantically to the room. The laden man hurried to the room and was in no more than a few seconds, when he came out, his face drained as he stuttered, 'Dear God, it's a child – somebody's killed a child in there!'

By the time the *Polizei* arrived, the corridor was filling with gawping spectators, guests and the two chambermaids. The manager of the hotel was trying to keep some semblance of order, shouting for people to stand back, but he was very unsteady on his feet, having been dragged out of his quarters. The tails of his collarless shirt hung out over his hurriedly drawn-on trousers.

Polizei Oberrat Torsen Heinz pushed his way through the throng, holding up his badge. Three uniformed officers followed behind him, shoving people away. Torsen Heinz was the first to arrive at the open bedroom door. He asked if the doctor or forensic teams had been there. He could see the tiny body, the small foot in the red sock, and his stomach turned over. He did not attempt to remove the congealed mess beneath the bedcover, and trod gingerly and carefully around the body.

The manager hung at the doorway, peering into the room, demanding to know who had torn pages out of the registration book.

The doctor arrived and took only a second to certify the body as deceased, which was all he was required to do, but until he had verified the obvious work could not commence.

The pathologist came in, followed by two technicians from the forensic department. They began yelling for everyone to clear out of the room.

Oberrat Heinz checked the room quietly, using a pencil to open a couple of drawers. The doctor looked over to him as he departed. 'It's not a kid, it's a dwarf or a midget and he's taken one hell of a beating, but that's rather stating the obvious. G'night.'

The pathologist carefully slipped plastic bags round the tiny red socks; he applied a bag to Kellerman's right arm and hand, and then reached for his left. He stood up rubbing his knee and, looking down, realised he was kneeling on a set of broken dentures. He beckoned Heinz. 'I'm sorry, I think I may have broken them. My mistake, but someone should have checked this area.'

Heinz stared at the broken teeth, and then stepped out of the way as the pathologist continued his work, about to wrap Kellerman's left arm in a protective plastic bag. 'Jesus, look at this, it's been hacked, a big chunk of skin removed, just above the wrist!'

Heinz sent one of the uniformed officers out to check for any rubbish that might have been removed. The pathologist finished wrapping the tiny body, and then his team slipped a plastic sheet beside Kellerman, rolled him on top of it, tied all four ends and lifted the body up.

'He booked in early yesterday,' Torsen Heinz said to no one in particular. He tugged at his blond hair, watched as two men dusted door handles and mirror, then made his way down to the so-called reception area. The manager, now wearing a jacket, insisted he had been on duty and had seen no one who was not an official guest. Heinz listened, knowing that local tarts used the place for their clients, but said nothing, simply asked to see the guest register. The manager shoved it towards him, pointing with a stubby, dirty fingernail to the torn pages. He scratched his greasy head, tried to recall the dead man's name, but the name escaped him.

'What about his passport, did you see his passport, retain it?'

The manager was sweating. 'I saw it – checked it, I know the rules. He had luggage, a sort of greenish carryall, did you find it?'

'But you don't recall his name?'

'No, he just signed, and I gave him the key, told him what floor. I was on the phone when he checked in.'

'What nationality?'

'American – Kellerman!' The manager beamed. 'I remember, it was Kellerman.'

No one Heinz questioned had seen anyone entering the room and he and his sergeant took off for the mortuary to see what they could learn there. It had closed for the night.

Heinz returned early the following morning. Tommy Kellerman's naked body was even more tragic in death than in life, his squat hands spread out palm upwards, his legs spread-eagled, his pride exposed, a wicked freak of nature to give this small, stunted body a penis any man would be proud to display: it was virtually down to the kneecaps on his twisted legs.

The bedcover had to be inched and cut away from his head as the blood had clotted like glue. There was hardly a feature left intact: nose broken, cheek, jaw and forehead completely concave; blood clotted in his eyes, his nose, his ears and his gaping mouth; the bottom row of false teeth had cut into his upper lip, giving him the look of a Neanderthal man, a chimp – even more so as his thick curly hair was spiky with his own blood.

The pathologist ascertained that Kellerman had died near to midnight the night before he was found and had eaten some four hours before he was hammered to death. He spent considerable time over the open wound on

Kellerman's left forearm: he could tell it had been made while Kellerman was alive, and that the skin cut away was probably a tattoo, judging by the faint edge of blue left along one skin edge. The pathologist added that whoever killed Kellerman must have been covered in blood, as the main artery had been cut on the tattoo wrist.

Kellerman's clothes were spread out on the lab tables; again they gave a tragic impression of the wearer as they were so small, so childlike. In his underpants semen stains mingled with the final evacuation of his bowels: it was ascertained that he had ejaculated shortly before he was killed.

His pockets were empty, apart from a rubber band and a Zippo lighter. His clothes were tagged and listed, his body washed and tagged, placed in a child's mortuary bag, laid on a drawer and pushed into the freezer.

Torsen Heinz hung around for a while, then returned to the hotel to question the hall porter.

The toothless decrepit man could recall no one entering the hotel while he was working, or at least no one who warranted any special attention. He did recall seeing a big man, wearing a black hat, outside the hotel – in fact, the man could possibly have just left the main entrance, he couldn't be sure, he had simply passed him on the street as he emptied the rubbish. He could not describe him in any detail, just that he was tall, wearing a black hat, and it was around eleven or perhaps a bit later.

Torsen Heinz returned to his office and sat at his large wooden desk. The station was in a baroque-style building in the Potsdam district of East Berlin, and for equipment there were half a dozen old typewriters and an obsolete telephone system incapable of connecting with West Berlin. The principal piece of modern technology was a microwave oven, installed two months before to heat up the officers' lunches. Torsen and his men had been unable to keep up

107

with the sharp increase in criminal activity since the fall of the socialist regime. Previously East Berlin's criminal behaviour had been hushed up by the Stasi secret police or played down by the state-controlled media. Now, Polizei Oberrat Heinz and forty-odd uniformed officers had to learn as fast as possible to make their own decisions.

Sitting with his microwave-heated breakfast sausages Torsen felt swamped. None of the officers he had assigned to the Kellerman case had made any report because they had clocked out promptly at six o'clock. No matter how much Torsen argued that they were no longer working from nine to six but if necessary round the clock, they were too used to the old regime to change their working habits. There was not one man on duty yet, and it was half past eight. Torsen had already been working for several hours.

Alone, he sifted through the statements and facts he had so far gathered about the dwarf. He surmised that Kellerman was possibly an American citizen as, according to the hotel manager, he spoke with an American accent. Without a passport or any documents to substantiate this, he decided he should first contact the US Embassy to see if they had any record of his arrival in Berlin. The next call would be to the main circus which was being heralded as the biggest event of the season. He tried to contact the embassy, but the telephone switchboard was still closed down, waiting for the telephonist to arrive. He finished his breakfast, carefully folded his cloth napkin and put it back in his briefcase, washed his hands at the cracked sink and returned to his desk. There was a photograph of his father on the wall behind the desk, wearing the same uniform as Torsen's. Gunter Heinz's picture was brown with age. Torsen gave the photograph a brief nod and determined that until it was absolutely necessary he would not go cap in hand to the West Berlin police; they had already been forced to assist him on a number of cases, and he had taken a lot of ridicule from his West Berlin 'colleagues' with their high-tech computers and fax machines. He wondered how well they would cope without so much as one single telephone connected after 6 p.m. or before 9 a.m.

He turned in his chair and looked at the memos taped to the wall beneath his papa's frowning face. 'Accept no coincidence – only facts.' He had stuck the typed scrap of paper up after he had been made chief inspector at exactly the same age his father had been promoted; his father's memo had been written when Torsen had first made the decision to follow his father into the *Polizei*.

Gunter Heinz was now residing in a home for the elderly, suffering from senility, for most of the time happily unaware of his surroundings – or for that matter who he was – but occasionally having strange flashes of recall, as if the clouds lifted, and in these moments Torsen was able to converse with him, even play chess. Torsen had arranged with the nurses that whenever his father was lucid, they call him. The last time he had hurried to visit, however, the old man had glared at him and asked who the hell he was. Torsen had replaced his chessboard in his case.

The nurse had apologised, whispering that she was sorry to have called him, but earlier in the day his father had asked to speak with his son on an important matter. Torsen had understood and was grateful for her kindness in contacting him. During Torsen's conversation with the nurse, his father was ripping small pieces of paper tissue from a box, carefully licking each tiny scrap, sticking it on his nose and blowing it off like a snowflake. A sad spectacle, but one that would have been laughable if it had not been his own father.

The desk phone pinged, signalling that the switchboard was now in operation. Torsen rang the US Embassy. They had no record of an American citizen named Kellerman in residence in East Berlin, but suggested that the border patrols be contacted, since if the deceased came across from Western Europe by train or even by bus then his particulars might have been recorded. The flow of refugees arriving in Germany was causing mayhem, and there was an attempt to record everyone travelling in by car or train. It was also possible that Kellerman had used the main airport and travelled to the East section; the airport authorities should also be approached.

Torsen sent two uniformed officers to try to discover Kellerman's origins and then set off with Sergeant Volker Rieckert for his first destination, the circus.

The patrol car got bogged down in the mud, but the attendant would not let them drive any closer to the private trailers and the performers' car park. Inspector Torsen displayed his ID, but it had no effect; the raincoated attendant simply pointed to a railing, also bogged down in the mud.

Torsen and his sergeant sloshed across the space that would eventually be used by the customers, but which now resembled a bomb site; deep holes and cinders made the long walk to the trailer sections and big tents a hazard. Their trousers were soaked at the bottom, their hair plastered to their heads, as they made their way towards the cashier's trailer.

The girl had dyed bright red hair, with a pink comb stuck in the top that matched her lipstick. She looked at his ID and blew a large pink bubblegum bubble, then pointed towards the manager's building. Torsen swore under his breath as he felt the mud squelch into his hand-knitted woollen socks.

The circus's administrator welcomed the men into his office. It was in a small building at the side of a massive tent, and the office itself was small and overheated. It was filled with neat filing cabinets, and the walls were covered in large circus posters. Romy Kelm, the administrator, a balding bespectacled man, introduced himself formally and ordered tea to be brought.

The two officers were settled on folding chairs, and Mr Kelm seated himself behind his pristine desk. He was quickly able to provide Torsen with a Christian name: the dead man could very well be Tommy Kellerman. Kelm hastened to add that Kellerman was not employed by the circus, but had been more than twenty years ago. He knew also that Kellerman had been in gaol in the United States, was prone to fighting and drunken brawls, and had stolen from his own people. He had absconded with a company's wages eight years previously when attached to the Kings Circus, a smaller touring company. The circus telegraph system of internal newspapers had given details of his theft and subsequent prison sentence. Kelm inferred that a number of people still resented Kellerman, to many of whom he owed money.

Torsen was given a detailed list of all the performers gathering for the opening night who may have known Kellerman or worked with him. Kelm told him that the dead man's ex-wife, Ruda Kellerman, was a star performer and was, in fact, still using the name Kellerman, although she had remarried long ago.

Torsen's head was reeling; it could take him a few weeks, even months, to accumulate all the data he was being handed. His sergeant was dumbstruck as he scrawled names and contact numbers endlessly on his pad. They spent more than two hours in the little office, and the small room became so hot that both police officers could feel their socks and shoes drying out, stiffening along with the bottoms of their trousers.

Finally, Torsen was assisted into his raincoat and handed a neat layout of the trailers, so that it would be easy for the two officers to get their bearings, and the dapper Mr Kelm reiterated his eagerness to help. The circus did not want any adverse publicity, their biggest show of the season was to open in a few days' time, their acts had come from all over the world, the opening night was to be a major occasion. Kelm was anxious to know whether anyone from his company was involved in the Kellerman incident and, if so, he wanted it dealt with as quietly and as quickly as possible. He was virtually saying to Torsen that if it was one of ours, get him, take him and get it over with. He kept gesturing to the posters as if to confirm what he was saying: 'Circus people often get a lot of ordinary folk against them, as if they are tinkers or gyppos. We are all good God-fearing people, who work hard for a living. Many of our people are world-famous and we are proud to present to a united Germany what we hope will be the finest display ever seen in this country. We have extended the main arena, and built a second and third ring . . .' As he ushered the policemen into the corridor, he said he felt sure no one in the present company was involved with Kellerman, that he was a man who had been virtually ostracised, a man who had turned against his people, who was unemployable . . . blacklisted.

Torsen suggested gently, without malice, that Kellerman's reputation surely meant that if many people detested him enough, perhaps one could have wanted to kill him. He received no reply, just a cold stare from the washed-out eyes behind the rimless glasses, but Kelm managed a tight smile, saying quietly he hoped Torsen was incorrect, and again offering any assistance necessary, saying that he was always available.

Torsen eased open the main exit door, and looked out at the downpour. He swore, then hunched up his shoulders and stepped out. His sergeant followed, tucking his thick notepad into his pocket, along with the free posters and cards that had been pressed into his hands by Kelm for his children – if they wanted to see the show, all they had to do was contact him and he would arrange tickets.

The inspector sloshed ahead and Rieckert quickened his pace, hunching his shoulders in his navy raincoat. 'Las Vegas, you see that poster on the high wire act! How much do you think a set-up like this costs?' He received no answer as he caught up with Torsen. 'That Kelm was pretty helpful, wasn't he?'

'Yeah he was, wasn't he? It's called get off our backs, schmuck! We've got our work cut out for us. You want to split up or shall we start it together?'

A string of horses draped in protective blankets was led past them on a single rein by a sour-faced boy. Rieckert stared with open curiosity, and then looked at four equally sour-faced men wearing dark blue overalls. They carried pitchforks, and one promptly cleared away some horse dung as the others hurried on towards the practice arena. Rieckert's jaw dropped again as coming up behind him were five massive elephants. He shouted to ask Torsen if he had seen them. Torsen looked at him – it was hard to miss five fully grown elephants.

The two men plodded on through the mud, heading towards the main trailer park. Torsen had decided he would interview the ex-Mrs Kellerman first. By the time he discovered they had been reading the trailer route upside down, he was sodden again and his hair was dripping. After asking a number of scurrying figures with umbrellas and waterproof capes, they arrived at the Grimaldi trailer. Torsen dragged his suede shoes across the grids outside and tapped on the door of the glistening trailer. Behind him Rieckert looked at it with admiration, wondering how much it was worth. The door opened, and Torsen looked up, still on the lower step.

'My name is Detective Chief Inspector Torsen Heinz,

and this is Detective Sergeant Rieckert. Would it be possible for us to come in?'

Grimaldi stared, Torsen hesitated, asked politely if Grimaldi spoke German, and received a curt nod of confirmation.

'We would like to speak to a . . . your wife. She was Mrs Kellerman, yes?'

Grimaldi nodded, and then stepped aside. Torsen moved up the steps to enter. The officers were instructed to take off their shoes, and there was considerable fumbling around at the door, as Rieckert couldn't undo his soaking laces. The two men's coats were hung on a hook at the back of the front door while both pairs of shoes were propped up outside, promptly filling with rainwater.

Grimaldi gestured for the men to follow him and, now abreast of him, Torsen realised they were of similar height, six feet, but that Grimaldi was a big, raw-boned man, with very broad shoulders, whereas Torsen was bordering on skinny.

Grimaldi sat on a thickly cushioned bench seat, and offered coffee, but both men declined, sitting side by side on the opposite padded bench seat, grateful for the cushion after the hard-backed chairs in the administration office.

'Ruda's feeding the cats, should be back shortly.'

Rieckert took covert looks around the spacious room, greatly impressed, while Torsen stared at the posters and photographs, then gave a charming smile of recognition. 'I saw you – saw you performing, do you call it? Many years ago. I was just a kid, but I have never forgotten it, you were fabulous.'

Grimaldi's dark eyes were suspicious, brooding; he hardly acknowledged the compliment, but flicked a look in the direction of the posters. He pointed to the one of Ruda, and then looked back. 'This is Ruda, you see, Ruda

Kellerman. She still uses his name. What's that little piece of shit done now?'

Torsen straightened his back. 'He's been murdered, sir, we are both from East Berlin *Polizei*. He was murdered in East Berlin some time the night before last.'

Grimaldi smiled, showing big even teeth, a little yellowish, wolfish, then he laughed out loud and slapped his cord trousers with his huge hand. 'Well, you'll have a lot of contenders. He was a detestable creature, real vermin, somebody should have smothered him years ago. What was he doing in East Berlin?'

'We don't know, sir, and as yet we have had no formal identification of the body, but we are led to believe it was Tommy Kellerman. Would you mind me asking where you were last night? I mean, the night before last.'

Grimaldi banged his chest. 'Me?'

Torsen nodded. 'We will have to ask everyone at the circus if they saw him. Did you, by any chance?'

'Me?'

Rieckert's jaw dropped slightly, he had never come across anyone as large as Grimaldi. The man appeared to be built like an ox, his hands twice the size of any normal man's.

Grimaldi leaned back and then looked at Torsen Heinz. 'You serious? Night before last? Oh, yes. I was here, all night, ask my wife – she couldn't sleep because of my snoring. As to Kellerman, lemme think, I've not seen the creep for maybe five ... no, more, I thought he was in gaol, last saw him – must be eight to ten years ago.'

'You have recently been in Paris? Was he working with you then?'

Torsen fumbled with his notes, giving Rieckert a cue to take out his notebook also. But it was in his raincoat pocket, so he excused himself and had a tough time retrieving it from the pocket – the pages tore slightly, damp from the rain. When he returned, he had to step over Grimaldi's outstretched legs.

Grimaldi was shrugging his massive shoulders. 'No one would employ him, he stole an entire week's wages, from ... can't remember, but no circus would touch him. Besides, he was in gaol! I think he got extra time for beating up some inmate, that's what I heard.'

The door opened, and Ruda walked in. She leaned against the door frame, looking first to Grimaldi, and then to the two men.

'Kellerman's been murdered,' said Grimaldi.

Ruda eased off her boots. 'What do we do, throw a party?'

Grimaldi grinned, and introduced Torsen Heinz and Rieckert. Ruda walked further into the room and shook the officers' hands as they both stood up to greet her. Ruda's hand felt like a man's to Torsen, rough, calloused. She was almost as tall as he was but, judging by the handshake, a hell of a lot stronger. They made quite a pair, Mr and Mrs Grimaldi.

'Is this true?' she asked.

Torsen nodded. He had never seen such a total lack of emotion. Kellerman had, after all, once been this woman's husband.

'Would you mind if I asked you some questions, Mrs Kell – er – Grimaldi?'

Ruda placed her boots by the door. 'Ask what you need to know. Is there coffee on, Luis?'

Grimaldi eased himself out of his seat, went into the kitchen and poured his wife coffee, again asking if either of the men would care for some. They both replied that they would, and he banged around getting the mugs and sugar together.

Ruda sat on the seat vacated by her husband, now

rubbing her hair with a towel. Torsen rested his elbows on his knees. 'When did you last see him?'

She closed her eyes and leaned back. 'That's a tough one. Let me think . . . Luis? When did he come to the winter quarters? Was it six, eight years ago? I can't think.'

Grimaldi set down the mugs of thick black coffee; he didn't offer any milk, but a large glass bowl of brown sugar. As the two policemen spooned in their sugar, Ruda and Grimaldi had a short conversation about one of the cats. Ruda was worried that she was off her food: if it continued she'd change her feed, maybe put her back on the meat instead of the meal. They seemed totally unconcerned about Kellerman.

'Do you have a photograph?'

Ruda looked at Torsen and raised her eyebrow. 'Of the cats?'

'No, of Kellerman.'

'You must be joking. Do you think I would want a reminder that I was ever in any way connected to that piece of shit? No, I do not have a photograph.'

Torsen sipped his coffee. It was odd that neither had asked how Kellerman had died. They continued to be totally disinterested, and Ruda, when asked where she had been at the time of the murder, lit a cigarette and rubbed her nose. 'The night before last, shit, I dunno. Last night I was here working the act until after twelve.'

'No, the night before.'

Ruda thought for a moment then frowned. 'Guess I was here, worked the routines, then had supper over at the canteen, then came to bed. What time did I come in, Luis?'

Grimaldi took a picture of himself from the wall. He handed it to Torsen. 'That was the last time I played Berlin. You said you saw my act, more than fifteen years ago—'

Ruda interrupted. 'It would be more than fifteen, lemme see.'

She looked over the wall of photographs, and Torsen put his mug down. They were both discussing the exact time they were last in Berlin. Ruda suddenly turned to face him. 'You're sure it is Tommy Kellerman? I think he's still in prison.'

Torsen stood up and straightened his sodden trousers, the crease no longer in existence. 'We would be sure if you would be so helpful as to identify him. We have no one formally to identify him, so we ask your co-operation.'

Ruda hesitated. 'Don't they have fingerprints for that kind of thing? Contact the prison. I don't want to see him, dead or alive. Get someone else, there's many around the camp that knew him.'

'But you were his wife . . .'

Ruda stared hard at Torsen. 'Yes, I was his wife, but I'm not now, and I haven't been for a very long time.'

'For me to cable America and wait for prints could take a considerable time.' He did not add that it could take months as he had no fax machine, nor for that matter any facilities to send cables or check which prison. Gaining permission from Interpol to assist him could entail more paperwork, more time.

'If there's no one else . . .' Ruda said, obviously not liking the situation.

'Thank you. Thank you for your time, I may have to question you again. Oh yes, one more thing, the tattoo. Kellerman had a tattoo on his left arm. Could you tell me what it was like?'

Grimaldi laughed. 'Probably gave the size of his prick, he was so proud of it. Don't look at me, I never let the creep within two feet of me. Ask her, she was – as you so rightly say – married to him.'

Ruda looked at the thick carpet, her stockinged feet

digging into the pile. 'A tattoo? He might have had it done in prison, he didn't have one when I knew him.'

Torsen shook their hands, and again felt how strong her grip was. 'Maybe he was looking for work. Ask at the main administration office,' Ruda suggested.

Torsen smiled his thanks, and just as he opened the door, Grimaldi asked how Kellerman had been murdered. Torsen dragged on his raincoat. 'Some kind of hammer, multiple blows to his head.'

Grimaldi wiped his mouth with the back of his hand. 'Ah well! Poor little sod had it coming to him.'

Torsen said tersely that no one had to be subjected to such a horrifying death. He then smiled coldly at Ruda, and asked if she would accompany them when he had finished taking statements from the rest of the people he needed to speak to. Ruda was tight-lipped, asking how long it would take – with the show due to open shortly she had very little time.

Torsen said he would be through as fast as he could, perhaps in two hours, if it was convenient. He did not wait for a reply, but left the trailer. The men's shoes were filled with rainwater, and they sat on the mud-caked steps to replace them.

From the trailer window, Ruda watched them hurry through the lanes between the trailers, pause to examine their map, and then head for the Giorgios' trailer. 'They've gone to the Giorgios'!'

Grimaldi chuckled. 'They'll last ten minutes. What do you make of it?'

Ruda sighed, making no reply, so he repeated the question. 'Maybe it isn't him!' she snapped.

'Well, you'll know soon enough, he'll not get anyone else to ID the body.' Grimaldi leaned back, then lifted his feet up to rest on the bench seat. 'You married him! Maybe he left some dough to you in his will.'

'Yeah. The only thing he's left is a nasty smell and a string of debts. He can get someone else to ID him, I'm not going.'

'But you were his wife.'

She swiped at him with the towel. 'You knew him, you identify him, it'll give you something to do.'

'Ah, but I didn't know him as well as you, sweetheart. You can't get out of that.'

Ruda sat down, pushing his feet aside. 'I can't do it, Luis. Don't make me, don't let them make me see him.'

Grimaldi cocked his head to one side. 'Why not? He's dead. You telling me it's affecting you? I thought you detested his guts.'

'I do, I did, but I don't want to see him.'

Grimaldi pinched her cheek. 'You use his name, sweetheart . . . Serves you right.'

Ruda swung out at him, this time with the flat of her hand. She caught his face hard, and he gripped her wrist, shoving her roughly aside.

'Give me one good reason why I should do anything for you!'

'Fuck you!'

Ruda punched him, and Grimaldi swung off the bench, landing a hard, open-handed slap to her face. She kicked him, he slapped her again, and this time she didn't fight back. Her face twisted like a child's, and he drew her to him. 'OK, OK. I'll take you, I'll go with you!'

He began to smooth her hair from her face, massage the throbbing scars at her temples. Her body felt strong in his arms, strong as a man's, and for her to be vulnerable like this was rare. He held her closer. 'Ruda, Ruda . . . why do we torment each other the way we do?'

She whispered like a child, 'Just be with me, Luis, just stay with me, I don't want to go by myself.'

'Stay with you, huh? Until the next time you want something?' He couldn't help himself – as soon as he said it he wished he hadn't. She backed away from him, her hands in fists, and he threw up his hands in a gesture of impotence. 'We have to get divorced, Ruda, you know it. I can't live like this any more, we're at each other's throats.'

'I don't want to talk about that, not now.'

'Because of that shit Kellerman? Jesus Christ, Ruda, who gives a fuck if he's alive or dead? What concerns me is us, we have to settle the future, settle it, sit down and work out what part of the act you want. I'm through, Ruda, through standing around waiting, at your beck and call.'

'You can't have the act!' She glared at him.

Grimaldi clenched his hands. Like two fighters, they faced each other. 'Fine, you want it, then we arrange a financial settlement. Simple as that, Ruda.'

He saw the way her face changed, the way her dark eyes stared at him, and through him. Her voice was as dark as her eyes. 'Every penny I have earned has been put back into the act. You want out then you go, take your tart, your stupid little bitch, your whore . . . take her and *fuck off*.'

Grimaldi smirked. 'Takes one to know one.'

She went for him like a man, punching at him, kicking, and then she grabbed his hair. He tried to resist, but he couldn't; in the end they were slugging at each other. Crockery smashed, pictures crashed off the walls, and in the confined space they fought until they both lay sprawled, panting, on the floor. She still punched him, hard blows that hurt like hell. 'Take your clothes, take your belongings and get out! Without me you'd have nothing! Without me you'd be a drunken bum!'

She spat at him, and he staggered to his feet, began to open the overhead lockers, throwing not his things, but her belongings at her, around her. 'You take *yours*, you take *your* belongings and get out, go sleep with the animals, sleep with your precious angel! Sleep with any twisted, fucked-up thing that'll keep you!'

Ruda kicked him so hard in the back of his legs that he slumped forwards, hit his head on the side of the cupboard and fell backwards. He lay half across the bunk, half on the floor and she was on top of him, spread-eagled across his body. For one second he thought she was going to bite him: her jaw opened and shut, she was snarling like a wild cat, and then he rolled her – her head cracked back on the floor – and heaved his body on top of her. He bent his head closer, about to scream at her to stop. He felt her body grow limp beneath him, and her arms wound round his neck as she drew him closer. They looked into each other's faces, and there was a soft low moan, in unison, chest to chest, breath to breath, both their hearts thudding with the exertion. The kiss was gentle, his lips softly brushing hers, and then she buried her head in his neck.

They lay together on the floor of the wrecked trailer, their clothes and crockery around them, like lovers having found themselves after a long separation. They lay together with broken glass and shattered pictures of the Great Grimaldi and the fearless Ruda Kellerman.

When he spoke, his voice was filled with pain. 'Let me go, Ruda, because this is where it always ends. I want you now, you can feel I want you, but it always has to end.'

Her voice was muffled, a low half-plea, begging him to take her, to have her. She eased her hands down his body, began to unhook his belt.

He leaned up, gently turning her face, forcing her to look at him. 'Do you want me? Or is this – Ruda, look at me. *Look at me!*' His big hand cupped her chin, forced her to face him. Her eyes were expressionless, glinting hard eyes, dangerous eyes. She couldn't fake it, she had never been able to, she couldn't even do it now when she needed him.

Slowly she let her hands drop to her sides. She made as if to turn over, for him to ease down her trousers, since she could not take him naturally, normally. Small slivers of glass cut into her cheeks, the pain excited her, but she felt no juices, nothing to prepare her body for sex, for his hard erection. She gritted her teeth, waiting.

Grimaldi eased himself up, carefully avoiding the glass, stepping over her, tightening his belt as his erection pressed against his pants; the hardness left him by the time he walked into his own room and quietly closed the door.

Ruda lay in the debris. It had always been this way, they had always fought each other, that part had always excited her, but she had never felt any sexual desire beyond the fight; sex pained and hurt her too much, hurt her insides like sharpened razors. She felt a tiny drop of blood roll down her cheek and she licked it, tasted the salt, the blood, as if the drop of blood replaced a salted tear. She never cried, hadn't for a long time, too long even to remember.

She got up and went into her own room, closing the door as quietly as Grimaldi had shut his. She showered, feeling the hot needles pummel her, then gently began to soap herself. Her fingers massaged her shoulders, her arms, her heavy breasts, and then she began to soap her belly, her strong hands feeling each crude, jagged scar. She massaged and eased the foam down, until she soaped between her legs; the ridges of the scars, hideous thick whitened skin, hard rough skin, skin always a dark plum red, like a birthmark. She rinsed the soap away with cold water, reached for the bath towel, her hair dripping. She hadn't heard him come in, but he was there, holding out the big white bath towel. Gently he wrapped her, as if she were a baby, trapping her arms in the big white softness. He held her close. Her eyes were frightened, childlike, as if the animal in her had gone into hiding; there was no longer any ferocity, no anger. He guided her towards the bed and

123

sat her down. She sat with her head bowed, her hair dripping, covering her face. Luis reached for a small hand-towel and began to dry her hair.

'I'll go to the mortuary, no need for you to do it, I'll go if they need someone.'

She nodded.

'Ruda, look at me. I need someone. I'm not talking about getting my rocks off, I'm talking about . . . needing – I need, you know? As it is now, I feel like half a man, and watching out for you every show isn't enough. It can't go on, this is my last chance. I'm old, maybe Tina can give me a few more good years, give me back my balls. I don't want to fight with you any more, I can't fight you any more. I will need to be able to keep Tina and the baby when it comes, so we have to work out an agreement, one we can both accept. I know how much money you've put in, I know how you've kept us going. I know, Ruda, but I can't go on like this.'

He rubbed her head gently, knowing the burn scars at her temples should not be irritated by the towel. He was so careful, showing more tenderness than he had in years.

There was a tap on the trailer door. It was the inspector asking if Mrs Kellerman could accompany him now to the mortuary. Ruda could hear Grimaldi asking if he could go instead, and she heard the inspector saying that Mrs Kellerman would be preferable. Grimaldi's voice grew a little louder as he said he also knew Kellerman. Then there were whispers, and the trailer door shut.

Grimaldi called out that she had better get dressed, they needed her, but he would accompany her. She began to dress very carefully, choosing a dress, high-heeled shoes and, for the first time in many years, she applied make-up other than her stage make-up. She took her time, a soft voice inside her telling her to stay calm, take things one at a time, she would deal with Luis when the time was right, this was not the right time.

Grimaldi had a quick shave and stared at his reflection, uneasy with the interaction between himself and his wife. He had felt such compassion for her, it confused him, she confused him, but then she always had. He rinsed his face and sat for a moment, remembering ... remembering Florida, how many years ago he couldn't recall, but shortly after they were married. Ruda had wanted a child so badly, he knew how she must feel now with the Tina situation. He understood, but what could he do? It was not his fault.

Luis had held her when she told him, wrapped her in his arms when she came out of the doctor's waiting room, but she had pushed him away. Then, he had so much love for her that he hadn't been angry, just saddened that she pushed him from her. He knew she was fighting to keep control of herself in that way she had – her head up, her jaw out. She didn't cry, he had rarely ever seen her crying; somehow it had been more touching, her desperation to speak matter-of-factly, as if she was not affected.

'I can't have a child, artificially or any other way, so that is that.'

She had put on her coat and walked out of the doctor's waiting room, and he had waited a moment to accept the news for himself, then followed her to the car. They had driven back to their winter quarters, Ruda staring ahead, giving him directions as she always did – Luis was never good at routes and their quarters were far out of the main city. But he would never forget that journey, the Florida heat, the quiet calm voice, flatly telling him to go right, then left ...

Ruda had become deeply depressed: nothing he said or attempted to do seemed to interest her. It was then that he had suggested she play a bigger part in the act; up until that point she had simply helped his boys muck out the cages. He had never contemplated her working in the ring with him, only suggested it to give her something else to think about. He had begun to train her, and to his relief her depression lifted, the dark sadness dispersed, but since then their personal relationship had deteriorated. Ever since the visit to the specialist she shrank away from him whenever he touched her. He let it go, hoping that in time she would come back to his bed.

The animals, his cats, had brought out a side in her that at first impressed him: she worked tirelessly, showed no fear, no regard for her own life. No matter how he reprimanded and warned her she continued to take foolish risks. She almost dared the cats to attack her, dared them to maul her. Luis was a good trainer, and a well-respected performer, a man brought up around animals. It was he who persuaded her that she must love the cats, nurture them; she would gain no results from threats or impatience. Everything took time but, above all, it was the caring, the loving which would pay off. At first, she had refused to listen to him, and the fights had begun then, the violent arguments, but he kept on warning her that unless she listened, showed him respect as well as the cats, she would never learn. Constantly he told her she was not to tame the animals, but to train them: there was a vast difference.

He gave her so much of his time, so much patience . . . and when she gained results, she began to smile again, and he heard her wonderful, bellowing laugh return. But she did not come back to his bed. When he took a mistress, one of the stable girls at the winter quarters, she had said nothing, and so the pattern had begun then, all those years ago.

And then Ruda bought Mamon, and their relationship took a terrible turn. They had been looking at cats to buy for the act, and they had seen a number, turned down many. Luis was intuitive when buying cats for his act: he had been taught by his father to be very choosy, often declining ten or twelve before he found an animal he felt would work well. One look and he could tell the young lion was trouble: Mamon had been in too many homes, too many circuses, moved too many times. His history would give any trainer a clue to his temperament, but Ruda had not listened – even when Luis had refused to pay for him – and argued to such an extent that he had driven off and left her.

A week later Luis had gone to inspect four Bengal tigers being sold by a trainer he knew well. These were four cats he was quick to buy because he trusted the owner and liked the act into which they had already been worked. He had bought them on a handshake, though his money was running short. Then he had returned to discuss the purchase with Ruda.

Ruda had taken the opportunity of his absence to go back to buy Mamon. Luis had been furious, but she had shouted that Mamon was not his but hers, and she would train him – with or without Luis's help – it had been her money, not his. Mamon was hers. The argument had grown into a fist-fight, and in the end he had given way. When she had said Mamon was her baby, he had walked away, walked into the arms of ... he couldn't even remember the girl's name now. He sat trying to recall it, and suddenly realised Ruda was calling him. She then banged on his door, shouting that she was ready, the *Polizei* were waiting. He fetched a clean shirt and began to dress.

Luis had never told Ruda that he had returned to the gynaecologist. He wanted to know for himself what Ruda's diagnosis had been, as she had refused to discuss it. He wanted to know if they should try for a second opinion. He had cared that much. At first the doctor had refused to discuss his patient with Grimaldi, even though he was her husband. He said that Ruda had asked him not to, and simply stated that there was no hope of his wife being able to conceive, and no amount of second opinions or other specialists could help.

Luis had accepted the gynaecologist's word, but at the same time, from his manner, he knew the man was not telling him the entire truth. When he tried to push for further details, the doctor, without meeting Grimaldi's eyes, said quietly, 'Your wife is unable to have normal sexual intercourse, and even if insemination took place, there is no possibility of her carrying a child. I am sorry.' Though he would not discuss Ruda's condition with Luis, he showed her X-rays and tests to two colleagues. He gave them no name, nothing to identify the woman, just the appalling X-rays and photographs of her genital area. All her organs had been removed, as if her womb had been torn from her belly. The internal scar tissue was even worse than her external body scars. Nothing could be done to eliminate them. The entire genital area had been burnt by what the surgeon felt was possibly an early form of chemotherapy.

The colleagues listened in silence – appalled silence. The clitoris had been severed, the vagina covered in scar tissue, the crudeness of the stitches and the scar tissue formation had left no opening. The only form of sexual intercourse the woman could have was anal; her urinary tract had been operated on to enable her to pass liquid, and a plastic tube inserted when the infected tract had festered. The anal area was large, denoting that sexual practice had obviously occurred on a regular basis over a period of years, stretching the colon.

The three men discussed the X-rays. What they had on their screens was a shell of a woman. She had been stripped of her female organs, and what made all of this even more horrible was that the butchery had been performed when the woman was a small child. They talked about the resilience of the human body to have withstood so much, but did not deal with the patient's present state of mind. They couldn't. Ruda Grimaldi had refused to discuss what had led to her condition, and she never returned to the gynaecologist.

Grimaldi knew something of Ruda's past, but she would never tell him all of it. Only Kellerman had known more, but Ruda had told Grimaldi the first night he had met her that she wouldn't have straight sex. She had told him in that stubborn way she had, head up, jaw stuck out. Grimaldi combed his hair. It was strange to think of it all now. At that time he hadn't cared, he had no thought of marrying her then. That had come many years later. He slipped his jacket on, brushing the shoulders with his hands. He had married her – not out of pity, Ruda hated pity. Grimaldi had married her because by the time she had come back into his life, he had been in desperate need of someone. He was slipping down the slopes, drinking too much, and his act was falling apart.

He sighed, knowing he was lying to himself. For a reason he couldn't understand, he had married her because he had loved her. He had believed she loved him, and it was many years before he realised Ruda loved no one, not even herself. No, that was wrong: she loved her angel, she loved Mamon.

By the time he was dressed and ready to leave the trailer, Grimaldi had talked himself into a corner. He had to leave Ruda, but fighting her and making ridiculous demands wouldn't work; he had to make it a fair split. He determined that after the Kellerman business was sorted out, he would discuss it calmly and realistically, and this time he would not back down.

'Luis, come on, what are you doing? You've been ages, that inspector is waiting.' Ruda banged on his door again. 'What are you doing in there?'

Grimaldi came out of his bedroom. He gave her a smile,

made her turn around, admiring her, flattering her; he had not seen her so well dressed for years. He had also not had a drink for more than twenty-four hours. He felt good, and he teased Ruda as he admired her dress. 'How come you dress up for a corpse?'

Ruda wrinkled her nose, and hooked her arm in his. 'Maybe I need to give myself some confidence. I'm scared.'

Grimaldi laughed, and assisted her down the steps. Then, because of the mud, he held out his arms and carried her to the waiting patrol car.

By the time Inspector Heinz and his sergeant had returned to their bogged-down patrol car, they were both reeling from the statements given by all the people who had known Kellerman. Not one had a nice word for him, all seemed rather satisfied he was dead, none had been helpful, none had seen Kellerman on the day or night of his death, and everyone had a strong alibi. Torsen was grateful that the ex-Mrs Kellerman had agreed to identify the dead man.

He held open the back door, and Grimaldi assisted his wife inside. She looked very different from the woman Torsen had visited in their trailer. She was also in a good mood, laughing with her husband – a strange reaction, considering she was being taken to a mortuary to identify her ex-husband's corpse.

Ruda had been determined to make sure she could not be recognised in case someone had seen her enter Tommy Kellerman's hotel. She had dressed carefully in a flowered dress and a pale grey coat. She had left her hair loose, hiding her face, and with her high heels she seemed exceptionally tall. Torsen looked at her through the car mirror. It was hard to tell her exact age, but he thought she had to be close to forty, if not more. It was her manner, the direct unnerving stare of dark, strange amber-coloured eyes: he felt as if they were boring into the back of his head as he tried to back out of the mud-bound parking area.

Ruda wasn't looking at the inspector, but past him, about fifty yards in front. Mike, one of their boys, was hurrying towards the canteen section, a rain cape over his shoulders, but what freaked Ruda was that he was wearing Tommy Kellerman's black leather trilby. She remembered she had left it in the meat trailer when she had returned – left it and forgotten about it. The car suddenly jerked backward free of the mud, turned and headed out of the car park. Ruda didn't turn back, she couldn't: her heart was pounding, her face had drained of colour. Grimaldi gripped her hand and squeezed it. He murmured it was all right, that he was there, and there was no need for her to be afraid.

The rain continued to pour throughout their entire journey to East Berlin. The patrol car's windscreen wipers made nerve-racking screeches as they worked. Grimaldi and his wife talked quietly to each other, as if they were being chauffeured. Torsen began to listen to their conversation. They spoke in English and he could only make out the odd sentence, wondering idly what the word 'plinth' meant. His sergeant sat beside him in the front seat, thumbing through his notebook in a bored manner, then he muttered, patting his pockets, that he had lost his pencil. Torsen continued to listen to Ruda, passing Rieckert his own pencil.

In an attempt to calm her nerves, Ruda was talking about the new plinths for the act, having tried them out that morning. She was telling Luis she had had a lot of trouble, particularly with Mamon: he seemed loath to go near them, had played up badly. Grimaldi said the return of the old plinths was out of the question, they couldn't get them returned in time for the act. They would tone the colours down. Ruda snapped at him, telling him the smell of the fresh paint would be just as disturbing, and to pull out the main part of the act would be insanity. They discussed asking for more rehearsal time before the show, and then both fell silent.

Torsen surmised that plinths and pedestals were the large seats the animals sat on and climbed up and down during the act. They drove on in silence for a while, through Kreuzberg, passing refurbished jazz cellars, Turkish shops, bedraggled boutiques and small art galleries.

It was the same town Ruda had passed through on the bus the night she had murdered Kellerman. A heavy foreboding in her mind reflected the greyness of the town.

Torsen looked back at them through his mirror. 'It was perhaps naïve of us to expect the new freedom would unleash some exciting new era overnight. People who have lived in cages get used to it and people in the East feel afraid – this new financial insecurity spreads a panic. The people here have been denied creative and critical expression for so long, they suffer from a deep inferiority complex. In the old regime many cultural institutions were built up, very well funded – we have good opera houses, two in fact, but now the West holds our purse strings and a number of our theatres have been closed for lack of funds.'

They continued to drive on in silence. The inspector felt obliged to talk, as if giving a guided tour. 'In the old days we had no unemployment – of course, there was much overstaffing, but that was the GDR's way of disguising unemployment. Everything has doubled in price since the Deutschmark took over but I believe we are on the threshold of a new beginning.'

Ruda sat tight-lipped, staring from the window, wishing the stupid man would shut up. They crossed into East Berlin. Ruda turned to her husband as her fear, mingled with the thought of having to see Kellerman, made her angry. She had to unleash it, she was going crazy. They passed a building with JUDA scrawled over its walls, and it was the perfect excuse. She suddenly snapped, her voice vicious, 'Some new beginning, look what they daub on their walls. He should stop the car and grab those kids by the scruff of their necks, better still take a machine gun and wipe them out! *Fuck you, bastards!*'

Inspector and sergeant exchanged hooded looks; the screech of the windscreen wiper was giving Torsen a headache, and the rain wouldn't let up.

Grimaldi stared at the anti-Jewish slogans, and touched Torsen's shoulder. 'How come this kind of thing is allowed?'

Torsen replied that no sooner did they wash down the walls than the kids returned. His sergeant turned. His pale blue eyes and blond crew-cut made him at first appear youthful, but there was a chilling arrogance about him. He spoke with obvious distaste, his pale eyes narrowed. 'The city is swamped with immigrants, the Rumanian gypsies have flooded in, women and children sitting on every street corner, begging. The Poles are not wanted either. They fight like animals in the shops, they park their tatter-demalion cars any old how, they steal, they urinate in the entrances of apartments – this new Germany is in chaos. Eastern Europe is poverty-stricken, and they come in droves. We have more illegal immigrants than we know what to do with. We have no time to wash down walls.'

They drove on, past peeling buildings, collapsing sewer systems, electricity cables hanging from broken cages on street corners. The patrol car passed vast acreages of grimy nineteenth-century tenements that had withstood the bombing, their occupants staring now from filthy windows in their grey shabbiness. Ruda was tense, shifting her weight, one buttock to the next, crossing and uncrossing her legs. She took out her cigarettes and lit up, her hand shaking. She opened the window. She didn't care if she got soaked ... just to be able to breathe. She tossed the cigarette out, breathing in through her nose, exhaling, trying to stay calm.

Torsen noted her discomfort and began pointing out sights, a few new art galleries. The atmosphere in the car was tense and he was trying to lighten it but now he had a gale blowing down the back of his neck. No doubt, to add to his headache he'd have a crick in his neck the following morning.

They went past a greystone hospital building, and around a drive to a low cement building, with empty parking places freshly painted in white, but there was no other vehicle to be seen. The inspector pulled on the handbrake, and turned to his passengers. 'We are here, this is the city mortuary.'

Ruda and Grimaldi were led to a small empty waiting room – green plastic seats and a low table with torn newspapers – and were asked to wait. Sergeant Rieckert remained with them, his eyes flicking over Grimaldi's jacket, his shoes, his Russian-styled shirt with its high collar, mentally sizing up how he would look in the same apparel.

Inspector Torsen Heinz walked down a long, dismal corridor into the main refrigerated room. 'Can you get Kellerman ready for viewing?' He shut the door again, returned to the waiting room and beckoned Ruda to follow him down the corridor. Grimaldi asked if he should accompany them, and Torsen said it was entirely up to him. The three walked up the long corridor, their feet echoing on the tiled floor. They reached a door at the very end, which was opened by a man wearing a green overall. He stood to one side, removing his rubber gloves. They entered the cold room. Three bodies were lying on tables, covered in sheeting, and Grimaldi tightened his grip on Ruda's elbow. Her heart was pounding, but she gave no other indication of what she was feeling. Grimaldi looked from one shrouded body to the other, then to the bank of freezers, with their old-fashioned heavy bolted drawers. He wondered how many bodies they kept on ice.

The inspector stood by a fourth table: the small figure, shrouded like the others, seemed tiny in comparison. In a hushed voice he addressed Ruda. 'Be prepared, the dead man had extensive wounds to his face and head . . .'

Grimaldi moved closer to Ruda and asked if she was all right. She withdrew her arm, nodding. Slowly the inspector lifted the sheet from the naked body, revealing just the head. Grimaldi stepped back aghast, but Ruda moved a fraction closer. She stared down at Kellerman's distorted face, or what was left of it.

'Is this Kellerman?'

Ruda felt icy cold, but she continued to stare.

The inspector lifted the sheet from the left arm. 'The tattoo was on his left wrist. As you can see, the skin was cut away. It would have been quite large.'

Ruda stared at the small hand, the open cleaned wound, but said nothing. Torsen waited, watching her reaction, saw her turn slowly to Grimaldi.

'Is this Kellerman, Mrs Grimaldi?' he asked again.

Ruda gave a hardly detectable shrug of her shoulders. She showed no emotion whatsoever. It was difficult for the inspector to know what she was thinking or feeling. She seemed not to be repelled by the corpse, or disturbed by the grotesque injuries to the dead man's face.

Grimaldi stepped closer, peered down. He cocked his head to the right, and then left. 'Well, I think it's him.'

He returned to Ruda, leaned close and whispered something, and she moved away from him, nearer to the dead man. She looked at Torsen. 'I can't be sure, I'm sorry . . . it has been so long since I saw him.'

'It's him, Ruda, I'm sure even if you're not.' Grimaldi seemed impatient. Turning to the three shrouded bodies he asked if they, too, had been murdered. He received no reply. Torsen lowered the sheet further to unveil Kellerman's chest.

Again Grimaldi whispered to Ruda, and this time he smiled. The inspector couldn't believe it – the man was making some kind of joke.

Grimaldi caught the look of disapproval on Torsen's face and gave a sheepish smile. 'The little fella was very well endowed, I suggested my wife perhaps could remember . . .' He shut up, realising the joke was unsuitable and tasteless.

Ruda touched Kellerman's hair, a light pat with just her fingers to the thick curly grey-black hair. She spoke very softly, hardly audible. 'He had a mole, on the left shoulder, shaped like a . . .'

The inspector pulled the sheet down, exposing the left shoulder to reveal a dark brown mole. Ruda nodded. She whispered that the dead man was Kellerman, then she turned and strode out of the room – had to get out because she could hear Tommy's voice, hear him telling her not to switch out the light. He hated the dark, was always afraid of the dark and of confined spaces. She had teased him, calling him a baby, but she had always left the lights on. He didn't need them now.

Back in the waiting room Inspector Torsen thanked Ruda for her identification. He opened his notebook and sat on the edge of the hard bench; he searched his pockets and looked to his sergeant. 'Have you got my pencil?' He snatched it from Rieckert and looked at Ruda. 'We have been unable as yet to trace any documents on the deceased, how he entered Germany, and if there are relatives we should contact. Was he an American citizen?'

Ruda nodded, told the inspector that Kellerman gained

his American citizenship in the early sixties, that he had no relatives and there was no one to be contacted.

'Where did he come from originally, Mrs Grimaldi?'

Ruda hesitated, touched the scar at her temple with her forefinger. 'Poland I think, I can't recall . . .'

Grimaldi frowned, almost waiting for her to tell the inspector that she had met Kellerman in Berlin, but then she surprised him: she suddenly asked about Kellerman's burial, suggesting he be buried locally as there were no relatives to claim the body. She also said that she would cover any necessary costs, and asked for a rabbi to be called. Although, Ruda said, Kellerman had not been a practising Jew, she felt that he would have wanted a rabbi present.

The inspector wrote down her instructions carefully, but looked up quickly when she said in a low sarcastic voice, 'I presume there is a rabbi in this vicinity. Or one left in Germany who could perform the funeral rites. He must be buried before sunset.'

Torsen said he would arrange it. Then he asked if Kellerman was the deceased's real name. Ruda looked puzzled, said of course it was. He saw at last she seemed disturbed. She lit a cigarette, inhaled deeply before she replied again to his question, apologising for her rudeness. As far as she knew it was his name, that was the name she had always known him under and the name she had taken when she married him. Torsen snapped his notebook closed officiously, and offered to have the couple returned to West Berlin. They refused the offer of a patrol car and asked instead for a taxi.

Grimaldi suddenly asked if they had a suspect, and Torsen shook his head. 'We have no one as yet. We have also not discovered his suitcase, the hotel room was stripped.'

'But didn't anyone see who killed him? That was some

beating the little guy took, I mean someone must have hated his guts, and surely someone must have seen or heard something?'

The inspector shrugged. They had nothing, possibly a number of motives. Kellerman was not a well-liked man.

'Well liked is one thing, but you don't beat a man's head in because you don't like him. It must be something else.'

Torsen nodded, said quietly that until he continued the investigation, there was no further information he could give. He excused himself and left his sergeant to arrange their transport.

The sergeant, irritated at having to walk back to the station, called two taxi companies but no cars were available. He suggested that they could get one from the Grand Hotel: it was not too far, if they wished he could walk with them.

Ruda refused his offer to accompany them, and turned back to stare out of the grimy window. Grimaldi came to her side, whispered to her that she should have kept her mouth shut – now she would have to fork out for the little bastard even in death. She glared at him in disgust and, keeping her voice as low as his, she murmured that what he was really pissed off about was her asking for a rabbi. She turned back to the window. 'That little blond-haired Nazi prick will probably send us in the wrong direction anyway, now he knows I'm Jewish!'

Grimaldi gripped her elbow so tightly it hurt. 'Shut up, just keep it shut! And since when have you been a fuckin' Jew!'

Ruda smirked at him and shook her head. 'Scared they may daub us on the way back to the trailer?'

Grimaldi glared back at her, he would never understand her. She was no more Jewish than he was, certainly not a practising one. She had no religion, and he was a Catholic

– not that he'd said a Hail Mary for more than twenty years.

The sergeant handed directions to Grimaldi and, with a curt nod of his head, left them. He'd heard what she had called him and he smarted with impotent fury: foreigners, they were all alike, and Detective Chief Inspector Heinz bowed and scraped like a wimp to that Jewish bitch! What kind of pervert was she to have been married to that animal on the mortuary slab? She repelled him.

Luis and Ruda walked together, arm in arm; it took a lot longer than the sergeant had suggested – over an hour to arrive at the newly refurbished Grand Hotel. It was such a sight that they decided – or Grimaldi did – that they should order a taxi and have a martini while they waited. At first Ruda resisted, but then, being told there would be no taxi available for another hour, she relented.

They walked into the foyer and headed for the comfortable lounge. They made a striking couple. Grimaldi began to enjoy himself. Guiding Ruda by the elbow, he inclined his head. 'Now, this is my style, and I think, since we're here, we might as well order a late lunch. The restaurant looks good, what do you say?'

Ruda looked at her wristwatch. She had to get back to rehearse and feed the cats, but they had to wait for the taxi so she suggested they just have a drink and a sandwich.

Grimaldi decided this was as good a time as any to have a talk, out of the trailer, away from the circus. In the luxurious surroundings they might have a civilised conversation. They sat in a small booth, with red plush velvet seats and a marble-topped table. Ferns hid them from the rest of the hotel residents, mostly American as far as Grimaldi could tell.

They sipped their martinis in silence, and Ruda ate the entire bowl of peanuts, one at a time, popping them into her mouth. Grimaldi took an envelope from his pocket and opened it. 'I have been working out our financial situation, how much the act costs, living expenses, and what we will both need to live on. Maybe we should sell the trailer and buy a smaller one each.'

She turned on him. 'Your priority is to get back the old plinths! I can't work with the new ones.'

'We've already discussed that, for Chrissakes. Just go through this with me, we have to sort it out some time.'

Ruda snatched the sheet of paper, and looked over his haphazard scrawl. It was quite a shock to her that even after their closeness, he was still intent on leaving her.

'She's pregnant, Ruda. I want to get a divorce and marry her.'

Ruda tore the paper into scraps. 'I'll think about it.'

Grimaldi signalled for the waiter to take another order. Ruda's foot was tapping against the side of the table leg. 'I don't want to have an argument here, Ruda. OK?'

She stared at him, her mind ticking over, telling herself to keep calm. She had to deal with things one at a time. She had dealt with Kellerman, next would be Grimaldi himself, but her main priority now was to get the act ready for opening night. One thing at a time, this show was the biggest she had done, and if she performed well she knew that with the television live coverage there would be no more second circuit dates: she would be an international star. She wanted above all to get to the US again and win a contract at the mammoth New York circus, Barnum and Bailey's big top, one of the finest in the world.

'Ruda, we have to discuss this . . . Ruda!'

'I'll think about it. We'll work out something.'

As the waiter arrived at their table, passing directly behind him was a very handsome man accompanied by an attractive blonde woman. They were both deep in conversation, not giving Grimaldi or Ruda a glance. They seated themselves in the next booth, and the waiter, after taking Grimaldi's order, moved quickly to the elegant couple's booth.

'Good afternoon, Baron.'

Helen Masters asked for a gin and tonic, and the Baron a Scotch on the rocks. He spoke German, then turned back to continue his conversation with Helen in French. They paid no attention to the big broad-shouldered man seated in the next booth. They could not see Ruda.

Grimaldi had ordered two more martinis. Ruda had said she didn't want another but he had ignored her. He looked around the lounge, then noticed she was playing with the bread. It always used to infuriate him, the way she would pick at it, roll it into tiny little balls, twitch it and pummel it with her fingers . . .

'Stop that, you know it gets on my nerves. We'll sort out the plinths when we get back. Now, can we just relax, Ruda?'

She nodded, but her hands beneath the table began to roll a small piece of bread tighter and tighter, until it became a dense hard ball, because she kept on seeing the boy, Mike, wearing Kellerman's hideous leather trilby. Mike, Grimaldi and his bloody divorce . . . It was all coming down on her like a dark blanket, and suddenly she felt as if her mind would explode. Her fingers pressed and rolled the tiny ball of bread as if out of her control. She swallowed, her mouth had dried, her lips felt stiff, her tongue held the roof of her mouth. It was seeping upward from her toes . . . she fought against it, refusing to allow it to dominate her – not here, not in public. 'No . . . no!'

Grimaldi looked at her, not sure what she had said. He leaned closer. 'Ruda? You OK?'

She repeated the word, 'No!' like a low growl. He could see her body was rigid, and yet the table shook slightly as her fingers pressed and rolled the tiny ball of bread.

'Ruda! *Ruda!*'

She turned her head very slowly; her eyes seemed unfocused, staring through him. He slipped his hand beneath the table. 'What's the matter with you? Are you sick?' He held her hand, crunched in a hard knot. She recoiled physically from him, pressing her back against the velvet seat.

'I have to go to the toilet.' Suddenly she rose to her feet. 'I'll meet you outside, I need some fresh air.'

Grimaldi made to stand, but she pushed past him and he slumped back down in the seat, watching as she walked stiffly towards the foyer, hands in tight fists at her side. She brushed past an elaborate display of ferns and then quickened her pace, almost running to the cloakrooms. There was only one other occupant, a tourist applying lipstick, examining her reflection in the mirror. Ruda knocked against her, but made no apology, hurrying into the vacant lavatory. She had no time to shut the door, but fell to her knees, clinging to the wooden toilet seat as she began to vomit. She felt an instant release, and sat back on her heels panting; again she felt the rush of bile, and leaned over the basin, the stench, the white bowl – she pushed away until she was hunched against the partition.

'Are you all right? Do you need me to call someone?' The tourist stood well back, but very concerned.

Ruda heaved again and forced herself once more to be sick into the lavatory bowl.

'Should I call a doctor?'

Ruda wiped her mouth with the back of her hand, and without even looking at the woman, snapped, 'Get out, just get out and leave me alone!'

Ruda slowly rose to stand, pressing herself against the partition, then crossed unsteadily to the wash basin. She ran cold water and splashed it over her face, then patted herself dry with the soft hand-towels provided. She opened her handbag and fumbled for her powder compact. Her whole body tingled, the hair on the back of her hands was raised, the same strange, almost animal warning at the nape of her neck. Was it this hotel? Something in this hotel . . . ? The white tiled walls, the white marble floor – had she been here before?

She seemed to step outside herself, look at herself. What was wrong? And then, just as she had always done, she began to work the calm, talking softly, whispering that it was just the whiteness, it was the white tiles, it was seeing Tommy, it was nothing more. It was a natural reaction, it was just shock, delayed shock at seeing him, seeing Tommy.

Ruda passed through the large foyer, her composure regained. She paused, wary, as if listening for something, to something, but then she shrugged her shoulders and headed towards the main revolving doors. She made no attempt to return to Grimaldi, just walked out, had to get out of the building.

As Ruda stepped outside, Hylda was scurrying towards the staff entrance, a small hidden door at the side of the large hotel. She stopped in her tracks, seeing the tall woman standing on the steps. For a moment she thought she was seeing the Baroness, but then she shook her head at her stupidity; this woman was much bigger, her dark hair long. Still, as she continued through the staff entrance, she wondered where she had seen the woman before. She unpacked her working shoes and slipped them on, carefully placing her other shoes in her locker. As she closed the door and crossed to the mirror to run a comb through her hair, she remembered. The circus poster. It was the woman from the circus poster, she was sure of it and rather pleased with her recall. She wondered if she was staying at the hotel; perhaps, if she was, Hylda could ask for her autograph.

A chambermaid coming off duty called out to Hylda, and scurried over to her. She asked furtively if it was true that the Baroness was insane; rumours were rife and she was eager to gossip. Hylda refused to be drawn into a conversation, and the young girl pulled a face and changed the subject, moving on to further news. Yesterday a dwarf had been found murdered in the red-light district just behind the hotel, his body beaten. They had first thought it was a child, his body was so small; she knew about it because her boyfriend worked with the *Polizei*. She came close to Hylda and hissed: 'He was a Jew!'

CHAPTER SIX

GRIMALDI LEFT the Grand Hotel, unable to find Ruda. He walked a while, then caught a bus back to the circus.

Baron Maréchal and Helen remained in the hotel bar. The Baron knew he had been rude to leave Helen waiting so long, and attempted to explain his reasons. She said no explanation was necessary, that if he needed to speak with Dr Franks alone, that was his business. He kissed her hand, saying that her understanding never ceased to amaze him.

The Baron sipped his drink, placing it carefully on the paper napkin. 'Franks knows that the present situation cannot continue.'

The manager approached their table, and excused his intrusion. For a moment the Baron half rose from his seat, his face drained of colour. 'Is it my wife?'

The manager handed the Baron a folded envelope containing faxes that had been sent that morning. Helen saw the relief pass over Louis's face, and he tipped the manager lavishly before he opened the envelope. He read through the five fax sheets, handing each one to Helen as he did so.

There was no record of a Vebekka Lynsey in Philadelphia, and the woman who had once run the model agency that first employed Vebekka confirmed that her real Christian name was Rebecca. Still, checks on Rebecca Lynsey in Philadelphia produced no results. Two girls who had once been employed by the same agency had been tracked down. They remembered Rebecca, and one thought her real surname was Goldberg, but could not be absolutely sure.

She had shared a room with Rebecca, and remembered her receiving letters in that name.

A Mr and Mrs Ulrich Goldberg had subsequently been traced to an address in Philadelphia, and though they had no direct connection to the Baroness, they were able to give further details. Ulrich Goldberg's cousin, Dieter, or David, Goldberg, had run a successful furrier business until 1967. He and his wife Rosa had arrived in Philadelphia from Canada in the fifties. They had one daughter, Rebecca Goldberg. Was Rebecca Goldberg Vebekka Lynsey? Ulrich Goldberg, when shown recent photographs of Vebekka, was unable to state that they were definitely of her, but admitted there was a great similarity.

According to Ulrich, Rebecca was last seen at her father's funeral in January 1972. She had been distant and evasive, speaking briefly to only a handful of mourners, and had soon departed. No one had seen or heard from her since. A number of photographs were being forwarded by express mail, taken when she was about ten or twelve years old.

Mr and Mrs Ulrich Goldberg had arrived in the United States in the late 1930s from Germany. They knew that David Goldberg's wife was or had been a doctor, born in Berlin, but the time when she had married and emigrated to Canada was something of a mystery. Although the two Goldberg families were related, Ulrich openly admitted that he and his wife had not been on close terms with David Goldberg – and found his wife a very cold, distant woman.

The Baron finished reading the last page and handed it to Helen. She read it in silence, then folded the fax sheets and replaced them in their envelope. The Baron lit a cigar, and turned to Helen. 'This could all be some kind of confusion. These are not from a detective, he's my chauffeur!'

Helen nodded, and then chose her words carefully. 'The date of the funeral, is that when Vebekka left Paris?'

The Baron frowned, picked up the envelope, and after a moment nodded.

Helen spoke quietly. 'First you have to deal with the lies Vebekka has told, or the cover-up. Perhaps she simply didn't want you to know anything about her family, for whatever reason, but if she really is Rebecca Goldberg, and her mother was born in Berlin, we can do some detective work of our own. Maybe there are relatives still living here, maybe someone who knew them. We could try to trace them.'

The Baron pinched the brow of his nose; everything was too much for him to take in.

Helen twisted the stem of her glass. 'Perhaps the reason, or a possible reason, was that your family were against your marrying Vebekka.' She hesitated. Would Vebekka's being Jewish have been one of the reasons why the Baron's family disapproved of the marriage? She decided not to broach the subject; after all, she was sure Vebekka was Catholic. She sipped her drink and put down the glass. Perhaps, as Louis himself had said, this was all a misunderstanding. But if Louis was hesitant to check out this Goldberg connection, there was no reason why she shouldn't.

Hylda had almost finished a sleeve and was beginning to check the measurements on her knitting when Vebekka stirred, and opened her eyes. Slowly she turned to face Hylda and smiled. 'Have I been sleeping long?'

Hylda nodded, said it was after two, but that she needed all the sleep she could get. She helped the Baroness out of the bed, and wrapped a dressing-gown around her thin shoulders. She assisted her into the bathroom, where big towels were warming on the rail. She had to help her into the bath, but Vebekka slid into the soap- and perfume-filled water with a sigh of pleasure.

Hylda had gently towelled Vebekka dry, feeling protective and motherly as the thin frame rested against her, and Vebekka seemed loath to let her go, clinging to her as they returned to the bedroom. Then the Baroness sat in front of her mirror and opened one of her precious vanity cases. 'I need my hair done, Hylda.'

Hylda said that she would try, but she had never done this blowing and combing and was not sure how to go about it. Vebekka had giggled and begun taking out small pots and brushes. 'No, no – my roots! I need my roots done. See, the grey hair is showing through.'

Hylda watched as Vebekka mixed her tint, stirring it into a plastic container. 'It's called Raven. It looks sort of purple, but it comes out black, see. Mix the two, now stir them together.'

With Vebekka parting her hair and clipping sections, Hylda began to brush the thick purplish liquid into the hair line. Then Hylda sat and waited, timing to the last second: the tint had to be left on for twenty minutes. Meanwhile, Vebekka manicured her hands, creamed her elbows and neck, then her legs, and her arms. Together they returned to the bathroom and Hylda shampooed and washed out the tint. Her hands were covered with the dye, but she soaped and rinsed and conditioned, under Vebekka's instructions. Then she wrapped a towel around the clean, tinted head and they returned to the bedroom. Next Vebekka directed Hylda to hold the dryer while she used the brush. 'I'm young again, Hylda, see? You were very good. Now I want to look beautiful, a little make-up, rouge . . .'

Hylda was fascinated at the transformation, even more so when she helped the Baroness into a flowing silk and lace garment, so delicate it floated when Vebekka moved, the lace on the sleeves trailing like a medieval costume.

Hylda ordered a light luncheon of boiled fish, some milk and vegetables, and she was pleased to see that Vebekka ate every morsel. Just as she was ringing for room service to take the trolley away, the Baron entered to find his wife sitting like a princess at the window. His face broke into a smile of delight. 'You look wonderful! And you have eaten? Good, good . . . do you feel better?' Hylda made herself scarce, entering the main bedroom to tidy the room and remake the bed.

The Baron bent to kiss his wife's cheek, she smelt sweet and fresh, her hair gleamed like silk. She smiled, and looked up into his concerned face. 'Did you come in to see me earlier?'

'No, I had a cocktail with Helen. If you need her she is in her room.'

She cocked her head to one side. 'Well, don't you two get too familiar!'

He turned away, irritated.

'I was just teasing you, Louis, it was just – well, strange. I was sure someone came in . . . maybe I was dreaming.'

With her husband's assistance she stood up, clinging to his hand. 'I think I will rest for a while now. You don't have to stay, I have Hylda. Maybe Helen would like to go sightseeing? She must be very bored.'

They walked slowly to the bedroom, and suddenly she leaned against him. 'Remember in that old movie with Merle Oberon, when she said, "Take me . . . take me to the window, I want to see the moors one last time!"' Vebekka did such a good impersonation of the dying heroine from *Wuthering Heights* that she made Louis laugh; he swept her in his arms and gently carried her to the bed.

He stood by watching as Hylda fluffed up her pillows,

remained watching as Hylda gently drew the sheet around her and then closed the curtains, leaving the room in semi-darkness. Then she asked if she might take a break for an hour as she had not had her own lunch. He nodded, dismissing her with an inclination of his head, and sat in the chair she had vacated.

Vebekka lay with her eyes closed, as if unaware he was there. She could have been laid out at a funeral home she was so still, the perfect make-up, the long dark lashes, her hair outlining her face, framing its beauty. The Baron took out his gold cigarette case, opening it silently, patted his pockets for his lighter, and kept his eyes on her as he clicked it open. Still she didn't stir. He inhaled deeply and let the smoke drift from his mouth to form a perfect circle above his head. Had she woven all these lies about herself? Why? He couldn't think of a reason for not telling him – unless she was ashamed, but ashamed of what? The more he stared at the still figure, the more unanswered questions crossed his mind. Was it his fault? He could hear her, as if she was saying it to him now: 'My father's dead. I have to go to America to see to the funeral.'

She had said it so matter-of-factly, as if suggesting she fly to New York for a dress fitting. He had asked if she wished him to accompany her and she had smiled, shaking her head, reminding him that he was flying to Brazil for a polo game. All he could remember was his relief at not having to alter his plans. He had not been in Paris when she returned, so the funeral was not discussed. She had bought so many gifts for the children and for him, and had laughed at her extravagance, saying she was surprised at how much her father had left. Louis knew it was a considerable amount, because his own lawyers had telephoned to discuss the matter, but she had been uninterested in the money, as he was. She had been happy, she had been well – above all, happy.

These infrequent episodes always remained vivid to him, because when Vebekka was happy the entire family's spirits lifted. She was so energised, arranging secret outings and surprise parties, like a child. Her good spirits extended beyond the family circle: she arranged dinner parties, dressed up for masked balls. As a hostess she was a constant delight, charming and making everyone feel immediately at ease.

He leaned forward, noting in the semi-darkness the contours of her face. The way her long exquisite fingers rested like an angel's, one hand on top of the other – the perfect nails, her tiny wrists. It was hard to believe that those long tapering delicate hands could become like vicious claws.

The Baron pondered on his conversations with Dr Franks. Was he in some way to blame? Was it his fault? In the quietness of the room he could honestly ask himself if he was guilty and why the glimpses of sun in her life were so shortlived now, so rare, and why, when she changed, there was such anguish.

He got up to stub out his cigarette. From the dressing-table he looked at the still sleeping woman; she had not moved. He had to think not just of himself, but of Sasha, the boys; they too had suffered, they had been forced to care for their mama, watch out for the signs. His eldest daughter had retreated into a social life that left little or no time to spend at home. The boys had drawn very close to each other. The real damage had been done to his younger daughter, so much younger than the others that she had seen fewer good periods.

Louis would perhaps never know what damage had been done to his sons and daughters. He sighed. It would be easy to slip the pillow from the side of the bed, press it to her face, and it would be over. No one could say he had not been driven to it, that she did not deserve it.

She stirred, her hands fluttered, lifted a moment, and then rested again. She turned her head towards Louis, slowly opened her eyes. He wondered if she knew he was there, wondered if anyone could understand what it was like to turn to someone you loved, and then face a stranger, and worse — be afraid. That awful moment of awareness when he knew it was happening. When the face he loved became distorted, the mouth he kissed pulled back like an animal, the voice he loved, snarled — and the gentle arms lashed out like steel traps.

He pressed his back against the dressing-table, watching. Was he about to see the transformation now? The slender arms stretched and she moaned softly, then smiled with such sweetness. 'I thought you were going out? How long have you been here?'

'Not long,' he lied, and sat on the edge of the bed.

'Where's Hylda?'

'She's having something to eat.'

'She's so sweet.'

'How do you feel?'

'Good . . . refreshed. Have I eaten? Where's Helen?'

'I don't know, she may have gone shopping, I don't know.'

Vebekka sat up and shook her head. 'We did my hair, Hylda and I. What time is it?' She looked at her bedside clock, and then threw back the sheet. 'We can call Sasha and the boys.'

He watched her slip her feet into satin slippers, and then yawn, lifting her arms above her head. 'I feel hungry, I am ravenous! Hot chocolate, I need something sweet, we call room service? Where is Hylda? Oh, you said . . . and Helen? Oh, shopping, my mind's fuzzy.'

Louis hesitated, then told himself not to draw back now, to go through with it. 'I'm glad you feel better, and hungry. Dr Franks will be pleased too.' He saw the cat-like reaction,

152

her eyes narrowed. He continued, 'Franks is waiting for me to call him. He said for me to contact him as soon as you recovered.'

'Really?' she said flatly, and turned away.

'Yes, really. So, my dear, shall I call him?'

She pursed her lips. 'Oh, I can't see him yet. I'm still too weak. Can you get Hylda for me?'

Louis opened the curtains, warned himself not to back off, not this time. 'Shall I tell Dr Franks maybe tomorrow?'

'Oh, I don't know. Is Anne Maria in?'

Louis crossed and took her hand, drew her to him. 'Come and sit down. I'll get Hylda and Anne Maria, but first we need to talk.'

She sat on the dressing-table stool, looking up at him.

'I'm going to call Dr Franks, right now. What shall I tell him?'

She hunched her shoulders. 'I can't see him for a while.'

He sighed and stuffed his hands into his pockets. 'What does that mean? A day? Two days? A week? How long do you expect us all to wait around here? This is the entire reason—'

She retorted angrily, interrupting him, 'I know why we came, and I have agreed to see him, but not just yet!'

When the Baron suggested they ask Franks to come and see her later in the afternoon, she pursed her lips. 'I have to rest.'

He walked to the door, saying he would call him anyway.

'I *don't want* to see him, I've changed my mind. Besides I feel as if I am getting stronger. Without all those pills that wretched woman makes me take, my system is getting cleansed – I am detoxifying, it's always a slow process, I am bound to have some withdrawal symptoms and—'

'That's right, keep on with the excuses, but this time I am not taking no for an answer. If you want to stay here a month I'll arrange it, but you are going to Dr Franks.'

'Don't be so nasty to me. Why are you being so nasty?'

'For God's sake, I am not being nasty, you are being childish. I'll call him now.'

'No.'

He looked at her, opening the door.

'I *said no*.'

He slammed the door shut – hard. '*You* have no say in the matter, do you understand?'

'I won't see him.'

The Baron crossed the room and gripped her arm. 'You will see him, do you hear me, you will see him, we agreed, *you* agreed and you cannot change your mind now.'

'Why not? It's my mind.'

He released her arm. 'Right, *now* it is! But for how long? I've told you, this is the last time, it's your last chance.'

'Don't you mean yours?'

He had to control his temper. 'We have nothing left, Bekka, you and I both know it. I am doing this for you – not for me, for you.'

'Liar. You want me certified and dumped.'

'I don't want to fight with you, Bekka, I want to help you. Can't you understand it? That is all I have ever wanted to do – help you.'

She stared at him, pouting childishly. He kept his voice low, trying to be controlled. 'You need help, you know it. If not for me . . .'

'Oh, shut up! I've heard that one too many times.' She mimicked him, '"If not for me, do it for yourself."' She turned on him. 'This is for you, Louis, I am here in this bloody awful country for *you*. *You* want to get rid of me, don't you think I know it? Well, one, I will not give you a divorce, two, I will go to see Dr Franks when I feel up to going to see him, in my own time when I feel fit and well enough, and I will not be pressured by you, or by that whore Helen. I will not be forced into seeing this crank because *you* want to get rid of me and run off with that tart.'

'Tart? You mean Helen? For God's sake, she is your friend, your doctor – and, Bekka, I am not running anywhere, I never have before, and I don't intend to now.'

'But you are leaving me? Aren't you? You've decided, haven't you?' She plucked a tissue from its container, and wiped her face, slowly removing her make-up. She had only done her hair and made herself look pretty for him. She murmured under her breath about Helen again.

'Helen has nothing to do with any decision I make.'

She smiled. 'Ah, you're making a decision all by yourself, are you? Well, that does make a change.'

He refused to be drawn into an argument, and their eyes met in the mirror. 'No, Bekka, you make the decision this time, it's up to you. If you refuse to see Dr Franks, then . . .'

She held his gaze with a defiant stare. 'Then what?'

'You cannot return to the children.'

'They are old enough to make their own decisions.' She said it with a pout, but he could see her eyes were beginning to flick, blinking rapidly.

'Sasha is not.'

Her hands trembled and she began to twist the tissue, but still she didn't look away from him. 'You can't do that to me! I love Sasha, she needs me.'

'You give me no alternative. I've told you, this is your last chance.'

He walked out. Even after he had closed the door, he felt as if her eyes were on him. He poured a brandy, his hands shaking as he lifted the glass, his body tense, waiting. Would she begin throwing things, screaming, was she going to come hurtling out of the bedroom? The brandy hit the back of his throat, warming him. He poured another measure, and then froze. The telephone extension rang once, he knew she was making a call, and he hurled the glass down, breaking the stem. Was she calling Sasha? He hurried to the bedroom, about to fling open the door. He could hear her talking; he pressed his head to the door to listen.

Vebekka's palm was sweating, small beads of perspiration glistened on her brow. She could feel a trickle of sweat slip from her armpit, but she waited, licking her lips, her mouth as dry as her body was dripping. She gripped the telephone tighter, afraid she would unconsciously replace it.

'Dr Franks? This is Baroness Maréchal, I—' She could hear him breathing, then asking how she was. She had to swallow once, twice before she could reply. 'I am very much better.'

'Good, I am glad to hear it.'

The sweating made her feel weak, her whole body trembled. Her hair was wringing wet – she could see the clear drops, became mesmerised by them.

'Hello? Baroness? Hello?' Dr Franks could hardly hear her, but he knew she was still on the line. 'Are you experiencing any adverse effects? Any withdrawal symptoms? Baroness?'

'Sweating, I am sweating—'

She gasped and had to reach for the dressing-table top to steady herself; she felt as if she was going to faint.

'That is only to be expected. You must drink, can you hear me? You must drink as much water as possible, spring water, keep drinking. Would you like me to come and see you?'

'No!'

Franks couldn't hear her. He asked again, 'I can be with you in half an hour. Would you like me to come to see you?'

There was a long pause. He could not tell if she was still on the line or not.

She whispered, 'I would like to come to see you.'

'Pardon? I can't hear you.'

'I want you to help me, I want to come to you.'

Franks punched the air. 'That is good, I can arrange for you to have the entire morning. Shall we say nine in the morning? Baroness?'

'Thank you.' Carefully she replaced the phone, it felt heavy. Her hands clasped tightly together. Vebekka felt nothing but fear, she had hardly been able to finish the call.

The Baron was elated that she had called Franks herself. He had not expected her to have the strength. He called down to the desk to ask for Hylda to come to their suite immediately. He then called Anne Maria to check on his wife. He was banking on Dr Franks, as if on a miracle cure; it was naïve of him, and he knew it. But even if Franks could not help Vebekka, at least the Baron could honestly tell himself that they had tried. And then he could, without guilt, have her placed in an institution. Facing the prospect no longer gave him any regrets, it was the only choice he had. From the open door to her bedroom, he watched for a brief moment as Anne Maria attended to Vebekka. He could see that her nightgown was sodden, her face dripping with sweat and she was mumbling incoherently. The Baron saw Anne Maria check his wife's pulse, then take her temperature. He continued to watch as Vebekka struggled a moment, her arms thrashing at her sides, and then she grew listless, still sweating profusely. He turned away as Anne Maria began to remove his wife's delicate nightgown. Vebekka seemed unaware of the nurse, and when Anne Maria realised the Baron was watching she hesitated, the gown half removed.

He bowed his head. 'I'll be in the foyer if you need me.'

He didn't go to the foyer but to the small bar at the rear of reception. There was no mistress for him to run to;

instead, he sat hunched in the corner of the bar with a cognac.

Vebekka seemed grateful when Hylda bustled in and quickly began to help Anne Maria change the bed linen. They changed her nightdress, and continued to place cold compresses on her head. Bottles and bottles of mineral water were brought up. Hylda helped her to hold the glass, encouraged her to drink as much as possible. Vebekka began to shiver, and more blankets were piled on top of the quilt.

Hylda was sitting close to the bed, wringing out the cold compress – Vebekka had gone from shivering with cold to sweating with fever. At least she was sleeping deeply now, but Hylda grew more and more concerned. She gestured for Anne Maria to move closer to the bed and watched as she took Vebekka's pulse. It was rapid, but nothing to be too concerned about. She felt the skin on the underside of Vebekka's wrist. There was a shiny area of skin, whiter than the rest. Anne Maria pointed it out to Hylda.

'What is that mark on her wrist from?'

Anne Maria whispered, 'She told me it was a burn, it looks more like a skin graft.' She continued whispering as she pointed out that it was the same wrist Vebekka had cut the night they had arrived. She smirked, suggesting that perhaps Vebekka had attempted it before. Hylda said nothing, she could see the fresh wound already healing, but the white, neat scar tissue was higher up, about four inches from the base of the Baroness's palm.

Ruda shouted out orders to Vernon and Mike, and they rushed to finish attaching the locks to the arena cages. She attempted to work on the new plinths for an entire hour but could not concentrate, could not give the rehearsal her full attention. She had a headache: the harder she worked the worse it became, and the cats picked up on her tension. Mike had not seen Ruda so obviously tense in the ring or take so many risks as she put the cats through their paces. She snatched a towel left stuck between the bars and wiped the sweat from her face and neck.

'And again, Mike. Let's go from the top again! *Vernon*, get Mamon's cage in position, *now* . . . move it the pair of you!'

It was just after four when Vebekka woke, and she reached out for Hylda's hand, struggled to sit up, drank thirstily from a glass Hylda held, then rested back on the pillows. She looked to the window, asked for it to be opened as she wanted some fresh air. Hylda obliged. 'Is this too much?'

'No, it feels good. Has it stopped raining?'

'Yes, just. But there are dark clouds, I think there could be a storm.'

Suddenly Vebekka's body went rigid and blinding colours flashed across her brain. Hylda rushed back to her side. 'What is it? What is it?'

The thin hands clutched the sheets, her body seemed in spasm, and Hylda ran out to call for Anne Maria.

The colours screamed in her head, red . . . blood red . . . green . . . they were coming fast, flashes of brilliant reds, greens and blues. When Hylda returned, Vebekka was struggling to get on to her feet, she kept repeating, '*Up* . . . *up!*'

Neither woman could restrain her; she struggled to get to her feet, her hands pushing them away. Then, as quickly as the spasm had occurred, it stopped. She flopped back on to the pillows, clutching her head as if in agony. Hylda tried to put an ice-cold cloth on her brow but Vebekka swiped at her, screamed for her to get away, to stay away from her.

Hylda stepped back, frightened by the force of that skinny arm. Shocked, she looked to Anne Maria, but she was well back, not attempting to go anywhere near the thrashing figure.

'Should we call someone?' Hylda asked.

Anne Maria walked out of the room, warning over her shoulder for Hylda to stay away from the bed. Vebekka was rubbing at her hair, banging her head with her fists. 'Stop it! Stop it! Make it stop, please God, make it stop!' The colours hammered, flashed, and she couldn't get her breath. Panting and gasping, she reached out to Hylda, trying to get hold of her. Anne Maria came back with the straitjacket, unwrapping it from its plastic case. 'I told them she could have one of her turns. That doctor should be here now, never mind her husband!'

Hylda stood guard by the bed, her arms open wide, protecting Vebekka. '*No*, no! Don't put that on her, I won't let you!'

Anne Maria looked at the bed, and tossed the jacket aside. 'They shouldn't have taken her off the sedatives. This has happened before. Well, I am not taking any responsibility, she'll attack you . . .'

She stormed out, and Hylda kept hold of Vebekka, calming her, stroking her hair, saying over and over that she was there, she wasn't going to leave her. The thin arms relaxed and Vebekka rested her head against Hylda's shoulder. 'Oh, God, help me, what is it? What happens to me, Hylda?'

Hylda coaxed her to lie back on the pillows, and Vebekka didn't struggle – she was too exhausted. She whispered, like a frightened child, 'It is closer. It is so close, I can't make it go away . . .'

Hylda made soft shushing sounds, as if to a little girl.

'What is it? What are you frightened of? Is it something in the room?'

'I don't know. It takes me over, controls me, and I can't fight it any more, I'm so tired . . . so tired.'

Hylda continued stroking Vebekka's hair. 'What do you think it is? If you tell me, then maybe it won't be so frightening.'

Vebekka turned away, curling her knees up, her arms wrapped around herself. How could she answer when she didn't know? All she knew was that it was closer than it had ever been before.

Hylda closed the window, drew the curtains, and in the semi-darkness returned to the bedside, bending down to try to see Vebekka's face. She talked softly all the time, saying she was there, nothing could come into the room, nothing in the room could frighten her. She stood by the bed, waiting, but Vebekka didn't move. Gradually, she crept out, closing the door silently behind her.

Hylda stood in the empty suite lounge, not knowing what she should do – stay or try to find the Baron or Helen Masters. She looked at her watch, it was almost five, glanced at Anne Maria's closed door and back to the bedroom. The suite was silent, she could hear the clock ticking on the marble mantelpiece, but outside the taxis tooted, the noise of traffic drawing up outside the hotel was intrusive and she was afraid it would wake Vebekka.

Hylda crossed to draw the wooden shutters closed. They were heavy and she moved from one window to the next before she lifted the fine white curtains to look into the street below. Hylda's hand was on the shutter when she saw the solitary figure. She could not see whether it was a man or woman, because a car drew up and obscured her view. The driver appeared to say something to the dark figure, who bent down then straightened up, gesturing for the car to drive on. Hylda could tell now that it was a woman, but her hair was drawn back tightly from her face. The collar of her thick overcoat was turned up. But what caught Hylda's attention was the way the figure seemed to be staring towards the hotel, her head moving very slightly from side to side, as if looking from window to window, floor to floor. At any moment now she would face Hylda, and Hylda could catch a better view of her – but just then the doors to the suite were thrown open.

Helen Masters strode in and asked brusquely if the Baron was with his wife. As Hylda turned back to close the shutters, the woman on the pavement below had vanished. 'No, Dr Masters, he is not.'

At that precise moment the Baron walked in. Helen smiled a greeting. He seemed a little unsteady. 'Helen, I called your room, have you been shopping?'

'No, Louis, you must come with me. I've traced a woman, a relative of David Goldberg's wife, Vebekka's mother. She said she would see us.'

'Excuse me, Baron . . .'

They both turned to Hylda, as if only then realising she was in the room. When she nervously repeated what had occurred, the Baron slumped into a chair, then turned to Helen. 'She called Franks herself, earlier this afternoon, said she would see him tomorrow. And now this!' He opened the bedroom door and went into the darkened room.

Helen asked if Anne Maria was with Vebekka, but Hylda shook her head. She was twisting her hands nervously, and Helen went to her side. 'Are you all right, did she frighten you?'

Hylda whispered to Helen that she would like to speak with her, that she did not mean to say more than she should, but felt Helen should know what Anne Maria's intentions had been.

Helen moved her further away from the bedroom, patting

Hylda's shoulder. 'It's all right, you can tell me. I want to know what happened. It's very important.' Briefly, and in a hushed voice, Hylda related to her the story of the straitjacket.

Louis bent down to try to see Vebekka's face. She appeared to be sleeping. He gave a feather-like touch to her head and then joined Helen. 'She's sleeping.'

Helen gestured for him to come close and repeated everything Hylda had told her. The Baron strode to Anne Maria's room, knocked and without waiting for an answer entered and closed the door behind him. Anne Maria looked up from her book, flustered, trying to straighten her blouse.

'I would like you to leave, you can arrange a flight at the reception desk.'

He opened his wallet, and before Anne Maria had time to reply, he left a thick wad of folded banknotes on her bed. She snapped her book closed, wanting obviously to discuss the matter, but he walked out. She stared at the money, her lips pursed. Then she counted it, looked at the closed door and swore under her breath.

The Baron and Helen Masters were sitting in the lounge when Anne Maria came out of her room, with case packed and coat over her arm. Her face was tight with anger. 'Thank you for your generosity, Baron. Perhaps when you return to Paris, you would be kind enough to give me a letter of recommendation.'

The Baron threw the straitjacket at her feet. 'There will be no letter of recommendation.'

Anne Maria stepped over the straitjacket, and crossed to the suite's double doors. She opened the right-hand side, about to walk out without a word, but then she turned back. 'I would be most grateful for a letter. I will require one for future employment.' Helen put out her hand to restrain the Baron. Anne Maria looked at them both with disdain. 'I will be only too pleased to give *you* a letter of recommendation – to enable you to have the Baroness certified. She should have been, years ago! Dr Franks is just another quack, another fool who'll take your money like all the rest of them. There will be no cure, it is a fantasy. Your wife, Baron, is insane. She has been since I have been in your employment. Next she will kill someone – and that will be entirely your fault.'

Helen's hand was thrown from the Baron's arm as he leapt up and strode across the room. 'You had better leave before I throw you out. *Get out!*'

'As you wish, Baron. I will collect my personal belongings from the villa.'

He pushed her out and slammed the door shut. 'I should have done that months ago.' At his feet was the straitjacket. He picked it up and stared at it. He seemed totally defeated.

'Don't give up, Louis, it isn't true. I believe in Franks.'

He sighed, laying the jacket on a chair. He kept his back to Helen. 'Maybe she is right, maybe this is all a waste of time. I am so tired of it all, Helen.' His whole body tensed. 'I wish to God she was dead!'

'That's not true.'

He turned to face her. 'Isn't it? I was sitting by her bedside, earlier today, thinking if I had the guts I would put a pillow over her face and end it, for her, for me, then—'

'Then?'

He sighed, slumping into a chair. 'She was lucid, understood that I cannot allow her to be with Sasha, and she did it. It was her decision to call Franks.'

Helen crossed to her handbag and took out her notebook. 'I am sure he will help her, but I think we should at least talk to this woman. The more we know of Vebekka's background the better. Franks will need as much information as possible. Louis?'

He cocked his head to one side and gave a rueful smile. 'Fine, whatever you say.'

Helen picked up her coat, heading for her own suite. 'I'll have a bath and change. We can leave when Hylda returns. Perhaps I'll order some coffee to be sent up.'

The Baron nodded, and then gave a delightfully boyish smile. 'Yes, I think some coffee would be an excellent idea.'

The coffee arrived moments later, and the Baron downed two cups before he felt at all revived. He checked the time, first on his wristwatch and then the clock on the mantelpiece. It was five-thirty. He put in a call to his sons, and spoke to Sasha for a while. He said they missed her, and that he would tell her mama that she was being a good girl. The high-pitched voice hesitated before asking if her mama was being a good girl. He told her that everything was fine, and her mama would talk to her very soon. He managed to keep his voice calm and relaxed, but he was crying.

'Will she be coming home better, Papa?'

Louis pinched his nose between thumb and forefinger. 'I hope so, but she hasn't been very well for a day or so, which means we may be here longer than we anticipated.'

Sasha sighed with disappointment, but then changed the subject, talking about school and her new pony and that she was practising dressage and entering a gymkhana – she was sure she would win a rosette this time. Angel – her pony – was living up to his name. 'Papa, we jumped a two-foot fence. He's wonderful!'

Louis congratulated his daughter, and then said he had to go, there was another call on the line. Sasha made kissing sounds, and he waited for her to replace the receiver before he put his down. He heard the click, then another click. He frowned, replaced the receiver and walked into Vebekka's bedroom. She was propped up on her pillows, very pale, deep circles beneath her eyes.

'I will go to see the doctor tomorrow, Louis, even if you

have to carry me there.' She sipped a glass of water, then replaced the glass on her bedside table. It took all her willpower to be calm, she needed something to help her, something to make her sleep, but she asked for nothing. She wasn't going to drug herself, not this time; she was determined she would see it through.

'I've dismissed Anne Maria. Hylda will be here shortly.'

She leaned back, closing her eyes. 'I never liked Anne Maria, she was so ugly. Will you hold my hand?'

He sat on the edge of the bed, lifted her hand to his lips and kissed her fingers; they were so thin, so weak.

'Will you promise me something, Louis?'

'Depends on what it is.'

She didn't open her eyes. 'I understand what trouble I cause, and I know I am always asking you to forgive me, but I always mean it, I always need your forgiveness. But if – if this doctor – if he thinks I will get worse, that these good moments will get fewer, and . . . you are right, that I shouldn't be with Sasha, I understand that, but you must understand, I never . . . I never intend to hurt anyone. I don't know what takes me over, but it unleashes such terrible—'

'I know . . . I know, but you must rest now, regain your strength.'

She withdrew her hand, turning away from him. 'Louis, if nothing can be done, you know, if after the hypnosis you find out things, I want no lies, no cover-ups, no new tests, because I don't think I can stand it any more. I'm getting worse, I know that, hours go by and I don't know what I have done, who I've hurt, so promise me.'

He knew what she was going to ask of him and he leaned over the bed to kiss her cheek. 'Sleep now . . .'

She opened her eyes: they pleaded, they begged him. 'Don't put me away, Louis, help me to end it – promise me?'

He kissed her again, tilted her chin in his hands, looked deep into her eyes. He didn't answer, and her eyelids drooped as she fell asleep, her chin still cupped in his hands.

They were still together like a loving couple when Hylda slipped quietly into the bedroom. Gently the Baron drew the covers to Vebekka's chin, and Hylda saw the way he brushed her cheek with the edge of his index finger.

'She was so frightened, sir, of the dark. Frightened someone was out there.'

The Baron patted Hylda's shoulder. 'Hylda, my poor darling is frightened of her own shadow. Thank you for your care and attention, good evening.'

Hylda whispered, 'Good evening,' as he quietly closed the door. She began to knit, then looked to the closed shutter and remembered the woman, the one she had seen outside earlier; she had been like a shadow, waiting, watching . . . The click-click of her knitting needles soothed and calmed Hylda.

Vebekka did not seem to be awake, but her hand moved closer to Hylda, and she said very softly: 'Ma . . . angel.'

Helen was still getting ready, so the Baron lit a cigarette, pacing the sitting room, tormented by his wife's request. He picked up the paper that Helen had left in the room, and a front-page article caught his attention. 'Murdered Man Identified.' He started to read the column. The man was called Tommy Kellerman, a dwarf, a circus performer, who had recently arrived in East Berlin from Paris. The *Polizei* requested anyone seeing Kellerman on or during the night of his murder to come forward.

Helen walked in, refreshed and changed. The Baron lowered the paper and smiled. 'You look lovely.' He was about to toss the paper aside when he passed it to Helen. 'Did you read this? A circus performer was murdered.'

Helen took the paper and glanced at the article. 'Yes, I

was talking to one of the doormen. The hotel is only a few streets away from here, in the red-light district. Apparently they have no clues as to who did it – it happened late the same night we arrived. He was horribly beaten, the doorman was very keen to pass on all the gory details.'

The Baron drew on his fur-collared coat, and said he would call down for a taxi. Helen went to the window, drew open the shutter to look at the weather, then had a moment of *déjà vu* so strong that she had to step back from the window. Vebekka had been curled by the window, her nightgown covered in blood. Helen recalled the exact words she had said – 'We have done something terrible tonight' – and remembered thinking she was referring to Louis. But now something else came back to her: she had seen a man, a tall man, passing in the street below. She was sure of it.

'Good heavens, Louis, is there a description of the man they are looking for?' She picked up the newspaper again, rereading the article, then something else jarred her memory, the word Paris leaped out from the paper, and she turned to Louis. 'When we were at Dr Franks's you said you remembered an incident with Vebekka and the children . . . something about a circus.'

But Louis did not hear her, he was on the telephone. 'There's a taxi waiting for us. I need to tell Hylda we are leaving.'

Hylda was given instructions that, should Vebekka awake, need anything, she should call Dr Franks. The Baron thanked her profusely for being such a caring companion and slipped some folded banknotes into her hand. She blushed and replied that she was happy to look after the Baroness. She added hesitantly, 'I hope she will be assisted by this Dr Franks, that whatever demons torture and frighten her will be driven away.'

*

The same taxi that the Baron and Helen used had just returned from the circus, having driven Ruda Grimaldi back to her trailer. The driver kept up a steady flow of conversation about the price of the circus tickets, and that there were already lines of people waiting for them. He was about to launch into telling them that the previous occupant of his taxi was one of the star performers, but Helen and the Baron began to speak to each other in French, ignoring him, and, as he couldn't understand a word they said, he concentrated on driving to the address in Charlottenburg. It was a long drive and he hoped the rain would keep off as they were about to get into the rush-hour traffic. The Grimaldi woman had been strange, said hardly a word, and she hadn't gone into the hotel but stood outside on the pavement, waiting, watching, looking up at the window, the collar of her big overcoat pulled up as if hiding her face. Then, after a while, she had asked him to return her to the circus. He thought it odd, because he had seen her leaving earlier in the afternoon – perhaps she had caught a bus then, been incognito, the famous often acted up – but, stranger still, was the fixed expression on her face. Standing, so still, almost as if listening for someone to call out to her. Ruda Grimaldi had ordered him to pick her up the following day. He wondered if he could ask her for a couple of complimentary seats.

CHAPTER SEVEN

After Ruda Grimaldi had identified her ex-husband at the mortuary, Inspector Torsen returned to his rundown station in the slum area of East Berlin. He and Rieckert proceeded laboriously to type out all the information about the people they had interviewed.

Kellerman's immigration papers had not been found at Customs. All Torsen knew to date was that he had arrived from Paris, booked into the hotel, eaten a hamburger and been murdered. Nobody seemed to have seen him or noticed anyone else either enter his room or leave it. Everyone who had known him from the circus felt his death was deserved. His ex-wife had not seen him since he had been in prison and was unable to describe the tattoo sliced from his left arm.

Rieckert put his typed report on Torsen's desk and since it was almost one-thirty went to collect his raincoat.

Torsen watched him. 'You know, for a few nights we may have to work overtime on this.'

'I have a date tonight. You coming out for a sandwich?'

'No, but you can have a toasted cheese and tomato sent over, just one round, rye bread, tell her I'll pay tomorrow.'

Rieckert shrugged and walked out. Torsen completed his own reports, adding that the hall porter from Kellerman's hotel should be questioned again. His stomach rumbled – he'd eaten nothing since breakfast and he hoped Rieckert wouldn't forget his sandwich. He put the kettle on to make himself an instant coffee and, waiting for the water to boil, he turned in his reports to the empty *Polizei Direktor*'s office, and filed a second copy for the *Leitender Polizei Direktor*, who was away on holiday.

The coffee jar was virtually empty and, someone having previously used a wet spoon, he had to chip away at the hardened coffee powder. He then fetched his own sugar supply, but could find no milk. He sighed, even thought about joining Rieckert, when his cheese on rye was delivered, wrapped in a rather grubby paper napkin but at least it was what he had ordered. He kept an eye on the delivery boy who hovered by the missing persons photographs, and not until he had left did Torsen return to his desk.

The bread was stale, he noticed as he chewed thoughtfully, reading the autopsy report. The heaviness of the blows indicated they were more than likely inflicted by a man – to have crushed Kellerman's skull must have taken considerable force. Whoever had killed him also ground his false teeth into the carpet. A heel imprint, retained in the pile of the carpet, was still being tested at the lab. The print was of a steel-capped boot heel, again probably a man's because of the size. Samples of mud and sawdust found at the scene of the crime were also still being tested.

Torsen made a few notes:

(a) Where did Kellerman go for his hamburger?
(b) How many dwarfs were attached to the circus?
(c) Were any dwarfs missing from Schmidt's circus? (Just in case they had lied about him not being employed there.)
(d) Sawdust – was it from the circus?
(e) Get the ex-Mrs Kellerman to give a written positive ID for burial to take place (Rabbi).
(f) Why was Tommy Kellerman in East Berlin?

Torsen wondered why she still used Kellerman's name and not Grimaldi's. Then he remembered something that had been nagging at the back of his brain. He scrambled for his notepad and scrawled a memo to himself. 'Check unsolved dossier – the magician.'

When Torsen's father had been detective inspector at the same station as his son, they had often discussed unsolved cases together. It had begun as a sort of test between the old policeman and his eager son, but the two men had eventually grown to enjoy discussing what they thought had happened, and why the case remained unsolved. One case they had nicknamed 'The Magician', because the murdered man had been an old cabaret performer. He too had been found brutally beaten and stabbed. The magician – he could not even recall the man's real name – had been discovered in the Kreuzberg sector; he had been dead for many months, his decomposed body buried under the floorboards . . . and his left arm had been mutilated. It was suspected that the mutilation had taken place because the discovery of a tattoo would have assisted police enquiries, may even have helped them identify him. They would have required a lot more assistance if his body had not been wrapped in a wizard's cloak. They had been able to identify him, but his killer had never been found.

It was, Torsen surmised, just a coincidence . . . but he could hear his father's voice, see that forefinger wagging in the air. 'Never believe in a coincidence when you are investigating a murder, there are no coincidences.'

Torsen picked up his notepad again.

(1) Discover any persons residing in East Berlin or in the vicinity of the dead man's hotel recently arrived from Paris.
(2) Call the Hospice Centre.
(3) Magician.

Torsen checked his watch, then demolished the rest of his lunch, carefully wiping the crumbs from his desk with the napkin. He sipped his coffee, draining the cup and then, unlike anyone else at the station, returned it to the kitchen, rinsed it out and left it on the draining board. He had a quick wash and brush up in the cloakroom before going back to his office, where he sifted through the work requiring immediate attention. Then he checked his watch again: he had taken exactly one hour, no more no less.

Rieckert was late back, by a good fifteen minutes. Torsen could hear him laughing in the corridor and snatched open the door. 'You're supposed to take one hour!' Rieckert held aloft a new jar of coffee as an excuse, asking if Torsen would like a cup. 'No thank you, now get in here on the double!'

Torsen left his door open and began to gather up all his half-completed vehicle-theft reports, at the same time shouting again for Rieckert to join him.

He was looking very authoritative when at last he strolled in. 'I was just going to get some milk. We haven't got any.'

'These are more important – get them sorted. I want the lot filed and checked.'

'But I'm off at five-thirty!'

'You can leave when these are completed and not before. I have to go out later myself so the faster we get through them the—'

'Where are you going?' Rieckert interrupted sullenly.

'The Grand Hotel. I am, in case you are unaware of the fact, heading a murder investigation. I have to have further discussions with the manager and list all guests and, if the hall porter saw someone leaving the hotel around the time of the murder, perhaps I should have a look at the alleyway – the distance the porter would have been from him, if that is permissible with you!' To bring home his point Torsen began furiously jotting down further ideas in his thick notebook.

(a)   How did the killer get to the hotel?

(b)   Question taxi drivers.

(c)   Question bus drivers.

(d)   Question doormen at the Grand: very well lit-up reception area outside, within spitting distance of Kellerman's hotel.

(e)   Discuss guests with hotel manager.

Ruda had been soaked to the skin standing outside the Grand Hotel yet she still went to see Mamon before she changed. As she turned to head towards her trailer, she saw Mike – and froze. He was still wearing Tommy Kellerman's black leather trilby. She swore at herself again, at her stupidity for not remembering to burn it along with the rest of Kellerman's belongings. She watched Mike heading towards the meat trailer, but she couldn't do anything about him. She had to change and get ready to rehearse the act, already behind schedule. When she reached the trailer Grimaldi was already there, with an open bottle of brandy.

'Why don't you stay sober, at least until I've worked the act?'

'I just need something to warm me up, all right? I'm freezing. I looked all over the place for you. Why didn't you wait for me at the hotel? You just upped and walked out. Where the hell have you been?'

Ruda pulled on her old boots, ignoring his question, and suggested nastily that all he had to do was try to retrieve the old plinths, then slammed out of the trailer. Grimaldi cursed at her as she passed the window. Ruda didn't even turn her head, but gave him a V-sign. So much for thanking him for going with her to the mortuary. He didn't know where the hell he was with her. 'And you never have, you old goat,' he muttered to himself.

He really had not intended getting loaded, but he had just one more, then another, and then Tina tapped on the trailer door. She wore a raincoat over tights and a glittering bodysuit, and carried a feathered headdress. 'I hear you and the bitch went to see Kellerman this afternoon.'

Grimaldi nodded, offered her a drink which she refused. She surveyed the broken crockery, the smashed pictures, and half smiled when she said, 'Did you talk to her about us, then?'

'Yes, and it's settled . . . well, up to a point.'

'What's that supposed to mean?'

'We discussed it. She's not going to be easy.'

'But you knew that. Did you show her what we worked out?'

'I reworked bits of it. I can't just give her an ultimatum. She's worked her butt off for the act. It'll take a while to sort out.'

'Take a while! *Take a while!* You've been fobbing me off with that line for weeks. I'm pregnant, Luis, how long do you think I can get myself bounced around in my condition? You promised – promised you'd talk to her about it, about us.'

He drained the glass. 'And I just told you we talked about it. She's got a lot on her mind.'

'And I haven't? *I am pregnant!*'

He sighed, opening his arms, but she wouldn't come near him.

'I want you to get it written down, on paper, I want her out of this trailer, I'm not rooming with the girls any longer.'

He hung his head, his big hands clasped together. 'As soon as the opening's over, you and I can sort out the living accommodation.'

'There's nothing to sort out – we agreed. You give her half, that's fair – it's your act, half those animals are yours, this is your trailer. Just see how far she can go without you and your name.'

'She doesn't use my name. Now shut up.'

Tina hit the wall with the flat of her hand. 'She just uses you, and I can't bear to see it, everyone laughing at you behind your back – and what are you drinking for? What are you getting pissed for at this hour?'

She was giving him a thudding headache. 'I am not getting pissed, I am just having a drop to warm me up – I've been standing around a freezing mortuary for half the fucking day. I've been wanderin' around lookin' for her, gettin' soaked to the bloody skin. She's been actin' like a bear with a sore arse. I dunno. Everybody is naggin' me, drivin' me nuts. So don't you start, just shut up! I dunno where she goes half the time, I dunno what she's doing.'

Tina sat down and began to pluck at the feathered headdress.

'Was it him, then?'

Grimaldi nodded. 'Yeah, it was him.'

'She must be sick in the head. How could she have married that grotesque, malformed creature?'

'Because he had a big dick.'

Grimaldi grinned, and she flung her headdress at him, but she smiled. 'So have you . . .' She went to him then, and sat on his knee. 'I want us to be married, and with me behind you, you could take over the act.'

He smiled ruefully. 'You think so?'

'I know so. You were the best, everyone tells me. They all say at your peak you were the best in the world.'

'Ah, yes, at my peak . . . that was quite a while ago, sweetheart. I've peaked and come up for air a few times, and I've plummeted. Maybe I'm too old.'

Her heavy breasts were pushed up by her costume and he bent forward to kiss them. She was so young, too young ever to have seen him perform. He had been at his peak before she was even born.

'I want to have the baby, and then you can begin to train me, teach me what to do. I want to be in the ring, I want my face in the centre of that poster.'

He laughed, a low rumble. 'I bet you do . . . but it takes a long time.'

'I'm young, I have time to learn.'

He eased her off his knee and filled a glass. 'She learned so fast, Tina. I've never seen anyone adapt to working with cats like Ruda.'

Tina pouted. 'Well, that was because she had the best to teach her – that's why I want you.'

He smiled. Sometimes she was so blatantly obvious it touched him. He leaned his back against one wall staring at the posters. 'See that one from Monte Carlo? That was her first solo performance. Then there's Italy, and France . . .'

Tina put her hands over her ears. 'I don't want to hear about her, all I want to know is if you are ditching her, getting a divorce.'

'Ditching her?'

'Well, separating, whatever you want to call it.'

The trailer door banged and Mike, wearing Kellerman's hat, popped his head round the door. 'We're almost set up, sir, if you want to come over, we're ready to go in about fifteen minutes.'

'Thanks, Mike. I'll be there.'

Mike gave Tina a good once-over, and she glared at him as he closed the door. Grimaldi was checking some of the broken pictures. One was of Ruda with Mamon, she was sitting astride him as if he was a pony – she was laughing. 'You know, she hardly ever laughed when we first met, was always so serious.'

177

Tina swung one foot up and down. 'Oh, please, no past glories. I get bored with all your past glories. All I am concerned with is the present, and the promises you make and don't keep.'

Grimaldi replaced the broken frame, hung the picture up without the glass. 'I'll talk to her some more after rehearsal.'

Tina clasped him in a hug from behind. 'Will we keep him?' She pointed to a picture of Mamon.

Grimaldi shook his head. 'No, she'll never part with him.'

She clung tighter. 'I'm sorry, I forgot, I'm sorry.'

He wanted to shrug her away, wanted her out of his way, but he stood there, her soft body curled around him, her pink young lips kissing his back, rubbing her nose across his jacket. 'You'd better go, I've got to get ready. We're trying out some new plinths, the cats could get tetchy.'

She picked up her headdress, and slung her coat round her shoulders. 'OK, I'll be by later. Can we have dinner?'

'Sure.'

She stared at his back, waiting for him to turn, but he didn't. She sighed, opening the trailer door. 'Be about nine, Luis?'

'Yes, nine's fine. See you then.'

'I'll talk to her with you, if you like.'

'No . . . no, that won't be necessary. I'll work it out.'

He sighed with relief when the door closed, and then bowed his head. 'You stupid bastard, what the hell are you getting into?' he asked himself.

Another glass and the bottle was half empty. Still he stared at the wall of photographs. Tina was such a child – he was old enough to be her father, he laughed to himself, her grandfather even. He lit a cigar knowing he should be going across to the arena, but he couldn't move. The more he drank the more each photograph recorded his past. He took sly glances at Ruda riding Mamon, as if he was drawn back to that single memory more than the others. He leaned over and unhooked it, ran his fingers across her face, and then smashed the frame against the side of the table, smashed it until the photograph itself was destroyed. 'I've got to get to the arena,' he kept telling himself – but he couldn't move. It was as if the brandy was opening up the scar down his body, opening it stitch by stitch until he felt as if he was on fire.

It had been late afternoon, winter quarters in Florida. He had watched her working the act, saw she was making extraordinary strides, knew he should have been in the ring with her. He saw her lifting the hoop, training Mamon to leap through it; the fire was lit on top, and Mamon jumped like the angel she called him. Next, he watched her edging the padding for the flames further and further around the hoop, each time Mamon leapt through. Now the entire hoop was alight. Mamon hesitated, and then he jumped straight through it. She hugged Mamon as if he were a puppy! And the hands standing around watching applauded and cheered. Mamon began a slow lope around the arena, and then on a command he moved closer and closer.

Luis had watched, genuine interest mingled with envy, as she held on to the massive creature's mane of thick black fur, and then sat astride him. One of the boys had taken the photograph, not Luis, but it was as clear a picture in his mind as it was in the frame. The way she had tossed back her head and laughed that deep, wonderful full-bellied laugh; he had never been able to make her laugh like that, had never witnessed her so free, so exhilarated, and he was consumed with jealousy.

Mamon was Ruda's baby, Ruda's aggressive, terrifying love. She worshipped him, and Luis knew she was too close to him, that no trainer should get so involved with one of the cats. The danger was that the animal could become too possessive of her, that when she was working with the others and fondled one, or gave it a treat, Mamon might become jealous and in his jealous rage he would attack.

Ruda and Grimaldi had argued about her training of Mamon. He had insisted she must refrain from treating him as if he was a pet. 'He is a killer, a perfect killing machine, if you forget what he is, then you place yourself in danger.' She had smirked at him, insinuated that he was jealous because he was too afraid even to get into the ring with Mamon – he was jealous of the way she was handling him. He had turned to her angrily. 'Wrong, Ruda. What I'm trying to do is to make you see. You treat Mamon differently. All the other cats, you're working as I taught you, but with that bastard you constantly give in to him. What you refuse to see is that he is dominating you and, lemme tell you, the first, the very first moment he sees he has you, he will attack. You must not treat Mamon differently, because he will automatically think he is stronger than you.'

Ruda had stood in sullen silence before she had answered. 'Mamon is different, I understand him, and he understands me.'

Luis had shaken his head in disbelief. 'You are being naïve, childish and foolish. He is not human, he is an animal.'

She had walked out, giving him one of her snarls, twisting her face. 'Maybe I'm one, too . . .'

But Ruda knew Luis was right, and she attempted not to be so familiar, to spend less time with Mamon. Still, he was the one she could train faster than the others.

They had introduced two more lionesses, and allowed Mamon to mate with both of them. Ruda watching him released into the compound, his powerful body loping round the two lionesses as he courted and showed himself off. The three disappeared into the huts, and she had sat outside all night, waiting. Luis had told her she should stay away from him the following morning, he would be all male, all animal – wild.

Mamon had walked out as the sun rose, his head low, his massive paws carefully crossing his pathway in a perfect, steady rhythm. His eyes caught the sun like amber lamps and Ruda stood up, her hands tight on the netting. Mamon rose up on his hind legs and roared, and she could feel his hot breath on her face. 'You perform well, my love? You screw the arses off them, did you? Who's a beautiful boy?'

He had banged his body sideways on to the meshing, and then loped off to drink at the trough, turning with water dripping from his mouth to see if she was still watching.

Both lionesses were pregnant, and Ruda watched over them until the birth. Two female Bengals were pregnant and a Siberian; Ruda had her time cut out watching over the cubs, and began to see less and less of Mamon. He became distant, defiant, more and more uncontrollable. Luis blamed Ruda, but she refused any assistance. Working in the ring with sixteen tigers, two lionesses and two lions, she was still confident that she could control her Angel.

Luis had been right behind her the first time she had taken over the main part of the act. Twice he broke up squabbles between two Bengals, but Ruda seemed to have the act under good control, until Sasha misjudged a leap and fell. She reared up as Jonah, a massive Bengal, tried to attack her, and Sasha fought back and somehow caught her right paw in the top of the meshing. Her claw held firm, and she hung, paws off the ground – open and vulnerable – as the tigers, only too ready for a scrap, moved in for a hoped-for kill. Luis shouted for pliers to be brought – and fast – and helped Ruda force the rest of the cats back into their positions on the plinths.

The lions remained seated, with Mamon at the top of the pyramid, seeming to survey the situation. Luis kept up his commands as Ruda obeyed him. The clippers were brought and with Ruda moving in front of Luis to cover for him, he unclipped the wire caught in Sasha's claw. She was away fast, unharmed, lashing out a warning to the others not to come near her.

'Keep them in position, Ruda . . . hold the positions, Ruda!'

She faced the cats, sweating, her whole body on fire with adrenaline. Sasha shook her head, became very vocal but moved back into position. The danger was over and Luis, at Ruda's side, put his arm around her. He was smiling. 'OK. You did OK!'

That was the moment Mamon chose to make his attack. He sprang down from the twenty-foot-high plinth, his body seeming hardly to touch the ground as he sprang again. Both front paws caught Luis in the chest, throwing him back against the railings, but he was back on his feet again fast. Mamon's right front paw ripped through Luis's shirt, cut open his chest and dragged him forwards. His face was close to the massive jaws, and Ruda was on Mamon's back, clinging to his mane, screaming her commands. Off his back again she lashed out with the whip, and Mamon turned his attention to her, stalked her, but she kept up the command for him to move off. Turning on her heels to keep the rest of the cats in her sight, she screamed out, '*Red* A-Gmamon . . . *Red!*'

Luis's hands clutched the open wound of his chest as he backed towards the trap gate. He managed to stay on his feet, still ordering Ruda to get the cats in line ready to be herded out, before he collapsed half in and half out of the trap gate. Mamon went for him again, Luis's blood dripping down his jaws as, snarling, Mamon shook him like a rag doll, his teeth cutting through Luis's leather belt, ripping open his belly, trying to drag him like a piece of meat further into the arena. The boys got him out just in time.

When Ruda got the cats back down the traps to their cages, Luis was already aboard the ambulance and on his way to the emergency ward. She arrived at the hospital shortly after he was brought out of the operating room. His wound had taken one hundred and eighty-four stitches: he had been ripped from his throat to his groin. He remained in intensive care for eight days, as the wound festered and he suffered blood poisoning.

Ruda was at his bedside when he regained consciousness. His voice was barely audible as he told her to shoot Mamon, that he had warned her the cat would do something like this. She had wept, promised she would get rid of him, had even lied to him at other visiting times, saying that Mamon was gone, that the most important thing was for Luis to get well.

Grimaldi had recovered slowly, very slowly; the wound constantly reopened and he suffered from persistent infections, caused by rancid meat caught between Mamon's claws. His weight plummeted, he caught hepatitis, and then pneumonia put him back on the critical list. The hospital bills took every penny he had. Ruda worked at making as much as she could, but nothing covered the costs of the feeding and winter quarters. She began to sell off the cubs – and anything else she could lay her hands on. Some of the cats were the prize part of Grimaldi's act, but she had no choice. The bills kept on coming in, even though many of Grimaldi's friends rallied round and helped.

Grimaldi's main man went to visit him in hospital, and announced that he was quitting. It was a severe blow, they had been together for thirty years. It was not that his wages had not been paid – that he could understand. What he could not deal with – and refused even to clean out his cage – was Mamon. Ruda, he told Luis, had never made any attempt to get rid of him: when any buyers came, he was towed to the back of the quarters.

As sick as he was, Luis had ranted and raged at her. Why had she lied to him? Lost him a man he had worked with for all those years? Ruda had listened with eyes lowered so that he couldn't see her expression and then had said it was not Mamon's fault; he had been vicious because he had an abscess on his tooth, and since it had been removed he was as gentle as a lamb.

Grimaldi languished in the hospital as the bills mounted. Ruda came less often, claiming she was too busy trying to keep a roof over their heads. She succeeded in retaining nine of the cats – and Mamon, of course.

On his release from hospital, she had driven Grimaldi back to the quarters. He was determined to see the cats, and with the aid of a cane he had walked from cage to cage. 'Where is he? *Where is he?*'

She had stepped back, warning him, 'Don't you touch him. I mean it, Luis, don't touch him.'

He had pushed her aside, determined to find him, and she had stood guard over the cage, arms outstretched. 'Please don't, Luis, please. I have never asked you for anything in my life, but don't touch him.'

Mamon was lying like a king, yawning, as Luis stared at him. Grimaldi had turned away and limped to their trailer. Ruda called out that she would show him just what a sweetheart Mamon was, he must watch from the trailer window. Luis got the shotgun, would have shot him then, but instead he had watched her, been afraid for her, loved her, and watched . . . until the fear crept up along the jagged scar, a fear that had crippled him. He had never been in the ring since, and Mamon had proved him wrong. He had never mauled or attacked Ruda, but she had never forgotten Luis's words. She used everything he had ever taught her, and went beyond it, working out her own methods and her own commands. Even if Luis could make it back into the ring now, she would have to teach him a new act, the complete new set of commands she now used.

As for Mamon, he was both an obsession and a constant test of Ruda's capabilities. The controller and the controlled. Theirs was a strange battle of wills that thrilled her beyond anything she could have imagined. Mamon was the lover she could never take, and they had reached the perfect union, one of total respect. But she knew if she broke their bond, weakened, if she gave him an opening, he would attack her. She liked that.

Luis stared at his bloodshot eyes, began to clean his teeth, angry at himself for drinking so much. He heard the trailer door bang and he sighed, hoping it wasn't Tina again.

'Yeah! What is it?'

Mike's voice called out and intuitively Grimaldi knew something was wrong. He ran out of the small bathroom. The boy was panting, waving his hat around. 'You'd better come over to the arena, she's having a really rough time. It's those new plinths.'

Grimaldi ran with Mike across to the big tent, Mike gasping that it couldn't have come at a worse time: the big boss was in, up in the gallery looking over the rehearsals.

Hans Schmidt, wearing a fur-lined camel coat, sat back in his seat, his pudgy hands resting on a silver-topped cane. Below him, way below, he could see the main ring, the cages erected and the caged tunnel. The spotlights were on, and Ruda's figure seemed tiny as she turned, calling out to the cats.

185

Mr Kelm eased into the vacant seat next to Hans Schmidt. 'You wanted to see me, sir?'

'This Kellerman business, has it been cleared up?'

'I don't know, sir, the *Polizei* were here, I told you. I gave them every assistance possible, but I heard they asked Mrs Grimaldi to identify him this afternoon.'

Schmidt nodded his jowled head, his eyes focused on the ring. 'Very disturbing, bad publicity. Very bad!'

'Yes, I know, but I'm sure it'll all be cleared up.'

'It better be. This is the costliest show to date. What do you think of the Kellerman woman?'

'She's stunning. I've seen parts of her act in Italy and Austria, she is very special.'

'Doesn't look so hot now . . .'

Kelm peered down, and then told Schmidt about the new plinths, that the animals were playing up, they always did with new props. Schmidt stood up. 'Jesus God, is that part of the act?'

Kelm looked down to see the cats milling around Ruda, he nodded his head and then waited as she did the jump, spinning on the tigers' backs. Schmidt applauded. 'I have never seen anything like it . . . she must be insane!'

Kelm nodded again, his glasses glinting in the darkness. 'She takes great risks.'

Ruda felt her muscles straining as she lifted one plinth on top of the other; the sweat was streaming off her, her hands in their leather gloves were clammy. She backed the tigers up . . . gave the command for them to keep on the move, and then tried for the third time to get them seated in the simple pyramid. They went up to the plinths, hesitated and turned away.

'Goddamn you . . . *up red edededddd! Roja!*' She knew if Roja obeyed her the rest would follow, but he was playing up badly. She was exhausted. Grimaldi moved slowly to the rails, asked if she was OK, and she backed towards him.

'The owners are up in the main viewing box, it's been mayhem. But I think I'm winning. Can you give me the long whip?'

Luis passed it through the bars. She took it from him without looking and began again, her voice ringing round the arena. '*Red–red–blue Sasha blooooooooot* . . . good girl, good girl, *Roja up* . . . *yup yup* . . . Red! thatta good boy . . . good boy . . .' Luis kept watch as at last she got them on to the plinths, leaving one vacant ladder to the top.

Ruda gave the signal and the tigers remained on their plinths as she gave a mock bow, looked to the right, to the left. The gates opened. In came one male lion and, a beat after, she heard the click again and knew the second one was hurtling down the tunnel. The two lions came to her, one to her right side, one to her left, and she herded and cajoled them on to the lower seats. They were unsure, backed off . . . but they were not as uneasy as the tigers.

She gave the signal, and Mamon, spotlighted in the long tunnel, came out at a lope. Ruda pretended she did not know he was there. Mamon was trained to come up behind her, to nudge her with his nose, and then in mock surprise she would jump, on to his back. She had a semi-circle to go before she gave him the second section command. The act centred on Mamon's refusing to do as he was told; it was always fun, the audience roaring their approval as Mamon played around.

Mamon refused, once, twice . . . Ruda called out to him but he swung his head low. Again she gave him the command: '*Up* . . . Ma'angel up Mamon . . .'

Mamon refused the jump. He began to prowl around the back of the tigers. They got edgy, started hissing, and then

187

two of them began to fight. Ruda called out, '*Down*,' herding out all the cats, leaving Mamon to her right. They behaved well, moving back down the tunnel, but Mamon refused to leave.

Luis waited, watching, swearing to himself about the plinths, but it was too late now. Ruda gave the signal for Mike to get the cats herded back into their cages. She was going to have to work Mamon with the new plinths, cajoling and talking to him, all the while trying to get him on the lower plinth. He refused, sniffing, unsure, smelling, circling, giving a low-bellied growl.

'Come on, baby . . . up up . . . *yup red red red red!*'

Mamon lay down, ignoring her, staring at her. She stood with her hands on her hips. They eyed each other, and Ruda waited.

High up at the back of the main circle seats Tina sat eating a bag of crisps, watching as Ruda sat on one of the plinths, patting it with her hand, softly encouraging Mamon to come to her. He refused. Ruda checked the time, knew she was overrunning, and suddenly stood up. 'Angel . . . *Angel up*, come on – *up*!'

Mamon slowly got to his feet, walked very, very slowly to the new plinth, sniffed it, walked around it, and just as slowly eased himself up and sat. Ruda looked at him. 'You bastard, now stop playing around – *uyup blooooo.*' He shook his head, and then just as slowly mounted the blue plinth. He sat. Ruda encouraged him, flattered and cajoled him until he had sat on each plinth and sniffed it – twice he pissed over them. He was in no hurry, his whole motion was slow, leisurely, constantly looking to Ruda as if to say, 'I'll do it. But in my time.'

Ruda gave him the command for his huge jump down; he hesitated and then reared up and sprang forward, heading straight for Ruda. Tina dropped her bag of crisps as she stood up, terrified.

Ruda shouted at Mamon, pointing the whip. 'Get back . . . back!'

Mamon paid no attention. Ruda spoke sharply to him – and suddenly he turned. Grimaldi gasped as the massive animal churned up the dust. Now he was not playing, now he was the star attraction. In wonderfully co-ordinated jumps he sprang from plinth to plinth, showing off, until he reached the highest point. Then he lifted up his front paws and struck out at the air.

By the time Mamon was moving back down the tunnel, Ruda had unhooked the latch to let herself out of the arena. She slumped into a seat, taking the proffered handkerchief from her husband to wipe her face. He sat next to her and she could smell the brandy.

'That was tough going!'

'You said it, Luis. I'm going to need double rehearsal time before we open, you could see. They're all over the place. They hate those bloody plinths. I hate them!'

'It was your idea to get new ones, I warned you but you wouldn't listen.'

'I said get them the same *fucking colours. These are too bright!'*

They argued and Tina looked on. Her vision of herself taking over the act had paled considerably. She watched as Grimaldi and the boys began to dismantle the arena cages, then she went over to the horses and got ready for their practice. Grimaldi hadn't even looked in her direction.

Ruda was still in a foul mood, and exhausted, when she walked into the freezer trailer. She began chopping up the meat for the cats' feed. By the time Mike appeared, still wearing the hat, she had all the meat ready.

'The arena cages are stacked, we got two extra hours tomorrow.'

'That's marvellous, this'll be a nightmare. You saw them, they were all playing up.'

Mike shrugged, giving a funny cockeyed smile. 'But you handled them. Word is that Schmidt was impressed! You want me to take the feed through?'

Ruda shook her head. 'No, I'll do it, just double-check that their straw is clean, their cages ready.'

'OK. Will you need me later tonight? I reckon if I get their night feed set out me and a few of the lads will go round to the clubs.'

'I hope not in that hat. Where did you get it?'

'Oh, I found it, it was in here.'

Ruda smiled. 'Well, just leave it, will you? It's one of Luis's I kept here so he wouldn't wear it, it's disgusting.'

Mike tossed Kellerman's hat aside. 'Sorry, it was just that it was pissing down earlier . . . Oh, about this guy Kellerman.'

Ruda froze, staring at the blood-red meat.

'Somebody said he was a dwarf, used to work the circus, is that right?'

Ruda nodded.

Mike flushed slightly. 'He was found in East Berlin. One of the lads told me he had been murdered.'

Ruda lifted the trays. 'Yes, he was, we had to go and identify him today. You ever meet him?'

Mike shrugged, shaking his head. 'Nope. I don't know anything about him, just that someone said he used to be your husband.'

'Yes he was, a long time ago.'

Mike watched her carry the trays down between the trailers, stacking them on to a trolley. She returned for the next batch and said sharply, 'You going to stand watching me work or are you going to earn your pay?'

'Oh, sorry.'

Mike began to put more feed trays out, and Ruda worked alongside him, until suddenly she banged down an empty tray. 'Mike, if you've got something to say, why don't you come out with it?' He flushed pink, unable to tell her what was bothering him. He was sure he had seen Kellerman the day he died, but he said nothing. She continued heaving out the hunks of meat. 'Maybe you can feed Sasha and the two buggers with her.'

'OK,' he said, already carrying out the second batch of feed. Ruda picked up Kellerman's hat and put it into her bag, then continued heaping the meat into the trays. Mike was still watching her and she stopped abruptly.

'OK, I married Tommy Kellerman. I needed a marriage certificate for a visa for the United States. Tommy offered it, I accepted, I went to the United States. End of marriage – or is that fertile imagination of yours working overtime?'

He laughed, and then paused at the open door. 'More kids arriving for the tour of the cages. Look at the little gawking creeps.'

Ruda walked with Mike to the loaded trolley. Stacking the last of the big trays, she chatted nonchalantly. 'There was one of those kids hanging around the cages the other afternoon, did you see me talking to him? Only came up to my waist, trying to put his hand into Mamon's cage. I had to give him a ticking off.'

Mike grinned. 'I remember, yeah. It was a kid then, was it? I wondered, you know . . .' He went on with his business and called to her that he would return as soon as he parked the trays. Ruda returned to the freezer. That was Mike sorted out, he hadn't known it was Kellerman with her, and now that she had the little bastard's hat, she was safe. Ruda stared at her hands, her red-stained fingers, the blood trickling down almost to her elbow. She was thinking of Tommy, seeing his crushed, distorted face on the mortuary table, and she whispered: 'I'm sorry I broke our pact, Tommy, but you just wouldn't stop.'

It was as if he was calling out to her from the cold marble slab, calling to her, the way he used to when she teased him, but hearing his voice in her mind, hearing it now, made her feel a terrible guilt.

'Don't turn the light out, Ruda, please leave the light on!'

CHAPTER EIGHT

THE RAIN had started again, the traffic jams had built up and the journey to Charlottenburg became a long and tedious drive. The Baron looked from his rain-splattered window and checked his watch. It was after six. Helen spoke to their driver in German. 'I have never seen so many dogs!'

Their cab driver looked into his mirror. 'We Berliners love animals, bordering on the pathological. There are more dogs in Spree than anywhere else in Germany – they say there's about five dogs to every hundred inhabitants.'

The Baron sighed, resting his head against the upholstered seat. Helen stared from her window. 'Why is that? I mean, why do you think there are so many?'

The driver launched into his theory, welcoming the diversion from the inch-by-inch crawl his car was forced to make. 'Many people living in the anonymous council flats, many widows, a dog is their only companion. A psychologist described the Berliners' love of animals, dogs in particular, as a high social functional factor.'

Louis grimaced, taking Helen's hand, and spoke in French. 'Don't encourage him! Please . . . the man is a compulsive theorist!' Helen laughed.

They passed by the Viktoria-Luise-Platz, heralding the West Berlin Zoo, and their driver now became animated.

'The zoo, you must visit our famous zoo. In 1943 the work of a hundred years was destroyed in just fifteen minutes, during the battle for Berlin. When the bombing was over, only ninety-one animals survived, but we have rebuilt almost all of it. Now we have maybe eleven or twelve thousand species – the most found in any zoo in the world!'

At last, they were near the centre of Charlottenburg itself. 'Bundesverwaltungsgericht,' the driver said with a flourish, and then he smiled in the mirror. 'The Federal Court of Appeal in Public Lawsuits.'

Helen passed over the slip of paper with the address of Rosa Muller Goldberg's sister, a Mrs Lena Klapps. The driver nodded, turned off the Berliner Strasse, passing small cafés and ale houses, and rows and rows of sterile apartment blocks, their shabby façades dominating the rundown street, before he drew up outside a building. He pointed, and turned to lean on the back of his seat. 'You will require for me to take you back, yes?'

The Baron opened his door, saying in French to Helen, 'Only if he promises to keep his mouth shut!'

Helen instructed the driver to wait, and joined the Baron on the pavement. They looked at the apartment numbers painted above a cracked wide door leading to an open courtyard. Their driver rolled down his window, pointing. 'You want sixty-five. Go to the right . . . to the right.'

The lift was broken, and they walked up four flights of stone steps. Dogs brushed past them, going down, and one bedraggled little crossbreed scuttled ahead, turned and yapped before he disappeared from sight. There were pools of urine at each corner, and they had to step over dog faeces. Helen muttered that perhaps the residents were all widows. 'Dogs are . . . what did he say? . . . a social function? More like a health hazard.'

There was a long stone balcony corridor, the apartments numbered on peeling painted doors . . . sixty-two, sixty-three was boarded up, and then they rang the bell of apartment sixty-five.

An elderly man inched open the door; he was wearing

carpet slippers, a collarless shirt and dark blue braces holding up his baggy trousers. Helen smiled warmly. 'We are looking for Lena Klapps, née Muller? I am Helen Masters. I called.'

The old man nodded, opened the door wider and gestured for them to follow him. They were shown into a room containing antique furniture mixed with a strange assortment of cheap modern chairs, and a Formica-topped table. The room was dominated by an antique carved bookshelf, covering two walls, its shelves stacked with paperbacks and old leather-bound books.

The old man introduced himself as Gunter Klapps, Lena's husband, and gestured for them to be seated. He stood at the door with his hands stuffed into his pockets. 'She is late. The rain – there will be traffic jams. But she should be here shortly, excuse me.'

He closed the door behind him, and Helen unbuttoned her coat. The Baron stared around the room, looked at the threadbare carpet, then to the plastic-covered chairs. Helen placed her handbag on the table. 'Not exactly welcoming, was he?'

The Baron flicked a look at his watch. 'Maybe we should call the hotel?'

Helen nodded, and crossed to the door. She stood in the hallway, calling out for Mr Klapps. The kitchen door was pulled open, and he glared.

'Telephone – do you have a telephone I could use?'

'No, we have no telephone.'

He continued to stare, so Helen returned to the room. The Baron was still standing, his face set in anger. 'I hope this is not a wasted journey. I am worried about Vebekka, leaving her alone.'

'They have no telephone. Shall I go out, make a call?'

He snapped, 'No,' and then sat in one of the ugly chairs. Helen took off her coat, placing it over a typist's chair tucked into the table. She looked over the bookcase; some of the leather-bound volumes were by classical authors, but many of the books were medical journals. She was just about to mention this to Louis, when they heard the front door open.

Lena Klapps walked in. She was much younger than her husband, but wore her hair in a severe bun at the nape of her neck. The grey hair accentuated her pale skin and pale washed-out blue eyes. 'Excuse me, I won't be a moment, my bus was held up in the rush-hour traffic. May I offer you tea?'

The Baron proffered his hand. 'Nothing, thank you. I am Baron Louis Maréchal.'

Lena retreated quickly, saying she would just remove her coat and boots.

She returned a few moments later. She wore a white high-necked blouse, a grey cardigan and grey pleated skirt. Her only jewellery was her wedding ring. 'I must apologise for my husband, he has been very ill.' She shook Helen's hand, and nodded formally to the Baron, gesturing for him to remain seated. She then withdrew the typist's swivel chair, lifting Helen's coat and placing it across the table. She seemed to perch rather than sit, her knees pressed together, hands clasped in front of her.

Helen looked to the Baron, but he gave a small lift of his eyebrows as an indication she should open the conversation. She coughed, and chose her words carefully. 'May I call you Lena?'

Lena nodded, looking directly at Helen. Her pale eyes were cold, ungiving, as unwelcoming as her husband's.

'The Baron's wife, Vebekka Maréchal – we are trying to trace her relatives, and as I said to you in my telephone call, we think she may have been your sister's daughter. Your sister was Rosa Muller?'

'Yes, that is correct.'

Helen continued. 'She married a David Goldberg? And they lived in Canada and then Philadelphia, yes?'

'Yes, that is correct.'

The Baron cleared his throat. 'Do you have a photograph of their daughter, of Rebecca Goldberg?'

'No, I lost contact with my sister before she left for Canada. I know they emigrated to Philadelphia, but we did not keep in touch. Her husband's cousin, a man named Ulrich Goldberg, wrote to me that she had passed away.'

Helen bit her lip. 'We need as much information as you can give us about Rebecca and your sister.'

Lena swivelled slightly in her seat. Her toes touched the ground, the folds of her pleated skirt falling to either side of her closed knees. 'I know nothing of . . . Rebecca, you say? I cannot help you.'

'But Rosa was your sister?'

'Yes, Rosa was my sister.'

Lena suddenly turned to the bookshelf, reached over and took down a thick photograph album. She began to search through the pages of photographs. She spoke in English, heavily accented, as if she was proving some kind of point. 'I find it somewhat strange that after forty years I am asked about Rosa. You say it is in reference to your wife, Baron? Is that correct?'

Helen went to stand by Lena. 'The Baroness is very ill, and we have come to see a specialist in East Berlin who may be able to help her. It is his suggestion that we should try to discover as much about her past as possible.'

Lena nodded. 'And this is Rebecca? Correct? But there must be some confusion. She could not be my sister's child.' She paused, turned back two pages, and then showed Helen the photograph. 'This was Rosa when she was seventeen, 1934 . . .'

Helen stared at the picture of a pretty blonde-haired

teenager, with white ribbons in her hair, white ankle socks and a school uniform. Next to her stood Lena, taller, fatter, and not nearly as pretty. She had been as stern-faced a teenager as she was now in middle age. Helen passed over the photograph album to the Baron. Lena hesitated, her hand out, obviously not wanting the Baron to take possession of the album. 'That is the only photograph, there is no point in looking at any others.'

'Lena, is there some way we could contact any of David Goldberg's friends or family? Do you know if any of his relatives are still living in Berlin?' Helen asked.

'No. I did not know Rosa's husband, they met at university. As I said, I have not spoken to my sister for more than forty years.'

The Baron turned over a few pages, and Lena got up and retrieved her book. She stared at the neatly laid-out photographs, some brown with age. 'Berlin has seen many changes since these were taken. My family home,' she pointed to an elegant four-storey house, 'it was bombed, all our possessions, we lost everything but a few pieces. The other photographs are just my family, my mementoes – nothing to do with Rosa.' She held on to the book, touched it lovingly before she replaced it on the shelf, and then hesitated. 'I agreed to see you, because I know Rosa was well off . . . as you can see, money is short. I thought perhaps she had made provision for me. Obviously I was wrong.' She stared from Helen to the Baron and then, tight-lipped, remained standing. 'I am sorry, but it seems very obvious that I cannot help you.'

Helen reached for her coat, making as if to prepare to leave. 'Rosa was a doctor? Is that correct?'

'She was a medical student. She did not qualify here, she continued her studies in Canada, after the war.' Lena folded her arms.

'Was her husband a doctor?'

Lena shook her head. 'No. My father, my grandfather were also doctors.'

'But Rosa and David met at university?'

'Yes, but he was studying languages, I believe. When they went to Canada, I heard he began to trade as a furrier.'

Helen looked at Louis, wishing he would say something, ask something; but he sat on the edge of his seat, obviously wanting to leave.

'Er . . . you said earlier that Rebecca could not have been Rosa's daughter. Was she perhaps David Goldberg's daughter?'

'I don't know.'

'But why are you so sure she could not have been Rosa's child?'

Lena pursed her lips. Then she carefully pushed her chair under the table. 'Rosa could not have children.'

Helen persisted. 'Could you give me the reason?'

Lena faced her. 'Because she had an abortion when she was seventeen years old, a backstreet abortion, paid for by that creature she ran off with and married. She nearly died, and she broke my father's heart. When he discovered her relationship, he would have nothing to do with her. He begged her to give David up, but she refused. He tried everything, he even kept her under lock and key to stop her from seeing him. She was obsessed by David and so she ran away, and my father never spoke to her again.'

'This was when?'

Lena rubbed her head. 'She ran off on the second of June. It was 1934 they ran away together. We discovered they had married.'

'They went to Canada?'

'Yes. His family were wealthy, they must have had contacts there to help him set up in business. They always help each other.'

Helen began to put on her coat. 'Did they ever come back?'

Lena nodded. 'I believe so, but not for a long time, not until just after the war. The Goldbergs had property here.'

'So they came back to Berlin?'

'Yes, yes, I believe so.'

'And you didn't see him or speak to him?'

'No.'

'Did you see Rosa when she came back?'

'No.'

'And you cannot give us any clue to relatives?'

Lena stared hard at Helen, her eyes expressionless. 'He had no one left but his cousin, Ulrich Goldberg, who was already residing in the United States. Rosa never contacted her mother, never visited her father's or her brother's graves. As far as I am concerned, my sister died a long time ago, the day she ran away. Now I should be grateful if you would leave.'

The Baron gripped Helen's elbow, wanting to get out, but she stood firmly. 'Do you think your sister could have adopted Rebecca when she returned to Berlin? Could she have adopted a child then, knowing she could not have children of her own?'

Lena pushed past Helen and opened the door. 'I have told you all I know, please leave now.'

Helen snatched up her handbag and walked out, as the Baron folded some money and handed it to Lena. 'Thank you for your time, I appreciate it.'

He followed Helen to the front door. Lena watched them, her hand gripping the thick wad of folded notes.

'She worked in a hospital for three months. I don't know where, I have told you all I know.'

The stale smell of cabbage filled the hallway, as they hurried along the stone corridor. The Baron guided Helen down the stairs, holding her elbow lightly in the crook of his hand. 'The family album was interesting. Did you get a chance to see any of the other photographs? The father was like an SS officer, the brothers were all in uniform too.' He shook his head. 'Can you believe it? She wouldn't see her sister for forty-odd years, and then thinks she may have left her something.'

Helen stopped and turned to him. 'We can get Franks to check hospitals, and we can contact someone from the Canadian Embassy to see if they can trace a birth certificate – but you know something, I don't think they'll find one. I think they adopted a child here. God knows, there must have been thousands of children needing help.'

The Baron snapped, angrily, 'We don't know if this Rosa was Vebekka's mother, adopted or otherwise. We're just clutching at straws.'

They came out from the apartment building, and their driver tooted his car horn, having parked across the street. Louis slapped his forehead. 'Dear God, I'd forgotten him! I don't think I can stand his guided tours all the way back.'

Helen found it a little strange. Louis seemed more relaxed, even good humoured, now they had left the apartment. They got into the car and he asked the driver to stop at the nearest telephone kiosk. They drove only half a mile before he went to call the hotel to check on Vebekka. Helen watched him from the window, and then leaned back closing her eyes. She was sure the jigsaw was piecing together: the Mullers had turned their back on Rosa not because she was pregnant, but because the father of her child was a Jew.

Louis returned and signalled for the driver to move on. 'She has eaten, she is resting, and Hylda says she is calm, sleeping most of the time.'

As they crossed into East Berlin, their driver became even more animated. 'You know the Communist regime may have tried to squash artistic freedom but, like the

West, we always had circuses – you like the circus? At one time it was all provided for, classical music, opera, everything funded by the state. Now we need many millions of marks to sustain it and all our artists, our best talent and producers run to the West. A leading ballerina from the East Berlin Ballet is having to find work as a stripper to cover her rent – it's true!'

Helen leaned forwards, trying to stop the constant flow of dialogue, and asked if he had heard about the murder, the dwarf found in the hotel not far from the Grand.

The driver nodded his head vigorously. 'Yes, yes I heard, the crime wave is unstoppable here, we don't have enough *Polizei*. Maybe he was working at the Artistenschule, you know, teaching circus acts. We have many famous circus performers from Berlin – you know there is a magnificent circus about to begin a new season? If you want, I can get you tickets, I have contacts.'

The car drew up outside the hotel, and still the driver talked. 'I have many contacts for nightclubs, for shows. If you want something risqué – you know what I mean – this I can arrange . . .'

He had exhausted them both. Helen rang for the lift while the Baron enquired at the desk for any letters or calls. He was handed a package, a special delivery, just arrived.

Standing next to the Baron was Inspector Torsen Heinz, also waiting at the reception, but he gave him no more than a cursory glance, more interested in the contents of the parcel. Torsen was mentally counting up the cost of the small salad he had eaten in the hotel bar: he'd never have another, not that it hadn't been fresh and well served but it had cost more than five times his cheese on rye at lunch.

Torsen had been waiting patiently for more than half an hour for the manager to give him a list of residents who had arrived at the Grand Hotel from Paris on or near the night of Kellerman's murder. The Baron and Helen stepped into the lift as the manager bustled across the foyer gesturing for the inspector to follow him.

He ushered Torsen into his private office, then closed the door. 'I have had to speak to the director of the hotel over this matter. I am afraid you place us in a very difficult situation. We do have guests, and they are from Paris, but whether or not I can ask . . .'

Torsen opened his notebook officiously. 'I have been able to gain a positive identification of the murdered man, sir, and I will require from you the date these guests arrived. Does it coincide with the dates I gave to you?'

'Yes, yes, but these guests are Baron Maréchal, his wife, a nurse and I think his wife's physician, a Dr Helen Masters.'

Torsen closed his book. 'Could I speak with the Baron?'

'I'm afraid that won't be possible. His wife has not been well and she is resting in their suite. I really don't like to disturb them. Perhaps if you return in the morning, I will speak to the Baron. He is not available now.'

'He just came in.'

'Pardon?'

'I said the Baron just arrived at the reception desk. I saw him.'

The manager pursed his lips, referred again to the conversation he had just had with the director, and suggested Torsen returned in the morning. In the meantime he would speak to the Baron.

Torsen was shown out into the elegant foyer, and checked the time by the array of clocks behind the reception desk. He wondered if he could squeeze in a quick visit to his father before interviewing the hall porter at Kellerman's hotel. It had started to rain again, and the inspector decided he would treat himself to a taxi. He asked the doorman to call him one, but he pointed at the waiting rank.

The Baron's and Helen's driver was snoozing, his cap drawn over his eyes, but he jumped to attention when Torsen tapped on his window. Torsen got into the passenger seat next to him, gave the address of his father's home, and was treated to a detailed blow-by-blow account of the rise in price of hospital beds and facilities for the elderly. 'This city will be in deep trouble – you know why?'

Torsen made no reply, knowing it would make no difference.

'The avalanche of poverty-stricken immigrants is heading this way. Our young have all flown to the West. I was telling the Baron, he was in my cab today, I was telling him about the circus, the Artistenschule, once the most famous in the world for training circus performers. It'll close, mark my words, it'll close . . .'

Torsen frowned. 'Did the Baron ask about the circus?'

The driver nodded. 'We were discussing the murder, the dwarf. He was asking about the murder.'

Torsen listened, interested now, and instructed the driver to change direction. He wanted to go to the Artistenschule.

The driver did a manic U-turn in the centre of the road. 'OK, you're the boss. I said to the Baron, I said, they'll never find the killer.'

'Why is that?' asked Torsen.

'Because we've got a load of amateurs running our *Polizei*, they never made any decisions before, they were *told* who to arrest and who not to, you can't change that overnight. This is it, the main door is just at the top of those steps.'

Torsen fished in his pockets for loose change, then asked for a receipt. The driver drew out a grubby square notepad, no taxi number or official receipt. 'How much do you want me to put on this? Travelling salesman, are you?'

Torsen opened his raincoat to reveal his uniform. 'No. I just need to give it to my *Leitender Polizei Direktor*.'

The driver said nothing, scribbled on his notepad, and shook Torsen's hand – too hard, too sincerely. For a brief moment Torsen saw fear pass over his face, and then it was gone. So was the Mercedes in a cloud of black exhaust fumes. In the old days he could have been arrested for slandering the state.

Torsen tapped on the small door marked 'Office Private' underlined twice. He waited, tapped again, and eventually heard shuffling sounds. Then a rasping voice bellowed to some animal to get out of the way. The door opened, and Torsen was confronted by a massive man wearing a vest and tracksuit bottoms. Clasping his hand was a chimpanzee. They rather resembled each other, the vest hardly hiding the man's astonishing growth of body hair.

Fredrick Lazars beckoned Torsen to follow him, saying he was just eating his dinner. Torsen was seated on a rickety chair, covered in dog hairs, as Lazars sat the chimp in his baby's high chair and fetched a big tin bowl and large spoon. He tipped what looked like porridge into the bowl, and then took out of an oven a plate piled with sausages, onions and mashed potatoes. He offered to share his dinner with Torsen. As the dinner looked started, the sausages half-eaten, Torsen refused politely, adding that he had just dined, 'At the Grand Hotel!' He made no mention that it had been just a side salad and, as Lazars didn't seem impressed that he had eaten there, dropped the subject. Lazars opened two bottles of beer and handed one to Torsen, just as the chimp swung his spoon, flicking Torsen's uniform with porridge. Only two years old, the chimp was called Boris, but was really a female – all this was divulged in a bellow from a food-filled mouth.

'Did Tommy Kellerman come to see you?'

The big hands broke up large chunks of bread, dipping them into the fried onions. 'He did . . . the night he died.'

Torsen took out his notebook, asked for a pencil, and

205

Lazars bellowed at Boris who climbed down and pottered to an untidy desk where he threw papers around. 'Pencil . . . *pencil, Boris*!' Torsen was half out of his seat, ready to assist Boris, when a pencil was shoved at him, but Boris wouldn't let go of the pencil, so a tug of war ensued before Lazars whacked Boris over the head and told her to finish her dinner. Boris proceeded to spoon in large mouthfuls of the porridge substance, dribbling it over the table, herself and the floor.

'Kellerman came to see me about six, maybe nearer seven.'

'Why have you not come forward with this evidence?'

'He came, he ate half my dinner and departed. What's there to tell in that?'

Torsen scribbled in his book. 'So what time did he leave?'

Lazars sniffed and gulped at his beer. 'He stayed about three-quarters of an hour, said he had some business he was taking care of, important business.'

'What did you do after he left? Or did you accompany him?'

'No, he left on his own, I stayed here.'

'Do you have any witnesses to substantiate that?'

'Yep, about two hundred. We were giving a display, just a few kids trying out, but I started at eight-thirty, maybe finished around ten or later, then we had an open discussion, finished after twelve. We went on to O'Bar, about six of us, then we stayed there.'

Torsen held up his hand. 'No, no more . . . if you could just give me some names of people who can verify all this.'

Lazars reeled off the names as Boris banged her plate splashing Torsen with more of her food. She started screeching for more, and received it, giving Lazars a big kiss as a thank-you.

'I love this little fella . . . mother died about a year ago –

you know we had to close part of the animal sector? Well, she's moved in with me until I find someone to buy her.'

Torsen asked Lazars what he knew of Kellerman's background, and the massive man screwed up his face, his resemblance to Boris even more staggering. 'He was an unpleasant little bastard, nobody had a good word to say about him, always borrowing, you know the kind, he'd touch a blind beggar for money, but, well he'd had a tough life . . . you forgive a lot.'

'Did he ever work here?'

'Yeah, long time ago – I mean, a really long time ago, early fifties, I think. He turned up one day, sort of learnt a few tricks, just tumbling and knockabout stuff, but he never had the heart. Got to have a warm heart to be a clown, you know? Kellerman, he was different, he was never . . . I dunno, why speak ill of the dead, huh?'

'It may help me find his killer. Somebody hated him enough to give him a terrible beating.'

Lazars lifted Boris down and carried her to the dish-piled sink. He took a cloth, ran it under the water, rinsed it and wiped the chimpanzee's face.

'Look, Kellerman was a bit crazy, you know? Mixed up. He hated his body, his life, his very existence. Kellerman was somebody that should have been suffocated when he was born. He couldn't pass a mirror without hating himself. And when he was younger, it was tragic – he looked like a cherub. Like a kid . . . See, when he first came here he must have still been in his twenties.'

Torsen nodded, finishing the dregs of his beer. Boris, her face cleaned, now wanted her hands washed. 'I'm trying to train her to do the washing up!' roared Lazars, laughing at his own joke. 'But she's too lazy! Like me!'

Lazars sat Boris down, and cut a hunk of cheese for himself. 'The women went for him, always had straight women – you know, normal size.'

Torsen hesitated. 'I met his ex-wife.'

Lazars cocked his head to one side. 'She's a big star now, doesn't mix with any of us, but then who's to blame her? She's been worldwide with the Grimaldi act. He's a nice enough bloke, part Russian, part Italian – hell of a temper, nice man, but I'm not sure about Ruda. But then who's sure about anybody?'

Torsen flicked through his notebook. 'Did you know them when they were married?'

'No, not really. I don't, to tell you the truth, even know where she came from. I think she used to work the clubs, but don't quote me. Kellerman just used to turn up, we never knew how he did it. I think he was into some racket with forged documents, he seemed to be able to cross back and forth with no problems. We had a bit of a falling out about it. You know, he'd come over here, check over the acts – next minute they'd upped and left. I think he made his money that way, you know – paid for fixing documents and passports. He always had money, not rich, but never short of cash either in those early days, so I just put two and two together. He had a place over in the Kreuzberg district, so he must have had contacts. Not circus people, he was only ever attached to circuses because of his deformity – when he couldn't make cash on rackets, he joined up with a circus.'

Torsen rubbed his head. 'Did he have money when you last saw him?'

Lazars shook his head. 'No, he was broke, told me he had been in gaol but I knew that anyway. All he said was he had some business deal going down. Maybe he'd got in with the bad guys again, who knows? I do know he let a lot of people down.'

'How do you mean?'

'Promises, you know, he'd get them over the border, get them work. They'd pay up front, end up over there, and no

208

Kellerman – he'd pissed off. Any place he turned up you could guarantee there would be someone waiting to give him a hiding.'

'Or kill him?'

Lazars had Boris on his knee; the chimp was sucking at her thumb like a tiny baby, her round eyes drooping with tiredness. Torsen reached for his raincoat; it was covered with animal hairs. 'There is just one more thing, then I'll get out of your way.'

Lazars stood up, resting Boris, fast asleep, on his hip.

Torsen almost whispered, afraid to wake Boris. 'Do you recall a tattoo on his left arm?'

Lazars nodded, and the bellowing voice was a low rumble. 'I remember it, they're the ones you never forget.'

Torsen waited, and Lazars sighed. 'Maybe that was why we all put up with his shit. Tommy Kellerman was in Auschwitz – the tattoo was his number.'

Torsen bowed his head, answered softly, 'I see. Thank you for your co-operation.'

For once the rain had ceased, and Torsen took a bus back to Kellerman's hotel. He sat hunched in his seat, making notes in his book. He put a memo for Rieckert and himself to visit Ruda Kellerman and question her again: it was important, he underlined it twice. She had lied about Kellerman's tattoo, she must have known what it was. He closed his eyes, picturing Ruda Kellerman as she touched the dead man's hair at the mortuary that afternoon. She had lied.

He spent the rest of the journey mulling over why she would have lied, but came to no conclusion. He stared from the grimy window of the bus at a group of punks kicking empty beer cans along the street. They had flamboyantly blue and red hair; they wore torn black leather jackets, and black boots that clanked and banged the cans along the street. He felt old, tired out, bogged down, trying to find the killer of a man nobody seemed to care about. Was it all a pointless waste of time? The men at the station had implied that it was; nobody would give any overtime to assist him.

He interrupted himself, swearing. He should have asked Lazars if the dinner he had shared with Kellerman was hamburger and chips. He'd have to call in the morning, and again he swore – he couldn't call him before nine because of the switchboard. He also wanted a telephone.

Torsen began another of his lists. He was going to start throwing his weight around; he wanted a patrol car for his personal use, plus fuel allowance, and, as from tomorrow, he was going to work out a rota – none of this nine to five from now on. They would work as they did in the West, day and night duty officers, round the clock. The bus rumbled on. Torsen sniffed his hands – they smelt of Boris, he smelt of Boris, and the remains of the chimp's food had hardened into flecks all over his jacket. The bus shuddered to a halt and Torsen stepped down, checking the time, sure the porter must have started work by now. He felt even more worn-out as he headed for Kellerman's hotel, passing the ornate and well-lit Grand Hotel's entrance, hurrying down the back streets tallying up how many girls he saw lurking in the dark dingy doorways, even wondering if one of them had seen the killer. But he didn't approach the girls because he was alone and didn't want his intentions to be misconstrued. He made a mental note to add to his lists: check out the call girls. No doubt Rieckert would jump at the chance.

The Baron had ordered dinner to be served in his suite, and the manager himself had overseen the menu. He bowed and scraped at the lavish tip, the Baron thanking him for his discretion; he understood the *Polizei* would have to take statements. He shut the door, sighing, and turned to Helen. 'This place is unbelievable. They want me to meet with someone from the police here because we arrived from Paris on the same night that circus dwarf was murdered!'

Helen frowned, but said nothing. She was sifting through the package of letters and photographs that had just been delivered. She held up a small blurred snapshot. 'I am sure this is Rosa Muller, she's even got the same pigtails, and you can see where it's been cut in two, so maybe we were right after all . . . Louis?'

He sat beside her. 'Yes, yes . . . I hear you.'

Helen pointed out the cut edge of the photograph, sent by the Baron's chauffeur from the US. 'I am sure Lena was on this photograph. It's very similar to the one she showed us, and just look at the other snapshot, Louis. I'm sure it's Vebekka.'

Louis looked again at the snapshot of a girl in school uniform who was glaring at the camera. She had two thick plaits, her arms rigid at her sides. And she was very plump: her face, even her legs seemed rounded. 'I just don't know.'

Helen took the photograph. 'We could always ask her, show it to her?'

Louis snapped, 'No, I don't want her upset, I don't want anything to upset her, she's calm, she's sleeping, she's eating, she's going to see Franks tomorrow. You talk to him about it, see what he says. I just don't want these games we're playing to upset—'

'Games? Louis, we're not playing games, for God's sake.'

He shoved the papers aside. 'I used the wrong word then, but we have come here to have Vebekka see Franks, she's agreed, now all this detective work . . .'

Helen pushed back her chair. 'This detective work was, if you recall, specifically requested by Franks himself. I don't understand your attitude. You have no knowledge of her past, and you have said it is your main priority to find out whether there is any history of mental instability in Vebekka's family. But, Louis, unless we try to trace her goddamned family, how do you expect to find out?'

Louis rubbed his brow, his mouth a tight, hard line. 'Perhaps some things are best not uncovered.'

'Like what?'

He stared at the ceiling. 'I don't know . . . but all these photographs, this woman this afternoon, what have we gained? We still know nothing of Vebekka's family. Her mother, or adopted mother, is dead, her father, or adopted father, is dead. How can they tell us what, as you said, is my priority? And it is not just *my* priority, but my sons', my daughters'.' He sighed. 'Look, maybe I'm just tired, it's been a long day.'

Helen carefully gathered the photographs together, the letters from Ulrich Goldberg, the lists of Goldbergs she had contacted to trace Lena, and stuffed them into the large brown envelope. 'Perhaps you're right. I think I'm tired too, maybe I'll make it an early night.'

The Baron poured himself a brandy. 'Do you want one?'

'No, thank you. I'll look in on Vebekka if you like.'

'No, that's all right. Hylda's staying overnight, she's using Anne Maria's old room.'

'What time are the police coming?'

'First thing tomorrow morning.'

'I'd like to sit in on the meeting, if I may, just out of interest. What time will Rebecca be going to Dr Franks?'

'Vebekka!'

'What? Oh, I'm sorry, what time is her appointment with Franks?'

Louis shrugged as he lit a cigar and began puffing it alight. 'I doubt if it will be before ten – he has set aside the entire morning.'

'Goodnight then.'

He stared at her, then inclined his head. 'Goodnight.' Louis noticed she took the envelope with her; it irritated him slightly, but he dismissed it. He turned the television set on, standing in front of it a moment, switching from channel to channel.

Hylda came out of Vebekka's bedroom. 'She is sleeping.'

He smiled warmly. 'Good, you are very good for her, and I am grateful for your assistance, also for agreeing to stay. Thank you.'

Hylda crossed the room, head bowed, and slipped into Anne Maria's room. As she went into the small adjoining bathroom, she could hear a bath being run from Helen Masters's suite.

Helen wrapped the thick hotel towelling robe around herself, and then sat at the writing desk, taking the photographs out, studying them and staring at the wall. She picked up the photograph of the plump schoolgirl, turning it over. On the back was written in childish scrawl, 'Rebecca'. She stared at the photograph angrily, and then let it drop on to the desk. Why was she so angry? Why?

She looked again at the photograph, and this time she took a sheet of paper and held it across the bottom part of the child's face, hiding the nose and mouth. They were Vebekka's eyes, she knew it!

Inspector Torsen had to wait at Kellerman's hotel until after eleven o'clock before the porter came on duty. He stood waiting impatiently as the scruffy man rummaged through the rubbish bins in the alleyway. Eventually, and very disgruntled at his work being interrupted, he led Torsen to where he recalled seeing the tall, well-built man.

He pointed from the alley towards the street – not, as Torsen had thought, the other way round.

'But it's well-lit, you must have got a good look.'

'I wasn't paying too much attention, I'd just started work. I clear the rubbish bins on a number of hotels around this area. I don't start workin' until after ten, but I remember seein' him, and he was walking fast, carrying this big bag – a sort of carryall.'

This was something new. The porter was able, after some deliberation, to describe a dark hat, like a trilby, worn by the man. 'It was shiny, sort of caught the light, yes, it was black and shiny.'

'Did you see his face?' Torsen asked.

The porter shook his head, asked if he could continue his work and Torsen nodded, standing a moment longer as the man turned on a hose and began to wash down the alley.

It was almost twelve, but Ruda worked on. She swilled around the sides of the sink, then rinsed out the cloths, filled a bucket of water, and carried it to the chopping table. She scrubbed the surface, shaking the brush, dipping it into the boiling water. Her mind raced, had she covered any possible tracks, any possible connection to the murder? As hard as she tried to concentrate she knew, could feel something else was happening. It had begun in the hotel, when she was sick in the toilets. Why did she feel the compulsion to return to that hotel? She hurled the brush into the bucket, yanked the bucket up, slopping water over the floor and herself as she tipped it down the drain . . . white tiles, splashes of the red, bloody water . . . white tiles. The same tingling started. Her hands, the nape of her neck, the dryness in mouth. She rubbed her hands dry on the rough towel, then, as she threw it into the skip used for the laundry, she saw the bloody towels and cloths and caught her breath. It wasn't Tommy, it wasn't the murder, it was something else.

She swore, muttering louder, she must not allow this to happen. She had controlled it for her whole life, she would not allow it to break into her mind, not now, and she punched out at the walls, punched with all her strength, right fist, left fist. But nothing would make the memory subside, return it to the secure, locked box imagined in her mind. Her fists slammed against the wall and she turned her fury to Kellerman: it was his fault, all his fault. Why did he have to come back? Why now? But Ruda knew it was not Kellerman who was back. It was the past.

Louis was sitting in a comfortable chair, a magazine held in his hands. He was wearing half-moon glasses, but he had been unable to concentrate. The glasses took Helen by surprise, she had never seen him wearing them. It was a moment before he realised she was in the room. 'Can't you sleep?' he asked softly.

Helen glanced at the clock on the mantelpiece. It was after twelve, she hadn't thought it was so late. 'No, no, I can't. I'm sorry, it's late but . . .'

He put his fingers to his lips, then indicated Vebekka's room. He gave no indication of his own surprise at Helen's intrusion, but he was none the less taken aback: she was wearing only a rather flimsy nightgown, her robe undone, and her feet bare.

'She's sleeping, she looks very well.'

'Good, I'm glad.'

Helen sat on the edge of the sofa. 'Louis, I need to ask you something, I am just not sure how to phrase it . . .'

'Do you want a brandy?'

'No, nothing, thank you . . .' She stared at his slippered feet, suddenly aware that in her haste she had not put on her own. 'Vebekka has said repeatedly that she is afraid of hospitals, nurses and doctors in white coats, yes?'

He nodded, pouring a glass for her even though she'd said no. He went over to the sofa and held it out. 'Here, it'll help you sleep.'

Helen took the glass, cupping it in her hands. 'So even though she was afraid of needles, of doctors, she had plastic surgery to her nose, her face. I read it in Dr Franks's reports.'

He frowned. 'Yes, it was not extensive, and I suppose when she had it done she was well. I never thought of it. It was done in a private clinic in Switzerland the first time, and then, I think, in New York.'

'Were you with her on these occasions?'

He touched his brow, coughed lightly. 'The first time, but not the second. She had no adverse effects – quite the contrary, she was very pleased with the results. She's always been very conscious of her looks.'

Helen sipped the brandy. 'The photograph is of Vebekka, Louis. The girl is plump, fat even, but her eyes – I recognise her eyes. She could never change her eyes.'

He slowly stubbed out his cigar, his back to her. Helen took another sip of the brandy, she licked her lips. 'But that is not what I wanted to ask you.'

As he turned to face her, he removed his glasses, carefully placing them in a case.

Standing up, she put down her glass. 'I think you were, to begin with, prepared to try to discover everything about her background until . . .'

He moved closer. 'Until what?'

She looked at him, met his dark blue eyes. 'Until you heard the name Goldberg.'

'What's that supposed to mean?'

Helen backed further away from him. 'I know how important your family is, your family heritage. I know you have put up with your wife's illness because they would not approve of a divorce.'

'They?' He said it quietly, but with such sarcasm. 'My dear Helen, I am the family, I am the head of the family, and I can't for the life of me think what you are trying to say.'

'I think you can, Louis.'

He shook his head in disbelief, and then walked to the windows, drawing the curtains to one side. 'You really think I would care?'

Helen cleared her throat. 'I think the old Baroness would have, perhaps your father. It was common knowledge that he allowed the Gestapo to take over your villas.'

He drew the curtains, patting them into place. 'I think, Helen, you should try and get some sleep, before you say or insinuate anything else.'

'You have not answered me.'

He was at her side, gripping her arm so tightly it hurt. 'You know nothing, nothing, and your insinuation insults me, insults my family.'

She dragged her arm free. 'It's always your precious family. I think you, Louis, hate the thought of your precious family being Jewish as much as you hate the thought of producing more insanity.'

His slap sent her staggering backwards, she cried out more with shock than pain. He rushed to her, touched her reddened cheek. 'Oh, my God, I'm sorry . . . but you don't understand.'

Helen put her hand up to indicate for him not to come close, and he flushed, gestured another apology with his hands. 'I am so sorry.'

She watched as he took out his handkerchief, touched his lips, the brow of his head, and then crossed to the window and unhooked the shutter. He remained with his back to her as he reached through the half-open shutter to the window. 'I don't care if Vebekka is Jewish. How could I? She's the mother of my children, I only care about their future.' He opened the window, breathed the cold night air, but still seemed loath to turn and face her.

Helen twisted her ring around her finger. 'Then surely you can understand my confusion. Why don't you want to try to find out as much as possible, Louis? Please, look at the photograph. Look at it.'

He walked briskly to the table and snatched up the photograph from where Helen had left it. He turned it over, then let it drop back on to the polished wood surface. He saw the childish looped writing, the name 'Rebecca'.

'Helen, if she is this little girl, if she is in some way connected to that dreadful woman this evening, to these people in Philadelphia, then we must do whatever you think is right. But please don't ask me to show enthusiasm. Show this to my wife, if you wish, or preferably ask Franks to, because if she looks at it and admits it is her, then she has lied to me, to everyone. Let Franks do it, but don't ask me to.'

'Don't you see, Louis? It is the reason *why* she has lied that may be important – it has to be, and when we discover why, maybe—'

He snapped then, his face taut with controlled anger. 'Maybe what? Everything will fall into place? Have you any idea, any knowledge of how often I have hoped for that? Let Dr Franks handle this photograph and any further developments.'

'As you wish.'

As Helen crossed to the door, he said her name very quietly, making her turn. 'I obviously appreciate all you are doing for my wife, and any financial costs to yourself will be met. I had no conception of how – well, how much we would be seeing of each other, or how much my own personal life would be placed under scrutiny. I ask you, please, to realise at all times that you are privy to very personal emotions, traumas – whichever terminology you wish to label them with. But please do remember that you are my guest, and that you are here because my wife asked you to accompany us. You are therefore free to leave at any time you wish to do so.'

Helen felt as if he had slapped her face for a second time; his cold aloofness made her feel deeply embarrassed. 'I arranged my vacation to enable me to spend time here.'

'How very kind. But I will, as I said, make sure you incur no extra costs. Now, if you don't mind my asking, in future, if you wish to join me in my suite, you will be good enough to dress accordingly. Hotels are notoriously scandalous places. My wife has already managed exceptionally well in making a spectacle of herself since we arrived.'

Helen gave a brief smile of apology. 'Anything we have discussed is, and will remain, completely confidential. Goodnight, Baron.'

He saw the glint in her eyes, and flushed, moving back to the shutters once more. He switched off the lights, leaving the shutters ajar, the street lamps outside giving the only light in the spacious drawing room. Helen would never know what a raw nerve she had touched, he assured himself. His mama had accused him of marrying not only a fortune hunter, but a Jewish bitch with no breeding, no education, just a pretty face. She had ranted at him, shouting that men in his position took women like Vebekka as a mistress, never as a wife, and the reason the bitch had never let him make love to her was because that was all she had to hold him, sex . . .

Louis could see his perfectly coiffured mama turning to point with her cane at the paintings, the tapestries. 'Your papa would turn in his grave. She is a tramp! And you cannot see it. What kind of name is Vebekka? Eh? Tell me that? I tell you, she is trouble. Marry your own kind, Louis, marry a woman who can run this estate, bring money to this estate. Marry a woman who will make a wife.'

Louis had ignored his mother, had married Vebekka and when he had confronted her, knowing it was too late for her to do anything about it, she had opened her Louis the Fourteenth writing desk, and tossed a thick manila envelope at his feet. His face drained of colour as he read the contents and his mother glared at him contemptuously. 'You should have learned this before you acted so rashly. Now it's too late. Now you have made your bed and you must lie on it. I hope for your sake it works, because there can never be a divorce. I don't want the family name dragged through the courts, the press outside the château. I don't want to know about your private life, that is your business. But if you want your inheritance, you will, in future, do as I ask.'

So Louis had learned that Vebekka had lied, had known all those years that she was really Rebecca Goldberg, but he had chosen never to find out the truth or face her with it. He had burnt the contents of the private investigator's notes, and then left for a trip abroad.

Now the ghosts were catching up with him, as his eldest son, wanting to marry, waited to hear if his mother was clinically insane, waited for the Old Baroness's inheritance to be released, waited to see if he was socially acceptable to marry one of the richest heiresses in France. Waiting – the entire family, most of all her son, had waited for the Old Baroness to die and she had never released his fortune.

Louis laughed softly: his whole life had been spent waiting. His mama had tied up the bulk fortune in trust funds for his children, leaving Louis an allowance for life. His second son, Jason, was courting the daughter of a rich German industrialist, his eldest daughter engaged to a Brazilian multi-millionaire. He laughed again, a soft humourless laugh, all waiting, the massive wealth their cross in life.

Dear Helen, how very little she knew. Louis had been able to continue his luxurious lifestyle, to create one of the finest polo stables in the world, only because of David and Rosa Goldberg's inheritance. It wasn't his money that he squandered so lavishly, but Vebekka's.

He yawned and rubbed his hands. He felt chilled – the window was still open. As he reached to close the shutters he saw a figure standing near the brick wall opposite the Grand Hotel. He could not see if it was male or female, just the dark outline leaning against the wall, waiting. He paid no further attention, thinking it was probably a prostitute from the red-light district.

Ruda stared at the window, saw the light extinguished. Her eyes flicked to the next window. It was still dark. What had compelled her to return to the hotel in the middle of the night? What was here? She felt cold as she walked slowly to the cab rank and stepped inside a waiting taxi, giving one last look to the dark window, the window with the shutters firmly closed.

Her driver was a small, withered-looking man, who seemed delighted to have a fare at that hour. 'Do you know what night it is tonight?'

Ruda lit a cigarette and made no reply.

'Tonight is November the tenth. In 1938 the Nazi mobs destroyed Jewish property and murdered and abducted twenty thousand Jews. They paved the way for the Holocaust – the Night of the Shattering Glass, the Kristallnacht. And tonight, you know what is happening in Leipzig? Fighting! Hundreds arrested, the outbreak of violence is a nightmare. Some of my friends they've gone there for business, but me? Nobody will shatter the windows of my cab.'

Ruda closed her eyes. She spoke not one word, remaining motionless in the centre of the back seat, aware of his dark eyes peering at her in his mirror – suspicious, darting black eyes.

When finally they arrived back at the circus, she paid him, leaning into his cab as he carefully counted out the change. Suddenly she touched his cheek. 'Keep it. If they break your windscreen, you get a new one.'

CHAPTER NINE

G RIMALDI HAD been drinking steadily all evening. He and Tina had been out for dinner, and now they went around the nightclubs. He had demanded that the taxi stop when he recognised a street, and then excitedly leaned against the driver to direct him to where there was loud music and crowds of kids thronging around a doorway. He couldn't believe the club would still be in existence. He had paid off the taxi before he realised he was wrong, that it was not the same club he remembered.

Tina moved down the murky stone corridor lit by a naked light bulb. She shrieked above screaming music that it was a terrible place. A young punk passed them, laughed at Tina and then shouted to his friends. 'What did he say?' shrieked Tina.

Grimaldi put a protective arm around her. 'He said, welcome to the Slaughterhouse!'

The club was throbbing with life where once it had been filled with the screams of slaughtered animals. Tina squealed happily and pushed and shoved her way to the bar. The music was so loud it was impossible to hear. Grimaldi felt his age among all these kids, dancing and drinking, smoking pot and openly passing drugs. He suggested they drink up and leave.

Tina pouted. 'Don't be so *boring*! This is the only opportunity I'll have. When the show starts, I won't be able to get out.'

Grimaldi shrugged and made his way to a small alcove where a couple of crude benches were stacked against the wall. Tina sat on his knee as he squashed himself on to the edge of a bench. She tipped back her bottle of beer, her feet tapping to the music. All around them young men and women prowled in black clothes, dark faces, white make-up. They screamed and they danced and Grimaldi leaned back on the old white tiles, giving a dig to the girl behind him as she fumbled with her boyfriend's trousers.

A boy asked Tina to dance, and she kissed Grimaldi, passed him her handbag and her half-empty bottle of beer, and dived on to the dance floor.

He sat waiting, getting hotter and hotter. He finished Tina's beer, and began to look around the crowd of thrashing kids to see if he could see her. He got up, looked over the heads of the dancers and saw her flinging her body around, dancing with her eyes shut, loving every minute of it.

Grimaldi made his way up the crowded staircase, and then he pushed and shoved like the rest. He heaved for breath on the pavement, and looked right and left. He was trying to get his bearings, sure that the old club he remembered had to be near. He grabbed hold of the beefy doorman and, shouting to make himself heard, tried to describe Tina if she came out looking for him, and said that he had her handbag. He said that he was looking for a club called Knaast, which used to be in the same area. The doorman pointed down the street, and Grimaldi thanked him and walked off, still carrying Tina's bag. He walked for about ten minutes, stopped, turned this way and that, had decided to give up and return to the Slaughterhouse when he saw the club door. He grinned, and crossed the road.

The venue was the same, but the clientele had changed a lot. It was now a well-known leather bar; he had never in his life seen so many chains and leather jackets crammed into such a small space. Beefy barmen, with T-shirts and muscles, wearing spikes and God knows what attached to their chests and throats, and chained to bars, served customers. Some men were chained to each other, yet carrying on animated conversations as if their chains were part of the décor.

Grimaldi pushed his way to the bar, asked for a beer, and turned to face the main club floor. Only then did he realise the occupants were all male. He was asked to dance by an ageing homosexual in a strange leather helmet, jock strap and white tights. He downed his beer fast, and tried to edge his way towards the exit but it took a great deal of pushing. Inadvertently he shoved a large, muscular man wearing an SS hat, who turned and gripped Grimaldi by the testicles. 'Don't push me!'

Grimaldi grimaced and the man's grip tightened. 'I just want to leave, I don't want any arguments.'

'You don't, cocksucker?'

Grimaldi was eye to eye with the SS officer's handlebar moustache. 'I don't, but you will get a lot of trouble if you don't get your fucking hands off me!'

'Make me . . .' lisped the pursed lips through the handlebar moustache. Grimaldi back-handed the SS queen, then gave him an elbow in his throat. He could still feel his testicles burning, as the man went sprawling.

Suddenly a blond-haired boy tried to swipe Grimaldi with his whip. Grimaldi snatched the whip and began to crack it, his actions creating a mixture of hysteria and applause. A bottle of champagne was waved at him from behind the bar, the chained barman screaming it was on the house, and Grimaldi suddenly broke up laughing. It was so crass, so hideous he had to laugh, and everyone joined in. He kept on saying he had only fallen into the place by mistake, he was straight. 'Just get me out of here, somebody get me out!'

Suddenly he could hear his name being shouted, bellowed: '*Luis . . . Luis . . . Luis!*'

Grimaldi shook his head. His name was being yelled by a bloody chimp!

Fredrick Lazars had Boris up on his shoulders, the little animal's arms and legs virtually covering his face, and she was pursing her lips. She looked as if she was the one calling Luis, not Lazars. Grimaldi broke up, roaring with laughter, and the two men clasped each other in a bear-hug as Boris whooped and screeched with excitement. Lazars introduced Grimaldi to a few of his friends, and ordered drinks, dragging Grimaldi to a brick alcove.

An hour later, Tina stood waiting outside the Slaughter-house Club in tears. She spoke no German, and was still with her young dancing partner, who was trying to per-suade her to come back into the club. She pushed him away and shouted she was looking for someone, but he couldn't understand and began to pull at her arm.

'I'm looking for somebody . . . *Leave me alone!*'

'I help you . . . I find for you, OK?'

Tina was so relieved he spoke English, she hugged him, and kept tight hold of his hand as he talked to the doorman, who pointed down the street.

'Your friend, ze big man, go there – you come? I show you, come with me, yes?'

Tina teetered after her young friend, looking back doubt-fully to the doorman, who then nodded, gestured back to the street with his hand. 'Zat way . . . he go zat way.'

As Tina disappeared down the dimly lit alleyway, Gri-maldi was staggering out of a taxi with Lazars. Boris was riding on Lazars's shoulders; the two men stumbled around the pavement, Lazars trying to get his wallet out of Boris's hand while Grimaldi took out a thick wad of notes and paid off the taxi. Tina's handbag was still hooked over his arm, but he seemed unaware of it. He was very drunk, lurching

226

against the side of the taxi; Lazars bellowed for him to follow as he entered his apartment.

Lazars passed Boris over to Grimaldi and opened two bottles of beer. He drew up two chairs and then, weaving slightly, opened both his arms, beaming. 'She's a good girl, you won't regret this, and I'm giving you a good price!'

'I don't want a fuckin' chimp!'

'But you know somebody who would want her! You got more contacts than me, somebody'd want her. She's two years old, lot of years in her, she's intelligent, sharp, an' I've got all her papers, her certificates, her inoculations, it's a hell of a deal, I can't keep her here, shake on it! Look at her. You don't have a heart for human beings and a heart for animals. A single sense of compassion . . . I love her, my friend, but I am willing to let you have her.'

Grimaldi shook his head. 'I can't . . .'

'Put her in the act.'

Grimaldi drank the beer, banged the bottle on to the table. 'Just leave it, I don't want a goddamned chimp!'

Standing Boris on the table top, and pulling a worn old cardigan over her head, Lazars showed the little chimp as much affection as if she was a child. 'She's toilet-trained, she could live in your trailer, heard it's like a palace.'

'You been up to the grounds?'

'No, Tommy Kellerman told me. You know he's dead?'

Grimaldi yawned, scratching his head. 'Ruda had to identify him.'

Lazars tucked Boris up in the old horsehair sofa, gave her a teddy bear to cuddle, patted her head, and waited for the animal's eyes to close before he opened two more beers. 'You know my attitudes have changed, I never thought they would, but . . . eh, you remember the mad Russian, Ivan the Crazy Horse?'

Grimaldi nodded. 'He's a tough one to forget, you been over there? I hear he's still with the Moscow Circus.'

'Yeah, he's still with them, earning peanuts and working in that jungle of concrete and glass. He's got eighteen tigers, ten lions and two panthers. Act's good, he's good – one of the best – but . . .' Lazars drank thirstily, and then stared at the bottle in his massive gnarled hands. 'Not the way it used to be. Ivan took me round his cages, steel cages on wheels, hardly enough room for the poor creatures to turn round in. You know, I dreamed of working with big animals all my life. I never had the money or the breaks, and then – just like that!' Lazars slapped the table with the flat of his hand. 'I changed my mind . . . my whole outlook changed. I didn't want it any more. I talked to the Soviet Union's society for the protection of animals, SSPA, I said there should be more control. You know they lost three, *three* giraffes a few years back. They transported them around in railway carriages. They couldn't stand upright, hadda travel with their necks bent, crouched on their knees, for five days. But they said to me that against the power of the Soyuzgostsirk – I mean, they run most of the circuses in Russia – they could do nothing. It sickened me! For the first time I began to think we should look again, try again to find the heart of the circus.'

Lazars opened more beer, and gulped half a bottle down before he continued. 'Then, my friend, my eyes were opened. You ever seen France's Circus Archaos? You seen it?'

Grimaldi shrugged. 'Yeah, but it's not everyone's taste.'

'They got chainsaws, punks, Mad Max and *fire*! Rock music – it's new, it's exciting!'

'*Bullshit*. What kids wanna see clowns in dirty mackin-toshes and rubber boots, *bullshit*!'

Lazars banged the table. 'No, you are wrong, my friend. They have got some of the finest performers because the heart of their circus is still juggling, the trapeze, tumblers – but it's all updated. It caters to the new audience, the kids, the teenagers that don't want to see fucking bears pedal bikes, chimps like Boris forced to become entertainers. They've seen through it, they know it's a fucking lie. You train a dog to sit and you've got to use force. Animals are no longer wanted.'

'*Bullshit again!* Don't give me this arty-farty crap about the French. They tried an animal-free circus in England and it flopped belly upwards. Nobody came . . . you stand by a box office and you hear every other caller, they all ask the same thing. What animals? *They come for the animals!*'

'No, not any more. They see, Luis, they see with their own eyes, they see man trying to prove he is top dog. They see man only wanting to dominate other species, they see the tragic animals hemmed into their cages, *they see* . . .'

'I should get back.' Grimaldi tried to stand up, and slumped back into his chair again.

Lazars took no notice, passing over a bottle. 'So, how is Ruda? She's come a long way – she's queen now, huh?'

Grimaldi nodded, and Lazars began to reminisce about the old days, referring back to the time when Grimaldi himself was a star attraction. They swapped stories, recalling past glories, the two massive men seated either side of the small table in the filthy cluttered kitchen. They laughed, they slapped each other's shoulders, and ploughed their way through the crate of beer. They fell silent, suddenly caught up in their own private memories.

The first time Grimaldi had seen Ruda was with Lazars: Grimaldi was with a group of performers having a night out. He had been drunk that night, had been drinking for the best part of the evening when they all stumbled down to the basement club. The bombed-out, crater-filled city – the abject poverty was everywhere, the only escape was in drinking and attempting to keep the show on the road. The people were dazed, hungry, and the aftermath of the terrible war hung like a sickening cloud. Memories of prewar times, of affluence, of dreams were pushed roughly aside; living and being alive was all that mattered, making a living the only priority.

Grimaldi had money then, one of the few who had. He had been just a young boy of fifteen when the war started, had travelled with his father to the United States. His father had died, and it was in America that Luis learned his two brothers had been killed on the Russian front. He built up the act, and was one of the first performers to return after the war. It was the mid-fifties, and already word had spread among the circus scouts that young Luis Grimaldi was someone to watch. Those he was out with that night had all seen his act, and everyone was slapping him on the back, toasting him. Then Ruda and the Old Magician had appeared on the basement cabaret stage in a pitiful puff of green smoke. This had caused general catcalls and yells, a bottle was hurled at the old man, but he attempted to continue his act.

The audience paid little or no attention to the act until there was a taped drumroll, and the old man with the ragged satin cloak asked for their participation. This was greeted with whistles and lewd remarks. Ruda had been dressed in a cheap black bra and panties, with laddered black tights and high-heeled shoes. She seemed disinterested in the entire performance, passing the tubes and hoops with a half-hearted smile on her face. The magician had drawn from various pockets small silk handkerchiefs, red, blue, green. With great showmanship he had thrown them into the air and called to the audience to hide the silks. Grimaldi's friends had taken a bunch of the silk squares, blown their noses on them, tossed them aside, and Grimaldi had tucked one down his right boot.

Ruda had stood impassive, her head half turned from the blinding spotlights. The silk squares hidden, the magician slipped a thick black blindfold around her eyes. He began to thread his way through the audience, as Ruda in a low monotone began to name the colours as each was retrieved. 'Red, blue, red, red, red, blue, green, red, blue, green . . .' She seemed at one point to be ahead of the magician as the coloured squares were caught and held aloft. She turned her head slightly as if listening, and yet kept on intoning the colours. The audience had grown quiet, caught up in the scene as the old man pushed his way through the club, gathering the squares fast; at times he had his back to her, it was impossible for her to cheat.

He stepped in front of Grimaldi. 'Red . . .' Grimaldi shrugged his shoulders, smiling, gestured with his hands as if he did not have a silk square. 'Red . . .' They had all cheered as he suddenly retrieved a red silk square from his boot.

Grimaldi and his friends had continued to another club until almost dawn, and then Grimaldi had hailed a taxi. As he waited he saw her, standing on a street corner; she still wore her costume, only now she had an old brown thin coat around her shoulders. He saw her stop two men, and then shrug as they passed on.

The taxi pulled up and Grimaldi got inside, then the cab did a U-turn coming alongside Ruda. She stared dull-eyed at it, and then stepped forward. Grimaldi wound down his window, about to say he had seen her act, when she stuck her head in the window and asked, 'Do you want oral sex?' He shook his head, reached for the handle to wind up the window. She hung on. 'Come on, you can name your price!'

Grimaldi had told the driver to move on, but she still clung on to the window. 'You were the guy, it was in your fucking boot, you like to make people look like shit? *Fuck you!*'

Grimaldi shouted for the driver to stop. He got out and she backed away from him, afraid. But he smiled and complimented her. 'You know, that was quite good, you should get rid of that old man, work up a real act, you're good! I know it has to be some kind of trick, but it works.'

She hung back, pressing herself against the wall until he returned to the taxi and drove off. But the following morning she was there, hanging around his trailer. 'I'm looking for work.'

Grimaldi had virtually brushed her aside, but nothing deterred her. Every day she came by, and he used to give her a little money, more to get rid of her than anything else, but she still turned up. He would find her sitting on his trailer steps, no matter what the weather, waiting, asking for a job, or if he wanted oral sex, masturbation. He had told one of the stewards to keep her out, but she still came back. If she wasn't hanging round his trailer, she was waiting by the cages. She seemed always to be available, always in the worn brown coat, and always hungry. Grimaldi had been having a relationship with an attractive trapeze artist, a cute little girl from Italy, who began to scream at him to get rid of the whore. He had got nasty with Ruda, physically shoving her away; but still she came back.

There were only a few more days left on his contract before he travelled on, and so he had given in, become more pleasant to her, tried to find out where she came from, if she had a home. She just used to shrug her shoulders. Then he had done a foolish thing. Seeing her huddled outside his trailer in pouring rain, he had asked her inside.

Once inside she seemed genuinely interested in his photographs and his reviews. He offered to take her sodden coat, but she refused, sitting in it, smoking, her wet hair hanging.

'Can you take me with you when you go?'

He had laughed, saying it was impossible, he was going

to Austria, then on to Switzerland, crossing back to Italy and then, he hoped, America.

She had offered to be a groom, sweep up, do anything if he could get her a job, and he had told her she would have to get permission from the circus bosses. But he had allowed her to follow him into the tent to watch the show.

She turned up the next day – he found her sitting in his trailer. He chucked her out, but after the show she was back. He was exasperated by her persistence, and then said that if she had the right papers, passport and exit visas, he would see what he could do, maybe ask the circus boss if he could get her a job. She had stood with her hands dug deep into the pockets of her coat, then had upped and left. But later that night she came back, tapping on his window to let her in. He shouted for her to get the hell away, but she kept on tapping and in the end he had dragged open the trailer door. 'Look, I said I don't want you around. If you got the papers, leave them, I'll see what I can do, now go. I'm taking a shower – go – just go!'

She had brazenly walked past him into the small bedroom, taking off her filthy coat. Beneath it she still wore the black brassière, black panties with a suspender belt . . . and the stockings were even more laddered.

'I've got someone with me, OK? So whatever you have to say, make it quick.'

'I've got no papers, I need you to help me. I need money.'

She stared at him defiantly, and he almost laughed at her audacity.

'My husband won't let me have any money.'

'Your husband?'

'Yeah, the old man. I work for him, it's his act – you know, the magic man?'

Grimaldi hitched up the small towel around his waist.

'Well, like I said, part of the act – the part with the coloured silk squares – you should work it up. I mean, I don't know what the signals are, but it's good.'

'Signals? What do you mean?'

'Well, how you do it, how you get all the colours in the right order, and so fast.'

'Oh . . . that's no trick, that's just something I can do. I can do that easy, ever since I was a kid.' She was looking around, peering into his bedroom.

'Well, it's good. The old boy's not so good though. You should get a new partner.'

The next moment she was in his arms, coiling around him. She pinched his cheek in her finger and thumb. 'You lied. There's no bleedin' woman here. You lied. Who's a bad boy, then?'

He didn't want to kiss her, touch her even, but he stood there, he let her go down on him, let her take him there in the middle of his trailer.

After it was done, she wiped her mouth with the back of her hand. 'That was for free! I'm going now.'

He had felt guilty, thrust money into her pocket. She seemed surprised, taking out the folded notes and counting them, and then she had looked up and smiled. He had never seen her smile before. 'Maybe next time I come I'll have a visa, you can take me with you then. Oh, my name is Ruda . . . R U D A, you won't forget that, will you? Thanks for the money.'

He travelled on the next day, but he didn't forget her – he was able to recognise her immediately five years later when she turned up again. This time it was in Florida and she was accompanied by her husband: Tommy Kellerman.

Grimaldi woke up. For a second he had no idea where he was, his head throbbed so hard he couldn't lift it. He felt something warm and hairy curled by his side, lifted a stinking blanket and peered into Boris's face. 'Whoop . . .

234

Whoop.' Grimaldi let the blanket fall back over the chimp. A loud snoring was coming from across the room. In the darkness he could just make out the sleeping Lazars, his legs propped up on the table, his head on his chest, still sitting in the upright chair.

Grimaldi swore . . . how in God's name had he got here? . . . he couldn't remember. He sighed, and the strong hairy arm patted his chest gently. He inched up the blanket again, and the round bright button eyes blinked . . . 'What time is it, eh?' Boris sucked in her gums, and Grimaldi tried to sit up – he slumped back again, better to sleep it off. He doubted if he could stand up anyway.

Ruda was wakened by the trailer door being banged and tossed her sheets aside. She lifted the blinds and saw a bedraggled Tina waiting outside. 'What do you want?'

Tina peered through the window. 'Is he here? I can't pay the taxi. He took my handbag. Will you let me in?'

Ruda pulled on an old wrap, stuffed her feet into worn slippers. She fetched her wallet, and opened the trailer door. 'You know what time it is? How much do you need?'

Tina was red-eyed from crying. 'He just left me, he took my bag.'

Ruda laughed. 'That's my husband. Here, take this.'

'Is he back? Did he come back?'

Ruda shook her head, about to close the door, her hand on her hip.

'I can't get into my trailer, the girls lock the door.'

'What do you expect me to do?'

'Can I come back, after I've paid him?'

Ruda shrugged and left the door ajar, returned to the bedroom and closed the door. She heard Tina return, then heard the clink of cutlery. She stormed out. 'Eh! What do you think you're doing?'

'I was making a cup of tea?'

'Oh, were you? Don't you think it would have been polite to ask? You wake me up, get money out of me and now start banging around in my kitchen. You've got a nerve, a lot of nerve.'

'I'm sorry, do you want one?'

Ruda hesitated. 'Yeah, white, one sugar.'

She got back into her bed and turned on the bedside light. It was after four; she leaned back, hearing the girl banging around searching for the tea, then she heard the rattle of teacups and her door inched open. Tina had a tray with the two cups, a pot of tea, sugar and biscuits. She poured Ruda's cup, spooned in the sugar, then stirred it carefully.

Ruda took the cup, watching Tina pour her own, then she laughed softly. 'Well, isn't this cosy? You fancy keeping the baby in my room, do you? Little pink elephants on the curtains, frilly crib, white baby wardrobes?'

Tina edged to sit on a small stool in front of Ruda's dressing-table. 'I got really frightened, he was with me one minute and the next he just disappeared, and he's got my handbag, all my money, my cards, chequebook – everything. I'm worried about him, do you think he'll be all right?'

Ruda opened her bedside drawer, took out a bar of chocolate and broke it into pieces. She sucked at a large piece, not offering any to Tina. Tina took a biscuit and nibbled it. 'I mean, he had been drinking.'

Ruda said nothing, kept on staring at Tina.

'Actually, I wanted to talk to you, Ruda. Is it all right if I call you Ruda?'

Ruda took another bite of chocolate, sipped her tea, felt the thick black slab melting slowly in her mouth. She found it amusing to watch the stupid little bitch squirming. She said nothing.

'I know he's talked to you about the baby, and we've never really spoken. He said you'd agreed to a divorce.'

Ruda licked around her mouth, leaving a dark brown chocolate stain.

'I know how much the act means to you, Ruda. I was watching you in rehearsal. I mean, I was really impressed. I don't know all that much about training, but—'

'Impressed! Well, I *am* flattered—' Ruda held out her cup for more tea, and Tina scuttled to the tray and poured, spooned in more sugar and then started for the door.

'I don't want any milk, never have milk in the second cup, thank you.'

Ruda smiled, and Tina sat on the edge of the bed. 'I love him . . .'

'You love him. How old are you?'

'Age doesn't matter.'

'Doesn't it?'

'No, and I think I can make him happy. He's really excited about the baby.'

'Is it his?'

Tina flushed, and her petal mouth pursed. 'That's a terrible thing to say. Of course it's his.'

Ruda slowly put her cup down and leaned forwards. Tina backed slightly, and then allowed Ruda to take her hand. 'What tiny little hands you've got. Let me see your palm. Oh yes, really interesting! My, my! What a lifeline.'

Tina moved closer, allowing Ruda to press and feel her open palm. 'Do you believe in that stuff? I think it's all mumbo-jumbo.'

Ruda suddenly gripped Tina's hand so hard it hurt, but she still smiled, as if she was joking. 'And I think everything you say is a load of crap – you little prick-teaser. You don't love Luis. You don't love that big bloated old man, that drunken has-been, you want . . .'

Tina tried to draw her hand away, but Ruda held her in

a vice-like grip, pulling her closer and closer . . . and then, there was no smile. Her face twisted with anger, and with her free hand she punched Tina's belly, pummelled it as if it was a lump of dough. Tina twisted and tried to drag herself free. She started screaming – terrified, trying to protect her belly.

Ruda hauled Tina almost on top of herself. Tina kicked out with her legs, but Ruda dragged her closer and covered her mouth. Tina could feel Ruda's body beneath her, and she twisted again, tried to turn.

'Don't struggle or I'll break your neck.'

Tina began to cry, her body went limp. She knew she couldn't fight, Ruda was too strong.

'Promise not to cry out? Promise me? *Promise!*'

Ruda jerked Tina so hard she gasped. 'I promise . . . I promise . . . just don't hurt me, don't hurt my baby, please . . .'

'If you scream or cry out, then I will hurt you, maybe even kill you.' Slowly Ruda released her grip, easing Tina from her, and then rolled away, leaned up on one elbow. She smiled down into the frightened girl's face. Tina was like a rabbit caught in the poacher's beam of light. Her eyes were wide, startled and terrified. She was transfixed, unable to move, too scared to cry out. Now, Ruda's strong hands stroked and caressed, with knowing assurance, gently easing down Tina's skirt to feel between her legs, her voice soft and persuasive, a half-whispered monotone, hardly audible.

'The nights when they had their entertainments, when they had their drinks, their music, we knew we were safe for one or two hours. We'd hear the laughter, we'd hear the singing, the applause, the shouting . . .'

Ruda unbuttoned Tina's blouse, cupping the heavy breasts in their white lace brassière. Her skin felt soft, so soft, and Ruda had an overwhelming desire to hold her, as if she was some long-forgotten lover she wanted to protect. She no longer frightened her, she knew that, and she cradled Tina in her arms, drawing her closer, her lips close to Tina's face. She gave gentle, almost sweet kisses to her neck, to her ears. Tina felt the sadness sweep over her like a wave, a terrible sadness. She could not stop herself giving a return, child-like kiss to Ruda's neck. 'Where were you?' Tina asked hesitantly, unsure what was happening, why it was happening.

Then Ruda rested her head against Tina's breast, and Tina continued softly to stroke the back of Ruda's head, as if to encourage her to continue. 'Where were you?' Tina repeated.

'Oh, I was some place, some place a long time ago. The older ones discovered there was a flap beneath the main hut, that we could wriggle beneath, hide under the trestle benches, hide and wait to see the show . . .'

Ruda moved to rest her head on the pillows. Tina could easily have got up then, but she didn't move. The big strong woman's sadness had mesmerised her.

'What was the show? Was it your first circus?'

Ruda sighed. 'Yes, it was a sort of circus. They had animals, they had dancers, and they had hunchbacks and giants. They had every imaginable human deformity, but they had chosen only the prettiest girls. They were thirteen, maybe a little older, but each one had their head shaved, their body hair shaved, and they were given coronets of paper flowers . . . red flowers, like bright red poppies . . .' Ruda's eyes stared to the ceiling, her face expressionless.

'They made the dwarfs fuck the giants, they made the hunchbacks fuck the pretty sweet virgins, they forced the dwarfs to ride the dogs' backs with their dicks up their arses . . . and they clapped and applauded, laughed and shouted for more. Then they began to beat the pretty, weeping girls and they kept on beating them until their

239

white bodies were red with their own blood, as red as the paper flowers on their scraped and scratched bald scalps ... One of the trestles moved, cut into my leg. The others escaped, they crawled back under the feet of the bastards, inching their way out. But I couldn't. I was trapped, I had to keep on watching. When I shut my eyes, it made it worse because I could hear them, hear the cries, hear the dogs ...'

Ruda seemed unaware Tina was there, and Tina inched away, slid from the bed until she knelt on the floor trying to retrieve her clothes. Ruda made a strange guttural sound, half sob, half cry, and she covered her face with her hands. 'Oh, God, my poor Tommy, poor Tommy!'

Tina slipped her blouse round her shoulders. Ruda remained on the bed, not attempting to stop her leaving. She wiped her cheek with the back of her big raw hand. 'Not until the show was over, not until they were too drunk to stand, too drunk to care, could I crawl back. Next morning, I saw what they'd done to the older ones. They were on the cart, the skin of their little bald heads burst open, clouds of flies stuck to their blood, purple-black-rimmed eyes. I only wanted to see the show, to see what made everyone laugh.'

Tina crawled towards her skirt. Suddenly Ruda rose from the bed, her hand outstretched. 'Don't go. Please stay with me, just for a little while.' She reached over and placed her hand on the unborn, the rounded belly of the young girl. 'I will see you have money to travel, but you are leaving.'

Tina backed away from Ruda: the expression in the woman's eyes made her afraid again. 'You will be leaving, Tina, but without my husband.'

Tina blurted out a pitiful, 'No. No!' She would never forget the look on Ruda Grimaldi's face, the strange hissing sound before she spat out the words: 'He is *mine*!'

The slap sent Tina reeling against the wall. At the same time Grimaldi eased open the trailer door, silently, so as not to wake Ruda. He heard the cry, turned towards Ruda's bedroom, inched along the narrow tiny corridor, opened the door, and for a moment was unable to comprehend what he was seeing.

He slammed the door, slammed out of the trailer and, still drunk, began to vomit. He turned as Tina ran out hysterically, half undressed, sobbing. She gasped, 'My handbag. I want my handbag.' She snatched it from him, and ran. She stumbled once, flaying the air with her hand, and then ran out of sight.

Ruda was at the trailer door, looking at him shaking, his vomit trickling down the trailer. 'You better get some coffee down you. Come on, I'll get Mike to clear up in the morning.'

Grimaldi, dazed, allowed himself to be helped back up the steps, stood as she took his jacket and peeled off his shirt.

'Christ, you stink. What the hell have you been doing?'

'I met Fredrick Lazars, we got drunk . . .'

'Sit down and let me take your trousers off, you stink like a dog.'

Grimaldi sat as she heaved off his boots and unbuttoned his trousers.

'I slept with Boris, a baby chimp.'

He curled up on the cushions. She fetched a blanket, dropped it around him, placed a bottle of Scotch ready for him to drink when he came round – she knew he would be unable to face the day without one. When she was sure he was asleep, Ruda returned to her own room and slumped on to her crumpled bed, confused by the evening's events. What had she just done?

She rubbed her arms with revulsion, growing more angry with herself. She had told Tina, stupid little Tina, about a part of her life that she had never told anyone before. Why? She bit her knuckles. Tina had made her feel something, the girl's soft body in her arms had reminded her of a warmth, a loving, she had forgotten. But it wasn't the same, it was stupid even to think of it now, she had to get her mind straightened out, had to think straight. She had even offered to pay Tina to leave. Why? 'What do you want, Ruda?' she asked herself. Whatever Grimaldi had become, even if she didn't want him, was the real truth that she didn't want anyone else to have him either? That surprised her.

'What do you want?' Ruda said it aloud as she started her pacing walk, up and down the small trailer bedroom. Her pace quickened, and she paused twice looking up to the cupboard. She could feel it drawing her, but every time she got to it she turned and walked back across the room. She paused by her own picture, her poster. She pressed her hand against her face, and then she couldn't stop herself. She stepped up on the small stool by her make-up mirror, and opened the small cupboard above. She had to balance on tiptoe to reach it. Her hands pushed boxes and hats aside until she felt the cold sides of the black tin box. She hugged it to her chest, secretive, child-like, and then got to her hands and knees, lifting the carpet until she found her hidden key. She always felt a strange sensation on opening the box: pain pierced her insides. The odd assortment of treasures, her secrets that meant so much to her, were of no value to anyone else. She spent a long time fingering, touching her things, unaware of the low humming sound she made, her body rocking backwards and forwards. 'Mine, mine . . . mine . . .' She licked the small oval grey pebble-like object, then replaced it, and looked to the poster of herself. 'Mine, mine, mine.' Her own face in the centre of the brightly coloured poster became a distorted skeleton head. She could see the loaded truck, weighted down, being dragged through the muddy yard, teetering dangerously to one side. Beneath a hastily thrown tarpaulin, she glimpsed the stacked, bloated bodies, and from the crushed bellies of the corpses came the hideous hissing sound of escaping gas. As the truck tilted a body slid from beneath the tarpaulin, and fell to the ground, rolling to one side. The guards shouted to the orderlies to get the corpse back on the truck, but then in the darkness something glittered on the fat bloated hand, with fat purple fingers. The guard tried to wrench the thick gold wedding ring free, but try as he would he could not release it. He picked up a spade and, holding it above his head, brought it down blade first across the dead woman's hand. The fingers jumped, as if they had a life of their own, and they rolled in the mud. The guard dug this way and that, swearing and shouting but unable to find the ring. He gave up and screamed for the truck to move on. An orderly unhooked his coat belt, made a loop and flicked it over the dead woman. He dragged her by her neck back on to the truck, and then tightened the tarpaulin down. The guards and the Kapos began to push and shove the truck forwards through the freezing muddy ground.

As it disappeared, the ragged men, hidden like nightmare shadows, appeared like a pack of dogs, scrabbling in the mud until one man, on his hands and knees, found the ring. 'Das gehört mir!' 'Mine!' But the others tore at him, beat him, he screamed and kept on screaming: 'Das ist der *meine*, *meine*, *meine*!' The pitiful man clung to his treasure, fought like a demon, then desperate to save himself he threw the ring and it shot through the air, sinking in a puddle not two feet away from a tiny little girl, a little girl crying with the pain in her leg, terrified by what she had just witnessed . . . a frightened Ruda, crawling between the alleyways of huts, safe from the shadow men, on the other side of the barbed-wire fence. The man clung to the meshing with his skinny hands, his mouth black, gaping and toothless, like a starving jackal he screeched, 'Das ist der meine, das gehört mir, das ist der meine!'

Ruda had crept back to her hut, silently lifting the worn blanket, slipping to lie beside her sister, needing her comfort, needing to feel the warmth of the tiny plump body and, in her sleep, Rebecca turned to cuddle Ruda, to kiss her with sweet adoring childish kisses. Ruda felt safe and warm, and they had a prize worth a fortune. A golden ring. The music, the red paper flowers, the screams and the anguished faces merged and distorted as Ruda, not old enough to comprehend the misery, felt only the burning pain in her leg, and she repeated over and over in her mind: 'Das ist der meine, das ist der meine . . . meine, meine . . .'

Ruda carefully relocked her treasure box, hid the key and returned the black tin box to its hiding place. She knew she could not sleep, and as it was after five decided she would shower and get ready for the first feed of the day. As she soaped her body, turning round slowly in the small shower cabinet, she felt the tension in her body begin to ease. But she could not rid herself of the deep anger which lingered inside her. She carefully wrapped herself in a clean soft towel, patting herself dry, then pointed her left foot like a dancer. The small scar where the trestle bench had cut into her leg was still there. She poured some body lotion into her cupped hand and massaged her leg with long, soothing strokes. The wound had festered. She had been so frightened of telling anyone and eventually she had been taken to the hospital bay. They had put a paper dressing on it. Days, perhaps weeks later the pain had become so bad that she had been carried back to the hospital by an orderly. Lice had eaten into her leg beneath the pus-soaked bandage and she had been forced into the de-lousing bath, screaming and crying out in pain. It was as a result of the festering wound that she came to the attention of Papa. She had been taken to see him that afternoon, washed, her hair combed, wearing clean clothes, her wound well bandaged with a proper dressing. That was the first time she had been alone with him, the first time he had asked her if she wanted to play a game, a very special game. He had sat her on his knee, given her a sweet and jiggled his knee so she bounced up and down. But she didn't unwrap the sweet, and he had asked why not. He had smiled, asking, didn't she want the sweet? He even playfully tried to take it away from her.

'Das ist der meine!' The little girl's fist clamped over the sweet and she glared into his handsome face, her determined expression delighting him, and he smiled, showing perfect white teeth.

Ruda tossed the towel aside. She continued to cover her body with the moisturising lotion, then she dressed. The anger had gone now. Thinking of Papa always made the anger subside. It was replaced, as it had always been, with a chilling, studied calmness. Ruda braided her hair, gave a cursory look at her reflection. She passed the poster of herself and, in passing, lightly touched it with her hand. That poster represented everything she had fought so hard to attain, and nothing would take it from her. She didn't even look at it as she passed, but she whispered quietly to herself, making a soft hissing sound: 'Das ist der meine!'

Luis was still deeply asleep where she had left him. She drew the blinds, pulled the blanket further round his shoulders, and left him. Outside she picked up the hose and washed down the trailer herself, then began to whistle, stuffing her hands into her pockets as she strolled over to the cages. She looked skywards, shading her eyes. It still looked pretty overcast.

Ruda passed between the trailers, calling out a brisk good morning to the early risers. There was movement now, trainers, performers, some heading to the canteen for breakfast, some, like Ruda, getting ready to prepare their animals' feed. She made her routine morning check, passing from cage to cage, calling every cat by name, and then she stopped by Mamon's cage. He was lazily stretching, easing his massive body away; he threw back his head and yawned. 'You're mine, my love.' She leaned against the rails, and he swung his head low, stared at her and then threw his black mane back with a roar that never ceased to delight her. He seemed to roar her inner rage. 'Everything's all right now, ma'angel!'

CHAPTER TEN

TORSEN WOKE refreshed and prepared to put everything he had listed into order. The moment he got into his office, he pasted up his memos, his suggested rota for the men. It was still only seven-thirty, but he had brought in fresh rolls and was brewing coffee. He typed furiously the past evening's reports and distributed them around the station.

At eight forty-five when the men began to trickle into the locker rooms, they saw a large memo requesting all station personnel to be in the main incident room for a briefing.

Torsen was placing his notebook and newly sharpened pencils on the incident room's bare table when he overheard Rieckert laughing as he entered. 'No, I said, it's not just a dwarf but a Jewish dwarf and . . .'

He beckoned to Rieckert to join him. He kept his voice low, his back to the main room. 'If I hear you make one more anti-Semitic remark – in the station, in the car, at any time you are wearing your uniform – you will be out, understand?'

Rieckert smiled, said that he was just passing on a joke.

'I don't care, I don't want to hear, now sit down.'

Torsen gave out the day's schedule, and suggested that they should all review the new rota of times for on and off duty periods, and anyone with any formal and reasonable complaint should leave a memo on his desk. He then discussed in detail his findings to date regarding the murder of Tommy Kellerman.

The meeting was interrupted by the switchboard operator, who slipped a note to Torsen. It was an urgent request to call his father's rest home. Torsen placed the call, and the nurse informed him that his father was exceptionally lucid, and had requested to see him.

Torsen returned to the incident room. 'I will not, as listed, be on the first assignment. Rieckert and Clauss take that, and I will join you at the Grand Hotel. Please remain there until I arrive.'

Torsen had made clear that they must all remain in contact with each other throughout the day so that they could confer and discuss their findings. He declined, however, to tell them where he was going, feeling that after his pep talk a visit to his ailing father should not, perhaps, take precedence over the murder enquiry. But everyone found out anyway – the switchboard operator told them. She was very miffed at being told to come into work an hour earlier than usual: she had children to get off to school, a husband to feed, it was all very well for Inspector Torsen to throw his weight about since he wasn't married.

Nurse Freda was a pleasant dark-haired girl in her late twenties; she was waiting for Torsen at the main reception. 'He seemed very eager to speak to you.'

'I appreciate your call, but I cannot stay long. I am involved in a very difficult case.'

He followed her plump rear end along a corridor, and into his father's ward. Nurse Freda turned, smiling. 'He's been put by the windows today. It's more private, you can draw the curtain if you wish.'

The old man was looking very sprightly, hair slicked back, checked dressing-gown and clean pyjamas. He had a warm rug over his frail knees, and his usually sunken jaw was less so today because they had put his teeth in.

'Took your time, took your time, Torsen ... I don't know, only son and he never comes to see his poor old father.'

Torsen pulled the curtain and drew up a chair to sit next to his father.

The old man crooked his finger for his son to come closer. 'This is important, woke up thinking about it and I've been worried stiff . . . can't sleep for worrying. Then I had a word with Freda, my nurse's name's Freda, and it clicked, just clicked.'

'What did, Father?'

'You need a wife, you've got to settle down and have a couple of kids. You've got a good job, good pay and a nice apartment. Now Freda, she's not married, she's clever, make you a good wife, she's got good, child-bearing hips.'

Torsen flushed, afraid they would be overheard. 'Father, right now I don't have a telephone.'

'Why haven't you got a telephone? Did they take it out?'

Torsen sighed – he had had this conversation before. 'No. Remember, when you moved here, I was delegated a smaller apartment. The telephone remained in the old apartment – I was not allowed to take it when I moved.'

'How can you work without a telephone?'

'With great difficulty, Father. I put in for one months ago, and today I left a memo to the *Direktor*. In fact today I instigated many changes, some I am quite proud of . . .'

The old man stared out of the window, plucked at his rug a moment, then turned frowning. 'No telephone? Tut tut.'

Torsen checked his watch, then touched his father's hand. 'I am in the middle of an investigation, I have to leave.'

The old man sucked in his breath and turned round, staring at the ward, leaning forwards to enable himself to see the row of beds. Then he sat back. 'Dying is a long time in coming, eh? There are many here, waiting, and afraid.'

Torsen held the frail hand. 'Don't talk this way, I don't want to go away worrying about you.'

'Oh, I'm not afraid, there are no ghosts to haunt me, but the dying here is hard for some. They have secrets, the past is their present, and they remember . . . You understand what I am saying? When you pass by their beds look at their faces, you'll see. You can hide memories surrounded by the living, but not in here. Still, soon there will be none left and then Germany can be free.'

Torsen wondered what his father would think if he saw the packs of skinheads screaming out their Nazi slogans. 'I hope you're right.'

The old man withdrew his hand sharply. 'Of course I am. We have been culturally and politically emasculated by Hitler, devastated by the Allies and isolated by the Soviets for more than half a century. Now it is our second chance, the city will be restored as the capital of reunified Germany. We are perfectly placed, Torsen, to become the West's link with the developing economies of the democratic East. You must marry, produce children, be prepared for the future . . .' The old man's face glowed, his hands clasped tightly.

'Father, I have to leave. I will come again this evening.'

'What are you working on?'

Torsen told him briefly about the murder of Kellerman, and the old man listened intently, nodding his head, muttering, 'Interesting, yes, yes . . .'

Torsen leaned close. 'In fact, I was going to ask you about something, remember the way we used to discuss unsolved crimes, Father?'

The old man nodded, rubbing his gums as if his teeth hurt.

'There was an old case, way back, maybe early sixties, late fifties, we nicknamed it the Wizard case . . . do you remember? The body was found midway between your jurisdiction and I think Dieter's. There may be no connection, it was—'

'How is Dieter?'

'He's dead, Father, ten years ago.'

The old man frowned, Dieter was his brother-in-law, and for a moment he was swamped with confusion; was his wife, Dieter's sister, dead too?

'Father, can you remember the name of the victim in the Wizard case?'

'Dieter is dead? Are you sure?'

Torsen looked into the confused face and gently patted his hand. 'I'll come and see you later.' He drew back the curtains and waved to Nurse Freda to indicate he was leaving. His father began singing softly to himself.

Torsen proceeded to walk down the aisle between the beds. He paused, watching Freda finish tending a patient, then waited until she joined him. 'I wondered if perhaps, one evening, we . . . if you are not on duty, and would like to join me, could go to a movie . . .'

Freda smiled sweetly. 'Your father has been playing Cupid?'

Torsen flushed and fiddled with his tie. She laughed a delightful warm giggle and then asked him to wait one moment. She disappeared behind a screen with a bedpan.

Torsen stared at a skeleton-thin patient, plucking frantically at his blanket, his toothless jaw twitching uncontrollably, eyes wide and staring as if at some unseen horror.

Torsen turned and hurried out, unable to look at the dying relic of humanity, too agitated to wait and arrange a date with Freda.

Rieckert was waiting in the hotel foyer. Torsen hurried to his side, apologised for his lateness and then crossed to the reception desk to ask if they could go to the Baron's suite.

The Baron himself opened the doors to the suite, and pointedly looked at his wristwatch. Torsen apologised profusely as they entered the large drawing room. Rieckert gaped, staring at the chandelier, the marble fireplace – the room was larger than his entire apartment.

The Baron had laid out his wife's and his own passport and visa on the central table; he then introduced them to Helen Masters who proffered her own documents. Torsen leafed through each one, and asked if they were enjoying their stay. The Baron murmured that he was, and sat watching Torsen from a deep wing armchair.

Torsen noted that their papers were in order. Then, standing, he opened his own notebook. 'Would you mind if I asked you just a few questions?'

The Baron shrugged but looked at the clock on the mantelpiece. Helen Masters interrupted to say they were late for an appointment. Torsen smiled and said it would take only a few moments. He looked to the Baron and asked whether the Baroness was feeling better.

'She is. Will you need to speak with her?'

Torsen coughed, feeling very uneasy, and drew up a chair to sit at the central table. 'If it is not too much trouble. But if it is not convenient for her I can return at a later date.'

The Baron strode towards the bedroom, tapped and waited. Hylda came to the door. 'Is the Baroness dressed?'

Hylda murmured she would only be one moment, and the door was closed.

Torsen directed his first question to Helen Masters. 'You arrived by car on the evening in question, that is correct?'

'No, I think we came just before lunch.'

The Baron sighed. 'We ate in the hotel restaurant, then returned to the suite. Then we left at about three o'clock to visit Dr Albert Franks's clinic. We remained with Dr Franks, and then returned to the suite. We dined here, and remained in the hotel all evening.'

Helen nodded as if to confirm part of the Baron's statement. Torsen looked to her, and she hesitated a moment before saying, 'I remained with Dr Franks and had dinner with him, but I returned here at about ten-thirty, maybe a little later.'

Torsen asked if on her return she had seen anyone in the street outside.

Helen laughed softly. 'Well, yes, of course, I saw a number of people – the doorman, the taxi drivers and . . .' She looked to the Baron. 'Your chauffeur, we have forgotten about him. He returned to Paris and then flew to New York, but he would have left before early evening.'

'On your return to the hotel did you see a very tall man, about six foot, wearing a dark raincoat, and a shiny, perhaps leather, trilby hat?' Helen shook her head. Torsen looked up from his notes. 'Did you see anyone fitting that description at or near the hotel entrance on the night in question?'

'No, I did not.'

'Did you see anyone fitting that description in the lobby of the hotel?'

Helen gave Louis a hooded smile. 'No, I am sorry. Is this man suspected of the murder?'

Torsen continued writing. 'I wish to talk to this man about a possible connection to the murder.'

Helen moved closer. 'Do you have any clues to his identity?'

Torsen folded his notebook. 'No, we do not. I think that is all I need to ask.'

'What time was the murder?' Helen asked.

'Close to eleven or eleven-thirty. We know he was carrying a large bag and that his clothes, if he was involved in the murder, would have been heavily bloodstained.'

Helen asked how the victim was killed, listening intently as Torsen described the severity of the beating. She asked if the victim was with the circus, and Torsen gave a small tight smile, wondering why she was so interested, but at the same time answering that the victim was not, as far as he had been able to ascertain, an employee of any circus.

The bedroom doors opened, and Torsen rose to his feet as the Baroness, assisted by Hylda, walked into the room. The Baron sprang to his feet, crossing to his wife, arms outstretched. 'Sit down, come and sit down. The car is ordered.'

Vebekka wore a pale fawn cashmere shawl fringed with sable, a fawn wool skirt, a heavy cream silk blouse and a large brooch at her neck entwined with gold and diamonds. She also wore her large dark glasses. Her face was beautifully made-up, her lips touched with a pale gloss sheen. She held out her hand to Torsen.

'I am sorry to inconvenience you, Baroness. I am Detective Chief Inspector Torsen Heinz, and this is Sergeant Rieckert.'

The Baroness's hand felt so frail he did no more than touch her fingers. She smiled at Rieckert. Hylda helped her to sit and brought her a glass of water. Torsen noticed how thin she was, how her body seemed to tremble, her hands shaking visibly as she sipped the water. He found it disturbing not to be able to see her eyes.

'I need simply to verify your husband's account of the day you arrived in Berlin.'

She sipped, paused, sipped again and Hylda took the glass.

'What day?'

The Baron coughed, drawing attention to himself. 'The day we arrived from Paris, darling.'

She nodded and then looked at Torsen. 'What did you ask me?'

'If you could just tell me what you did, during the afternoon and the evening.'

She was hardly audible, speaking in a monotone, as she recalled arriving, taking lunch, and then going to see a doctor. She reached for the water again and this time Hylda held the glass as she sipped. 'We dined in the suite, and then I had to rest, I was very tired after the journey.'

Torsen placed his notebook in his pocket, gave a small nod to Rieckert as an indication they were leaving.

'Why are you here? Has something happened? Is something wrong?' She half rose, looking at the Baron. 'Is it Sasha?'

The Baron hurried to her side. 'No, no, nothing wrong, just something happened close to the hotel the night we arrived, and the *Polizei* have to question everyone who booked into the hotel from Paris.'

Torsen noticed that he spoke to her as if she was a child, leaning over towards her, touching her shoulder as if shielding her from harm. 'There was a murder, everyone in the hotel is being questioned.'

'Is this true?' the Baroness asked, and looked in concern at her husband. 'But why? Why have we to be questioned? I don't understand, did I do something wrong?'

The Baron patted his wife's hand, gently telling her they were asking all the guests in the hotel the same questions.

'You didn't happen to see anyone, perhaps looking out of the window down to the street, at about eleven o'clock – a tall man wearing a shiny hat, carrying a holdall?'

The Baroness seemed unable to comprehend what he was talking about. She stared at her husband. 'I didn't do anything, did I? I was in the suite, I never left the suite.'

Torsen shook Helen's hand and thanked her. He gave a small bow to the Baron. His sergeant was already holding open the door. As they waited for the elevator, Rieckert whispered to Torsen, 'She's a sicko. That doctor, Albert Franks, he's a famous shrink. Deals with crazies, hypnotises them, that's what they must be here for, she's a sicko . . .'

As Rieckert went to collect their patrol car, Torsen waited on the whitewashed steps. He saw the line of taxis

255

waiting for hire and recognised the driver from the previous night. He crossed over to his Mercedes. The driver jumped out, started to open the rear door.

'No, no, I just wanted to ask you to spread the word around for me – ask if anyone saw a tall man, wearing a shiny trilby hat, dark raincoat, boots, carrying a bag on the night the dwarf was murdered, it was—'

The driver stopped him with an outstretched hand. 'I know the night, we've all been talking about it, but I never saw anyone fitting that description, sir.'

Torsen persisted. 'You ever pick up Ruda Kellerman? The lion tamer? Her husband is Luis Grimaldi.'

The driver nodded his head vigorously. 'Yeah, picked her up from this hotel yesterday, took her back to the West, to the circus.'

Rieckert drew up in the patrol car giving an unnecessary blast of the horn. They drove off as the driver went from cab to cab asking if any of them had seen or given a ride to a huge man in a big trilby, with high boots – the killer! As he conferred with each driver his description grew ... scarred face, huge hands and covered in blood. One cab driver recalled driving Ruda Kellerman from the hotel, and then remembered it was after the murder, so he didn't mention it, or that he had seen her standing on the opposite side of the road, looking up at the hotel windows. He didn't think it was of any importance.

Ruda was feeling a lot happier. The act had run smoothly, the animals getting more used to the new plinths. She saw to the feeds, checked that the cages were clean and the straw changed, and then, still in her working clothes, went to Tina's trailer. She rapped on the door, and waited.

A big blonde woman with gapped teeth inched open the trailer door.

'Can I see Tina?'

'She doesn't want to see anyone, she's been very sick.'

Ruda stuffed her hands into her pockets. 'Tell her it's me, will you.'

After a moment the girl returned, said Tina's room was at the end of the trailer and she had half an hour before practice. The girl stepped down and walked off. Ruda went inside.

The trailer was small and cramped, costumes and underwear littering the small dining area. Ruda stepped over the discarded clothes and pushed open the bedroom door. Tina was huddled in a bunk bed, her face puffy from crying, and she wore a flowered cotton nightdress.

Ruda hitched up her trousers. 'You seen him?'

'No . . . I can't face him. What did he say?'

Ruda shrugged. 'Nothing much. Actually, he sort of suggested I come and check on you. If you want I can fix you something to eat.'

'I'm not hungry, oh, God!' She buried her head in her hands and sobbed. 'It must have looked disgusting. I mean, I dunno why I let you.'

Ruda began to tap the toe of her boot with her stick. 'Look, I didn't come here to talk about last night. I just want to tell you something. He will never leave me, Tina, and I will never divorce him. He's old, sweetheart, he's an old man, he's washed up, and without me he's fucked.'

Tina stood up. 'I don't want to hear any more. Just get out, leave me alone.'

Ruda leaned forwards and pressed Tina's belly. 'How far gone are you?'

Tina backed away, her hands moving protectively over her abdomen. 'Three and a half months.'

'You're lucky . . . they don't like terminating after four months.'

Tina gasped. 'What did you say?'

Ruda smirked. 'You heard me, now stop playing games and listen.'

'I don't want to listen to you – you are evil, you are sick. Get out – *get out!*'

Ruda cocked her head to one side and kicked the bedroom door closed. 'I am here to help you, you stupid little bitch. I can help you, I can give you names, good people you can trust, they'll take care of it for you.'

'I want my baby! I want my baby.'

Ruda shrugged her shoulders. 'OK, that's up to you . . . but I am going to make you an offer. Now, listen to me. I am going to give you fifteen thousand dollars – dollars, Tina! You can leave Berlin, go back to wherever you came from, you can have the baby, abort it – whatever you want. But—'

'I don't want your money.'

Ruda dug into her pockets. 'It's the best offer you'll have, sweetheart – fifteen thousand dollars, in cash, but the deal is, you leave before twelve. If you hang around, the money goes down every hour, so . . . you got until twelve o'clock noon, Tina. Think about it. I'll be in our trailer. OK?' She half opened the bedroom door, then hesitated, swinging it backwards and forwards slightly. 'You know, I'm doing you a big favour. I was married to an old man once, as old as Luis . . . decrepit, senile, pawing at me. You turn the offer down, Tina, and I guarantee your life will be a misery. He's a failure, he's washed up, and you wouldn't last a season with any act he tried to get together. He's scared, Tina, he'll never go into the ring again. Everything he's promised, all the lies, are just an old man's dreams.'

Tina sat hugging her knees, rocking backwards and forwards. Big tears trickled down her cheeks. She cringed as Ruda stepped towards her, looked up, almost expecting to be slapped. Instead, Ruda gently brushed the girl's wet

258

cheeks with her thumb. 'Take a good look round this hovel. Now, imagine a cradle, a little baby bawling and clutching at you, needing you, and your body feels bloated, your face all blotchy. You want to bring it up in this? Get rid of it, walk away. It won't even hurt.'

Tina turned her face away. 'I want my baby.'

Ruda swallowed. Tina surprised her. 'Then go home, Tina. Take the fifteen thousand dollars and get out.' Ruda was almost out of the door.

'Make it twenty.' Tina tried hard to meet Ruda's eyes, but they frightened her. She bowed her head, but quickly looked up again when she heard the big deep laugh.

'You're gonna be OK, sweetheart. An' you know somethin' – I like you. It's a deal.'

Ruda whistled as she threaded her way between the trailers. When she reached her own, she eased off her big boots, stacking them outside. She looked skywards, the rainclouds were lifting. She let herself in silently and eased open drawers as she collected the money, counting it. She slipped it into an envelope. She heard Luis stirring.

'Hi, how you feeling?'

He needed a shave, his eyes were red-rimmed. She gave a quick look at the bottle – it was a quarter full – and crossed to him, pulling up the blanket. 'Sleep it off, then I'll fix you something to eat, eh? Rehearsal went well, they're calming down, getting used to the plinths. You were right, you said they'd work out OK.'

'That's good . . .' he mumbled. 'Do you want a chimp? Lazars's got a chimp.'

She cocked her head to one side, handed him the bottle. 'Here, is this what you want?'

He moaned, said he didn't want a drink, but he took the

bottle, drank. Some of it trickled out of his mouth. She walked out and left him, turned on the shower for herself and began to undress.

The bottle fell from his hand, he stared at the ceiling, one arm across his face. In his drink-befuddled mind, he kept on seeing the fear on Tina's face, her wretched submissiveness, but worse – he couldn't forget the way Ruda had looked at him, because Ruda had looked at him the same way, the exact same way, when she had ridden on Mamon's back, daring him, mocking him. He lowered his arm, tried to sit up, but the room began to spin, he couldn't get to his feet, couldn't stand. He sank back, then reached for the bottle. He held it by the neck, unable to focus. '*Rudaaa! Ruda!*'

Ruda came in and held the bottle out for him. He eased himself up, and stared at her. 'Thank you.'

She was soaping herself when she heard the light tap on the door. She smiled and peeped round the shower curtain. It was almost twelve. She wrapped herself in a towel, was about to call out, when she heard the main trailer door opening.

Tina walked in. It was dark, the blinds drawn. She stood in the doorway, unable to adjust to the darkness.

'Want a drink?' He was stretched out on the bench seat, his fly undone, his shirt hanging out. Tina edged further into the room as he held out the bottle. 'Have a drink?'

Tina took a step back, whispered his name and then, in a half sob, repeated it. She had somehow not expected him to be there.

'Chimp . . . got a two-year-old chimp, called Boris . . . *oi Boris!*' He laughed, and continued to drink, he didn't even know she was in the room.

She jumped when she felt a light touch on her shoulder, and Ruda drew her close. 'Look at him, take a good look, Tina.'

Tina squeezed past Ruda into the tiny corridor by the front door. 'I did love him. I did.'

Ruda pressed the envelope into her hand. 'I know ... I know you did but, you know as well as I do, it would never have worked out.'

Tina fingered the thick envelope. 'Because you would never have given us a chance. I'll take your money, Ruda, not for me but for my baby – Luis's baby.' The young girl's eyes stared up at Ruda. This time she didn't look away. 'We agreed twenty, don't make me have to count it. You said twenty.'

Ruda smiled, touched Tina's cheek with her hand. 'Don't push your luck, little girl. I have done only what I had to. It's called survival. You got off lightly. Now get out of my sight before I kick you out.'

Tina let herself out. Ruda shut the door fast, even faster than she had intended, because right outside the trailer she could see the wretched little inspector. She swore under her breath. Why had she been so foolish? She should have just smiled at him. It was getting rid of Tina that had made her react suspiciously. She took a deep breath and waited. Was he coming to see her?

Torsen and his sergeant were looking at the large pair of boots outside the Grimaldi trailer. They had steel tips. Torsen gave Rieckert a few instructions, had to repeat them as Rieckert was so interested in the pretty girl who had just left the trailer, then tapped on the trailer door.

Ruda inched open the door and smiled.

Torsen gave her a small bow. 'Mrs Grimaldi, could I please speak to you for one moment? Oh! Are those your husband's boots outside?'

Ruda hesitated, and then drew her gown tighter around herself. 'Yes, why, do you want to borrow them?'

'No, no. May I come in?'

'I'm afraid he cannot see you right now, he's indisposed.'

Torsen cocked his head to one side. 'It is you I wished to speak to, Mrs Grimaldi.'

Ruda shrugged her shoulders and stepped back from the doorway. She gestured to her husband, still sprawled out, and then suggested they go into her bedroom. She tossed the duvet over the unmade bed. 'What is it this time?'

Torsen remained in the doorway. 'It is with reference to your husband.'

'He won't be able to talk sensibly for hours, maybe days. He's drunk.'

'No, it is about Mr Kellerman. You see, when I questioned you, both here and at the city mortuary, I asked about the dead man's left wrist. You said you had no knowledge of a tattoo, and you repeated that at the mortuary. I have subsequently discovered that the dead man was a survivor of Auschwitz, and the tattoo was his camp identification number. So you must have known what the tattoo was when I asked you. Now I ask you, why? Why did you lie to me, Mrs Grimaldi?'

Ruda sat for a moment, her head bowed, and then slowly she began to roll up her left sleeve, carefully folding back the satin, inch by inch, until her arm was naked. She looked at Torsen. 'Is this a good enough reason for not talking about it?'

She turned over her wrist, her palm upwards, displaying a jagged row of dark blue numbers: 124666. Her voice was very low, husky. 'When they reached 200000 they began again – did you know that? They were confident that by that time there would be no confusion, no two inmates carrying the same number. You know why? Because they would already be dead.'

Torsen swallowed, shocked by the confrontation. He had never met a holocaust survivor face to face. He had to cough to enable himself to speak. 'I am so sorry . . .'

She stared at him, carefully refolding the sleeve down to

cover the tattoo. Her eyes bored into his face. In great embarrassment he stuttered that she must have been very young, so very young. 'I was three years old, Inspector. Is there anything else you want to know?'

Torsen shook his head, mumbled his thanks and apologies, and said he would let himself out. He hurried to the patrol car, where Rieckert grinned at him. 'I did it, took a shoe box, one of the performers gave it to me. I filled it with mud, then pressed the boot down hard. We've got two good clear prints. I took the right and the left because I wasn't sure which heel we got the original print from.'

Torsen started the engine. 'Left, it was the left heel, and they're Grimaldi's boots.'

The car splashed through the mud and potholes and on to the freeway. Rieckert opened his notebook. 'I got samples of sawdust from the cages, from all over the place, got it all in plastic bags as you told me. So, what did she say? Why did she lie?'

Torsen stared ahead, continued to drive. After a moment, he said, 'She had a reason for not wanting to remember. One I accepted.'

Ruda carried her boots to the main incinerator, the one used for the massive amount of rubbish left after a show – old ice-cream cartons and leaflets, chocolate boxes. She checked the grid: the fire was low, it wouldn't be built up until after the show opened, but she tossed the boots inside the oven and waited by the open door to see them catch. They took a long time – the leather was tough, hard to ignite. Gradually they began to smoulder, to give off a heavy odour. She slammed the oven closed.

So many years she had controlled the images, fought them, but the smells . . . they were the worst, they could sneak up on you unexpectedly, and they were stronger because they were unexpected, more difficult to repress. The pictures they conjured up were more powerful, more horrific . . .

Ruda walked blindly through the lanes of trailers, her hands in fists, taking short sharp breaths to keep herself from falling into the darkness. She made her way to the cages as if by instinct, until she was at Mamon's cage. He sprang to his feet, swinging his head from side to side, and she clung to the bars, gripping them so tightly that her knuckles turned white. 'Ma'angel, ma'angel!'

Mamon's tongue licked at her through the bars, rough, hard. She closed her eyes, comforted by his growled affection, a low heavy-bellied growl, and she answered him, releasing a part howl, part scream of release, as the pictures faded.

Vebekka had been calm all the way to the doctor's, seated between Helen and Louis, holding their hands. She clung to Louis as they went into the reception, where Maja greeted Vebekka warmly. Dr Franks, wearing a green cardigan and an old pair of grey flannel trousers, sauntered in, kissed Vebekka, and said he felt they should talk in his private lounge area. She allowed herself to be led along a corridor into the comfortable room. Vebekka was relieved: there were no white coats or nurses.

'Sit where you will, my dear, and Helen, Baron, if you wish to stay with us, by all means do. We are only going to have a friendly discussion.'

Helen touched Louis's arm; she knew Dr Franks wanted them to sit in the adjoining room and watch through the glass. Vebekka seemed a little afraid when they left, but then sat in a comfortable easy chair.

'And how are you?' Franks asked softly.

'A little better, still weak, and thirsty. I keep on drinking as you told me to.'

'Good, good.' He drew up a chair, not too close, but within touching distance, and then fetched a stool, winking at Vebekka. 'Make myself nice and comfortable. Now, let's get you some nice iced water, do you want a cigarette?'

Vebekka began to relax. He would not offer her a cigarette if he was going to hypnotise her, would he? She opened her case and he clicked open his lighter. She bent her head, inhaled the smoke, at the same time easing her body back. Franks settled himself in his chair, and propped up his feet.

'Tell me,' he said quietly, 'if you were to describe, with only one word, how you feel mostly – like happy, moody, sad – what word would it be?'

She let the smoke drift from her mouth, and then cocked her head to one side. 'One word? Mmmm – that is very difficult.'

The room fell silent, Franks sitting with his arms folded over his chest, Vebekka cupping her chin in her hands.

She flicked the ash from her cigarette. 'One word?' she asked again and he nodded. She continued to smoke for a while, obviously thinking, then she sipped the iced water and replaced the glass.

'Can you think of a word, Vebekka?' He looked at her directly, and she turned her face away from him, sighed.

'Longing.'

He savoured the word, repeated it, and then smiled. 'That is very interesting, nobody has ever said that to me before . . . longing.'

'I long for . . . always I feel I am longing for . . .'

His voice was soft and persuasive. 'What, Vebekka, what are you always longing for?'

'I don't know.'

265

The clock was ticking, ticking. She could hear a soft voice telling her not to be afraid, she had nothing to fear, and that perhaps she would like to lie down, rest for a while. She wasn't sure if she got up, or if she floated, but she was glad to lie down, it was so comfortable . . .

Helen and the Baron watched intently, saw Vebekka smiling, smoking, and then saw Franks help her lie down on the couch. He took a soft blanket and gently covered her up. Her eyes were open, wide open.

Franks now flicked on the microphone connecting the two rooms, and looked to the two-way mirror. He said, very softly, 'She is under. I am going to begin now.'

CHAPTER ELEVEN

D<small>R</small> F<small>RANKS</small> began by asking Vebekka simple questions, what she liked to eat, what her favourite drink was, and she answered coherently and directly. Then he reached for his notes, made reference to doctors she had visited and asked for her reactions to the tests. Again she answered directly, referring to the last medical diagnosis with sarcasm. Franks asked what she understood to be meant by panic attacks, did she feel she suffered from some form of panic? No answer, so he asked if she often felt afraid.

'Yes, I am afraid.'

'Do you know what you are afraid of?'

'No . . .'

'How does the fear begin?'

'As if someone I am frightened of has entered the room.'

Franks pursed his lips. He did not want to push Vebekka too far on their first session so he changed the subject, directing his questions away from her fear. He asked how she liked to travel, what cases and clothes she liked to take with her, and he was given a long list of favourite items from her wardrobe: shoes, wraps, furs. She continued for ten minutes, and he saw that she was relaxed again, her hands resting on the top of the blanket.

The Baron looked at Helen, raised his eyebrows and sighed. He could see no point in the session whatsoever. Helen whispered, 'Wait . . . just wait.'

'Now tell me about your cases, your trunks, Vebekka.'

She described her various handmade leather cases, how

she liked to pack everything with tissue paper. Franks asked her about her small boxes, her many vanity cases, and without any sign of undue stress, she listed her jewellery, her make-up, the photographs of her children and her medicine.

'Do you feel these cases, or boxes, have any other meaning, that you separate everything you own into compartments?' He received no reply. He asked, 'Do you have similar boxes inside you? For example, shall we say the make-up box is your head. Do you think that way at all?'

She hesitated, and then smiled. 'Yes, yes I do.'

'Can you explain this to me?'

'I have many compartments inside me.'

'Do they all have keys?'

'Oh, yes!' She seemed pleased.

'Will you unlock them for me? Tell me what is inside each layer? Can you do that?'

She sighed and moved to a more comfortable position. 'Well, there's the first compartment, that contains my special make-up, make-up I use only on rare occasions.'

'Tell me about the second.'

'My children, their letters, their photographs, things I treasure. I have Sasha's first baby tooth and I have . . .'

'Tell me about the third box . . . what's in there?'

'My jewellery, all the pieces I am most fond of, the most precious pieces. There is an emerald and diamond clip and a bluebird made of sapphires and—'

'Go to the next box . . . open the next box.'

'Medicine, sleeping tablets and my pills . . . I have them all listed.'

'You make a lot of lists?'

'Yes, yes, lots of lists.'

'Go to the next. Open the next box.'

Vebekka began to become a little agitated, her hand clutched at the blanket.

'Go to the next box.'

'No.'

'Why not?'

'Because it's private.'

'Please, open it. Or does it frighten you to open it?'

'No, it's . . . just personal, that's all.'

Franks waited, she was breathing very deeply. 'Open it, Vebekka, and tell me what is inside.'

'Rebecca.'

Franks looked to the two-way mirror, and then turned to Vebekka. 'Rebecca?' he asked softly.

'*Yesss*, she's in there.'

'Do you have any more boxes?'

Vebekka was more agitated now, chewing her lips.

'Go to the next box, Vebekka, tell me about the next box.'

'No . . . it is not a box.'

'What is it?'

'Locked, it is locked, I can't open it.'

'Try. Why don't you describe it to me?'

'It's hard, black, it's chained, I don't have the key.'

She began to twist, her hands clutched tightly together. 'Rebecca won't open it.'

Franks talked to her softly, saying he was there to help her and whatever was in the box he would deal with – all she had to do was open it.

'*It's not a box.*'

'Whatever is there, we'll leave it for a while. No need to get upset, if you don't want to open it then we won't. But tell me about Rebecca, who is Rebecca?'

Her breath hissed, she seemed exasperated. 'She guards it, she protects it, so nobody can open it, nobody must know.'

'Know what?' Franks could feel her strength of mind, it astonished him. She was fighting his control. She began breathing rapidly, her eyelids fluttering, she was trying to surface, trying to come out of the hypnosis. Franks changed the subject. 'Vebekka, tell me about Sasha.'

Vebekka relaxed and began to tell Franks about her daughter, that she was riding, and had a pony. She described Sasha's bedroom and her clothes, giving Franks a clear picture of the little girl.

'Tell me about Sasha's toys. Her dolls.'

Vebekka described the different dolls, where they had been bought. How many were for birthdays, for Christmas.

'Why did you destroy Sasha's dolls, Vebekka?'

'I did not.'

'I think you did. You took all Sasha's dolls, you took their pretty frocks off and you stacked them up like a funeral pyre, didn't you? You set light to them, you burned them—'

'*No, she did that!*'

'Who? Who burnt the dolls, Vebekka?'

She tugged at the blanket, her body twisted. 'Rebecca . . .'

'Who is Rebecca?'

Vebekka vomited, her whole body heaved and she leaned over the couch. Franks fetched a bowl and a towel. He pressed for assistance and Maja entered. She went quickly to Vebekka as Franks put down the bowl.

'I am so sorry . . .' Vebekka turned to face him, their eyes met for a moment, and then she looked away.

Franks checked her pulse, frowning, and helped her to lie back on the cushions. He drew his chair up. She smiled and whispered again she was so sorry, then she closed her eyes. Franks touched Maja's shoulder and whispered for her to clean up the room. He slipped out.

He joined the Baron and Helen Masters. 'Firstly, I have to tell you I have never known this before, she is able to move into the waking cycle by herself. She forced her vomit attack, her will is quite extraordinarily strong. I had quite a hard time taking her under – usually it's a matter of seconds but she took a considerable time, did you notice, Helen?'

Helen looked at the Baron, and then asked if she could speak to him alone. Franks seemed slightly taken aback, and then said by all means, he would wait in the corridor. Helen turned to the Baron and said quietly that considering what Vebekka had already said during the session she felt they should now pass on the information to Franks regarding the discovery of the photograph.

She went to Franks, who was talking quietly to Maja. She told him about the photograph, passed him the black-and-white snapshot. He studied it, turned it over to read the inscription 'Rebecca', then asked if Vebekka was aware of the discovery. Helen was sure that she was not. The Baron came out into the corridor. Franks looked at him. 'I must ask if you are sure your wife has had no hypnotherapy treatment before.'

'None that I know of.'

'I ask because I feel that she is very aware, and I did not take her too deeply. But now, now I would like to try.'

The Baron gave a shrug of his shoulders. 'You are the doctor, I will go along with whatever you suggest.'

Franks returned to Vebekka. Helen and the Baron took their seats again in the viewing room. She whispered, 'He was trying to find out if she could be a multi-personality . . . the boxes, taking her through the different internal protective layers.'

He sat tight-lipped, irritated when Helen added softly, 'I was right, Vebekka is Rebecca!'

Vebekka sipped the iced water, resting back on the cushions, and Franks checked her pulse again. She was very hot, and he removed the blanket. Returning to his seat he paused a moment before he began to hypnotise her again.

'Longing, repeat the word to me, Vebekka.'

She did, but it was hardly audible, and she did not resist him.

'So you feel a longing . . . yes? Listen to me, Vebekka. Just listen to my voice, don't fight my voice, just listen . . . you feel very relaxed, you feel calm and relaxed, you know no harm will come to you, and the feeling of longing . . . longing . . .'

She was under again. This time her eyes were closed, and she breathed very deeply, as if sleeping. Franks waited a few moments before he asked if he could speak to Rebecca. Would Vebekka allow him to speak to her?

She sighed. 'You don't understand.' She sounded irritated, as if he had asked her something stupid.

'Then help me, let me talk to Rebecca.'

'I am Rebecca,' she snapped.

'I'm sorry, you were right, I didn't understand.'

'Oh, that's all right, you wouldn't like her anyway. She's not very nice, she has very bad moods, very dark moods and a very bad temper. She is ugly and fat, always eating, always wanting sweet things – not nice, Rebecca is not nice.'

'But you said you are Rebecca?'

Again there was the irritable sigh, as if his incomprehension of what she was telling him annoyed her. Her voice became angry. 'I *was* Rebecca, but I didn't like her. Don't you understand? I am Vebekka, I am not Rebecca any more.'

'I see. So which of you would you say was the stronger? Rebecca or Vebekka?'

She hesitated, then gave a strange sly smile. 'Rebecca was, but not any more.'

Vebekka went on in a low unemotional voice, describing how she had made the decision to shut away Rebecca because she did not like her. She left home, left her parents and went to live in New York. Nobody knew Rebecca there, so it was very easy; she created a new person, someone she liked. She lost weight, became slim and joined a model agency as Vebekka.

'How did Rebecca feel about this?'

'Oh, she couldn't do anything about it. I locked her up, you see, I shut her away.'

Franks began to try to pinpoint dates and times, discovering that the change of name or personality change occurred when Vebekka was seventeen. Then, because she had changed, she did not want any connection with her old self, and as she became successful in her career as a model she started to travel on modelling assignments, eventually securing work in Paris.

'When did Rebecca start to come back?'

Vebekka turned on the sofa, wriggled her body, her face puckered in a frown. 'She started to get out, you see, she wouldn't stay locked up.'

'I understand that, but when did you find she was very difficult to control?'

She held her hands protectively over her stomach. 'My baby . . . she said there wasn't enough room inside me, not enough room for the two of us, she kept on trying to get out, but I fought her, she said terrible things, terrible things about the baby, she said it would be deformed, it would be deformed . . .'

Franks spent over an hour with her, and then decided he needed a break. He did not wake her because he wanted her to rest as much as possible. He replaced the blanket and tucked it around her, checked her pulse, and told her she would sleep for a while.

Helen poured a black coffee for the doctor. He sipped it,

sighing with pleasure, and then slowly replaced the cup. 'Let me explain something to you, Baron. What you have heard may seem extraordinary to you, that your wife created another being, but it is a very common thing. Every person, at some time or another, has his or her mind split into two factions. The easiest way to understand it is to think back to a moment of fear – for example a near miss in a car accident if you have ever had one – a voice will begin talking you down, talking your fear down, telling you it's all over, everything is fine, that it was a narrow miss etc. etc. Your wife created Vebekka because Rebecca was as she described, moody, bad-tempered, fat. She was, in other words, someone she did not like, did not want to be associated with. As yet we do not know the reasons for Rebecca's moods, or why she needed to become a split personality. All we do know is that for Vebekka to be able to exist, to live normally, she had to lock Rebecca away. There will be a reason, one that will come out, but it will take time. I will begin taking her back to her childhood, perhaps something occurred with her parents that instigated this dual personality.'

The Baron drained his cup and replaced it on the tray. 'You mean she was mistreated?'

'Quite possibly. Often the safety barrier created is due to sexual abuse. We shall find it out – but as you can see it is slow, a gradual stage by stage process to ascertain the truth.'

Helen was excited. 'If Rebecca began to resurface when she was pregnant, it ties in with what Louis has discussed, that her breakdowns began when she was three to four months' pregnant.'

Franks nodded. 'We shall see.'

Helen looked at the Baron, then told Franks about the meeting with Vebekka's mother's sister, and that she was sure Vebekka was adopted.

Franks said, 'You know you must keep me informed, I

have asked you to report back any information you gain, as everything could be of value. Have you received the newspapers, the ones I asked for?'

'Not yet,' said the Baron.

'Please try to contact whoever you have working for you in New York to send you copies. I would now like to be left alone for a while. If you would care to take some lunch and return, you may go straight into the viewing room.'

Franks walked out, and went first to sit with his sons, who worked with him and were recording and filming the session. They discussed what they had seen and heard to date, then Franks went to lie down in his office. But he did not sleep, just allowed the interaction between himself and Vebekka to replay slowly in his mind. He was sure he would discover severe child abuse, sure that it would have taken place over a period of years. What amazed him was that none of the many therapists and doctors who had already seen Vebekka had been able to uncover such a simple, basic and very common trauma. He hoped there were more layers to be uncovered, something deeper, because in truth he was somewhat disappointed.

Vebekka slept deeply, totally relaxed. Maja checked her pulse, and drew the blanket closer around the still figure. She emptied the ashtrays from the viewing room, and then went to have a quick lunch herself, peeking into Franks's office to tell him she was leaving. He was fast asleep on his own couch.

Grimaldi slept like a dead man. Ruda had opened the trailer windows, thrown out the empty bottles, and he had not stirred. She prepared to get ready for the afternoon's rehearsal. That evening would be the big dress rehearsal for the opening of the show, full costumes, lights and ringmaster. And she still needed as much time as possible to get the cats working with the new plinths. She hung up her costume, got the ironing board out ready to press the jacket. She opened the blinds and looked skywards. The sun was still trying to break through, but more rainclouds had gathered. She crossed her fingers, hoping that the storm which had been forecast would not happen, and then she left to feed the cats.

Grimaldi heard the door close, as if from some great distance away. He slowly opened his eyes, and moaned as the light blinded him. He lifted his head and fell back with a louder moan. His body ached, his head throbbed, if he shut his mouth his teeth came together like hammer blows. He let his jaw hang loose; his tongue dry and rough. One hand gripped the edge of the bunk seat and slowly, inch by inch, he drew himself into a sitting position. The room spun round and round, and his heart pounded in his chest. He needed another drink. He looked around bleary-eyed, but could not see a bottle within reach.

He got to his knees, moaning all the while, and then pushed himself upright. He fumbled in a cupboard for a bottle, knocking over glasses, sauces, tins of food. He began to retch uncontrollably and staggered into the shower. Turning on the cold water he slumped again on to his knees and let the icy water drench him, the sharp jets bouncing on to his tongue.

Grimaldi peeled off his soaking shirt and trousers. His head was so bad that tiny white sparks were shooting, dancing around his eyes. He moaned and swore but eased his pants off and propped himself up under the shower, turning on the hot water. He began to feel the life coming back into his limbs, his chest, but the headache was as if unseen hands were pressing his ears together. He could not remember how he had got into such a state and did not begin to piece it together until he sat hunched up in a towel sheet with a mug of black coffee and began to recall the previous night. He hung his head and half sobbed, but the action made his head scream, so he gulped more coffee, and more coffee and a handful of aspirin. The pills stuck in his gut and he burped loudly. Weaving unsteadily to the wash basin, he looked at himself. His eyes were bloodshot, his face unshaven with a yellowish pallor. 'Dear God, why do I do this to myself? Why?'

He began to shave. Jagged memories of the past evening made him feel disgusted . . . poor little Tina, he had to see her, had to talk to her . . . and then he saw Ruda's face smiling at him, he saw little Tina huddled half naked against the wall, and he bowed his head with shame. He remembered now he had left her in that club, the Slaughter-house; no club could have been better named, he had led her like a lamb to the slaughter. He finished shaving and got himself dressed. The effort exhausted him. He sat morosely, trying to find the strength to get himself out of the trailer and across to Tina's. He put on a pair of dark glasses and, still unsteady, crossed the trailer park, knocked on Tina's door and waited. He knocked again, and a voice inside yelled for whoever it was to wait. Tina's girlfriend opened up, she was wearing jodhpurs and pulling on a sweater over a rather grubby bra. She looked at Grimaldi and tugged her sweater down.

'What do you want?'

'Tina in?'

'You must be joking.'

'Where is she?'

The girl went back into the trailer and came out again carrying a rain cape. She slung it around her shoulders, and he stood there like a dumb animal. The girl looked at him with disgust. 'She's gone, packed her bags and gone, you bastard!'

He tried to reach out for her arm, to stop her moving off. 'I don't understand, what do you mean she's gone?'

'Ask your wife, shit-head, ask your bloody wife!'

'Gone where?'

'Home. She's gone back to the States.'

'Did she leave a letter?'

'What you want? A forwarding address? Dickhead! She's gone – left, understand? You'll never see her again.'

His mind reeled, and he leaned against the side of the old trailer. The girl sauntered off, calling out to two lads leading a couple of horses through to the ring.

Grimaldi walked a few paces and then stopped, turned back to the trailer, sure for a moment the girl was lying.

'Tina? *Tina!*'

He kicked at the set of steps in a fury. He felt impotent, angry, unable to believe she would walk away, leave him without a word. He turned towards the big tent and began to weave his way towards it, swearing loudly, striking out at the sides of trailers as he passed.

Mike ran into the meat truck, shouted for Ruda, and was told she was feeding, was in the cages. Mike took off, calling out for Ruda, dodging this way and that past the animals as they were led into the ring.

She came out of Sasha's cage, locked and bolted the door, and wheeled the feed trolley on to the next cage. Mike was shouting for her and she turned to look in his direction. She entered the next cage and put down the food, talking softly to the tigers as they came towards her. She rubbed their heads, tossing chunks of meat to them. Mike continued to call, and she let herself out and bolted the cage again, wheeling the trolley to the next cage. 'I'm here, Mike.'

He ran towards her, his face flushed. 'It's the guv'nor, he's screaming and yelling over at the main ring, you'd better get him out. The big boss is walking around, and there's a party of schoolkids just arrived.'

Ruda muttered to herself, 'I have to finish the feed.'

'He looks kind of crazy, Ruda, breaking up chairs, no one can get near him.'

Ruda picked up Mamon's big bowl and unbolted his cage. She stepped inside. 'Be right with you . . . Ma'angel . . . come on, dinner time, come on, baby.'

Mike leaned against the bars. 'He's thrown a punch at Willy Noakes, kicked a hole in his trailer.'

Ruda's attention wavered from Mamon to Mike, and the big cat snarled, swiping a paw at her, as if demanding her entire attention. 'Get back . . . *no* . . . don't you dare! Here – eat.' She tossed another hunk of meat. Mamon caught it in his jaw and lowered his head to rip it apart.

'*Rudaaa . . . Ruda!*' Grimaldi bellowed for her and Mike turned, startled. He was heading towards them, carrying a pitchfork, dragging it along the cage bars. '*Ruda!*'

Ruda moved further into the cage, still facing Mamon, but tossing out more meat. She rested her back on the bars, turning to her right. She could see Grimaldi staggering along with the huge pitchfork. 'Mike, get him away from the cages!'

Mike, terrified of the big man, stuttered out to him to keep back.

'You want to make me?' Grimaldi shoved the boy aside, and came to Mamon's cage. 'She's gone, she's left me, she's gone!'

Ruda threw another chunk of meat, but Mamon lowered on to his haunches, no longer interested in eating. He began a low rumbling growl; Ruda was trapped in the small cage, the exit door behind Mamon. 'Good boy, back . . . back off . . . *get back!*'

Grimaldi banged the bar with the pitchfork. 'What did you do to her, *you bitch! What have you done?*'

Mamon was up at the bars, snarling, trying to slice through with his paws, snarling and snapping at Grimaldi.

Ruda dodged around him and out of the trapdoor. She slapped it shut, bolted it and ran to the front of the cage. 'Get away from the cages – *get away from the cages!*'

Grimaldi turned all his pent-up anger on the big lion snarling and snapping at him. He pushed the pitchfork through the bars and caught Mamon on the rump: the cat went crazy, lunging and screaming with rage at the bars.

Ruda tussled with her husband, trying to get the pitch-fork out of his hands. They fought like two men, the big fork between them, pushing and shoving each other. 'Let it go – *Luis, let it go!*'

'She's gone, she's left me, you did it! You did this to me!'

Ruda brought her knee up, slammed it into his groin. He gasped with pain, let go his hold on the fork and doubled up in agony. She dragged the fork clear and then turned it, the sharp iron prongs at Grimaldi's chest. 'Get back – *get out of here!*'

He tried to grab hold of one of the sharpened prongs, gripping it with his bare hand, and Ruda yanked it free – the prong sliced into his palm. He stumbled back, blood streaming from his cut hand.

Ruda tossed the fork to Mike and pushed Grimaldi with her hands. 'Get out – go on, go back to the trailer – *back, get back.*'

He stared at her, but took two steps back. 'I'm not one of your lions, one of your cats. *You pushed too far this time, you pushed too far!*' Grimaldi turned on his heels and stumbled away.

Ruda turned on Mike. 'What the fuck you gaping at? Get that fork back to the truck and bring the feed trays – go on!'

Not until she had fed every cat personally did she take off to her trailer, but half-way there she was stopped by the administrator. Mr Kelm asked that she come over to the offices immediately. The chairman wished to speak to her. Ruda followed, the sweat still dripping off her.

The big man was standing, his coat draped over his shoulders, his silver-topped cane propped against a large oval table. Ruda walked in and he snatched the cane. Brought it down with a crash on the highly polished table.

'*We pride ourselves – understand me, Mrs Grimaldi – we pride ourselves* . . . that everyone working here is the best, the best in the world! We have millions riding on this show, millions in advertising – we have school parties coming through, I want every child to go home and say they want to come to the show, that's parents, sisters, brothers. And today those schoolchildren witnessed a brawl – *a brawl*! involving one of my top acts. Now, if you and your husband have domestic problems, sort them out in private – *not* in a disgusting public display. You may be a top act, Mrs Grimaldi, but I will not have the name of my company – this circus – damaged, even if it means ending your and your husband's contract. Do I make myself clear?'

Ruda nodded, furious at being spoken to like a child. She turned as if to leave.

'Every act is replaceable, Mrs Grimaldi – remember that!'

She faced him. 'Not every act. You show me one cat trainer, one act on a par with mine—'

'Yours?'

'Yes, mine. My husband no longer works in the ring.'

'I see. If your husband has a problem – get rid of it! Do I make myself clear?'

She nodded, and stood glaring at him. He dismissed her with a wave of his hand. She turned and walked out, carefully closing the door behind her.

Schmidt turned to Kelm. 'That woman is trouble – any further problems and they both leave. We can hire the lion act from Moscow Circus. Just keep your eyes on the pair of them and feed it back to me!'

Ruda tore back to the trailer in a rage, only to find Grimaldi, his hand wrapped in a towel, clumsily loading one of his rifles. As soon as she saw what he was doing, she slammed the door shut and locked it. 'Put that away, Luis, put it away!'

He turned, sneering, cocked the gun and released the safety catch. He then pressed the barrel to his neck. 'I was going to shoot that beast, that crazy fucking animal. Then I decided I should kill you. Now I think I'll blow my own head off, because that's what you want, isn't it? *Isn't it?*'

She sat on the bunk, forcing herself to remain calm. 'If that's what you think, then do it – go on, shoot.'

He wavered, but did not remove the gun.

'Why do you think I want you dead?' she snapped.

'Give me one good reason you don't.'

She shrugged. 'That might be tough, but if pressed I'd have to admit that maybe I need you.'

He lowered the gun. 'You haven't needed me for ten years.'

She watched the gun lower with relief – she couldn't take a scene, not after that lecture. 'I don't need you for the act, that's true . . . but maybe I need you.'

He slumped down, the gun loose in his hand. 'Bullshit, you don't need anyone, you never have – unless you want something, *then* you pretend to need.'

Ruda stared at him. 'Why don't you give me that gun and stop playing around? Come on, give it to me.'

He cocked his head to one side, asked why she had done it.

'Why did I do what?'

'Make Tina run away.'

She laughed, shaking her head. 'I made her? *I* made her? You don't think maybe you had something to do with it?'

'I loved her, I loved her . . .'

'You left her without money, without anything. Left her in the middle of the shittiest place in Berlin, and now you tell me *you loved her*? The only thing you love is booze. She came here crying her heart out and all I did was comfort her.'

'Comfort? *You filthy whore!*' He lurched to his feet and came closer. 'I saw you together – *I saw what you were doing to my little girl.*'

'She wasn't your little girl, and don't think for two seconds that baby was yours – she told me it wasn't. She came here asking for money, threatened to tell that fat slob Schmidt about you, about you screwing all the young kids, and you know what he just told me? He told me that if you play around with any more of the teenagers then you and I will be out, contract or no contract.'

'I don't believe you.'

'Ask him, go and ask him. Kelm was there, he heard, I just got a lecture from the fat-assed bastard. Tina was a little tramp. I am telling you the truth, the baby was not yours – she admitted it to me.'

Grimaldi leaned back, closing his eyes. 'I don't believe it.'

Ruda moved quickly, grabbed the gun from him, and put the safety catch on. He made no effort to stop her. He held his face in his hands, saying over and over that she was lying to him. Then he looked up. 'I could have had a life with her, I could have started again.'

'Doing what? Changing someone else's brat's nappies?'

'I could have been happy with her.'

Ruda sighed. 'And what was going to keep you? You

know I would never have parted with the act. I tell you something, you would have had to shoot me to get them, it was just a fantasy on your part.'

He got up and poured a glass of water for himself. 'I talked to Lazars, spent hours talking to him. We argued and yelled a lot, but he's changed, too, he's changed.'

'I don't follow. Can I have a drink?'

He handed her a glass of water, and then stared at the posters. 'I tell you, the circus, as we know it, it won't last, it can't last. You remember the Russian, Ivan? Spent fifteen years of his life training his tigers, been in the circus business since he was six years old, but he couldn't afford to keep them in the out-of-season periods. He shot the poor bastards, shot all twenty-four of them so nobody else could have them . . . said they were no use to anyone and he wouldn't let a zoo have them, didn't think it was fair . . . he told Lazars he shot them because he loved them. Now what crazy mind is that?'

Suddenly he laughed his old rumble laugh, leaning back, his eyes closed. 'Maybe I should have shot myself – can't be put out to grass, can't get any other work.'

Ruda's heart was hammering. She had never heard him talk this way, ever. She sat next to him, close to him. 'Don't . . . don't talk like this.'

'It's the truth, maybe I've known it for a while now. I see them cramped in their cages. I keep on telling myself that it was different when I was working the rings, that it was better, but I know it wasn't, if anything it was worse. You, we, are living on borrowed time, because it will come, one day soon, when all wild animals will be barred from being used as cheap entertainment.'

'No, no, I don't believe it. I love them, I care for them, I love every single one of them.'

Grimaldi cocked his head to one side, gave a slow sad

284

smile. 'No, you don't. You love the feel of dominance, you like the danger, the adrenaline, but you don't love them.'

'I do, you know I do.'

'Caged, locked up twenty-four hours a day, you call that love?'

He stretched out his long legs, resting his elbows behind his head. 'You know this little Boris, the little chimp Lazars had? Well, he got it from a troupe of Italians, spent his savings on her. Boris was too young to work in the ring, she was being trained, and Lazars sat in on one of the training sessions, kept on watching the Italian rubbing the chimp's head . . . he thought it was with affection. But the little fella got very upset. After the rehearsal Lazars checked her over. Boris's head was scratched, it was bleeding – this so-called trainer, his little finger, he'd got the nail sharpened to a point, like a fucking razor – he wasn't patting his animals and encouraging them out of kindness, he was sticking his nail into their heads . . .'

Ruda stared at the toes of her boots. 'Lazars was always a second stringer, a soft touch, you shouldn't listen to his bullshit.'

'I haven't before. I just think what he's saying may be true, that acts like ours have a short time to go.'

Ruda sprang to her feet. 'I won't listen to any more . . . I've got to go and get ready to rehearse.'

'Yeah, make them jump through hoops of fire – great, they love it. Get their manes singed, they fucking love it . . .'

Ruda paused at the door. 'Will you give me a hand in the ring? They're still nervous about the plinths.'

He looked up at her. 'You don't need me, Ruda.'

'What are you going to do?'

He turned away, unable to face her. There was such a helplessness in the big man, it touched her, unexpectedly. She hesitated, then went and slipped her arms around him.

'You're hung over, go and lie down. I'll come back later and cook up a big dinner, yes? Luis?'

He patted her head. 'Worried I'll run off, go after Tina?' She wriggled away from him, but he pulled her close. 'You are, aren't you? Is it me you want?'

She tried to get away from him, but he wouldn't let her go. 'Is it me?'

She eased away from him, her face flushed red. 'I guess I'd miss you, I've got used to you being around.'

He watched her reach for the door, unlock it. He gave a hopeless smile, he knew she didn't really want him – she just didn't want anyone else to have him. The door closed behind her and he sat down, once again staring at the posters and photographs over the wall.

The forensic laboratory had made a plaster cast of the mud and heel print taken from the Grimaldi boots. They were good impressions, very clear, but the print off the carpet was not. Even so, they were reasonably sure the heel print had been made by the same boot. Torsen asked whether it could be used as a piece of evidence, would it stand up in court? He was told not: the print taken from the victim's hotel room had only a section of the heel.

'But you think it was from the same boot?'

'Yes, I do, but that is just my personal opinion.'

Torsen sighed. It had been a long, fruitless day of waiting for results. The second disappointing non-evidence was that the sawdust taken from the victim's hotel room matched with fifteen samples taken from the circus, all from different cages. The sawdust was also discovered to be similar to samples brought in from the Berlin Zoo. The main sawdust factories had sent supplies to both the zoo and the circus.

Torsen's next enquiry was at the bus station. The night-duty staff had still to be questioned regarding bus passengers the night Kellerman was killed. The three conductors could remember no man fitting the inspector's description; two could recall no passengers alighting from a bus on the night in question at or near the Grand Hotel; the third conductor could only recall a female passenger who had picked up the bus from the depot and alighted at the stop close to the Grand Hotel; but he could recall little about her except long hair, dark. He remembered that it had been a particularly unpleasant journey, mostly filled with Polish women and children who had been greatly disturbed by a group of young punks hurling bricks at the bus, shouting Nazi slogans. The conductor spent considerable time berating the *Polizei*, saying they should give the buses, their drivers and passengers better security.

Torsen returned to the station, heated up a bowl of soup in the microwave and ran down his lists on the Kellerman investigation. He had a motive – the man was disliked by everyone he seemed to have been in contact with, possibly owed money to whoever killed him. But from there on it went downhill; not one person had seen a man fitting the description of the possible killer.

Torsen sipped his soup . . . it was blindingly hot and he burned his lip. He almost knocked it over when his desk phone jangled. It was the nurse, Freda, she was coming off duty at five and wondered if she could see him, or if he could come to the hospital. His father had written a note which he had made Freda promise to deliver. Torsen suspected it his father's ploy to get him to Freda. He stuttered that he would try to pass by the hospital, asked again about his father's health and Freda laughed, said he was making snowflakes again. He did not find it amusing – the vision of his father plucking the bits of tissue, licking them, sticking them on the end of his nose and blowing them off again. He spoke rather curtly, repeated that he would call by when he had an opportunity, but that he was very busy investigating a murder.

'I know, the note has something to do with it. Would you like me to read it to you? It would save you a journey.'

Torsen fumbled for his notebook.

'Are you ready? Shall I read it?' Freda asked.

'Yes, yes, please go ahead.'

Freda coughed, and then said: '"One" – it's very scrawled – "no coincidence". Would that mean anything to you?'

Torsen muttered that it did, and asked her to continue.

'"Two" – and this is very hard to decipher, it looks like "magic man", or "magician" – does that make sense?'

'Yes, yes, it does. Please continue.'

'It's a name, I think . . . Dieter? Yes?'

'Yes, yes, that was my uncle, is that all?'

Freda said she was trying to puzzle out the next few words. 'Ah, I think it says, "Rudi" . . . "R – U – D – I". Yes, it's Rudi and then there's a J. I think the name is Polish, Jeczawitz. Yes, I am sure it's Rudi Jeczawitz. Would you like me to spell it for you?'

Torsen jotted down the name, thanked Freda, and apologised if he had sounded brusque. She laughed and said no matter. She replaced the phone before he plucked up courage to ask to see her. He let the receiver fall back slowly. He swivelled around in his desk chair to look at the photograph of his father, murmured 'Thank you!' and finished his soup. He had to think carefully how to set about tracking down the old records of Jeczawitz. He would have to go cap in hand to the West Berlin *Polizei* with a story to cover his enquiry.

Torsen and Rieckert crossed the old border and passed through Kreuzberg, drew up outside a new building housing a section of the West Berlin *Polizei*. The building was a hive of activity, the reception area alone busier than the entire station the pair had just left. They were directed towards the records bureau through a long corridor. Outside was a counter at which a stern-faced woman heard Torsen's request for the record of a Rudi Jeczawitz, checked over his identification and handed him a formal records request sheet to fill in.

Torsen hesitated, as if uncertain whether it was necessary. 'The man is deceased, perhaps twenty to twenty-five years ago.'

He was told he must fill in the form, so he pored over the list of questions and alongside the request for case details he wrote 'last will and testament of relative query'.

They did not have to wait long as the station was fully computerised and the grey-haired, dog-faced woman soon returned with three sheets of paper clipped together. They had to sign the release request to say they had received the documents and Torsen asked if they wanted them returned.

'They are just copies, computer printouts. You can keep them.'

They hurried back to their patrol car, Torsen skimming the pages as they walked. He got in, and continued to read. He then sat bolt upright, turning back one page, returning to the next.

Rieckert waited patiently, having no idea why they had come to the station in the first place. 'Where next?'

Torsen lowered the paper. 'Better head back to the station. I have to speak to the *Leitender Direktor*.'

'He's still on holiday.'

'I have to speak to him. Just drive.'

Rieckert drove to their station, flicking looks at Torsen who read, lowered the pages and muttered to himself. His cheeks had two bright pink spots. The car had hardly drawn to a halt before he was out and running up the steps.

The records gave details of the dead man. The corpse had been found in a derelict building used by vagrants for many years and considered 'unsafe'. His body had been squashed inside a small kitchen cabinet, not, as Torsen had thought, under floorboards. The body, because of the freezing temperatures, had barely decomposed – yet Torsen was sure his father had described the body to him as exceptionally badly decomposed. It was almost intact, apart from deep lacerations to the left wrist and forearm. The victim was naked, apart from the cloak he was wrapped in. The skin had been hacked off with a crude knife with a serrated edge, but no weapon had been found. They had been unable to identify the body for a considerable time until a newspaper article requesting information on the deceased gave a clear description of the strange cloak wrapped around him. A club owner had come forward, identified the dead man as 75-year-old Rudi Jeczawitz, a one-time magician who had performed in his clubs. The man was an alcoholic, known to deal in forged documents. He had also been a procurer of very young girls, and shortly after the war had run a string of prostitutes. His drinking had made him fall on hard times, and at the end he had been working for little more than free drinks, using his wife as part of the act. His wife, a known prostitute, had disappeared; she had not been seen after the murder. It was supposed that she, too, may possibly have been murdered. No one was ever charged with the murder of Rudi Jeczawitz, his case remained on file. A few further details were listed: informants had said that he had been held in the death camp at Birkenau. He had survived the camp by entertaining the camp guards with his magic act.

Torsen felt his heart hammering inside his chest as he kept staring at the name, reading and rereading the name of Jeczawitz's wife: Ruda. Coincidence number one. Coincidence number two: Rudi, like Tommy Kellerman, had been involved with forged documents. And then there was a third coincidence: all three were survivors of concentration camps. He paused, the fourth coincidence: both men had been tattooed, and both had had their tattoo slashed from their arm.

Torsen scribbled down a list. He had to find out if they were legally married, find out the maiden name of Ruda Jeczawitz, see if there was still anyone alive who knew the old magician and could describe him. But most important was that he had to find out whether Ruda Kellerman was in fact the woman involved with Jeczawitz . . . Torsen was sweating, his lists growing longer. Next he scribbled 'boots'; he had supposed the boots had belonged to a man because of their size, had even asked Mrs Grimaldi if they were her husband's boots. But what if they were her boots? Torsen let out a small whoop. He thumbed through his book, until he found the page he had written that morning. A conductor was sure no male passenger had alighted from his bus the night of Kellerman's murder, only a woman, described as . . . he stared at his scrawl, for a moment unable to read it, then snapped the book closed. He knew he would have to go back: all he had written was female, dark-haired. He grabbed his coat, shouted for Rieckert, his voice echoing in the empty building.

He stormed through the vacated offices and then banged into the switchboard operator's small booth. 'Where in God's name is everybody?'

She looked up at him in astonishment. 'Tea break! They have gone across to the café for their tea break. It is four o'clock, sir.'

CHAPTER TWELVE

'I AM GOING to take you back now, Vebekka. You can see a calendar, the years in red print, we go back, '91, '90 . . . can you see the red date, Vebekka?'

'Yes, I can see it.'

'Go back, '89, ten years before, go through the dates . . . what year do you have on the calendar?'

Vebekka sighed. '1979 . . . it is 1979.'

Franks looked towards the two-way mirror, and then turned back to Vebekka.

The Baron tapped Helen's hand. 'That was the year of the newspapers . . .'

Franks continued. 'Go to the morning in New York when you were reading the newspaper, sitting having breakfast with your husband. Can you remember that morning?'

She sighed, gave a low moan, and then nodded. 'I am reading the real estate pages . . . Louis is reading the main section. I talk to him, but he pays no attention. I tell him . . . an apartment is for sale, but he doesn't listen to me.'

'Go on.'

She sighed and her brow furrowed as if she was trying to recall something.

'Go on, Vebekka, you see something in the paper?'

She breathed in quickly, gasping. 'Yes . . . yes . . . Angel, *Angel, Angel.*'

She twisted and turned, shaking. 'They have found him.'

'Who, Vebekka? Whom have they found?'

She ran her hands through her hair. 'It's in the paper,

it's in the papers, I have to find all the papers, I have to know if it's true. Angel, the Dark Angel of Death will find me, he put the message in the paper to find me.'

'It's all right . . . it's all right, no need to be alarmed. Who is the angel? Is it the angel who makes you so frightened?'

She thrashed the sofa with her hands, fists banging at the upholstery. 'They will know what I have done. *He knows what I have done! . . . Oh! God help me!'*

Franks lifted his voice, and told her to go to the next morning, to tell him what happened the next morning. She calmed, said that the next day she remained very quiet, said nothing to anyone about what she had seen. But she had a nightmare, she had thought the Angel had come into her bedroom and was going to make her tell, but it was just a shadow, it was just the curtains, he wasn't there.

Franks scribbled in his notebook that they must trace the newspaper. He was sure he was dealing with a woman traumatised by an event in her childhood, but when he began to discuss her childhood she became very calm again, seemed relieved. And when he asked if she was Vebekka or Rebecca she giggled, told him not to be stupid, she was Rebecca.

She began to talk quite freely to Franks as Rebecca. She described her home in Philadelphia, discussed her parents. She said they were kind but never very affectionate. She said that they were very close to each other, that she had often felt like an intruder.

'Did this upset you?'

'Not really, they always gave me what I asked for, they just seemed more interested in each other. My mother was often unhappy, she used to say she missed her home, her family, but they would never speak to her, they sent back all her letters unopened. She was often crying, and often ill

293

– she used to get bronchial troubles, that was why they moved from Canada, it was very cold, and Mama was always ill.'

Franks asked if she loved her parents. She hesitated, and then shrugged with her hands. 'They loved each other, and they fed and clothed me.'

'So you never felt a great affection for them?'

'No . . . just that they kept me safe, they watched out for me, no one could hurt me while I was with them, they told me that.'

'Who wanted to hurt you?'

She wafted her hand. 'I don't know.'

Franks asked her to recall her first memory of her mother.

She pursed her lips and said, 'She gave me a blue dress, with a white pinafore and a teddy bear.'

'How old were you then?'

She seemed to be trying to remember her age, but in the end she shrugged her shoulders and said she was not sure. He asked if she was afraid of her parents, and she said very promptly that she was not. 'They were afraid of me! Always afraid, afraid . . .'

'Had they reason to be afraid of you?'

'Yes, I was very naughty, had terrible tantrums.'

'What did they do when you had these tantrums?'

'Oh, Mama would talk to me, get me to lie down, talk to me, you know, so I would calm down.'

'Did they try to stop you leaving home?'

She laughed. 'Oh, no, they were pleased, I think they were pleased, when I left.'

'Did you miss them when you left home?'

'Yes . . . yes, sometimes, but Mama helped me often, told me how to handle Rebecca.'

'What did she tell you to do?'

'Oh, put her in a cupboard, throw away the key, forget her.'

'So it was not your idea to change your name?'

'Yes, it was, it was all my idea. I never told Mama what I had done, and I never told Papa. I just did what Mama said, put her away.'

'Is the other box inside you?'

She started to twist her hands, plucking at the blanket. 'Yes, yes, that is always there.'

'Did your mama put somebody in the box?'

'*It's not a box!*'

Franks was growing tired; he rubbed his head, checked his watch. 'What is it, then?'

She remained silent, her face taut as she refused to answer.

'Why don't you want to tell me about it?'

She seemed to be in terrible pain, her face distorted. She opened her mouth as if to scream, but no sound came out.

Franks stood close by the couch. 'It's all right, ssh, don't get upset, I won't ask you about it any more. It's all over . . . unless you want to tell me. Do you want to tell me?'

She cried, her mouth wide open like a child's, her face twisted, and the blanket was wrung into a coil between her hands. He waited, and in the viewing room the Baron rose to his feet. He hated the way his wife seemed to be in such pain; he pressed his hands to the glass. 'Stop him, tell him to stop this!'

She was clawing at her arms, trying to get up; Franks gently held on to her shoulders. The scream made him step back; it was a scream rising in such pitch, a terrible howling, her body shook in spasms. Franks asked over and over again what was happening to her, but the torture continued, her body thrashed around, she was out of control.

'Vebekka, listen to me, the longing time, come back into the longing . . . can you hear me? Longing . . . come on, come on, awake, everything is all right, you've just been sleeping, you'll wake up refreshed, relaxed.' But her body was stiff, he was not able to wake her. He began again to give her the key word between them, but whatever it was held her, and she was fighting it, fighting to get it out of her.

The Baron turned helplessly to Helen. 'It's as if she were possessed. Can't he stop it? Tell him to stop!'

Vebekka gasped, panting, that she was coming up the stairs, rounding the spiral staircase, but she could not find the door . . . Franks picked up fast, said the door was in front of her, she could open it. She began to relax, her breathing quieted down, and she sighed. He moved back as she sighed again and her eyelids fluttered.

Awake, she stretched her arms above her head and yawned, like a cat. She stretched her whole body, and then curled up. 'I am so thirsty . . .'

Franks rang for Maja and poured her a glass of water. She drank thirstily and held out the glass for more. He refilled it and she drained it again. Maja came in, smiled at Vebekka and asked how she was feeling. Vebekka laughed. 'Good, I feel very relaxed and refreshed.'

Franks was exhausted, Helen and the Baron drained. They left Maja with Vebekka while they conferred in the small office.

'She has been through deep hypnosis before – when, I don't know, but she knows how to hypnotise herself, bring herself through the waking cycles. I had no control over her for some considerable time. I have never witnessed anything like it, it is quite extraordinary. But we must try to ascertain when this occurred because it can be very dangerous. You saw for yourself her own internal trouble. Whatever she has locked away inside she refuses to unleash. God only knows what she was involved in, or subjected to – the key to her lies in that box, chest, the thing that is so hidden inside her, with chains, locks, God knows what else . . . but it is inside her. It is imperative that we find out what hypnosis she has been subjected to on previous occasions. Somebody at some time treated her, made her lock away horrors, and what you have witnessed, Baron, what we have both seen here today, is the danger of enforcing this. Vebekka, Rebecca, has pressed down a trauma inside her, hidden it deep inside her mind, and it rears up. When this occurs, it sends her to the edge of a breakdown. If we find out what it is, your wife may, with time and medical attention, be able to face and deal with the trauma. But also we must face the fact that we are dealing with the unknown. Others may argue that she has only survived by locking this trauma away. It will have to be your decision whether we continue or not. I would only add that I sincerely hope you will agree to continuing the sessions.'

The Baron stared, nonplussed. He could not tell whether Franks believed he could help his wife, or whether he was saying that to continue would cause irrevocable mental damage. He turned helplessly to Helen, who looked away.

'It must be your decision.'

'But what about Vebekka, doesn't she have a say in this matter?'

Franks stared at his shoes, his hands stuffed in his pockets. 'Your wife will have no memory of what occurred in that room, none whatsoever. As her husband, it must be your decision.'

'But what happens if she goes crazy? As you said, if you open up this trauma, and she cannot face it, then what?'

Franks still refused to look up. 'Then she will continue as she has done, sane periods, insane periods, spasmodic logic, violent moods. Who knows how this can continue? All we know is that she has, in your own words, grown steadily worse over the years, has attacked your daughter, you, your sons.'

The Baron pinched his nose, looked again at Helen,

wanting, needing confirmation – anything to assist his decision, but she turned away.

'What time would you like to see her tomorrow?'

Franks shook his hand. 'Good, you have made the right decision. Let's say nine, to have an early start.'

Vebekka felt better than she had for a long time, even though she had taken no drugs for two, almost three days. She wanted to dine out, go to some of the clubs, and Louis conceded. But first they should return to their hotel in case there were any messages. Perhaps she should call Sasha. Then, when they had dined, they could decide what they wanted to do. He was exhausted, had no desire to go clubbing. Nor had Helen, but she giggled. Their patient was filled with energy, having slept most of the day. She suggested to Vebekka that maybe she should rest, take care of herself, and she got a pinched cheek. 'Don't be such a fuddy-duddy, Helen. If my darling husband is too tired, then you and I will go on a trip. Some of the clubs here are the most famous in the world.'

There were letters and two packages for the Baron at the hotel desk. Helen went up in the lift with Vebekka, but returned to her own suite for a shower. Louis read through the further details pertaining to his wife's background: names of school friends who could be contacted, school teachers.

He tapped on the door of Helen's suite and entered with the parcels. She read over the letters and then asked if the newspapers had arrived. The Baron nodded, they would have to check through them. Helen had already decided that she would see what she could find out about Rosa Goldberg, née Muller. He asked if they should dine in the suite or in the restaurant, and Helen said she would prefer the restaurant. He booked a table for eight-thirty and

298

returned to his own room to shower and change. He heard Vebekka on the telephone in her suite talking to Sasha, and called out to send his love, said they would be dining at eight-thirty.

Shortly before eight Louis went to see if Vebekka was ready to dine, but she was not in her room. She had changed clothes; those she had been wearing were left on the bed. He called down to reception to see if she had gone ahead of them into the restaurant, but she was not there. Helen came in and they searched the suite, and spoke to Hylda, who said she had dressed the Baroness and presumed she had gone down to the restaurant.

The manager signalled to the Baron as soon as he saw them walk out of the lift. He gestured to the main foyer. 'The Baroness has just left. I am so sorry if I misled you, but I did not know she had ordered a car.'

The Baron went pale. 'Did she say where she was going?'

'No, Baron, I think she took a taxi from the rank outside. Would you like me to enquire?'

The Baron shook his head, gripped Helen by the elbow and guided her through the circular door. He was furious, swearing under his breath. As they stepped on to the red carpet, he spoke curtly to the doorman and was told that the Baroness had just taken a taxi.

'To where? Do you know where?'

The doorman looked perplexed and hurried to the rank, signalled for the Baron to join him by a waiting taxi. The driver popped his head out. 'She asked to be driven round the clubs, I heard her asking. We can catch them, no problem.'

The Baron turned back to the hotel, and Helen hurried after him. 'Louis, what are you doing? Don't you want to go after her?'

'I have been going after her all my life. She can do what she wants. I am hungry, I want to eat.'

Helen hesitated; she could tell that despite his attempt to appear unconcerned, Louis was very distressed. He made a half-hearted approach to the dining room before he stopped. 'Perhaps I should wait in the suite, have something sent up. I'll wait half an hour and if she has not returned I'll contact the *Polizei*.'

They turned back to the reception, the Baron reaching out to call the lift, then his hand moved back to his forehead. 'Why? Dear God, why does she do this? I don't understand . . . I had hope, I hoped . . .'

Vebekka sat in the back of the taxi feeling like a naughty schoolgirl who had escaped from her teachers. She wore her dark glasses, her sable cape and a pale green cashmere top with matching trousers. She had also taken great care in applying her make-up: thick eyeshadow, a dark, obvious foundation, her lips outlined in a bright, unflattering crimson. Make-up from her special box, make-up she only used on special occasions. She lit a cigarette and as she dropped the lighter back into her bag, realised she had no money. She tapped the glass. 'I have no money. Can you give me some?'

He stopped the car, turned back to her. 'You want to go to the hotel? Yes? Get money? Yes?'

She shook her head. 'No, you pay for me, OK? I am borrowing from you.'

The driver turned and hit the wheel with his hand. 'You must have cash? *Cash only, understand?*'

Vebekka opened her bag, took out her solid gold lighter. 'Take this, gold . . . good gold.'

The driver looked at the lighter, back to Vebekka, then put the car in gear with a beaming smile. 'OK . . . where you want go?'

Vebekka looked from the window. 'Clubs, take me to clubs.'

CHAPTER THIRTEEN

Torsen's eyes were becoming bloodshot reading the screens; he had been at the bureau for hours and still had not traced the marriage certificate of Jeczawitz. Many of the files were incomplete, and the further back he went, the worse they became. Listed time and time against names was 'no document available to establish birth certificate granted'.

Torsen looked up as the woman in charge of the records bureau gestured to her watch. She wished to leave. 'The building is empty, Inspector, and the watchman wishes to lock up the main gates before nine.'

He began to collect his belongings. She came to stand by his side. 'You still have four more files on the Js. Will you return tomorrow?' When Torsen said he would, she promised to have the files set out for him. 'Without knowing the year this man was married it is very difficult, especially in the fifties – so many refugees, so many homeless.'

They walked to the door, and she sighed as she turned off the overhead lights. 'Four million inhabitants, more, and you know how many were left after the war? Just two million, this city was devastated, everywhere corpses, burnt-out tanks. You are too young to remember, but the survivors were mostly children, old men and old women, making homes in streets buried by rubble, in the cellars, in the old bunkers.'

They walked to the main building exit doors. She went to a small closet and opened the door. 'There was something so frightening about the terrible emptiness in the city

301

– even the survivors crept about, no one believed it was over, and behind the half-alive were vast cities of dead ... I lost my father, my brothers, my family home – all my possessions ...'

Torsen waited while she collected her coat and hat and rang through to the watchman to lock up. He took her arm, and they walked slowly across the courtyard.

'I began working here just after the war and I have worked here nearly all my life, recording the marriages, the births, and trying to trace the dead. I think that was the worst, trying to get the papers organised. You see, the building caught fire, there was nothing left. In those days the main priority was to find food, everything was so scarce, and without documents people could get no food coupons. So the black market trade flourished, forged documents, so much confusion. And still it continues, but now we have people arriving from all over the world trying to trace their relatives, coming back year after year to learn about a son, a daughter. It is impossible, but we do what we can.'

Torsen paused and took out his notebook. 'May I ask you a great favour? If you could, when you have a spare moment, see if there is anything recorded for Rudi Jecza-witz's wife? All I have is a Christian name, Ruda, I don't know her age.'

They walked on, she seemed glad of his company. 'Ruda? Is that Polish? Maybe Russian? We had many, many refugees, they poured in daily, they were starved ... many so young, and all they had was their body. Now we have them again, refugees from the borders – they come every day, no papers, no money. It is getting bad, begging on the street, gypsies – Romanian, Czech, Polish. Dear God, it seems it will never end!'

Torsen nodded. 'I have been told she was a prostitute. Perhaps they did not marry legally, I don't know ...'

'Many did marry for papers. If they had none they would

302

marry for a name, for an identity. You know, many children roaming the streets in those days knew only their Christian name, nothing more – and some only a number. It was a terrible sight to see these young children everywhere, their shaved heads, their skeleton bodies, and now when I see these punks . . . this new fashion it stuns me, they do not remember. Maybe, maybe it is best they don't, because it haunts the living, I know that.'

Torsen continued walking. 'My father said that to me, he's in a clinic. He said there were many there finding dying hard, that they had memories, they clung to life afraid to die.'

She turned to him, a tight smile on her face. Her blue eyes searched his for a moment, and then she pointed to a bus stop. 'I leave you here, my friend, and I will do what I can, but no promises. I have enjoyed speaking with you.' They shook hands, and Torsen was apologetic, he did not know her name. 'Lena. Lena Klapps.'

Torsen waved to her as she stepped on to her bus, and then got on at his own bus stop, in the opposite direction. He felt worn out, and wondered if he had been wasting his time; the days were passing and he had made no arrest. He was behind in his daily *Polizei* work – all the paperwork he knew must be piled up in his trays. He closed his eyes. 'There is no coincidence in a murder enquiry.' And then, by an extraordinary coincidence, he looked out of the bus to see Ruda Kellerman stepping from a taxi. He craned his neck to see more clearly, sure it was her, but he could not see her face as she wore dark glasses, a fur draped around her shoulders. She was standing outside Mama Magda's – a notorious nightclub, a hang-out for gay, lesbian and mixed couples. He moved to the back of the bus to see more clearly, and watched her entering the dark paint-peeling doorway. He wondered what she was doing in such a place, then returned to his seat, his mind churning over the day's events, asking himself if there was some connection between Ruda Kellerman and the two murders? Suddenly he realised he was almost at his stop and rushed from his seat calling out to the conductor as he rang the bell. Hurrying along the aisle he came face to face with the night conductor he wished to question again. As he paid his fare, he asked if they could halt the bus for just a few moments.

For privacy they conferred on the pavement. Torsen asked for a better description of the woman who got off his bus near the Grand Hotel the night of Kellerman's murder. The conductor removed his cap, rubbed his head and tried to remember what he had first told the inspector while the disgruntled passengers glared from within the bus.

'She was foreign, dark-haired, definitely dark-haired . . . and wearing a dark coat – no, a mackintosh. It was raining, and she was tall, yes, tall . . . taller than me, say about five foot eight, maybe a fraction more.'

Torsen moved in close. 'That is very tall, are you sure she was that tall?'

The conductor backed off and sized up Torsen, asking him how tall he was, and they then stood shoulder to shoulder, until the man was satisfied he had been correct . . .

Torsen let himself into his apartment, put on his electric fire. He checked his empty fridge and swore, slamming the door shut. He brewed a pot of tea, sat at his kitchen table, and began his laborious notes again. He had a suspect, one he underlined three times. Ruda Kellerman-Grimaldi – but where were the reasons?

(1) Motive: None.
(2) Gain: None.
(3) Alibi: Good.

304

    (4)   Did she have help?
    (5)   Could she have inflicted the hammer blows?

Torsen rubbed out number five, then wrote it down again. He just remembered her handshake, she was very strong, she was also very tall. Could she have been mistaken for a man leaving Kellerman's hotel?

    (6)   Check if Ruda Kellerman has a trilby.
    (7)   Check if Kellerman had a trilby.
    (8)   Stock up fridge – coffee and milk.

    The more he thought of food the hungrier he felt, so in the end he took himself off to buy some rolls from the all-night delicatessen. He ate standing at the window at a small bar provided by the shop for their customers.

    When he returned to his apartment it was after ten, and a note was pinned to his door. Freda, the nurse, had popped by to deliver the note from his father in case he needed it. She had also left her home phone number and address, and a neat list of duty times, days on/days off, evenings on/evenings off. He liked that, liked that she was methodical, made lists like himself. He decided he would call her in the morning and ask for a date.

    That same evening, Ruda was ironing her jacket lapels, the iron hissing over the wet cloth. Luis woke up and sniffed. He loved the smell of freshly ironed clothes: they reminded him of his mother. He wrapped his dressing-gown around himself and wandered into the lounge. 'How did rehearsal go?' he asked.

    'I thought Mamon was adjusting, but he still hates the new plinths. He's been playing up again, I really have to push him.'

Grimaldi looked into a large frying pan left on the stove. There was bacon, sausages and onion rings, all of it now cold in its grease. She turned off the iron. 'I did call you, but decided not to wake you. There's a baked potato in the oven. Do you want a beer?'

He forked out the food on to a plate and refused the beer, said he'd stick to water – for that night. He carried his plate to the table and sat down. She called out that he would have time to shower and change, the dress rehearsal was not until nine as some of the acts didn't have their time during the afternoon. She came in zipping up her tight white trousers. 'We're the last act before the intermission, and we open the second act. It's a good spot – well, the one before the intermission is. I'd like to close the show, but he won't let me have the time to reassemble the cages.'

She put on her jacket, checked it in the mirror, and then arranged her hair in a tight braid down the back. She oiled it away from her face, so it looked sleek, almost Spanish. She leaned against him as she put her boots on, stamping her feet into them. He looked sidelong at her, and gave her bottom a pat.

'Don't!' she snapped. 'Your fingers are all greasy.'

'You look good,' he said with his mouth full, and she did a small pirouette, then gathered up the short whip, her stick and, with a final glance at her reflection, went to the trailer door.

'Get dressed, Luis, I want you on display, sober and looking good. Everyone heard about that scene, so let's put up a good front. It's almost seven-thirty.'

He laughed. 'This crowd thrives on what the Grimaldis did, what they said, who hit who – tell them to go fuck themselves.'

She picked up her hat, twisted it, and placed it on her head. 'Over and out, big man! See you in the ring.'

Grimaldi shaved and dressed, and stood in exactly the

same position she had, to give himself the once-over. He looked beat, even after a shave and a long sleep: his eyes bloodshot, his skin puffy. He checked the regrowth in his hairline. He needed a tint, the grey was showing through.

He tightened his big thick belt, aware that his belly hung over the top, and hitched the shirt up so it almost disguised the extra pounds. And as he stared at himself in the long mirror, he asked himself where it had all gone wrong. He couldn't blame it all on the mauling: it was falling apart – he was falling apart – a long time before that. Out of habit he looked at the wall of photographs, saw his papa, his brothers, remembered holding tightly to his dying father's hand. 'You keep it going, you marry, you have sons, don't let the Grimaldi name die. Have many sons! For your brothers, Luis, God rest their souls.'

He thought about little Tina. It had been a foolish dream, and yet he had been thrilled to think at last he would have a son, an heir. He had even wondered what it would feel like to hold his son. He never considered it could be a girl, it was a son he had always wanted. Yet he had married Ruda . . .

Luis opened a drawer and took out an old folder, small snapshots. He sifted through them, not even sure what he was searching for – memories maybe?

He inched open Ruda's wardrobe door and looked inside, wondering where she had stashed all his albums. He looked up: there was a row of cupboards on top of the wardrobe. He was tall enough to reach up and open one. It contained her show hats; he flipped open the second, it had an old winter coat, a plastic rain cape. He slapped the doors shut and tried the next. It was stuck firm, so he stepped up on the stool and pulled hard. He almost lost his balance as the albums tumbled out, paper clippings spilled everywhere, loose photographs. He swore as he bent to retrieve them.

He sat on her bed and began to flip through the books,

chuckled and smiled as the memories flooded back. His had been such good times, he had had a wonderful childhood. She never talked of her past; she had said without any emotion that some things are best left buried. She would talk about her life with Kellerman, even the old magician up to a point, but then she would change the subject, as if her life before that was not worth mentioning, or, as he guessed, too painful to mention, because, if he pressed, she would roll up her cuff, thrust the scar in his face. 'I have this to remind me. I am reminded every time I stand naked, every time my head aches, that is enough. Why talk about it, why open up memories I have fought to forget?'

When she had been in one of her moods, when she had thrown one of her rages because money was short or his drinking out of hand, she would turn on him with a fury, screaming that whatever pain he was in, she had known worse. She would thrust her tattoo under his nose, use it like a weapon. 'This is my proof, what is yours, Luis? What right have you got to complain about anything?'

She had taken over. He slowly turned the pages, asking himself how he had allowed it to happen. The first time he had met her, he was a star act, he had money – he had success.

He lay back on her hard pillow, closed his eyes, seeing the old winter quarters he had booked in Florida, remembering how he had stood in front of the cages as the vet went from one animal to the next. He had been working in England, just before all the quarantine laws came into effect, and his act had gone down well. He had travelled to Manchester, to Brighton, and then to Wembley for the big Chipperfield contract. He was at his peak in the early sixties – what a time that had been – and then he had returned to America, on the invitation of Barnum and Bailey's scout. With the winter season coming on he had arrived in Venice, Florida, confident that he was a star: the great Luis Grimaldi was an international act.

Knowing the contract was forthcoming, he continued to spend freely, and even bought two more tigers. Then the bombshell: first to go down was his lead cat, a massive Siberian tiger trained by his father. The big animal began sweating, his eyes running, and his coat quickly began to look dull. The vets diagnosed a virulent, dangerous flu – perhaps one of the animals in England had been contagious.

The cat flu spread like a forest fire, they went down one by one; the act was disappearing before his eyes. He worked every hour God gave him, but no matter what care and attention he gave to his beloved animals, they were dying. No injections saved them, his only hope was to segregate the animals fast. Then he had a second nightmare, the surviving animals had been placed in spare cages with hay from a farm barn where they had used poison to extermi-nate rats and mice. The fittest of his cats now became dangerously ill, and Luis worked himself into a state of exhaustion, remaining in the contaminated areas all day. He watched his beasts sweating, coughing, their breathing rasping as they choked and grew listless, eyes and noses running, paws sweating, refusing their food. They died in his arms. A funeral pyre was built, and he stood by watching as the prize and the pride of his life burned in front of him. He felt as if it was his own life blazing.

Out of eighteen tigers only four were left, with one fully grown male lion and a small sickly panther. The cost of replacing the animals was astronomical and no insurance covered the epidemic.

Then, when he believed nothing else could go wrong, a hurricane swept through the state. His trailer and two more cats perished. He lost his home, his cages were wrecked, his props and plinths crushed.

Luis Grimaldi could not sign the contract, his most coveted prize; he had not the finance to buy new cats. He was finished. He moved into a run-down trailer donated by the circus folk residing at the winter quarters. His drinking began then, and for weeks his old retainers fed and cleaned the few remaining animals, without wages, understanding. Eventually they had to seek work elsewhere – they had wives and kids to support – and the only one left was Johnny Two Seats, so nicknamed because of his wide, fat ass. He cared for Grimaldi as best he could, saw that at least he ate the odd meal or two.

Winter came and went, the circus performers moved on, and Grimaldi stayed. He had nowhere else to go and, out of pity, the owners and managers let him stay on. Ruda Kellerman had appeared, in a rusty old jeep, with her obnoxious husband. They were travelling on to Chicago: Kellerman had a contract to join a troupe of acrobats. She wasn't skinny or half-starved any more, but well filled out – twice the size of her diminutive husband. Kellerman was only there a few hours before he got into a brawl and was asked to leave. He yelled that he hadn't wanted to come to the rundown shithole, he'd only come because his wife wanted to see Grimaldi.

Ruda appeared at Grimaldi's trailer – or shack, as it didn't have any wheels. She banged on the window and, hung over, unshaven and stinking to high heaven, he flung open the door, shouting for whoever it was to leave him alone. She was shocked to see him in such a state, this man who had been her fantasy figure for years.

She brought him food, brewed some coffee, told him how she made pin money doing astrological charts, reading palms. She had laughed at how easy it was to make money. Grimaldi wasn't listening, he sat in a stupor, drinking the thick black sweet coffee. She dug deep into her old trouser pockets, took out a wad of dollars and stuffed them into his hand. 'Here, you were kind to me once. I've never forgotten that.'

Kellerman had banged on the door and yelled they were on their way. She had shouted back for him to wait in the truck, and stood staring at Grimaldi, her face concerned. 'I got to go, you take care now, maybe see you around some place.' She had offered her hand to shake, like a man, and he had turned away, embarrassed at taking her money, but unable to give it back.

For the next four months Ruda and Kellerman had travelled around, stopping off at small-time circuses, never for long. Kellerman held on to his dream of working in one of the main venues in Vegas, but when they eventually arrived there they were so broke that he had to sell all his so-called props. He had no act to offer, at least, not one that would earn them any cash, and none of the high-class acts would consider his type of performance. Ruda had to work as a waitress, at a roadside truckers' stop, doing twelve-hour shifts to earn enough for them to live on.

The gambling bug took hold of Tommy: slot machines attracted him like a drug, and he began to borrow more and more money. Then he made the mistake of getting in with loan sharks. He owed thousands, and gambled in a feverish panic to try to cover his losses. Three weeks after their arrival in Vegas, Ruda returned home, worn out after a late-night shift, to discover Kellerman had sold their mobile home at the trailer park – sold it, when they didn't even own it. But he had at least left word where he had bolted to and she tracked him down to a small, seedy rooming house. The only possessions he had been unable to sell were a few of her clothes. Ruda had told Grimaldi, albeit a long time after, how she had opened her cheap trunk, rummaged through her things, and then slammed down the lid. She told him how angry she had been, demanding to know what Kellerman had done with her albums and notebooks. Kellerman, so Ruda had said, didn't seem to care, he had simply got out as fast as he could.

Grimaldi remembered asking Ruda if that was why she had left Kellerman, why she had eventually come back to Grimaldi, and she had told him . . . He frowned, trying to recall exactly what reason she had given, then suddenly it came to him, he remembered exactly what Ruda had said: 'I was pissed off so many times with Kellerman, and the thought that he had left my boxes, the ones with all my letters, my contact numbers, my box numbers for when I wrote out my customers' charts – that really got me mad.'

She had grown silent, and Grimaldi had asked about the boxes. Had Ruda got them back? She had shrugged, tried to sound dismissive. 'Yeah, the little shit had that much decency – *he*'d got my boxes. Oh, Luis, I was so angry, I beat the hell out of him and I really went crazy when I found out he'd searched through them. He knew I didn't have any money, but what got me so mad was that he couldn't even leave my boxes alone. I guess it was that that finally made me leave him – that he didn't give me any respect. You see, they're mine. They're all I got.'

Grimaldi could have no knowledge of the importance of the boxes to Ruda. He could not know that Kellerman had watched her checking each item: the little pebble, a piece of string, a heavy gold wedding ring and all the tiny folded squares of newspaper, some of them brown with age, their edges tattered from being opened and refolded so many times. Ruda had never told her husband of the fight that had followed.

Ruda was always placing adverts in newspapers. In every city, every town, she would always place the same one, just two lines: 'Red, Blue, Green, Ruda, Arbeit Macht Frei' and then the box number where she could be contacted. Kellerman had given up trying to persuade her it was a waste of time. Finally he had been so angry he had torn up the neatly cut square of newspaper, ripped it into shreds and screamed: 'She will never contact you. She is dead, *dead*, *dead*!'

Ruda had looked at him, then calmly opened the kitchen drawer and taken out a carving knife. She seemed to fly at him from across the room, and he had only saved himself by crawling beneath a table. She kicked at him, began to stab the knife into the wooden tabletop; her frenzied attack continued until she had slumped exhausted on to the floor beside him. She had allowed him to take the knife from her hands and, like two children hiding, they huddled together under the table.

Kellerman never brought up the subject again, or admitted how much it hurt him to see those words: 'Arbeit Macht Frei'. They had been the words printed above each hut in the concentration camp. He knew, therefore, more than anyone else, the importance of the black box, but he had not realised it meant more to her than he did.

The morning after the fight, Ruda had given Tommy some money from her previous evening's tips. He had promised he would not gamble, he would look for a job. But he hadn't even attempted to find one, he had already planned what he was going to do. He used Ruda's money to buy a gun.

Kellerman and two men he had befriended planned the robbery together. They would travel to a circus where he had once been employed. Kellerman knew when and where the takings were counted. The robbery, seemingly so simple on paper, got out of hand and the cashier, a man who had himself lent money to Kellerman at one stage, was shot and died on his way to hospital. Kellerman had planned to move on fast with Ruda, but he had barely arrived back at

313

the rooming house with the takings when the police came for him. Ruda had been arrested along with Kellerman and held in gaol on suspicion of being his accomplice.

Perhaps one of the few decent things Kellerman had ever done in his grubby, miserable life was adamantly to deny that Ruda had played any part in the robbery. She was released. She saw him only once, and had listened as he begged her to find a good lawyer. Then she had looked at him and asked how she was to pay for a lawyer. He had pleaded with her: 'You got to help me, Ruda, please. Help me get out of this! I got a contact, guy runs a decent whorehouse, please . . . Turn a few tricks – help me.'

She hadn't even waited for the visiting time to be over, instead she had said, with a half-smile: 'No, Tommy. I'm finished helping you. You see, Tommy, you should never have opened my box. It's mine.'

Ruda never tried to contact Kellerman. She read in the newspapers he had been sentenced to eight years in gaol. By this time she was already heading back to Florida, having used his contact to make some quick bucks. It had been easier whoring than in the old days, and, as Kellerman had said, it was a decent brothel. Ruda had almost enjoyed the whips and domination scenes she had created for the fetish clients. They were always easier to take care of and they paid better than the straight ones. Ruda could have stayed on but she had no intention of returning to whoring full time. She had made up her mind to return to Florida, to Grimaldi.

She arrived at Grimaldi's winter quarters on the same day he had been asked to leave. Grimaldi was as broke as Kellerman: the people who had befriended him could extend their charity no longer.

Ruda acted as if he was expecting her, putting down her suitcase at the side of the table, picking up his notice to leave, and walking over to the manager's office. She paid

314

over two thousand dollars in cash and asked if she could use Grimaldi's shack as a contact base for her fortune-telling business. They all knew about Kellerman, about the robbery and his arrest – he had stolen from his own people – but Ruda stood her ground, saying although she was his wife she had walked out and filed for divorce as soon as she knew what he had done.

Grimaldi had run up huge debts, and just to have some rent paid off made Ruda's appearance in some way acceptable. She promised that, from that moment on, she would take care of Grimaldi. As if she had substituted one loser for another. Now, Luis asked himself, why? Why had she come back to him?

Ruda had returned to the rundown trailer and ordered Luis out while she began to clean the place up with buckets of water and disinfectants, washing and scrubbing as he sat on the steps drinking beer. She borrowed a van and carried the filthy sheets and laundry to a launderette in town; she ironed and tidied, brought in groceries and cans of paint. She was up at the crack of dawn, painting the outside of the old trailer, forcing old Two Seats to lend a hand. Grimaldi never lifted a finger.

Ruda slept on the old bunk bed in the main living area of the trailer; Grimaldi had the so-called bedroom. She was never still, stacking bottles and garbage into big rubbish bags, carrying them to the bins. One morning, Grimaldi leaned against the open door, watching her working and sweating with the effort. It was a blistering hot day and he had caught her arm as she was about to push past him.

'Where's Kellerman now?'

'Still in gaol. We're finished. He's history.' She released her arm and went inside. It was dark, flies everywhere. She poured water from a bucket into the sink – they didn't have running water. 'We got a quickie divorce, only cost a few dollars. If I'd known how cheap it was to get rid of him, I'd have done it years ago.'

Grimaldi slumped into a chair. 'So you married him?'

She turned, hands on hips. 'Yeah, I married him. I had no way of getting out of Berlin – he was my way. That answer your question?'

He looked up at her helplessly. 'I don't know what you want from me. Why are you doing all this?'

'You got somebody else?'

He laughed. 'Does it look like it? I'm just trying to get a handle on what you want.'

Her eyes were a strange colour – amber – they reminded him of his cats, and even in his drink-addled mind he felt she was dangerous. She had moved close to him: it was not sexual, it was a strange closeness. She put out her hand and covered his heart. 'Marry me.'

He had started to laugh, but her hand clutched his chest. 'I'm serious, marry me. I'll get you back on your feet, I'll get you started again. All you need is money, I can make money, I can get enough so you can start again, but I want some kind of deal, and if I am your wife, that's a good enough contract.'

'My wife?'

She returned to the sink, began scrubbing. 'Think about it. I don't want sex, sex doesn't mean anything to me. It'll just be a partnership.'

Grimaldi grinned, not believing what he was hearing. 'You any idea how much cats cost? Feed? Transportation? Then there's the training – it'll take months to get an act, any kind of a decent act, together.'

Ruda scrubbed a pan with a wire brush. 'Yeah, I'm sure it's a lot, but we can do it gradually, and I am willing to learn. I can muck out, do anything you tell me to do. I've been around circuses now for long enough, I know the ropes, and I know it's hard work, but I can do it.'

He sighed, shaking his head. 'No way, I couldn't do it
. . . I'm finished.'

She threw the pan across the room. 'You were the best,
the best, and you can be again. I'm giving you a chance.'

He grabbed her hand, dragged her out of the trailer and
crossed to the back of the sheds, to the pitiful remains of
his once fine act. He shoved her against the bars. 'Look at
these animals. They're as fucked and as finished as I am.
You don't know what you're talking about, you have no
conception of what an act the likes of mine took – *years. My
father, his father before him* . . . and that's what I'm left with.'

She back-handed him one hell of a punch. 'They'd turn
in their graves if they heard you. Go on, get another bottle,
go on, get drunk . . . you weak bum!'

He stormed off in a rage, wanting to hit out at her, but
wanting even more to hit himself. Left alone, she had stared
at the bedraggled unkempt cats, their cages filthy, their
ribs showing through their matted coats. She grabbed a
bucket of water, and headed back to the trailer.

The water hit him in the face, then the bucket. 'You
bastard. You can get yourself as drunk as you want, you
can let yourself go, but what you've done out there is a
crime – they're starving to death.'

'*I have no money to feed them. I got no money, and nobody wants
to buy them!*'

She rolled up her sleeve, shoved her tattooed arm under
his nose. 'See this? I've been caged, I've been starved, I've
been beaten, I've been to hell and back and I am still here.
I am still fighting, and I have enough for the two of us.
You've got ten minutes before I take a gun and shoot
what's left of those poor creatures, and then I'll leave a
bullet for you. You don't let them suffer another hour, you
hear me? *You hear me?*'

She had slammed out of the trailer, banging the door so
hard it came off its hinges. She went around to the cages.

317

Having never been inside a cat's cage in her life, she unbolted the door, stepped in, and took out the empty meat trays. She then rebolted the door and went back to the trailer. He was sitting, head bowed, hands held loosely in front of him.

'What do they eat?'

'Meat, horsemeat. Maybe I should put myself in there, let them have a go at me.'

Ruda stormed out and went into town. She came back an hour later, carrying a stack of wooden boxes. She found him mucking out the cages, Two Seats using a hose to wash them down. She cleaned out the bowls, and carried the fresh meat to the cages. Two Seats gave a toothless smile to Ruda, and he touched her hand with his gnarled, crusted fingers. 'I don't know what you said, but I thank God for you, young woman.'

They mucked out and cleaned, fed the cats and went back into town for fresh bales of hay and sawdust. Neither of them brought up the question of marriage. Luis began to exercise the cats. Two Seats collected the old plinths from the storage huts and dusted and washed them down. The heat was oppressive and the small trailer airless; they continued to sleep separately.

Four months after Ruda had arrived, Grimaldi disappeared into town. Old Two Seats sat on the steps glumly muttering that he doubted if the guv'nor would come back that night, he'd be getting plastered at the local whorehouse.

Ruda went and sat down on her bunk, flopping back. 'Shit! *Shit!*' She had traded one bum in for another. She wondered if she had made the wrong decision in coming to Florida, but then she heard Grimaldi calling out for her. Luis had returned, stone cold sober, and he placed on the kitchen table an envelope and a small red box. It was a marriage licence and a wedding ring. He said nothing, just pointed to the table.

He hovered outside the trailer watching her from the window as she opened first the envelope. He saw her smile – she who so rarely smiled – and then slowly she opened the ring box. She snapped it shut, was about to walk out to him when she heard Grimaldi ask the old man if he had a suit.

'A suit! You must be jokin', it's at the pawnbroker's.'

'Well, get it out, and by Wednesday, 'cos you're gonna need it.'

'What fer?'

'Wedding, you old bugger.'

'What?'

'We need a witness. Me and Ruda are getting married, next Wednesday.'

There was a loud guffaw, and then a lot of back-slapping. She came to the door, and Grimaldi held out his big hand. She took it, gripped it tightly as the old man wrinkled his nose and then threw his hat up in the air with a yell.

'By Christ – that's the best news I've heard in years!'

The wedding had been a quiet affair with just a few people from the winter quarters. They had lunch at a local restaurant, and then returned to feed the cats. Ruda had been very quiet; she had smiled for a photograph, but as the day drew to a close she continued to make excuses, anything to keep busy, delaying the marital consummation, even unsure if that was what he wanted. She had arranged a platonic partnership with Kellerman, but after six months in the States he had demanded sex with her. Kellerman revolted her, the thought of his touching her made her shiver with revulsion, but nevertheless the marriage had been consummated, in so far as it ever could be, but then Kellerman liked kinky sex. Her physical problems had never bothered him: he liked to have her give him a blow job, liked her on her knees in front of him.

Luis had brought flowers and champagne, and she noticed her bed linen had been removed from the couch she had always slept on. He was in high spirits, partly as the aftermath of the wedding party, and although he wasn't drunk, he was obviously merry. Also, having made the decision to marry Ruda, he was now more than willing to take her into his bed. He opened the champagne, and then produced a box, presenting it to her with a flourish. She opened the gift, and the delicate nightdress, its lace and frills carefully snuggled in white tissue paper, made her bite her lips – she didn't want even to take it out of the box.

'Don't you like it? It's silk, the lace is from France, is it the right size? Take it out, go on take it out . . .'

Slowly she had held the delicate nightgown against herself.

'You like it?'

She whispered that it was beautiful, and he asked her to put it on. She hesitated, and seemed so distressed he wanted to put his arms around her, but she stepped away from him. 'Nobody ever gave me anything . . .'

'So let me see you in it,' he said gently.

'You want this to be a proper marriage?'

Luis was a trifle confused; he said that he thought that was what she wanted, and she had turned away from him, hunching up her shoulders.

'I guess that is what I want, Ruda, I mean . . . maybe I've not been the best person to have around, not said the right things, but you wanted to marry me, didn't you?'

She nodded, but remained turned away from him, and when he tried once again to hold her she fended him off. 'I want to tell you something, I sort of thought you knew . . . but I guess you don't.'

Again he tried to make her turn to him, look at him, but she hunched further away. 'Don't, please don't touch me.'

She held the soft silk to her face, almost caressing the gown, and then she sighed. 'Luis, I *can't* have normal sex. Something was done to me when I was a child. I can give you . . . make it all right for you, but that is all.'

Luis had visions of her having had a sex change, that she was a man. He couldn't hide his revulsion, his confusion. 'Jesus Christ, what a fucking time to tell me. Are you kidding me?'

She turned to him, unbuttoning her shirt, her face rigid. 'You don't think this is something to kid about, do you?' She began to undress in front of him, and he now backed away from her. She undid her blouse, took off her bra, and then began to unzip her trousers. 'Look, don't, Ruda, don't do this to me, I can't deal with it, please, Ruda!'

She continued to undress, easing her trousers down, and then kicking off her shoes. She had a pair of thick cotton pants on, and he really believed she was going to show him a penis. Instead, she drew down the pants and showed him the terrible scars on her belly. He stared in disbelief, deeply shocked but not repelled.

Ruda then held up her wrist, showing him the tattoo. He looked from the row of numbers to her belly; he couldn't look into her eyes.

'I'm surprised you've never seen it before, the tattoo.'

He swallowed, and gave a half-smile, but his hands were shaking. 'I guess I'm just not very observant.'

She stood before him with such helplessness, such shame, her head bowed. He picked up the gown, and slipped it over her head. Then he stepped back. 'Now you look like a bride.' The small space between them was like a chasm; he did not know how to cross to her. Seeing her standing there in the white floating gown made him want to weep, but she shed no tears.

Her voice was husky, her head still bowed. 'I'll make up a bed for myself on the sofa. You don't have to be with me. I understand, I can understand.'

He gathered her in his arms and held her tightly. His voice was thick with emotion. 'What kind of a man do you think I am? We said to each other for better or worse, didn't we? Well, I don't think you got such a great bargain, so maybe you're a bit damaged too, that's OK, we'll make out.'

Ruda had clung to him, her whole body shaking, and when he cupped her face in his big hands, two tears rolled down her cheeks. He told her then that he loved her. Maybe it was those two tears – he had never seen her cry before – and he had carried her into the small bedroom and gently laid her down. He undressed as she watched, and then he got in beside her, and he reached out and cradled her in his arms.

'Don't ask me about it, Luis, don't ever want to know what was done to me, because it might open up a darkness inside me that I could not control. It happened, and now it's over.'

He had never felt so protective to any living soul. He kissed her head as she rested against his chest. 'I will always take care of you, Ruda, nobody will ever hurt you again. You are my wife, this will be our secret, no one will ever know.'

He made her feel secure, a strange new emotion. She felt warmed by this big soft man, and gently she stroked his chest, and then rolled over to lie on top of him. She smiled down into his face, and then whispered to him, that she could make him happy, there were ways, she would teach him how to make love to her, he would like it, he would be satisfied.

The old hand and the few workers left at the winter quarters gave knowing winks and nudges as a very happy Grimaldi greeted them the morning after the wedding. He was a man who appeared infatuated with his new marital status. Maybe it was indeed love.

The big album dropped to the floor, and Grimaldi woke with a start. For a moment he was disorientated, couldn't even remember coming into Ruda's bedroom. 'You're gettin' old, you soft bugger, noddin' off . . .' He yawned and leaned back. He could smell Ruda on her pillow. He nuzzled it and then slipped his arm round it sighing. 'Oh, Ruda, where did I go wrong, huh?' He knew she would play hell with him if she found him in her room, but he chuckled and eased himself into a more comfortable position. His last thought before he fell into a deep sleep was of Ruda, his wife. 'What a bloody wife.'

Ruda had intended to apply for a divorce as soon as she had the opportunity. That she had married Grimaldi bigamously never concerned her. With Kellerman in prison, he would not find out; by the time he was out she would have secured a divorce. She wished she had done it in Vegas, as she had told Grimaldi she had, but then she had been in such a hurry to leave that divorce had been the last thing on her mind.

Grimaldi began to earn money by training other acts, travelling around the United States. He returned with gifts, and cash to begin buying new cats for his own show. Ruda worked at the winter quarters, learning how to groom and feed the animals, and they thrived under her care and attention. She and Luis began to breed the tigers and their first summer together as man and wife saw four new cubs born. Ruda was a doting surrogate mother, bottle-feeding two lion cubs, and was heartbroken when Grimaldi sold them. He said they needed the sale because it would help build up their savings, but he also demonstrated his knowledge of the cats – the cubs were not a good colour. He taught Ruda how to detect the best of the litters, how to test their strength, their health always the main priority, and she was a willing pupil. She worked tirelessly, nothing was too much trouble. Everyone said that Grimaldi had found the perfect wife and that Ruda was getting him back on his feet.

Ruda continued with her star-gazing sideline. The letters arrived every week and she would spend hours every evening typing replies, giving predictions. She typed very slowly with two fingers, her face puckered with concentration. She had a dictionary beside her, always thumbing its well-worn pages. Grimaldi used to tease her, and at times was stunned when she asked him to spell the simplest of words. He believed at first it was because she was German and typing in English, but then watching her studied concentration, he understood she was almost illiterate. She had caught him watching her and given him a V-sign. 'I never went to school, dickhead, so no jokes!'

He leaned on her chair, and began to read a letter. She tried to cover it with her hand, and he snatched it out of the roller. '"Dear Worried From Nebraska", my God, what in God's name is somebody writing to you from Nebraska for?'

Ruda had tried to grab the letter back, but he held it away from her. 'I've done her charts, now give it back.'

Grimaldi dangled the letter jokingly. 'Her charts? What in Christ's name do you know about all this junk?'

He continued to read on, and roared with laughter as he read Ruda's predictions. She folded her arms. 'You laugh, but they pay ten bucks a letter, and they pay for the cats' feed. You got any better ideas how to make dough that fast?'

Grimaldi slapped the paper down, and rubbed her head. 'Keep working, keep working!'

She carefully rolled the paper back into the typewriter and he was about to walk out when he paused at the doorway. 'You never did tell me how you did that scarf trick, you know, with that old magician.'

She began typing again, and without looking at him said that it wasn't a trick. He told her to pull the other leg, but she turned to face him. 'That wasn't a trick, I'm telepathic.'

'Oh, yeah? Prove it!'

Ruda shrugged and said she couldn't be bothered, but he had hovered around, teasing, asking her to prove it. She sighed, pushed the typewriter away. She had picked up a stack of envelopes, containing all the letters she had received that week. She handed them to him, first flicking through the stack like a pack of cards. She then turned her back and told him to flick each envelope up and she would tell him what colour the stamps were. She repeated, in rapid succession: red, blue, red, red, green, blue, red, red, red, red . . . then swivelled round in her chair and cocked her head to one side.

'You already knew! You cheated!'

She held out her hand and shrugged. 'Yeah . . . now can I get on with my work?'

'Don't let me hold you up, carry on.' But he remained leaning at the doorway watching her, until she looked up at him and pulled a funny face.

'Is it just the colours, then? I mean, can you do anything else?'

She laughed. 'If I was to say yes, what are you gonna

do? Set up a booth and make me wear a turban? Just get out, go on, don't you have anything to do?'

Grimaldi laughed. As he stepped down he called out, 'I'll get myself a cloak like that old boy you worked with. Old Two Seats can bend over and give us a good fart, I'll set light to it!'

She could hear him laughing as he passed by the window, and then he stuck his head against the glass. 'I tell you today how much I love you, gel. Eh? Cross my palm with silver . . . and I'll tell you how much!'

She stuck up her finger, shouted for him to 'Sit on it!', and he gave his marvellous, deep-bellied laugh, as at last he went about his business.

Ruda began her laborious typing once more but, after a moment, she sat back and slid out from beneath the typewriter a slip of paper. It was another advertisement, another place: Florida. She stared at the two lines, remembering how Tommy Kellerman had told her she was crazy. Slowly she crumpled the paper, then straightened out the creases, kept on reading and rereading the two lines, 'Red, blue, green, Ruda . . .' and the message Tommy had hated so much.

Ruda crossed to her dressing-table, opened a drawer, eased her hand to the back and drew out the small black tin box now fitted with a new lock. She fetched the key, hidden behind a book in the bookcase and unlocked her treasure box. She looked at the stack of small, folded slips of newspaper clippings. The date of the last one, Vegas, was the longest time between all the many cuttings, perhaps because, for the first time she could remember, she felt a sense of security.

She locked away her treasures again, carefully hiding the tiny key, and returned to her typewriter. She sat staring at the white sheet of paper in the roller and lifted her hands, about to begin work, but she couldn't concentrate. She

326

went into the bedroom, slipping the bolt across as she passed the trailer door, and drew the curtains so the small room was in semi-darkness. She sat in front of the dressing-table mirror, a three-sided, free-standing mirror that she slowly drew towards herself, closer and closer until she could see her breath form tiny circles on the glass. By turning her head a fraction she could see her left profile, turning the opposite side, see her right, and then she stared directly ahead. She breathed deeply through her nose, mouth shut, and kept on breathing until she felt the strange, dizzy sensation sweep over her. Her shoulders lifted as her breathing deepened . . . first came the red, as if a beam of a red light focused on her face. She breathed deeper, concentrated harder, until the red merged into a deep green, then a blue. The colours, dense now, began flashing and repeating: red, blue, red, red, green . . . They never merged, each was a clear block of single colour. Her body began to shake, her hands gripped tightly the edge of the dressing-table. The bottles of cologne shook, the entire dressing-table began to sway, and she held on tightly, held on for as long as she could, before she regulated her breathing again, bringing herself slowly out of the trance.

Her body felt limp, exhausted, but she remained sitting, then tilted her face forward to kiss the cold glass, kiss her own lips. Slowly she sat back, and traced with her fingers the faint impression of her lips lingering on the mirror.

She had received nothing back, and she was consumed by an overpowering feeling of longing; the desire to feel warm lips return her kiss was like a pain inside her, a pain that, like her scars, would never heal. She could never give up, never, because on three occasions she was sure she had felt a contact.

She lay down on the bed, closed her eyes, needing to be enveloped by sleep. But now a low, nagging pain at the base of her spine made her feel uncomfortable. She turned on her side, but the pain grew worse, began to feel like a dragging sensation, as if something was being drawn out of her belly. Ruda panted, became frightened as she sweated, the pain intensifying. She gripped her stomach – it felt swollen and she began to rub her hands over her belly. As quickly as the pain had begun, it subsided. Ruda lay back. Then the pain began once more. She called out for Grimaldi, her body twisting in agony, the rush of pain centred in her belly and as she tried to sit up, she screamed with all the power in her lungs.

Grimaldi was in the barn, using a pitchfork to heave up the bales of hay. He paused, listened, and looked towards the barn doors. 'Did you hear that? Eh, you toothless old bastard, was that one of the cats?'

Two Seats shrugged and carried on working. Grimaldi stood for a moment, listening intently. Hearing nothing more he resumed his work, but after a moment he tossed down his pitchfork and walked back to the trailer. He peered in through the window, saw the typewriter, then crossed to the door, dragging his feet on the grid to wipe off the mud. He was just about to enter when he heard the bolt on the door drawn back. 'Ruda? You OK? Ruda?'

She opened the door, her face pale, shiny with sweat.

'What you lock the door for?'

Ruda gave a weak smile. 'I just didn't feel too good. I think it must be something I ate. I've been sick.'

'You running a temperature?' He reached out to touch her face and she stepped back.

'No, I'm fine now, you get on with your work. I'll lie down for a while. Go on.'

'I'll check on the cats, I swear I heard screaming. Did you hear anything?'

'Get back to work, you lazy old so and so. I'll bring over some food. It was just something I ate, now off . . . go on!'

He smiled, walking back to the barn, calling her a slave-driver. He didn't notice that she hung on to the door for support, so weak she could hardly stand.

As soon as Grimaldi was out of sight, Ruda inched herself back to the table and slumped into the chair by her typewriter. She had felt this same pain before, although she couldn't remember the exact date, but the pain had been the same, the terrible dragging sensation. She tried to type, forcing herself not to think about what had just occurred, because it frightened her. She was terrified of doctors, especially hospital doctors in their white coats – they made her shake with terror.

She felt her energy returning and just as she had pushed the pain from her, she forced herself to continue working, listing what the week's itinerary would be, what work she had lined up for Grimaldi. Almost immediately she felt better. She never did make an appointment to see a doctor, but a few months later she went to see a specialist, not at her own instigation, but her husband's.

With Ruda pushing him, Grimaldi continued taking on more training work. As the money came in, they began to buy more and more animals. At weekends he would begin training them, and she sat and watched his every move. Gradually she began to work alone when he was away, putting everything she had seen him do into practice.

They bought a new trailer and a truck, and then one night he sat her down. 'I know your injuries, the scars, but I was wondering, with you being here, and me away working until we have enough finances, whether maybe this would be a good time . . .'

'For what?' she had asked, dragging out the typewriter.

'Maybe we should see a specialist. They have all kinds of newfangled equipment now, and maybe we should go see someone about having a baby.'

She continued fetching papers, stacking them neatly at the typewriter, carrying her boxes of mail to the table. Over the past few months her little sideline had grown into quite a lucrative business. Having a semi-permanent address helped, and she worked each evening after the animals were settled. Grimaldi sometimes sat and watched her – he never read any of the letters, he was never that interested. Tonight, though, he wasn't prepared to sit. He didn't want her working, he felt this was too important.

'Ruda, listen to me. Maybe, just maybe, you can have this done medically, you know, artificial insemination. We could at least try.'

'I have enough work cut out for me, without bringing a kid up.'

'I want a son, Ruda. I mean, we're breaking our backs to get an act back together, so why not? We'd have a hell of a boy, Ruda. Don't you want even to give it a try?'

She rolled a sheet of paper into the typewriter, and started to type. He came and stood behind her, massaging her shoulders. He felt her shoulders shaking. She tried to type, and then folded her hands in her lap.

'If it hurts you, then we walk away. I don't want anything to hurt you, but we should just go and see somebody.'

He kissed the top of her head and left her. Slowly she began to type. 'Baby-baby-baby-baby . . . MY BABY. MY BABY. MY SON.'

She stared at the word until it blurred. She touched the paper, the word 'baby'. Nothing had prepared her for this, for Luis wanting a child, her child. She whispered, 'My child, he would be mine. My baby.' It had never occurred to her that perhaps there was a way. The more she thought about it, the more excited she became. Would it be possible? Dare she think it could be?

She ran out of the trailer, shouted to old Two Seats asking if he'd seen Grimaldi, and he pointed to the barn. She ran, calling for him, and hurtled into the barn. He was using a pitchfork, heaving the bales of hay. She dived at him, throwing him back on to the bales.

'Luis, Luis, I want a baby! *I want a baby. I want I want I want!*'

They had kissed, and held each other tightly. She was excited, almost feverishly so, asking him to fix an appointment. She would do anything necessary, and then she had leaned up on her elbows, looking down into his delighted face. 'You love me, don't you? You really love me!'

Luis knew what it meant to her the day she learned she could not conceive. She had not spoken a word since they returned from the clinic, and he was incapable of comforting her, needing comfort himself. Even when he tried to reach out to her in bed she had turned her back on him. 'Don't touch me, please leave me alone.'

He was almost grateful that he had to leave for a two-week stint in Chicago.

After he left she didn't want to get up, didn't even open the blinds, and remained in the darkened trailer. She remembered little Eva then, a girl she had hardly known, but a girl much older than herself. Eva had been in the camp too, had survived like Ruda, but when Ruda had been taken to the mental institution after the liberation, when the doctors at the hospital no longer knew what to do with her but certify her as mentally deranged, she hadn't known Eva was still alive – not until she caught sight of her in the mental ward. Eva had a beard, like a man. The teenage girl who had always had stories and jokes to tell the little ones now sat on a stool with her head bowed and her face covered in hair. Her eyes stared to some distant place.

Like Ruda, Eva had not spoken since she had been found, but Eva was docile while Ruda showed violent signs that she was greatly disturbed. They had to sedate her. Ruda found it impossible to speak, impossible to believe it was over; every night she had waited for the men in white coats to take her back to the hospital ward in the old camp. She had forced herself to remain awake. The screams and weeping from the inmates didn't frighten her – she was used to screams. What she was terrified of was being taken back – back to the camp. A key turning in a door sent bolts of terror shuddering through her body, and she could not speak her fear, could not cry tears. If they tried to comfort her, she was sure it was a ruse; if they spoke kindly to her, they had another motive. She spat out the pills they gave her, refused the food. Suspicious of everything, everyone, from the moment she had arrived in the institution, her paranoia manifested itself when she saw Eva. Poor little Eva Kellerman. At least Ruda had spared Tommy that, she had never told him, but it was because of Eva she had run. Eva had put an end to her own misery: she had torn a strip of cloth from her hospital gown and hanged herself in the showers. Ruda had discovered her pitiful body and knew then for sure that it was not over. She had run, had to escape some way, because any day, any hour, it could be her turn and she would become an animal, become like Eva, whose only freedom had been death.

In the end, Ruda made herself think that her inability to conceive was for the best. Maybe she could only produce a monster, an Eva. She would not think of a baby, her baby, any more, she would forget. As it was, the entire episode had dragged her back again to the darkness of her childhood; she was angry again, she was fighting again, determined that nothing would ever drag her back, it was to be forgotten.

Ruda had no real idea of how long she had been unreachable, how many times Luis had attempted to embrace her, show his love and concern. She wasn't aware he had slept on the couch, tried to tempt her to eat, or that she had kicked the tray from his hands. She was oblivious that when Luis had tried to tell her that he had to leave for a few weeks she had told him to fuck off, go wherever he liked, she didn't care . . .

Grimaldi had discussed her behaviour with old Two Seats, who suggested that all Ruda needed was time, she was just hurting, and this hitting out at Luis was her way of dealing with it. 'She's just like one of 'em cats, Luis. They get injured, and by Christ you'll know it, they'll go fer you! She's just hurtin'.'

Luis punched the old man's shoulder, said perhaps he was right. He never mentioned his own hurt, how much he had wanted a son . . . and he had left. He hadn't said goodbye because he hadn't wanted to disturb her. Ruda had been sitting on the bunk bed, with the old tin box.

Luis sighed, his face still pressed into Ruda's pillow. He rolled over, awake now, and sighed again. 'I wanted a boy, a son, so bad, Ruda, but, most important, I wanted him to be ours.' He sat up and ran his hands through his thick hair; it stuck up on end. He got off the bed and straightened the cover. The photo album had fallen open at an old picture of himself with his father. He picked it up, touching the picture lightly with his finger. 'Ah, well. Maybe the circus days are numbered, and, maybe I'd get a kid who wouldn't want to go into the ring. It happens . . .' Luis stepped up on the stool, talking away to himself. 'The Karengo brothers got a kid who's studying law! Mine'd probably end up in gaol some place . . . who knows? Can't all be warriors, eh, Dad?' About to shut the cupboard door, he saw the box, the old square black tin box at the back. He stretched and reached out, drew it close, and then stepped down with it. He tried to open it – it was locked. He went into the kitchen and took a knife, but when he tried to prise the box open, he buckled the lid. He swore as he wrenched and pulled, but it wouldn't open.

The trailer door banged. Luis turned guiltily: he was

behaving just like Kellerman – had he reached this point with Ruda, too?

Mike called out that they were due on in ten minutes. 'Ruda said to get over to the ring, the big boss is in the viewing room, and he's got a scout from Ringling Brothers' Circus with him. We're all set to go.'

Luis shouted he would be right there, and quickly hid the box under his own mattress. Mike was waiting at the door, and raised his eyebrow to Grimaldi; he admired the old man's resilience, there he was all done up like a Christmas dinner, and not long before he had been well plastered.

'Your hand OK?' Mike asked, as they walked towards the big tent. Grimaldi gave a big rumbling laugh and hooked a huge arm round Mike's slim shoulder. 'Son, I've been slashed by a lot more dangerous species than a pitchfork!'

Mike laughed, then lifted the tent flap. 'She's all steamed up as usual, pacing out there like a panther. Mamon's playing up, I hope to God he'll play ball tonight. It's those plinths, he hates them. Did I tell you the Ringling scout is in?'

Grimaldi nodded his head. 'Yeah, you told me, son. You know once I had a contract with them, some years back, but they offered me a . . .'

Mike had gone, and he was alone, talking to himself. He stood in the semi-darkness amid the empty rows and rows of seats. A juggling act was moving through its paces in the ring, the coloured costumes spangled, catching the spotlights. He looked to the lighted viewing box; he could see Schmidt conferring with a man sitting next to him, gesturing down to the ring. Then Grimaldi saw a third man, seated just behind Schmidt. He shaded his eyes to get a better view. It was Walter Zapashny, rated as probably one of the finest animal trainers in the world. Grimaldi wondered why he was up there; it made him feel uneasy.

Grimaldi inched down the aisle between the empty seats; he saw one of the hands standing by to erect the cages around the ring. He moved quietly to his side. 'Have you seen who's in the viewing tower?'

The man nodded, he whispered that everyone knew, it was the big Ringling scout. The word was out that the great Gunther Gebel Williams was about to retire. It meant that the most lucrative circus job, a possible ten-year contract with the powerful Ringling Brothers of New York was coming up for grabs. Williams had been top of the bill as one of the greatest showmen for almost twenty years.

Grimaldi nodded, his heart pounding in his chest. What he had dreamed of all his adult life, that coveted position for himself, could now be Ruda's. He felt a rush of pride. 'Tell Ruda I'm here, tell her to make this the best show she has ever given. Hurry!'

CHAPTER FOURTEEN

A s RUDA KELLERMAN prepared to begin her act, Vebekka Maréchal sat at the cramped dingy bar, its red light giving everyone an eerie pinkness. It was still only nine, and the club was almost empty; three girls wearing mini-skirts and tight lace tops chattered quietly at the end of the plush plastic-covered bar. Vebekka had gone from club to club until she found Mama's. A doorman came out of the men's toilet, looked at the elegant woman sitting alone, gave her a good once-over; he was sure she was after young blood – male or female. He sniffed, she'd get it – if she had enough Deutschmarks. He passed through the arch, its green and red beaded curtain held back by a ribbon, went up the flight of stairs leading to the main club entrance, then flattened himself against the wall as Mama began her heavy descent. He saw the swollen ankles first, the fat rolling over her gold sandals, as the tiny feet moved down one step at a time.

Mama Magda Braun's massive frame squashed against her doorman, but she didn't even acknowledge him. She was talking loudly to a small queer who had followed her down, clutching her poodle. 'I am sick to death of those ugly bastards, I don't wanna see those bitches stealing my girls' jobs. The smell of them! Emptying the store shelves, bringing crime and bad taste, I hate them! Everything used to be a good tight scene. Now, Jesus Christ what a mess!'

His high-pitched lisping voice squeaked out from behind her bulk. 'Now, Magda, the shops are doing a roaring trade, you know it, I know it . . .' He was referring to

Magda's sex and porn shops in East Berlin. She was making money hand over fist, but hated it when the girls from the East tried to come to her clubs in the West. Magda was the biggest single porn-shop owner in the West. Now with the Wall down, she had been one of the first to see the potential money-making machine; the sex-starved Easties, as she called them, needed an injection from the Westies, and she was giving them what they wanted in the form of shops – but they didn't have to come swarming over into her clubs. Magda Braun owned four nightclubs: she was a multi-millionairess.

Magda's peroxide curls turned bright pink in the light, her diamonds glittered, as did the large beaded necklace dangling over her massive bosom. But she gave a bad-tempered glance around the half-empty club. It was early, she told herself, but she hated it when it was empty. This was her main club, the one in which she had her small cramped office. Eric, her diminutive husband, called out to the girls, waved to a few couples and continued to follow Magda, to a door marked private. The effort of walking across the small dance floor had exhausted what little breath was able to squeeze through her nicotine-polluted lungs. Her chest heaved, and she gave a phlegmy cough. She could still be heard coughing as the door closed behind her.

Magda checked the takings on the computer, a cigarette in her crimson-painted lips. Years of smoke had created a yellow tinge on one side of her jowled face. 'Our take is down again this week. You think those bitches are at it again? I tell you, Eric, you have to watch them like a hawk. Give me a barman any day, trust a man better than those tarts.'

Eric was peering through a small spyhole. 'You seen the class act at the bar?'

Magda paid no attention, continued tapping out the

accounts. The boys handling the girls over in the East were short-changing her, she knew it. They'd have to have a short sharp lesson.

'I'm gonna check on the class, be back in a minute.'

Magda picked up a pencil and dialled, hooking the phone under her chin. 'It's Magda, can you get over here, bring a couple of the boys, and the handy ones, yeah? . . . Yeah, he'll do. No, . . . give me another.' She listened and agreed to three of the names supplied by the caller, then replaced the phone, sighing. They never learn their lesson, they should know you don't get to be near eighty, and as rich as she was, without learning every trick in the trade.

Eric scuttled back, gesturing for Magda to come to the spyhole. 'She's asked for water, just sits there, she may be a fruit. You want to take a look? She's wearing good jewellery – that's sable on the edge of her wrap, Magda.'

'I don't give a fuck about her, if she's paying, then what's the problem?'

'That's it, she's been there over half an hour, said she's not got any money she just wants to sit. She didn't pay any entrance money, doorman wasn't on duty . . . Magda!'

Magda shoved him aside, peered through and kept on looking, her heaving breath seeming to stop suddenly. She straightened up. 'I just seen a ghost. Fuck me!' She laughed, and thudded down into a wide cushioned seat. 'Eric, bring me a bottle of champagne, good stuff, and ask the lady to come in.'

'You know her?'

Magda nodded, 'I know her, she may look like class now but, honey, believe you me that was one hell of a tart. You know something, Eric? They always come back . . . some day, one day, they come back, maybe to see where they came from, or how far they've left us behind . . . but they always come back to Mama. Get her in. This one I've been waiting for, so long now I can hardly remember.'

Eric crossed to Vebekka, asked if she would join Madame Magda for a drink. He pointed back to the office, the door left ajar. Vebekka hesitated and looked towards Magda, who was smiling, beckoning her to come, but Vebekka shook her head. 'Thank you, no. I don't speak German.'

Eric asked if she was English. She told him she was French, and he attempted to repeat his invitation in French.

'*Ruda!* Come in here, Ruda!'

Vebekka felt strange, a little faint, as the fat woman kept calling to her, waving her over. She slid from the stool. 'Excuse me, I must go.'

Eric ordered champagne, took Vebekka's elbow. 'Please, you come.'

'No, thank you, no . . .'

'*Ruda! Ruda!*'

Eric insisted, holding her arm firmly, as one of the girls carried a tray with a bottle of champagne and two glasses across to the office. Vebekka was ushered into the small room and the big woman held open her arms. 'Come here. Come and give me a kiss!'

Vebekka stepped back, repelled by the grotesque woman. Eric pushed her further into the room, the waitress squeezed out, and Magda wafted her hand at Eric. 'You, too, get out.'

Disappointed, Eric walked out, pouting. He crossed to the bar and ordered a martini. The club began filling up, and he perched himself on the stool vacated by Vebekka. He noticed she had left her handbag on the bar.

Magda poured the champagne. Vebekka remained standing. Magda handed her a drink, but she shook her head. 'No, I don't.'

Magda smiled and set the glass down, lit another ciga-rette from a stub, offering the case to Vebekka. She took one, and Magda flicked a Zippo lighter across the desk. 'You look very good, I didn't recognise you at first.'

Vebekka remained standing. 'I am so sorry, I don't understand, I don't speak German.'

Magda smiled again, shrugged her plump shoulders. 'What then?'

Vebekka spoke in French, introducing herself as Baroness Vebekka Maréchal, asking if they had met before. Magda kept her eyes on Vebekka, heavily made-up eyes, the mascara so thick her lashes were spiked. 'You want to speak in French, Italian, Spanish that's OK by me. You been away so long, huh? That long?'

'I don't understand, I am so sorry, but I think there is some confusion, I don't think we have ever met.'

Magda leaned her fat elbows on the desk. 'OK, I'll play, have a drink, sit down.'

Vebekka eased herself on to the proffered chair; she felt very uneasy, but she sipped the champagne. Magda suddenly reached out and took Vebekka's left wrist, turned it over. Vebekka tried to withdraw her hand, but the old woman, for all her heavy breathing, was as strong as an ox. Her long nails scratching at Vebekka's wrist, she turned her palm upwards, and traced the fine skin graft with the tip of her nail. She let go, and smiled.

'Why did you do that?' Vebekka rubbed her wrist.

'So I know I am sure. Drink, drink – it's good, the best money can buy,' Magda answered in French.

Vebekka sipped the champagne, the old woman looking at her, scrutinising her. Magda tapped her own nose, and then pointed to Vebekka's face, said that the work was good, she looked good, looked young. She asked where she was staying, why she was in Berlin, and Vebekka said she was with her husband.

'And you couldn't resist it? Had to come back and see Magda? And now you're a what? A Baroness? Well, well – face changed, name changed, what did you call yourself? Vebekka? What kind of name is that?'

Vebekka smiled, a sweet coy smile, and sipped more champagne. Magda picked up her vodka, drank thirstily, and shook the glass. 'I still take it neat, with ice, but now I own a warehouse full! Times change, huh? Times change, Ruda, little Ruda. Just look at you, and married to a baron! Does he know you're here?'

Vebekka began to feel uneasy, a little frightened. Why did the woman keep on calling her Ruda? But all she said was that her husband did not know.

'I bet he doesn't. So you got to America? I heard you had, and then what? You met a prince and a baron – all the same thing. Is he rich?'

Vebekka drained her glass. Magda poured more and asked again if her husband was rich. Vebekka shrugged. 'I suppose so, I don't know, I never think about money.'

Magda laughed, her body shook and she had a coughing fit that seemed to be calmed by a drag on her cigarette. 'You don't think of money. I do, every second of every day, I count it every night on this little baby computer – cuts a lot of time, and accountants' fees.'

The two women drank in silence. The sounds of a Madonna record could be heard from the club, the low murmur of voices and shrill laughter. Magda's eyes watered. 'You know, it hurt, Ruda, it hurt when you ran off – I never thought you would steal from me, not after all I did for you. I never thought you would do that to Mama, maybe that's why I have never forgotten you. You forget lovers, forget husbands, forget children even, but when someone hits your pocket, you don't forget. I never forgot you, Ruda, and maybe I just guessed one day you would come back.'

Vebekka listened, her head cocked to one side. Sometimes she understood what she was saying, but Magda's French kept slipping back into German. 'I don't understand what you are saying, but I know I have never met you before. I am not this – Ruda? You are mistaken . . .'

Yet Vebekka felt a strange sensation when she said the name Ruda, it seemed to ring through her brain like a tiny ominous bell. Magda heaved herself to her feet and looked at Vebekka with distaste. 'Don't play games with me, I am a master player, sweetface. You don't speak German? We've never met? Who the fuck do you think you are kidding, eh? Because you got a few fancy clothes on, call yourself a Baroness?'

'I don't understand.'

Magda was losing patience. She slapped the desk with her fat hand. 'Don't make me angry, it's been a lot of years, a lot of changes, Ruda. I run this city, hear me? You stop this act right now – *I have had enough!*'

Vebekka gulped at the champagne. The woman frightened her. 'I have never met you before! Please, there is some misunderstanding, perhaps I should leave.' She started to stand but Magda was up beside her, pushing her into the seat, leering over her.

'You want something to refresh your memory? Huh? I didn't want to do this, I was prepared to be hospitable, maybe forget, but me? Never, I forget nothing, no one. You owe me a lot, Ruda, you owe me!'

Magda waddled to a large built-in cupboard, heaving for breath as she opened up the double door. The cupboard was stacked with boxes and files, she stared up and down, up and down, reached out for one box, and then withdrew her hand. Suddenly she yelled at the top of her voice. 'Eric. *Eric!*'

The club was in full swing now, Madonna still blared out from the speakers.

'Just sit, sweetface, I'm gonna jog that memory of yours.'

Eric tapped and entered, looked to Magda, to Vebekka, then asked if everything was all right.

'There was a box, old cardboard box from the Kinker-litzchen, taped up, big brown cardboard box.'

342

'What about it?'

'I want it. Where is it? It used to be stashed in there, in that cupboard. Where is it now?'

Eric hovered at the open cupboard doors. 'I haven't moved anything for years from here, everything you wanted brought over should still be here, unless when they computerised the club somebody threw it out. What do you want?'

'*I never gave permission for one thing to be chucked out!*'

Magda was heaving for breath, and Eric got down on his hands and knees. 'Shit, this place is filthy. It's dusty in here.'

Magda stood behind him. 'Just find the fucking thing.'

Vebekka looked on, not understanding what they were saying, looking from one to the other. Eric suddenly heaved at a box beneath a stack of files. 'Is this it?'

Magda peered over his shoulder and told him to put it on the desk. Eric dumped the dirty dusty box on the table and then restacked files as Magda tore it open. She rooted around, hurling things to the floor, and then took out an old torn thick envelope. 'Put it all back and get out!'

'Shit, Magda, I'll have to take all the files and restack them again, it won't fit now.'

Magda screeched at him to leave – she would sort it out later. Eric tripped over the dog, which yelped and scuttled under the desk, then slammed out of the office, very peeved.

Magda filled Vebekka's glass again, then settled herself back on her cushions, lighting another of her cigarettes. 'You don't remember Mama, huh? You don't remember what I did for you, what Mama did to help Ruda? Well, tell me, you remember this, sweetface?' Magda tore at the envelope and pulled out a parcel wrapped in old newspapers.

Again Vebekka felt the name pass across her mind . . . Ruda? She suddenly turned to stare behind her, she had the sensation that someone else was in the room . . . close to her; but there was no one. Ruda, she repeated to herself, not even listening to Magda. Then she sipped the champagne; it was chilled, icy cold, it tasted good. She had not been allowed to drink for years. She turned again, sure someone was near to her, but as she turned she saw Magda watching her, and she gave a nervous laugh. 'I have not been allowed to drink. I had forgotten how lovely it tastes. Are you all right?'

Magda was coughing, ripping open the newspapers. She withdrew an old wooden-handled carving knife, a knife with serrated edges, and snarled, 'You forgotten this?'

Vebekka looked at the knife, puzzled. 'I don't understand.'

'You don't understand, and you are not Ruda? And you didn't come bleating to Mama? Didn't come begging me to help you clean up? Help you to strip him, help you hide him? You couldn't even lift him, you had to come running to Mama, stuffing him into the kitchen cupboard? That perverted piece of shit still moaning and begging us to save him, begging you, begging me, but you couldn't do it, you were fucked up, so you started begging Mama – *you remember Magda now, tart?*'

Magda staggered slightly, heaving for breath again. Vebekka began to shake, both hands clasping her champagne glass. She could hear Louis shouting at her, he was dragging her to their car, she was trying to button her blouse, pulling at his hand. Where was it? Was it here? She couldn't remember. All she could hear was his voice as he pushed her roughly into the car. 'You tart! *You cheap tart!*' He had driven off so fast, the car tyres screaming, his face white with pent-up anger, shouting how he had been searching for her, and then he had pulled over and punched the steering wheel with his hands. 'Why, why do you do this?'

'You remember, tart? *Answer me!*'

Vebekka's head began to throb. She gulped the champagne. 'Did my husband tell you?' she asked Magda. She felt hot, the cramped office was stifling and she began to sweat. 'Water, could I have a glass of water?'

Magda leaned back in her chair, clinking the ice cubes in her tall glass of neat vodka. 'What you had done to your face? You done something to your face . . . you had a nose job? That's what's different, you had some work, sweetface?'

Vebekka touched her face. 'Yes, yes . . . I had, er, surgery.'

Magda chuckled patting her own fat jowled cheeks. 'I knew it, I knew it, I can always tell . . . Ruda.'

'Please, I need a glass of water!'

Magda reached over to the champagne bottle and banged it down in front of Vebekka. 'You want a drink? You need a drink?' Her fat face twisted, and she leaned forwards and threw the contents of her glass into Vebekka's face. The vodka burned her eyes, and she knocked over her chair as she sprang to her feet, her hands covering her face.

Magda dragged herself up. 'Get the hell out, and think about this!' Magda waved the carving knife in front of her. 'Think about this, Ruda, then come back and see me, you owe me, maybe now's the time to pay me off. *Out – get out!*'

Vebekka stumbled to the door, fumbled, trying to open it. Magda pressed the button at the side of her desk. The door buzzed open, and Vebekka ran out, as Magda picked up the phone and screamed for Eric to come in to her.

Magda's face was sweating, her eye make-up running. She didn't even give Eric time to shut the door, but snapped at him to follow the tart, find out where she was staying and report back. 'I want to know everything about that one, you understand me? Go on, get out!'

Eric straightened his hand-printed silk tie, smoothed his hair with his hands and made his way quickly to the club exit, not even acknowledging the calls from customers he knew. He thudded up the stairs, looked for the doorman and saw him examining two young kids' driving licences. 'You see a woman come out, dark-haired woman, few seconds ago?'

The doorman nodded, jerked his thumb along the street, and Eric took off, swearing loudly that he should have got his overcoat. It started to rain, coming down in a deluge; the doorman swore and huddled in the doorway.

Magda opened the small soft leather clutch bag. It contained only a gold and diamond embossed compact, a matching lipstick and a gold cigarette case. There was no wallet, no credit cards, nothing. She felt the lining, sniffed it; there was a faint smell of expensive perfume. 'You sure it was hers?'

The barmaid who'd brought the bag in nodded, said the woman had left it on the bar in front of her when she came into the office. 'OK, you can go.'

The girl departed as Magda took a magnifying glass from a drawer and examined the compact. She squinted, then lifted her eyebrows; it was gold, so the diamonds must be real. She checked the cigarette case; it too was eighteen carat. Maybe the bitch wasn't lying, maybe she was a baroness. Magda laughed, lit another mentholated cigarette, then turned the cigarette case over in her hand. She'd hang on to it and the compact; they would cover what the little bitch had stolen all those years ago. Hell, she sniffed, nowadays the leather bag would cost two hundred dollars. She opened a drawer and placed the bag inside, slamming it shut. It was funny, but she wouldn't have turned nasty, wouldn't even have wanted her debt repaid, so much water had passed under the bridge since then.

Magda sucked at her cigarette, the room stinking of

346

smoke. It was the way the bitch refused to admit who she was that really pissed Magda off. Who did she think she was kidding? All the handouts she'd given, all the helping hands to the young slags; they always turned round and slapped you in the face. She thought about the girls and the pimps she had set up, buying their trailers out of her own pocket, all they had to do was stand outside them, pick up their customers. She paid off the police, she, Big Mama, covered everything, even the bitches' clothes – and they still robbed her when they could.

Magda picked up the carving knife. The blade was eight inches long, the handle carved but worn; Ruda probably stole even that, or found it in one of the bombed-out houses in the rubble of the old cellar she had lived in. In those days it was surprising what you could find, picking around in the rubble. Magda ran her fingers along the serrated edge; it was brown with rust. She had always given a hand, helped the kids get started, and somehow had always survived, even the total wipe-out of the city.

It was after the war that she had come into her own. She gulped her vodka, slowly feeling herself calm down as she remembered the good times. The Americans, the English . . . those soldier boys wanted women, young, fat, thin, they wanted them, and Magda supplied their needs, every sexual need she could fill from under-age kids, boys and girls. The children were roaming the streets, hundreds of them, hungry and homeless; they'd turn a trick for a meal, for a crust. That's how she got her nickname 'Mama', even that bitch Ruda had called her Mama.

Magda squeezed her eyes closed, could see Ruda as clear as yesterday. Ruda, no more than eight or ten years old, crawling with lice, dressed in rags, her skinny legs covered in open sores. She had been like a stray dog. No matter how often Magda and her boys sent her packing, she returned, hand out, begging. Magda had taken pity on her, let her scrub out the cellars she had started to convert into makeshift brothels. She clothed her, fed her, and the child never said a word. They never even knew her name for weeks – or was it months? She couldn't remember how long it was before the girl had started talking, and when she did she had an odd gruff voice, used a strange mixture of languages, Polish, German, Yiddish. They never even knew her real nationality; all they knew was that she had survived one of the death camps, because of the tattoo. Which camp they never discovered.

They nicknamed her Cinders, after Cinderella, and they wondered if she was deaf as she spoke so infrequently. Then one day she hit one of the young lads who was messing around with her, hit him with the broom, knocked him unconscious and Mama Magda had been called in to attend to him. Ruda had huddled in the corner, clutching the broom, and then in her odd gravelly voice said that her name was Ruda. Magda had clipped her hard, told her she had to behave herself if she wanted to be fed.

'My name is Ruda.'

Magda asked if Ruda had another name; she always worried about the police checking up on her kids, rounding them up. At every bomb-blasted corner there were long notices of missing children, and Magda always kept an eye on these lists just in case one of the missing children was working for her; if any were she got rid of them fast, even dragged them to the depots. If the children had families searching, they could cause a lot of aggravation; soldiers, convoys of doctors and nurses from all the orphanages being set up tried to get the kids off the streets. It was a difficult operation; they were no sooner picked up and housed than more took their place, the pitiful, bedraggled aftermath of war, diseased and sickly. Some kids simply died on the streets. The ones who knew their way around landed with Mama Magda.

Magda often asked Ruda if she had another name, but the child acted dumb. Then once she had lifted her wrist, as if the number was her surname. Maybe that was what had touched Magda, that the kid didn't even know her own name. Maybe that was what made her take such an interest in the skinny wretch. Magda began to let her work in her own apartment, washing and cleaning. She was all fingers and thumbs, but the good thing about her was she still didn't talk, just got on with her work. She put weight on, her hair was cleaned of the lice and her sores healed. She was never a pretty girl, but there was something about her, and Magda's men friends soon started to take an interest in her.

She would probably have kept Ruda on as a maid, but she had one of the usual visits from the health inspectors, checking on missing kids. They had a long list with them of kids who had absconded from the orphanages. Magda listened to the names, shook her head. 'I check the lists, I make sure none of them are around here. I find one, you know me, I drag them to the depot. I'm known there.'

Then they asked if she'd come across a girl called Ruda, they had no surname and they were still trying to trace any living relative. She had been held in a mental institution for four years directly after the war. She was a survivor of Birkenau, would be recognised by her tattoo; they described her as possibly eight to twelve years of age. They had a place for her in an orphanage but she had run away. Magda said she had no girl of that age working for her; she was sorry she couldn't help but would keep her eyes peeled. For a moment she was scared they were going to start searching her squalid apartment, but they folded their papers.

'I hope, Magda, you haven't got any under-age girls working for you, because if so, we'll keep on coming, and we'll bring the *Polizei* with us.'

Magda had passed over a black-market bottle of Scotch, laughing and joking, telling them she drew the line at kids. 'You think I'd use kids? What kind of a woman you think I am?'

They had no illusions about her, but what could they do? They had no search warrants, no time to look properly, there were too many . . . Even the threat of the *Polizei* was empty, but they had to make a show, at least try to salvage some of the young children roaming the streets. They took their Scotch and left.

Afterwards, Magda had to search for Ruda, guessed she was hiding somewhere. She went into her bedroom and opened the wardrobe. Ruda was scrunched up inside. 'Don't send me back there, Mama, please. Please don't.'

'I can't keep you here, sweetface, they'll close me down. I don't want trouble. I said I didn't know you – they find out I lied and I get aggravation.' Ruda had clung to her, sobbing. It was the first time Magda had seen her shed a tear. 'I can't keep you here, but I'll see what I can do.'

Even though she now knew just how young Ruda was, she got one of the older girls to start taking her around the brothels, got her to break Ruda in. But then, after a few weeks, Magda was told that there was something wrong with the girl's vagina. She couldn't have straight sex. Magda had shrugged; she was still a kid, maybe too tight. She suggested they teach her a few other tricks, to get her working. 'Just don't bring her back, I don't want her here. If she can't earn her keep, kick her out.'

Ruda was taught about oral sex. She was grateful it didn't hurt her insides. She would do anything to prevent being sent back to the mental institution. She learned fast, and was given a small percentage of the money she earned. She ate well, and started living with a few of Magda's whores in a rundown house. The customers often asked for her, since she was exceptionally young. But she was forever stealing from them; no matter how often she was beaten she still stole wallets and food coupons. Magda put her on the streets, to see if that would teach her a lesson – out on the bombsites, giving head wherever there was a dark corner, a derelict truck or car. It was a step down from Magda's filthy cellars, at least they had mattresses there, but being on the streets Magda never knew just how much she earned, even though she sent her heavy thugs around to collect. Ruda could always lie, hide a percentage of her takings, even put up her price.

Ruda worked the streets for almost three years, scrimping and saving her money, never buying the black-market clothes the other girls coveted; she couldn't care less. She wore the same old brown coat Magda had given her and her underwear, opening her coat as a come-on to the soldiers. The few items of clothes she bought from second-hand dealers were neatly folded and pressed in a battered case she salvaged from a tip. She found a derelict house occupied by a few tarts, girls so low down they didn't even have a Magda to look out for them. These girls would fight and claw at each other to safeguard their lamp-post, doorway, wrecked car. The house had no electricity or running water and no roof, but Ruda's room was dry, and she slept on a burnt mattress she had also retrieved from a tip. She began to bring back clients to the room, but then one night a US Marine had wanted more than oral sex. When she had said she couldn't have straight sex, he had tried to rape her. Unsuccessful, he had buggered her. It had hurt her, made her bite the edge of the mattress to stop herself from screaming out loud, but after it was done, he gave her a handful of dollars, tossed them on to her naked body. The pain went, as she sat counting her money, realising that she could ask more, she could do more.

Ruda used to pay for a bath a week at the local bath-house. She always paid more for a private, number one bath – this meant she was the first to use the water. The bath was her only luxury; she saved, hoarded her earnings, dreaming of one day going to the United States. She plied any American soldier she met with questions about America. She was naïve enough to believe that when she had enough money saved she could just buy a ticket and leave. When she discovered that without documents, visas and a passport she could never go anywhere, she stayed in her hovel for two days, then went to talk to Magda.

'You want papers? Visas? You any idea how much that kind of thing costs, sweetface? There's lines, hundreds, thousands lining up waiting ... go find somebody with papers, marry them – that's the fastest way you can get a legitimate passport. You'll have to wait in line, but you'll get one eventually.'

Ruda begged Magda to help her. Where was she going to find anyone who would marry her? Magda asked how much she had saved. Ruda halved it fast, knowing she would be suspicious. Even so, Magda asked if Ruda had been holding out on her, it was a lot of money. Ruda had opened her coat. 'I got no clothes but these, I don't cheat you, not any more. I don't smoke, I don't drink, Jesus Christ, Magda, I hardly fucking eat, I save every cent, I wanna go to America.'

'What's so special about America?'

Ruda buttoned her coat. 'I need some surgery, I can't pee straight, I get pains every time I piss. I'm not going to any hospital here, they'd drag me off to some mental hospital, but they can fix me up in America.'

Magda arranged for Ruda to meet with Rudi Jeczawitz, a cabaret artist, who knew certain people dealing in forged papers. Jeczawitz had been in Auschwitz and maybe he'd be prepared to help Ruda.

Magda made a deal with him; he needed a girl to help him in his act. Magda made a deal with Ruda. She wanted half Ruda's savings for setting it up, so Ruda was pleased she had not told Magda the exact amount she had saved. In some ways Magda was relieved she had got rid of her – she had a girl working Ruda's pitch within the hour. She knew Jeczawitz had contacts, but as to whether or not he could get Ruda to her beloved America was neither here nor there. Magda pocketed the money, she did nothing for anyone for free.

Jeczawitz was not actually involved with forged papers. He worked the clubs, and anyone needing forged papers passed their requests to him. Then he forwarded the requests to a man named Kellerman, a dwarf.

Jeczawitz took Ruda into his act and for the rest of her savings agreed to marry her. That way she would have a marriage licence and a surname. Ruda paid, believing that it would only be a matter of time before her husband gained the visas and documents for her to leave for New York. Rudi Jeczawitz was in his late sixties, and crippled with arthritis. He had lost his wife and children at Auschwitz. He made no sexual approach to Ruda; it was a marriage of convenience. She cooked for him, washed his tattered belongings, and he moved into her derelict room. He had nowhere to go; he had been sleeping rough for years. He had a battered cardboard suitcase filled with his hoops and magic tricks – he had been allowed to keep them when he was in the camp. The officers had even found him a cloak to wear, and a wizard's hat. The case represented everything to him and he guarded it obsessively. He always wore his cloak, the hat was kept in the case.

It was Ruda's job to hand him the hoops, the hats, the silk scarves he dragged from his sleeves, night after night. The clubs were seedy, rundown, most of them only employing him because of his contact with Kellerman. If they were caught passing on illegal papers they could be closed down, but by using Jeczawitz as the go-between they could always

353

plead innocent, and he would take the blame. After every show there would be some desperate figure waiting to speak to him.

One night, just before a show, he had been arguing with Ruda about preparing his handkerchiefs when she had grabbed them, called out the colours, and stacked them in a heap. He began to notice how quickly she could get them into order; he tried it out a few times, holding them up to her, then behind his back – she was able to tell him the order of colours. If he spread them on to a table, she needed look only once and then she could tell him each colour in rapid succession. He asked how she was doing it, and she had shrugged, told him they used to play games in the camp, it was a test they did.

He stared at her. 'You played games? My babies died, my wife died, thousands died – and you played games?'

That was the first time he beat her, took a stick to her and kept on hitting her. She took his beating, she was used to them, she just shut her mind off. No incoming pain signals registered on her brain. She just waited for him to exhaust himself. Bruised, she had gone on stage, hating him, but held him to his promise of getting her papers.

Jeczawitz beat Ruda regularly, and then he would weep inconsolably for hours, calling out names. Jeczawitz was as pain-racked as his wife, bleeding internally, his mental wounds never healing. He had no peace, but he lived somehow, day to day, dragging his old suitcase to the clubs and brothels. At night he passed on the pitiful messages, the folded money, the names. Some nights he was so drunk she had to help him to their room.

One night he was too drunk to make it to the club. Kellerman arrived at their hovel in his flashy clothes, and Rudi offered him Ruda for a night.

'I don't want your whore, hear me? I want names, money that's been paid to you.'

Ruda had followed Kellerman out on to the wasteground outside their house, offered herself. He turned and spat at her; he never paid for women, he didn't want a whore.

'I want papers,' Ruda said. 'Can you get them for me? My husband said you could, I have money.'

He had stuck his thumbs into his braces. 'I can get anybody anything they can pay for. You got the money – I'll get you the visas, passport, anything you want.'

'I've got my marriage licence, I've got proof of who I am.'

He had laughed in her face, told her he needed nothing but money. He would supply a name, get tickets for anywhere in the world she wanted to go – all she had to have was money.

When she learned how much, her heart sank, but she tried to earn as much as she could. But then Jeczawitz's drinking got out of hand, they lost two spots, and she got him sober enough to do the third. Their audience that night was a rowdy bunch, all shouting and yelling. She was told they were performers from the big circus. Ruda discovered who the big man was, she even tried to pick him up after the show, but he had virtually knocked her off her feet before his taxi drove off. She had found his trailer, learned by now he was important. She was certain he could get her out of Berlin. She had pushed her way into his trailer and he had given her money, told her he was leaving, that he couldn't get her a job.

When she got back to her room she found Rudi huddled on the bed. 'Kellerman's been here. He's not coming back, they kicked me out of the club, Ruda.' He opened his arms up to her, wanting comfort, and she slapped his face.

'He was my only hope. You've ruined everything. Where is he? Tell me where I can find him!'

Rudi lay down, said there was no way Kellerman would do business with her, he hated whores.

She went to her hiding place, tore at the ground with her hands. Her tin box had gone. All the money she'd saved had gone. 'Oh, no, please – please tell me you didn't take my money, please tell me you didn't.'

He hung his head, shamefaced. 'I owed Kellerman, I had to give him money, it had been paid to me. I'm sorry, I'm so sorry—'

She punched him, and he fended her off. He screamed out that Kellerman had a place in the Kreuzberg district, that was all he knew. He never went to his place, Kellerman always contacted him. He began to cry, covering his face with his hands, blubbering his children's names.

'Shut up. I don't want to hear about your fucking children, your wife, your mother – you survived. *You're alive!*'

He sat up. 'No. I am dead, I wish to God I was dead, like my babies, my wife – oh, God, help me, why did they have to die?'

Ruda smirked at him. 'You made them all laugh, didn't you, playing out your stupid tricks, Mr Wizard? What else did you do, huh? With your act you had to do something else at the camps. You think I don't know? *You named names . . . you gave those bastards names. You killed your own babies, you bastard!*'

'So help me God I did not!'

Ruda danced around him. 'Liar, why would they let an old man live?'

He reached for his stick, but she snatched it from him, started thrashing him, and he fought back, kicking out at her. He raged at her, screaming, 'You played games, you were his children, in your pretty frocks. I saw you all, I saw you all fat and well fed. My babies died, but you—'

Her rage went out of control. How could he know what they had done to her, what they had forced her to do? She kept on hitting him with the stick, over and over. She hit his head, his weak bent body. She was panting, heaving for breath, but at last he was silent, and she began to panic. She felt for his pulse – and then ran out.

Magda could hardly understand what she was saying, begging her on her knees to help, asking what she should do – somebody had to help her. 'Mama, please, he lied to me, he took all my money, and he never got me papers – all my money – please, please help me. He said he would go to the *Polizei*, tell them about you, tell them about the forged papers, he's really sick.'

Magda sighed, threw on her coat, said she would look at the old bastard, get a doctor if he needed one. 'This is the last time, Ruda. You don't come to me for anything ever again, understand?'

Magda looked over the old man. He was alive, just, but she doubted that he would last long. She told Ruda to strip him and stuff his clothes into his case. Ruda did as she was told. Magda began to collect all the pitiful possessions from around the room, scooping everything into an old sack. She then opened a cupboard. Jeczawitz moaned, his eyes opened, and he begged Magda to help him. She gestured for Ruda to grab his legs, and they heaved him into the cupboard, drawing his legs up, pushing and shoving him into the tiny space.

'He's alive, Magda, he's still alive, what if he gets out?' Magda snatched a piece of rag, stuffed it into his mouth. 'Hold his nose – *hold his nose so he can't breathe, you stupid bitch!*'

Ruda pinched his nose as he twisted, made weak attempts to push her away, and then his chest heaved, once, twice . . . still Ruda held his nose, then he gurgled.

357

There was no more movement. He was dead. Magda looked around the room, saw the old knife, picked it up. 'Use this, cut it out.'

Ruda was panic-stricken, not understanding.

'The tattoo, his number, they can trace who he is. Cut it off his arm, and hurry up. I'll take his case, dump it, just clean everything out, cover him up, shut the door.'

Ruda averted her face as she sliced into his frail arm, hacking at the skin. The knife was serrated, it seemed to take a long and terrible time. Magda shouted for Ruda to hurry. 'Gimme the knife, come on, hurry!' She tied a knot in the top of the sack.

Magda left Ruda, telling her to make sure to leave nothing that could be traced back to her. Ruda cleared everything up, and pushed the cupboard door shut, pressing her body against it. His hand was caught between the doors, and she had to open them again. Then she saw his old cloak and threw it over his head, slamming the doors shut. She got a block of wood and dragged it against the cupboard, then bricks, anything she could lay her hands on. She scrabbled in the filth and dirt. Ripping up newspapers, she lit the fire, stacking wood on top of the papers. She heaved the heavy broken door to the room closed, and prayed the fire would ignite.

The fire smouldered, and it was the smoke that eventually drew the attention of a passerby. The fire was extinguished, having only partly gutted the room. Anything of value left intact was swiftly taken, and a new occupant was ready to take over the squalid blackened room, but then it was boarded up, as unsafe. The dead man would remain undiscovered for weeks.

Magda seemed almost surprised when Ruda showed up; she poured her a vodka, neat. Ruda was still shaking, thanking Magda, grovelling to her, saying she would do anything – she would work for free if that was what she wanted. Magda laughed, told her she just wanted her gone, that she should clear out fast.

'I've no money, I've nothing.'

'That's how you came, sweetface, so that's how you leave. I reckon I've done more for you than for anyone else in my life, why I dunno, but I'm a Gemini. What star are you?'

'I dunno, I don't know when I was born, we were in hiding when they took us, my sister—'

Magda cocked her head to one side. 'You got a sister, sweetface?'

Ruda felt icy cold, as if her body was slowly freezing over. She couldn't speak, the room began to spin. 'Sister? Sister?'

When she woke up Magda was sitting next to her and she was lying on her red satin bedcover. 'Jesus Christ, sweetface, where in God's name have you been? You went out like a light. I've had smelling salts under your nose, even lit a feather . . . you gave me a fright. I thought you were dead!'

Ruda smiled weakly and reached for Magda's hand. Magda held the dirty skinny hand in hers. 'You got to go, Ruda. I can't let you stay here, I want no more troubles than I got. You can have a bath, get some food from the kitchen, but then you are out.'

'Don't throw me out, Mama, please, please, I need you.'

Ruda had reached up, held the big fat woman, smelt her heavy perfume. She wanted to lie in this woman's arms, wanted her to comfort her, and Magda rocked her gently. 'I can't let you, it's too much of a risk, just get yourself cleaned up, like a nice good Mama's girl.'

Magda had cupped Ruda's face, and then kissed her lips. Her tongue thrust into Ruda's mouth, she was smothering her, pulling Ruda's hand beneath her skirts, between her big fat thighs. 'Oh, yes . . . yes, press your fingers inside me, Ruda, yes . . . yes!'

Ruda let the woman paw her body, rip off her cheap dirty clothes, lick at her, and when Magda began to peel off her own tent dress, when she saw the mounds of flesh, the mountainous breasts released from their brassière, she closed her eyes. She felt nothing but revulsion, but Magda kept on talking, kept on telling what she wanted her to do, her breasts flattened against Ruda's face, as she demanded she be sucked. She wanted her nipples sucked like a man's cock, she knew how good Ruda was, all the men said she was the best.

Magda sweated and moaned, and Ruda pressed and could feel the wetness dripping from Magda, seeping down her thick thighs. She began to moan and groan as she climaxed, and then she sighed, her body shuddered. Ruda prayed it was over, she could hardly breathe.

Ruda had to wait for Magda to bathe before she was allowed to wash. Magda tossed a few clothes from a trunk, told Ruda she could have them. They were good clothes, hardly worn, and Ruda clutched them tightly. Magda was dressed in one of her tents, slipping on gold bangles, and redoing her make-up. 'Go on, sweetface, get yourself all cleaned up and out of here. When you're through, come into the office. I'll give you some money, don't expect a lot, I need every cent I earn, but I'll see you have enough to get to another big city, maybe give you a few contacts.'

Ruda slipped into Magda's water in the bath, it was still quite warm, and she soaped her body, leaned back. She dreamed of the lion tamer, dreamed of Luis Grimaldi. She had to get to America, she had to find Kellerman, she had to find Luis Grimaldi wherever he was.

She buttoned up the dress: it was too short and the neckline gaped on her thin shoulders. She had on a pair of silk camiknickers, the crotch hung low and they were many sizes too large, but they were silk. She pulled on the nice checked coat with padded shoulders, then crossed to the dressing-table to brush her hair and see if she could find a safety-pin to fix the neckline of her dress. She looked over the powder-strewn dressing-table, with pots of cream and make-up jars littered everywhere. There was a large box of coloured beaded necklaces and cheap bangles, but no safety-pin.

Ruda inched open the small drawer beneath the mirror; a leather jewel-box was open. She stared at the rows of rings, picked one up and squinted at the shaft. It was gold. She looked at the rings again. They were Magda's famous diamonds, the rings she wore on every finger.

Ruda took a handful, then started for the door. She went back and took a necklace, stuffing it into her pocket. Her heart was pounding. She eased open the door and crept down the stairs, past the kitchens, past the lavatories. She saw no one, but as she reached the entrance to the club she heard voices. Magda was giving the barman hell about not watering the drinks enough.

She was out and down the street, running in a panic, not sure which way to go, or where. She kept putting her hands into her coat pocket, making sure the rings were there.

She returned to a club where she had worked with Rudi and spoke to the manager who gave her the once-over. She was looking very classy – he fingered her coat. 'Found yourself a rich American, have you?'

Ruda smiled. 'No, something better. I got people, a family with money, and they want a contact for passports.'

The manager shrugged and said he couldn't help her; he knew of no one dealing in any foreign documents or currency.

'Kellerman. I want to talk to Kellerman. I know you

know him and I know he's somewhere in the Kreuzberg district. Now you tell me, or I tip off the authorities. I know this club is a contact drop . . .'

Ruda found Kellerman sitting in a bar playing poker. It had been a long walk, four hours. She didn't have money for a taxi, even for a bus. He didn't recognise her, and she didn't remind him of where they had last met. He took her into a back room and eyed her, leaning against the wall, like he was some American movie star – all three feet of him.

'So what do you want?'

'Visa, passport, ticket to America.'

He laughed out loud. 'Oh, yeah, what makes you think I can get them?'

Ruda sat down and swung her leg. Her legs were good and she inched up her skirt. 'Friend told me. I got something to trade.'

Kellerman touched her knee. 'Baby, if it's your cunt, forget it. What you want costs a lot more than a fuck.'

'Maybe I've got a lot more . . .'

Kellerman shoved his hands into his tiny pockets. 'Let's see what you got.'

Ruda was no fool, she had already stashed the bulk of the stones under a broken-down truck outside the bar. She brought out a couple of rings and held them in the palm of her hand. Kellerman picked one up, examined it, then prodded her palm with his short squat finger. 'Good stones . . . but this isn't enough.'

'I have more, a lot more, and I've got a marriage licence.'

'You'll need a birth certificate, inoculation, visa, passport, then a ticket.'

Ruda deflated. How much was this going to cost? She held out her hand again. 'I've got more, a necklace, diamonds. How much do I need?'

Kellerman touched her palm again, and then drew up

the sleeve of her coat. He saw the tattoo. She tried to withdraw her wrist, but he held on to her. "S OK, I won't hurt you. Where were you?"

Ruda bowed her head. 'Does it matter?'

'I guess not, all that matters is you survived, eh, I'm not prying, see, I got one too.' He pulled up his shirt-sleeve. Then he flushed and pulled his cuff down. 'I don't show it to anybody. I was at Birkenau.'

'So was I . . .' She virtually whispered it.

He looked up into her face, reaching to touch her cheek with his short stubby hand. He had no need to say a word, there was mutual understanding in their eyes. It was not compassionate, or loving, it was a contact. Ruda bent down, to kneel, and he cradled her in his arms. Still they did not speak, and it was Kellerman who broke the embrace. Stepping back he said, softly, 'You never get down on your knees to anyone. Look at me, show me a fist, show me some fire in those eyes. I'll get us out of this shit. Get up, up on your feet, girl.' He began to pace up and down, strange blunt, short steps. 'We got to find a buyer first, sell the stones, turn them into cash, then we can do the deal. If you got more like the ones you showed me, we can get enough.'

'We? I don't understand, what's with this we?'

He gave her a cheeky wide smile. He had perfect white teeth, his face was cherubic under the thick black curly hair. 'Yeah, that's the deal – Ruda, you said your name was?'

'Yes, Ruda—' She could not mention the last name.

'The deal is, Ruda, I get the documents, make all the arrangements, but I want to come with you. We both go to America, and I'll get us a licence. We get married, you go as Ruda Kellerman, it'll make it a lot easier. I already got my papers, I just never had enough dough to get out of this shit-hole.'

She hesitated, and then smiled. He looked up at her. 'You know, when you smile it changes your whole face.'

'Same could be said of you.'

He chuckled. 'I guess maybe we've neither had too much to smile about, but have we got a deal?'

She nodded, but then held up her hand. 'But it's just a marriage of convenience, right? And where the stones go, I go? Agreed?'

He laughed and then, reaching up, swung the door open wide with a flourish. 'Let's go, partner, and America here we come!'

It had taken two months, a nerve-racking time. Ruda and Kellerman stayed together in his small rented room. He never made any advances towards her; instead they played cards together, and he started to teach her how to read and write. They felt safe with each other, they liked each other. He found out about the magician, and said she would come to no harm, he would take care of her. And he did. He pocketed a lot of the money for himself, but he kept his promise. He got them to America.

Magda had sent all her boys searching for Ruda, sure she would turn up on some street corner some place, some day. The days turned into weeks, months, and Magda had to admit she was wasting her time and money searching for the little bitch thief. But she never forgot Ruda: every time she slipped a ring on to her finger she remembered the little bitch thief. She had never told anybody of her part in the murder, but she had kept the knife – as a memento, a warning never to turn soft on any of her tarts, on anybody else for that matter. The knife had travelled from apartment to apartment, club to club, until she had stowed it away. She somehow knew that one day Ruda would come back, one day she would see her again . . . and when she did, she would think about cutting her throat open.

Magda ran her nail along the serrated edge. She had been right, she had come back. But when she had seen her . . . it was strange, she hadn't hated her, had really wanted to talk to her. She had been ready to forgive but Ruda had played a stupid game, pretending she couldn't understand German, that she didn't know Magda. Well, the Baroness, or whoever Ruda pretended she was, would be sorry. This time she wouldn't be able to hide away, there would be no place in Berlin she could hide. Remembering made her head throb and she searched for her tablets.

Eric slammed back into the office. He was soaked, his hair dripping wet. 'I lost her, she was going from club to club, she was very drunk. Then I went in one door, and she must have walked out another. She disappeared.'

Magda hurled papers from her desk. 'You fucking little queen, all you had to do was follow the bitch!' Her face was puce with rage.

'I followed her, I've been up and down the fucking streets. I'm soaked – it's comin' down in torrents out there!'

'Get out of my sight, you useless piece of shit!'

Eric leaned on her desk. 'I'm all you've got – you big fat cow. You haven't got a friend in the world, Magda. I am the only person who can put up with you.'

'There's the door, Eric, and that thing attached is the handle. Turn it and walk. Go on, I don't need you, I don't need anybody – I never have. I have never depended on anyone or anything but *me*! Because that's all I've ever had, *me. I made me and my money is mine!*'

Eric hesitated, and she laughed, her heavy phlegmy laugh. How many years had he put up with that hulk? But he had no other place to go, she kept him, and he had an easy life. Besides, she couldn't last many more years. She was eighty, maybe even more. So he laughed, and she held open her arms, her mammoth body shaking.

'Come on, make up, come and give me a hug.'

He let her embrace him, her beads clanking against his head. He could hear the rattle of her chest, her heavy hideous breathing that he had lain next to for fifteen years. She settled back on the cushions, and said she'd start calling the clubs, she'd soon trace her.

'Who is she? I mean, what's so important about her?'

Magda dialled, and waited. 'She stole from me, Eric. I was like a mother to that girl, and she pretended she didn't know me. Well, she's going to know who I am.'

Eric eased off his tie, removed his Gucci loafers with their little tassels. They were stained round the edges. Magda made call after call, club after club, getting more angry, breathier, lighting a cigarette, puffing and panting, describing Vebekka, even the clothes she had worn, down to the cape with the sable trim. She kept on saying it was urgent, she had to find her.

Eric pulled off his socks; his feet felt cold. He was so intent on inspecting his feet he didn't even hear anything strange; he only looked up because the room was so quiet. She sat well back in her chair, her head lolled on her bosom, a cigarette still burning in her fat hand.

'Magda? Magda?'

Eric inched around the desk, peering at her. The poodle suddenly started clawing at her leg, wanting attention. Eric took the cigarette from her fingers, stubbed it out. He called her name again, then felt for the pulse at her neck. He withdrew his hand and gave her body a little push. She slowly sagged to one side, and her arm slid from the desk and hung limply over her chair.

He gave a brief, dry laugh like a hiccup, and quickly

covered his mouth. He shooed the dog away and it scuttled beneath the desk. He was about to rush out of the office when he remembered he was barefoot. As he slipped his feet into his loafers, he had another good look at Magda and giggled. It was his club, all his now, and he wanted to hug himself.

The phone rang. He hesitated, deciding whether or not to answer, and in the end he snatched it up. It was the barman at the Vagabond Club returning Magda's call. The woman she wanted to know about had just walked in. 'It doesn't matter, Magda's dead,' said Eric. He heard the shocked voice asking how and when, and he beamed, but kept his voice to a hushed whisper. 'I have to go, I have to get the *Polizei*.'

'Jesus Christ, what happened?'

'Heart attack, I think.'

'My God, when?'

'Oh, about five minutes ago.'

'Oh, shit, will you be closing the club?'

'No . . . no, I don't think so, she wouldn't have wanted that. Nothin'll change, just that I'll be running the show from now on. So, if you'll excuse me . . .' Eric carefully replaced the receiver, looked at the peroxided head of his wife. He couldn't see her face – he was glad about that. He whistled to the dog, and grabbed it by the scruff of its neck. 'Your life, sweetface, hangs on a thread. You had better be very, very nice to me.' Eric didn't even notice the carving knife on Magda's desk as he walked out of the office.

CHAPTER FIFTEEN

VEBEKKA EASED her way to the bar. This was the third she had come to. The champagne had dulled her senses, she was confused and disorientated but she wanted something, anything, to wake her. The rain had begun again, a downpour. Her hair was wet, her cape soaked, but she pushed her way through the customers, calling to the barman.

She felt a man brush against her. He smiled apologetically and then signalled to the barman, clicking his fingers impatiently. His heavy gold bracelet and thick ring gleamed, his cheap suit and white polyester shirt were picked out in the fluorescent light.

'It's raining again?'

He said it pleasantly and smiled, his teeth as white as his shirt. She could see speckles of dandruff on his shoulders, and she giggled. 'I don't speak German, I'm American – or French.'

He spoke in pidgin English, leaning his elbow casually on the bar facing her. He asked Vebekka if she would like to drink with him. She nodded, asking for champagne. He hesitated, and moved closer.

'It's very expensive here.'

She looked at him with a half-smile, and asked for a cigarette. He patted his pockets in search of his packet but she leaned against him, slipped her hand into his trouser pocket, withdrew the cigarettes and giggled. Confident, he slipped his arm around her shoulders and then, as the barman came over, asked for champagne.

She drank the entire glass in one gulp and banged it on to the bar.

'Let's sit down.'

She shrugged and wandered off. Taking her hand, he guided her to a booth and she tossed her cape on to the seat.

'What's your name?'

'Vebekka.'

She drank another glass, again gulping it down as if it were water. He moved alongside her; his hand began to feel along her thigh. She suddenly felt sick, and she pushed his hand away, mumbling that she needed to go to the bathroom. He eased her past himself, feeling her thighs and backside. She stumbled, and he caught hold of her. 'Maybe you need some help . . .'

They headed towards the door marked 'Toilets', and by this time he had one arm around her, the other feeling under her cashmere sweater. The door led into a small corridor, ladies' and men's toilets to either side.

Vebekka staggered into the ladies'. She vomited into the toilet, the room began to spin, her legs went from beneath her. She swore, pushing herself up against the wall. She began to pant, trying not to be sick again. The cubicle door opened – she hadn't bothered to lock it.

'You OK?'

'I have to go. Can you call me a taxi?'

He closed the door behind him and locked it. 'Sure . . . in a few minutes.'

She didn't even attempt to stop him pulling down her panties, heaving up her sweater, she just leaned against him. He undid his flies and pulled her hands to hold his penis. Her head lolled against him, and he rammed her against the wall. She half laughed: it was as if she was on a train, her back thudding against the wall. She kept on half laughing, as he forced himself inside her. It was over, and she laughed louder. He buttoned up his trousers, listened in case anyone had come in, and then unlocked the door.

'You call that a fuck? When's the next train through here?' She laughed loudly, and then slowly slid down the wall, her underwear round her ankles. The tiles felt nice and cool; she lay down and rested her cheek on the nice cold tiles.

She was hauled to her feet. The man literally dragged her out – she was only semi-conscious. He dumped her in the corridor and went back into the club. He crossed to the bar, told the barman there was a drunken woman lying outside the toilets, went back to the booth, snatched his champagne bottle and made his way out.

The barman crooked his finger to the bouncer hovering at the main club entrance.

Vebekka was thrown out of the club, fell into the gutter, staggered up and stumbled away. She managed to pull her pants up, but she had lost her cape and her sweater was still half off. She kept on walking in the pouring rain. She stopped and looked upwards, holding her mouth open to catch the water: she felt almost happy.

Three skinheads passed and, seeing she was drunk, began messing around with her, pushing and shoving her until she fell against a wall. She put up her hands in a pitiful attempt to save herself, but one of them kicked, kept on kicking her, called her a filthy tart, and they walked on.

Vebekka sat hunched for a while, and then helped herself up by the wall; she began to be violently sick again.

The Baron slammed the taxi door. Helen didn't ask if he had found Vebekka, but instructed the driver to go to the next club he knew of: so far they had been to four, each one more tawdry than the last. They sat in silence, the Baron clenching and unclenching his hands as Helen stared from the window, glancing this way and that in the hope of seeing Vebekka. Then she leaned forwards and asked the driver to stop. Turning to look out of the back window, she could see the reeling figure stumbling along. Helen shouted, 'We've found her!' She was the first out, catching Vebekka in her arms as she fell again.

The Baron took off his coat and wrapped it around his wife. 'Put her in the back.'

Vebekka rested her head against Helen's shoulder.

'Dear God, look at her face. Have you got a hankie, Louis? She's bleeding.'

He snatched his handkerchief from his pocket. 'Aren't we all? Here.'

Helen gently dabbed the cut on Vebekka's forehead. 'She's been drinking.'

'I would say that is obvious.'

They arrived back at the Grand Hotel, Louis and Helen holding Vebekka between them; they almost had to carry her in. The manager rushed forwards, his face concerned, and the Baron brushed him aside. 'My wife fell, but she is all right. Just call the lift please.'

The lift operator stared hard: the woman was so drunk she virtually fell to her knees. He eased open the lift gate and stepped back. The Baron scooped up Vebekka in his arms and Helen hurriedly opened the doors to their suite. She followed Louis to the bedroom, and he called out for Hylda, dumping Vebekka on the bed. She moaned, and turned her face into the pillow.

Helen tapped on Hylda's door, and she whispered she would only be a moment, she had changed for bed.

'It doesn't matter, Hylda, just put on a dressing-gown. It's the Baroness. She . . . she's had a little accident, she fell.'

Helen rejoined the Baron, who stood staring down at his wife. 'Look at her, take a good look, Helen. So much for your damned doctor.'

He had such fury building inside him that he had to walk out – he couldn't speak to Hylda. He didn't even want to face Helen, but she followed him out, closing the door behind her. 'Hylda's bathing her, she's bruised all over her stomach, as if she's been kicked. Louis? Did you hear what I said?'

He stood with his back to her, his hands in fists at his sides. 'She stinks like a whore.'

Helen poured a drink, asked if he wanted one, but he shook his head. She sighed. 'I blame myself, the moment we knew she had left the hotel we should have gone out and searched. We wasted time.'

He whipped round. 'Have you any idea how many times, how many nights I've had to go looking for her? Searching every seedy rundown club, every red-light district? She's been found in alleys, in back rooms, she's been fucked for the price of a drink, and tonight was probably no different. You smelt her, she smelt of sex and booze – vomit. She sickens me, disgusts me, she's been picking up men—'

'You don't know that!'

He looked at Helen as if she were an idiot. 'I don't? She has played these games for years – *for years!*'

'I don't think she knows what she's doing. Are you asking me to believe she *likes* what she has been doing? Likes to be beaten up, kicked . . . She looks as if she's been kicked.'

He snapped, 'That's what she goes out for, Helen, she wants to be beaten, she *wants to be treated like a whore, she likes it – she is a whore!*'

Helen faced him, becoming really angry. 'Don't shout at me, Louis. I'm right here, OK? No woman likes to be treated like a whore – that is a male chauvinistic, ridiculous statement! Women who work the streets don't necessarily like what they are doing.'

'Oh, please, Helen, don't. Don't give me your psycho-analytical theories, I don't want them tonight, I don't want them period.'

'It is not a theory, it's a fact. No woman likes to be beaten, but if you beat her long enough, you will——'

He gripped her tightly. 'I have never beaten, struck or hurt her, I have had reason to, God knows, I have had reason, you don't understand . . .'

'I am trying to.'

The scream made them both freeze. Helen ran to the bedroom, as Hylda ran out. Her face was stricken. 'It is happening again! Please——'

Vebekka was rigid, her hands clenched, her teeth clamped together. The colours were cutting across her mind, terrible bright flashing colours, reds, greens . . . and she felt each flash. They kept on coming, blinding, as if her brain was going to explode . . .

Helen tried to talk to her, but the pain was so intense Vebekka didn't know who was there. All she wanted was the pain in her head to stop. Louis went to the other side of the bed, leaned over his wife, and she rose up. The scream was low, as if trapped inside her, her hands were like claws as she hit out, attacked the pain, clawed at the pain. Louis backed away, his hand to his cheek. She had scratched his face, drawn blood. Helen ran to the door, shouting that she would call Dr Franks. Vebekka was thrashing at the bed, her body rigid.

Hylda was terrified, she hung back at the door, shaking, holding one hand in the other. Helen called Franks, who said he would be there within half an hour, then slipped her arm around Hylda, whispering that she could go back to her room. Hylda clutched her hand. 'She bit me, she bit my hand!'

Helen forced Hylda to show her hand, and was shocked – the toothmarks were clear, the blood forming in deep red bruises. 'Dear God! Run cold water over it, Hylda, and I'll get you a bandage.'

Louis stood at a distance from the bed, searching his pockets for his handkerchief, then remembered he had given it to Vebekka in the taxi. He drew out a tissue from a box on the dressing-table and dabbed his face. He stared at Helen in the mirror.

'Franks will have to take her into his clinic. I'm finished, Helen, this is it.'

Helen nodded. 'Yes, yes, I think so too. I'll pack her things, maybe if I call him back now I can catch him before he leaves. Perhaps he will be able to make arrangements tonight.'

The first spot had made even Schmidt stand and applaud. Ruda was on form – she was brilliant. She had been flushed with excitement as Grimaldi had helped her change. 'Ringling's scout's in, did you know, Luis?'

He told her he did. 'You got them to their feet. It was the cartwheel – you should have seen Zapashny's face, he was open-mouthed. I could feel his envy!'

She began to redo her make-up. 'Zapashny? What's he doing here?'

Luis laughed. 'Getting jealous! I've heard Gunther Gebel is retiring. They must be looking for someone to replace him at Ringling.'

She turned in a panic. 'Oh, God, he's not here to replace me, is he?'

'Don't be stupid, you'll see them coming here in droves to get to Ringling's man – get him to see their acts, bribe him, you know the scene.'

Ruda brushed her hair, her hands shaking. Luis held out

her black shirt, but she pushed it away, drawing on her tight black jodhpurs. She stamped into the gleaming, polished boots, then held out her arms as he eased the shirt over her head, careful not to disturb her hair. She buttoned the collar. 'God, I'm so nervous. This is supposed to be a dress rehearsal!'

'Everyone else will be nervous, too, you can bet on it. You look wonderful! Now – make them get on their feet for the next spot. You pull it off and we'll be in New York, guarantee it!'

Ruda checked her appearance and tightened the wide black leather belt. She breathed in deeply, forcing herself to relax. All in black, her hair drawn away from her face, her eyes thick with black eyeliner, she looked like a cat herself – her strong lithe body was taut with nerves.

'OK, I'm ready. How long have I got?'

Luis checked his watch, told her she had plenty of time. All the acts were running over time, everyone playing to the visitors, pulling out the stops. She pulled down her shirt, seemed to give herself a small nod of approval. 'OK, I'm ready.'

Luis stood back and gave her a smile. 'Good luck! I'll be right by the ringside. You'll need an umbrella, it's pouring.'

Ruda carried a large black umbrella and carefully side-stepped the puddles as she hurried to the tents. Luis ran from the trailer and entered the big tent via the audience flaps. He made his way down to the ringside and sat waiting. The clowns were throwing their foam-filled buckets, chasing and tumbling, skidding on the plastic protective floor covering, an electric car bursting into smoke and flames as they reached their finale. The lights dimmed . . . It was strange to end in silence; usually the sound of thunderous applause accompanied the clowns, along with the high-pitched shriek of children's laughter.

Luis looked up to the viewing box, could see the Ringling

Brothers' scout standing with his back to the ring, talking animatedly, drinking champagne.

The crew moved like lightning, clearing the props, buckets and ladders, rolling the floor covering, raking up the sawdust. As the ringmaster announced the Polish group of bareback riders, they virtually stampeded into the ring, twelve of them, wearing brilliantly coloured American Indian headdresses, whooping and screaming, covering the last inches of clearance of the ring. Then the lights beamed on the riders, picking them out as they formed a fast-moving semicircle. Luis moved into position, saw their boys carrying in the cages, getting ready to erect the safety cage around the ring.

Dr Franks waited impatiently by the lift at the Grand Hotel, carrying a small medical bag. He barely gave the operator time to open the gates before he snapped out that he wanted Baron Maréchal's suite. As the lift moved up, he checked his watch, hoping the ambulance would arrive quickly.

Helen let him in, and they hurried to Vebekka's bedside. 'She's been quieter for about fifteen minutes.' Franks nodded, and Helen closed the bedroom doors. 'She left the hotel, she's been drinking.'

Franks held Vebekka's wrist and took her pulse, his face set in concentration. 'How did you let that happen?'

Helen blushed. 'She seemed so well, we were going to dine in the restaurant, and she was dressing. Next moment she had gone.'

Franks withdrew the bedclothes. 'Have you given her something? Anything to sedate her?'

'No, nothing, she was behaving as if she was having some kind of epileptic fit and then she calmed.'

Franks took out his stethoscope, examined her chest. 'How did she get these bruises?'

'We don't know. We were out looking for her and found her in the street.'

Vebekka moaned softly. Franks sat by her. 'Are you awake? It's Albert, Dr Franks.'

She opened her eyes and whispered softly that she knew who he was. He explained that he just wanted to examine her bruises, to make sure there was no internal damage. He rolled up her nightdress, saw the dark bruises on her belly, and gently pressed her body. 'Well, what have you been up to, huh?'

He eased her nightdress down, and drew the covers over her. She smiled sweetly. 'I went out. I had too much to drink.'

She looked past Franks to Helen, and turned away. 'Do you want to leave us alone, Helen, do you mind?'

Franks waited until Helen had left the room, and then he leaned close. 'What were you up to?'

The Baron sat impatiently in a chair, his foot tapping, waiting, waiting for Franks to come out of the bedroom. 'What in God's name is he doing in there?'

Helen looked towards the bedroom. 'They're talking.' The telephone rang and she answered it. The ambulance was downstairs, she told them to wait.

Franks came out of the bedroom, closing the door quietly. 'The ambulance is downstairs.'

He nodded, placing his bag down. 'I don't like to disturb her, she's sleeping now, she didn't need anything, she's exhausted.'

The Baron kept his voice low, afraid to wake her. 'I want her out of here, tonight.'

Franks sat on the edge of the sofa. 'She remembers everything she did, where she went, even the name of the clubs – Mama Magda's! Notorious old woman. She remembers, Baron . . .'

The Baron pointed to his cheek. 'She knows she did this?'

Franks shook his head. 'No, she remembers up to the point she was brought into the hotel. Would you like me to look at the—'

The Baron interrupted, 'It's just a scratch, but Hylda – she bit her hand! Don't you think you should call whoever is necessary and take my wife away?'

'I am not sure—'

'I am, doctor. I want her out of the hotel – tonight.'

Franks looked at Helen and asked what she felt. She hesitated. 'If I hadn't seen with my own eyes, seen how violent she was, how incredibly strong – neither of us could hold her down.'

'I see,' he said, not waiting for Helen to finish. He pursed his lips. 'You know I am loath to lose her to a hospital, be it mental or otherwise. I really think we had some interesting things come out of the session today, and I would very much like to continue.'

The Baron stood up and straightened his jacket. 'I refuse to take any further responsibility for my wife. If you wish her to be taken to your clinic, that is up to you. I want her out of the hotel.'

'Out of your life, Baron?'

'Yes. *Yes!*'

Franks nodded and looked at his watch. 'Very well, I will take her. She can stay at my clinic.' He opened his bag, and sifted through it, taking out papers. 'I will need you to look these over and sign them, releasing Vebekka into my charge. This will mean it will be my decision to certify her if, and only if, I feel there is nothing more I can

378

do. If this is the outcome, you will have to cover all financial costs for her to be sent to—'

'Doctor, just give me the papers.' The Baron took them to the writing desk and searched for his pen. Franks looked at Helen, raised his eyebrow slightly and then went into the bedroom.

Vebekka was lying with her hands resting on the cover. She turned to him and smiled. 'I'm hungry.'

Franks took her hand. 'Vebekka, I am going to take you with me to my clinic. There is no need to be afraid, but I think it would be for the best.'

She closed her eyes. 'Oh, God, what did I do?'

Franks kept hold of her hand. 'Nothing too bad, but you need to be cared for, need to—' Her hand began to grip his tighter, tighter, he was astonished at the strength.

'It's coming back—'

Franks could not release his hand. Her body twisted, he tried to stand but she was so strong that she pulled him down beside her. She was panting and her body began to go into spasm. The pain in her head – it was coming again, the bright lights, the colours. Franks wrenched his hand free and ran to the door. He shouted to get the ambulance attendants up immediately, then he returned to the bed. She gave him such a helpless look, opening and shutting her mouth, unable to tell him what was hurting so much. Her hands were shaking as she touched her temples. On and on went the piercing flashes of colour.

Franks leaned over her. 'Tell me. Tell me. What is it?'

Her mouth opened wide, but she was becoming rigid. The terror on her face became a frozen mask, the cement was creeping upwards, reaching her knees, her belly, pressing down on her chest. Any moment it would reach her neck, and though she could hear Dr Franks, could see him, she could not communicate, could not tell him that

379

the oozing thick whiteness was inching up into her throat, suffocating her. Franks saw her eyes glaze over but remain open, her hands become rigid. He turned with relief as the attendants carried in a stretcher.

Standing by the open doors was the Baron. He watched as they wrapped blankets around his wife, eased her stiffened hands to her side and then strapped two thick leather belts around the stretcher.

Luis moved closer to the caged arena. A massive single spotlight picked out Ruda. The tigers moved in a circle around her in the darkness. Twice she gave the command for the circle to break, for the tigers to begin forming the pyramid on the stacked plinths, still in the darkness. Their faces entered and disappeared from the carefully orchestrated spot, its light spreading inch by inch as the electrician saw the cats obey the command.

Ruda was sweating. She gave the command to Roja again and he kept on running, picking up speed. '*Roja, uppp uppp* . . . *blue* . . . *blue* . . .' Roja suddenly sprang back, and Ruda kept up the commands as, one by one, the tigers moved to their plinths. Blue, red, green . . . the spotlight spread and they were all in position. Ruda gave the command for 'Up!' and they sat back on their haunches, their front paws swiping at the air. She gave the command 'Down!' and they perched. With her left hand she gave Mike the signal to release the lionesses. They came down the tunnel within seconds, and she had to give her commands over and over again as they refused the plinths.

Luis could feel the sweat trickling down his back; he gripped the steel bars, swearing at himself. It was his fault, she had been right, the new plinths were putting them all off their stride. Luis looked up to the viewing room. Zapashny was deep in conversation with the Ringling

Brothers scout, pointing to Ruda in the ring, back at himself. He would know she was in trouble, and Luis guessed he was taking pleasure in giving his professional opinion to the scout, eager to tell him how much better his own act was.

The lionesses had reached their plinths. Ruda gave them the command to rest their front paws on the pyramid above them. Once, twice, they refused, snarling and growling; the tigers began to spit, but they held their positions, and Mike got the signal for the two massive male lions to enter the tunnel.

Three positions on the top part of the plinth were still vacant. The two lions ran to either side of Ruda, as rehearsed and, as rehearsed, she looked to the tunnel, bent down to one lion as if asking him a question, back to the plinths: three places, only two lions. She walked to the tunnel, followed by one lion, turned back to admonish him – all rehearsed. As she looked down the tunnel, she got a push from the lion – rehearsed. She turned and wagged her finger.

The children would be screaming by now, hysterical with unabashed delight at the big lions teasing her. Ruda had her hands on her hips in mock temper; she gave the two lions strolling around their command to get up on the plinths, calling out down the tunnel.

It happened again. Both lions refused their jump, once . . . twice. Grimaldi wanted to scream out, but Ruda was holding her own, keeping calm. Again she gave the command; now they obeyed and Grimaldi sighed with relief. He looked up to the viewing tower, the Russian was staring into the ring; he had to know what exceptional training it took to retain the pyramid of sixteen tigers, four lionesses, two lions, all seated.

Ruda gave the signal for Mamon to be released. He came down the tunnel at full run and galloped in. As soon as he entered the ring he came to Ruda as if he were late, and lay down in front of her – again perfectly rehearsed. He rolled over, legs in the air. Ruda stamped her foot, pointed to the plinth, and Mamon rolled and rolled.

Unrehearsed, two tigers started to swipe at each other. She crossed over and shouted, and they turned on her. Again she yelled at them and they calmed down. Now she began the carefully practised act with Mamon, pointing to the top twenty-foot-high plinth. He looked up and shook his huge head, she wagged her finger at him. He turned round and made as if to run back down the tunnel. Ruda grabbed his tail, began to pull him back – all rehearsed.

Mamon and Ruda had a tug of war; all the while she was feeding the commands to the cats still waiting on the plinths. Mamon appeared to be on form, he didn't hesitate over a single command, he was on time, in position, even when she rode his back. To the onlooker, he was performing faultlessly, but Ruda could detect he was impatient, as if pacing himself; like any star, he seemed to be withholding an energy. She kept an eye on him, but he continued working well, right up until the final command for him to jump to the highest point of the pyramid. All the cats were seated, all under control, waiting. Ruda gave the command, then a second time. '*Red – yup . . . Ma'angel, up, up!*' Mamon tossed his head.

Luis knew Ruda could not hold the pyramid formation much longer: they were starting to pick up on Mamon's unrest. Suddenly Mamon backed away, prowled around the back of the plinths. He stared at Ruda from beneath the pyramid, and then went low, crouching on his haunches.

Up in the viewing tower, all three men were standing, looking down into the ring. Ruda stared angrily at Mamon, '*Red, red, red . . . Ma'angel!*'

He suddenly leaped forwards, as if he were going to

spring at her, then he veered off, and like lightning he sprang from one step to another, up and up, until he was on the top plinth, up on his haunches. At a command they all rose up, some placing their paws on the plinth next to them. They looked like a mountain of brilliant colours. On command they moved again, jumping down in perfect order, and Roja led them out and back down the tunnel.

As rehearsed, Mamon held his position at the top. Ruda stood by the plinths, slapping the bottom one with her hand for Mamon to come down. He shook his head, refused to move – rehearsed. Ruda sat down giving a shrug of her shoulders to the audience as, behind her, Mamon moved down plinth by plinth. Ruda was giving him commands: *'Red – green – blue'*, but pretending she did not know he was directly behind her, within a foot of her. The children would always scream out, at this point, aided by the ringmaster, *'He's behind you!'*

Mamon eased his body back, balancing himself, and then gently placed his front paws on her shoulders. Ruda feigned surprise, turned virtually in his forelegs. Mamon was dependent on his own balance – in no way would Ruda be able to take his weight – it appeared as if he was resting against her. Slowly she slipped her arms around him in an embrace. The spotlight shrank down, down, until the two were framed like lovers, the huge lion's body swamping Ruda's. She gave the command for him to know she was stepping away, and then he came off the plinth. As she took her bow, she held her left hand out, towards Mamon's mouth. This was very dangerous, more dangerous than putting her head into his mouth – then the trainer would place a hand over the animal's nose, who wouldn't shut his mouth if he couldn't breathe! Mamon held her hand gently in his mouth, as she continued her bows. Finally, she pretended he was dragging her to the tunnel.

Blackout, the lights went, and the hands ran to dismantle

the arena. The lights came on, Ruda took her bow, and then left the arena. Grimaldi looked up to the viewing tower, the scout from Ringling Brothers was applauding, even though they couldn't hear him as the box was soundproofed. Grimaldi punched the air with his fist.

Ruda made sure the animals were back in their cages, fed and settled down for the night before she made her way back to the trailer. Luis had helped take down the cages, stack and prop them up ready for the show the following night. He returned to the trailer with a bottle of champagne. Ruda came in, her shirt soaked in sweat, and he swept her up into his arms. 'They were applauding, they were cheering you!'

She smiled and slumped on to the benches. 'They asked to see me, want to see me right away but get me the bandages and the disinfectant, quick!'

Luis looked puzzled.

'Do as I say, they want me over there in a minute.'

Ruda unbuttoned her shirt cuff, removed the protective wad beneath her sleeve. There were deep indentations of toothmarks, the dark bruises forming fast. 'Jesus Christ! Did he break the skin?'

Luis carried over the first-aid box and knelt down beside her.

'No, no, it's just bruised. It was really tough out there, they were all playing up.'

Luis looked up at her, and carefully pushed her sleeve up her arm. 'You mean your fucking angel was, you'll have to cut that part of the act. Jesus God – he could have taken your arm off.'

'But he didn't. Just put some antiseptic over it, then get me a clean shirt.' She wrapped a bandage around her arm, and got into a clean shirt, an identical black one. The old one was torn, Mamon's teeth had sliced the silk. She flung a coat around her shoulders; he went to get his, to accompany her, but she patted his cheek. 'They just want to talk to me, Luis, you wait here. I won't be long.'

He stepped back and flushed, saying he understood. He'd wait, maybe cook dinner. She smiled, said that she was hungry and then left him. He watched her holding the coat above her head against the steady rain.

Luis knew her arm must hurt like hell. She never ceased to amaze him, all the cuts and knocks she'd taken during training and never complained about. He stacked the first-aid equipment away, and then remembered the black tin box he had taken from her wardrobe. He had better replace it before she discovered it was missing. She'd know he had tried to open it: he had damaged the lid – maybe he could fix it.

Luis was about to press back the damaged lid without opening it, but then his curiosity overcame him. He took a screwdriver and began to loosen the tiny screws at the back. He inched the lid open. There was her wedding ring, still in its box: she had only worn it for a year, then said she had to take it off because she used the stick and whip and the ring cut into her finger. There was another wedding ring, maybe the one Kellerman had given to her; he had never seen it before. There was their marriage licence from Florida, still in the envelope, and then beneath that, tied up in a pale blue ribbon, were newspaper clippings, brown with age, neatly folded, as if treasured. Luis thought at first they would be reviews from one of her shows. He untied the ribbon; the cuttings smelled musty, the creases almost splitting the paper in two. He carefully unfolded the first, and stared at the headline: 'MENGELE STILL ALIVE IN BRAZIL'. He checked each tiny scrap of paper; every one of them referred to Joseph Mengele, the Angel of Death. He read snatches of the articles, one describing how Mengele had made sure the chimneys of Birkenau always blazed, heated by thirty fires. The ovens had large openings, one hundred and twenty openings, and each one could take three corpses at a time; they could dispose of three hundred and sixty corpses every half-hour – all the time it took to reduce human flesh to ashes. Seven hundred and twenty people per hour, 17,280 in twenty-four hours. Dr Joseph Mengele made sure the ovens were filled to capacity; he and he alone had the power to choose who lived and who died, to direct the terrified masses to the ovens with his murderous efficiency.

Luis felt his blood grow cold, as he read the dates and figures. May 1944, 360,000; June 1944, 512,000; July 1944, 442,000.

Ruda had written over some articles, in her childish scrawl: 'Joseph Mengele, Papa'.

Grimaldi refolded one scrap after another. Some were articles cut from journals, describing the diabolical experiments the Angel of Death had performed on tiny children, with or without anaesthetic, depending on his mood or the availability of medication. Article after article described Mengele's passion for furthering the Aryan race, this fanatical killer of babies, of women, of men – all defenceless, desperate human beings. He had embraced cruelty beyond a sane person's credibility, had been a madman let loose. One newspaper piece was around a small pebble, or stone, he couldn't tell; as he opened it, the cracks made the paper split in two, as if this particular piece had been read and folded, opened and folded. The article described the reported death of Dr Joseph Mengele, his body found on a beach in Brazil; the paper was dated 1976. The article discussed the possibility that it was not the real Joseph Mengele; forensic scientists had left for Brazil to begin tests.

Luis began to restack the clippings, wrapping them in the same way as he had found them, tying them with the worn ribbon. She had kept them as a woman would keep love letters, as if they were treasures. He carefully replaced each item in the tin box, rescrewed the back, and returned the box to her wardrobe. As he stepped down from the stool in front of her dressing-table, he remembered some of the things she had said to him, often in rage: how he would never know what pain she had suffered, that the worst scars were those inside. He bowed his head and sighed, he had never even attempted to understand. But, he told himself, Ruda had never wanted to discuss the past.

He looked around the kitchen, opening cupboards to see what he could cook, wanting to do something special for her. He decided he would go out and buy some groceries from one of the all-night shops, maybe get some champagne. He felt a need to start afresh, wanted a second chance and, if she got the Ringling contract, they could have a new life. He wouldn't fight her any more, he would fight alongside her, for her.

He passed the meat trailer. The lights were on, and he went inside.

'Mike? I'm going out for some groceries, taking the jeep. If you see Ruda, tell her I won't be long.'

Mike grinned, said the word was already going round, the Ringling Brothers scout was having talks with Ruda. Grimaldi winked, said not to count their eggs before they hatched. He looked out, the rain was still pouring down. 'You got a spare umbrella, Mike?'

'No, guv'nor, I dunno where they all disappear to, but I got a rain cape you can borrow.'

Grimaldi shook his head, drawing his collar up. Mike continued chopping up the meat, saying that his hat was around somewhere – in fact, he had borrowed it. Grimaldi held his hand out. 'OK, I'll pinch your hat, give it back later.'

Mike shook his head. 'No, I said I used yours, that old black leather trilby. Ruda said she hated you in it, so she stashed it in here someplace. Caught me wearing it!' He looked at the row of rubber aprons on the hooks and searched under the table. 'I dunno where it is now. I tell you what, wrap one of the rubber aprons round your head.'

Grimaldi laughed, hunching his shoulders. 'I'll wrap it around yours, son. Never mind, I'll make a dash for it.'

Grimaldi ran to the jeep and started to drive out. He passed the lighted administration offices and slowed down to look over at the window. He could see Ruda with the boss, the Ringling scout . . . they were drinking champagne, talking, and the Russian was with them. He stared for a while, he couldn't help feeling hurt, even rejected, but then he punched the wheel. 'Go get dinner, go and cook for your woman. Come on, get your fat ass into gear!' He had started the engine and was about to drive off when Ruda shouted out to him. He turned, she was running from the administration office, leaping over the puddles like a young girl. She yanked open the passenger door. The rain still poured down, but she wasn't even wearing a coat.

'I did it, Luis! *I did it! They want me to go to New York straight after this contract ends!*' She spun round, hands up, face tilted to the rain. '*I did it!* . . . I did it!'

'And if you stay out there any longer you're gonna catch pneumonia. Come on – get in the jeep!'

She dived inside and slammed the door, flung her arms around him. 'Luis, I did it! He loved the act, he thought it was great!'

Luis said he would drop her off at the trailer, and go on in to pick up groceries, maybe some champagne.

'I've had champagne. Just take me to the cages!'

'But you're soaked.'

'I don't care, I want to see my baby. I want to tell him!'

Grimaldi drove to the animal tent, and she was out running to the entrance. 'Get me chocolate, *black chocolate!*' She turned back, as he started to roll up the window, and she cupped his face in her hands. 'I told you Mamon was a good guy, didn't I? Was I right?'

He had thought she was going to kiss him, for a second he'd hoped she would, but then she was off running full pelt to the cages. Mamon leered at her from the back of his cage, bared his teeth, and she pressed close to the bars. 'Angel, ma'angel – what's the matter, huh?'

His eyes glittered, and then he went back to ripping his meat apart, his whiskers and his jaws bloody. She rubbed her arm, as if only now conscious of it. He had held too tightly; tomorrow she would have to rehearse him, rework him, make him know she was stronger than he was. She remembered always Luis's instructions: never let them know how strong they are, never let them know their own power, never give them the opportunity to know. Ruda stared hard at Mamon. 'Until tomorrow, my angel.'

CHAPTER SIXTEEN

VEBEKKA'S ATTACK was unlike any other Dr Franks had ever witnessed. He was convinced it was not an epileptic fit, but he looked through her files to make certain. He was sure he recalled a reference to a test for epilepsy. He found the date. In 1979, the doctor had written: 'Nervous system characterised by periods of loss of consciousness, with serious convulsions. Epilepsy brain scan negative.' Franks rechecked: the date of the attack coincided with the newspaper incident, and he called the hotel.

Helen Masters answered the phone; the newspapers were in the package that had just arrived, but they had not as yet checked through them. Franks requested she do so and call him first thing in the morning. Helen replaced the phone, feeling inadequate: seeing Vebekka taken away looking so defenceless had upset her more than she liked to admit. Yet she couldn't talk to Louis – he had asked her to leave him alone. Helen knew that the package containing the newspapers was in Louis's room; she would leave it there until morning.

She sat for a while thinking about the meeting with Lena Klapps, then frowned and went to her desk. She had Ulrich Goldberg's phone number in Philadelphia. She placed a long-distance call to him. She told him that she was sure the Baroness was Rebecca, his cousin's daughter, that she was very ill, and they needed to know as much about her background as possible in an attempt to help her recover. The line went silent. Then after a moment Ulrich said that he did not understand what assistance he could give. 'My cousin and I were not on very friendly terms, it is a personal matter and one I decline to speak of to a total stranger.'

'Rebecca is very ill, Mr Goldberg.'

There was a pause, but then he told her that the rift had been to do with the fact that his family were Orthodox Jews. His cousin's wife Rosa had never converted, and they had not made any attempts to bring up Rebecca as a Jew. It became a matter of bitter contention between the cousins, who had once worked together but split up. David Goldberg moved on to more successful ventures whereas Ulrich failed, and when he asked his cousin for help, it was offered only on the understanding that they invite his wife to their house, that they accept Rosa.

'You perhaps cannot understand what this would have meant to me, to my wife and my sons to have to accept Rosa. My wife was the daughter of a rabbi, one of my sons was to be ordained. My brother left me with no option but to ostracise him. It was a sad day.'

'Can you tell me what Rosa was like?'

Ulrich hesitated, and then said sharply, 'She was a very cold, aloof woman. Exceptionally intelligent, but deeply disturbed. She felt we were persecuting her husband when nothing could have been further from the truth. She was exceptionally cruel to both myself and my wife about some small debt. She was bedridden for the last fifteen years of her life. She was not a happy woman – in fact, Rosa was a deeply unhappy woman.'

When Helen asked again about Rebecca, there was the hesitancy. 'I was told they had a great deal of trouble with her in Canada. She seemed to settle down when they came to the United States, but I saw her very rarely, maybe three or four times.'

'They adopted her?'

Ulrich Goldberg coughed, asked her to repeat the question.

'Rosa Goldberg could not have children, did you know that?'

'I believe so.'

'Then you *knew* they had adopted Rebecca?'

'I was never told that was the case.'

'Was it, perhaps, because she may have been adopted illegally?'

'I was not privy to my cousin's affairs. We lived here, we did not see my brother and his wife until they arrived in Philadelphia.'

'Mr Goldberg, I am very grateful to you for talking to me. If you think of anything which may help my patient, would you contact me? Can I give you my hotel number?'

Helen passed on the hotel and suite extension, and then almost as an afterthought asked how well he knew Lena Klapps. She was surprised when he answered that he had never met her – had traced her via Rosa Muller's address book. The only telephone number they had for Lena Klapps was at her workplace, the Bureau of Records. After the death of his cousin he wished to contact anyone who might know who was his cousin's heir. As he had not heard anything of Rebecca, he did not even know if she was still alive. 'As it turned out, my cousin left everything to Rebecca, and it was at his funeral that I last saw her. She refused to allow me to enter the house. At the funeral she spoke to no one, and when we went to hear the reading of David's will, she left almost immediately after she was told she was the only beneficiary. We were obviously disappointed, had a perhaps misguided belief that David would forget our past differences . . . but he left everything to her. We knew he was wealthy, but the fortune was far and above anything I had ever contemplated. I believe her husband's lawyers settled the sale of the house and business.'

After Helen hung up, she began to pace the room. Louis

had remarked on a number of occasions that his wife had inherited her father's estate. What he had never disclosed was the vast amount of wealth. Helen knew he had lied about not knowing Vebekka was really Rebecca. If his lawyers settled her father's estate, it was obvious that he had to know. She found herself wondering if Louis intended to divorce Vebekka, or simply have her placed in an institution so he would gain total access to her money – or had he access to it already? Did he control her fortune?

Helen's mind reeled, so many unanswered questions, and such unpleasant ones. She knew she had to speak to Lena Klapps knowing she had no home telephone number. She decided the best thing to do was get a taxi first thing in the morning before breakfast, before Lena went to work.

Helen jumped as Louis tapped on her door. He seemed almost embarrassed, and excused his interruption by saying he had seen her light was on and knew she was still up. He was very hesitant. 'I wondered if you'd like a drink – I feel in need of some company.'

Helen smiled, said he was not interrupting her, in fact she was glad that he had appeared as she wanted to read through the newspapers. Louis looked puzzled for a moment, and then remembered the package. 'Oh, yes, of course.'

'I promised Dr Franks I would check them through before tomorrow, he wants to know the dates. We can do it together.'

Helen followed Louis into his suite. He asked if she was hungry, and she realised that she was. 'Yes, maybe a sandwich.'

Louis picked up the phone and asked room service to send up some coffee and some chicken sandwiches, then went to get the newspapers.

They sat at the large oval table. Louis opened the package and took out five newspapers, chose the *New York Times*. 'OK, I was reading the front few pages, and Vebekka was

393

reading the real-estate section. Helen? Helen, did you hear me?'

Helen stared at him, folding her arms. 'Why did you lie? You've known all along she was Rebecca Goldberg. I just don't understand why you have lied to me.'

Louis searched in his pockets for his glasses. Finding them, he slipped them out of their leather case. 'Haven't we been through this?'

She leaned towards him slightly. 'No. Why did you never tell me Vebekka was an heiress?'

His eyes flashed angrily over the half glasses, but he spoke with calm detachment. 'Perhaps, my dear, I did not think it was any of your business.'

Helen was stunned. 'Not my business? I see. Why am I here, Louis?'

He opened the paper. 'Because, at your suggestion, we brought Vebekka to Dr Franks.'

'And you didn't think it was *important* that I know who she really is? Louis, Ulrich Goldberg told me about the money, he said your lawyers settled the estate.'

'They probably did, and very well. They have cared for my finances since I was a child.'

The room service arrived and the coffee and sandwiches were placed on the table, but Louis continued to look through the paper, not acknowledging the steward or Helen as she poured his coffee and placed it by his elbow. She sat opposite him, and reached for the paper.

'If Vebekka is certified insane, institutionalised, will you gain access to her personal fortune?'

Louis still did not lift his head from the paper. 'It will be immaterial, there is not very much left, I have not given it much thought either way, and I would presume the costs of keeping her in a home, any kind of nursing establishment, would eat into what little money remains.'

He continued turning the pages of the paper, muttering

394

that he could see nothing of any importance, or possible significance. His refusal to look at her or speak to her directly infuriated Helen. She suddenly reached over and snatched the paper. The Baron's right hand tried to retrieve it but knocked over his coffee, which spilt on him. He sprang to his feet swearing. 'That was a bloody stupid childish thing to do!'

Helen hit him with the newspaper. 'Was it? *Was it?*'

He stared at her coldly. 'Yes, it was.' He removed his glasses, placing them on the table, picked up a napkin and began to wipe the coffee from his dressing-gown.

Helen patted the table dry with her napkin. 'I keep trying to understand you, Louis. You knew all along Vebekka was David and Rosa Goldberg's child, but you never admitted it to me. You let me continue making enquiries, like an idiot, a total waste of my time. Now I find out your wife inherited millions – another small fact you deliberately did not tell me.'

Louis swiped the air with his hand and snapped in fury, 'Leave me alone, just leave me alone!'

Helen watched in exasperation as he slammed into his bedroom. She reached down to try to salvage the papers. The front page of the *Times* had fallen beneath the table. She was not really concentrating, but telling herself she should pack her belongings and leave. She could explain to Dr Franks.

Helen folded the page. It was stained with coffee and she dabbed at it with her napkin. It was a small article at the bottom right-hand corner: 'ANGEL OF DEATH FOUND'. Helen glanced over the single paragraph, which stated that Joseph Mengele, the most wanted Nazi war criminal, had been found dead on a beach in Brazil . . .

Helen began frantically to open the other papers, searching each page, tossing them aside, as Louis returned, shamefaced.

'Helen, I'm sorry. You are right, perhaps we should talk.'

She turned to him. 'Louis, I think I've found it. Remember you told Franks how terrified she was about a dark angel? You heard her sobbing that night, just after the newspaper incident. Look at the bottom of the front page.'

Louis looked at the stained paper, picked it up. 'What am I looking for?'

Helen leaned over his shoulder and pointed. 'Angel of Death, Joseph Mengele, it's mentioned in two papers, just small paragraphs, but it's all that links with her screaming, with her nightmare of the Dark Angel!' He scrutinised the articles as Helen paced up and down. 'If she was adopted from Berlin, maybe that is the connection, and I am sure she was adopted, Louis.'

He held out his hand to her. 'I did not know she was adopted, I *didn't* know . . . and I don't understand where all this is leading to, but if you think there is a connection, then tell me what to do.'

'Be honest with me. And trust me, you must trust me, because if you don't then there is no point in my being here.'

He kissed her hand, gave a small bow. 'I apologise, and believe me, I am truly grateful for your presence. I don't really know how I would have coped without you.'

He gave her one of his boyish smiles, and his hesitancy was touching, he seemed so vulnerable. 'I know how her wealth must appear to you, Helen. But my mother left me a small allowance – everything is tied up in trust funds for my children. When the money came, it was a relief, it meant I could care for Vebekka, continue to live as I always had, but my decision to have her taken away is in no way connected to her fortune – it's gone. In fact, I will be dependent on my sons for the upkeep of the château, the apartments. They in turn will need the added finances of their brides.'

'And your life, Louis? What about your life.'

He drained his coffee, returning the cup to saucer

thoughtfully. 'I still have my allowance, I can sell the polo stable. It will break my heart, but if it comes to that, then so be it. Now I think it is time I went to bed, if you will excuse me.' He slipped his arm around her shoulder. 'Goodnight, Helen.' He kissed her cheek lightly.

She walked towards her own bedroom, not even turning back as she said, 'Goodnight, Louis.'

Helen knew how easy it must be to be drawn into a life of luxury, the Rolls-Royces, the fabulous restaurants, the flowers and expensive gifts. Louis was a very handsome man, his light, almost careless kiss to her cheek made her realise that he excited and attracted her, too, and it would not be hard to take their relationship a step further. She knew he had mistresses, but she knew, too, that such a life could not satisfy her. What she had to face was her own loneliness: before she had been only half aware of it, always able to justify being alone because she determined it was her choice; she even made the excuse of being a very private person. 'You are so private, Helen, that no one even knows you exist!' She said the words out loud, to herself, to her own reflection in the bathroom mirror. She cleaned her teeth, washed her face, and returned to her bedroom – everything neat and tidy, the bed cover turned down in expectancy. She lay for a long while staring up at the ceiling. It was time she returned to Paris. This was her vacation, she had given enough of her time – and with very little thanks. But then, guiltily, she thought of Vebekka. It had been at Helen's instigation that Vebekka had come to Berlin; she was too deeply involved to extricate herself. But from now on she would distance herself from Louis.

Helen left the hotel very early the next morning. She did not wake Louis, but left a note saying she would meet him at Dr Franks's clinic and to be sure he took the newspapers with him.

She looked along the taxi rank, and found the overtalkative driver who had taken them to Charlottenburg. He was dozing in his Mercedes. She tapped the window, and got in beside him.

'Same address as before?'

'Yes, the same address. Lena Klapps. I want to get there before she leaves for work.'

'We'll do it easy, no traffic at this hour, we'll miss all the rush.'

Inspector Torsen was at his desk by seven-thirty. He began to plough through the vast amount of paperwork; there were more reports of cars stolen in the West and brought to the East than they could handle. He worked on until eight-thirty, then opened the morning paper. There was a large article on the front page with a picture. 'MAMA MAGDA DIES'. He read the article, turned to the next page, and then flicked back. Now there was a coincidence: he had seen Ruda Kellerman the same night Mama Magda had died – entering Mama's club. He scribbled a note on his ever-ready pad, and continued to read, checking on the time as he wanted to be at the records bureau when they opened at nine.

Rieckert appeared, with a black eye and plaster on his cheek. Torsen looked at him, asked if he had been in trouble. Rieckert slumped into a seat. 'Acting on your orders, sir! We tried to clear up some of the hookers working from the trailers, we warned them to clear off, get their trailers out, and the next minute four big bastards jumped on us – the girls' pimps – and they had iron bars . . . bloody beat up Kruger, he's in hospital.'

'Did you make any arrests?'

Rieckert swore. 'You must be joking – we only just made it into that station courtyard. We radioed for them to have the gates open. They chased us, were on our tail for miles, their car was a hell of a lot faster than ours, it was a big four-door Mercedes! We only just made it back in time, and they banged and hammered on the gates. Have you seen the damage they did?'

Torsen rubbed his nose. 'This is madness, are you telling me the pimps *chased* . . . *chased* the patrol car?'

'Yeah! Overtook us twice, it was a near thing, one got me through the window – I had to have a stitch, cut my head open!'

'Would you recognise them again?'

Rieckert sat bolt upright. 'I'm not going back there, they'd bloody kill me, they're huge blokes, musclemen!'

Torsen returned to his desk. He flipped open the paper. 'There will be war out there soon. Mama Magda's dead, last night, and most of those trailers are hers, so God knows what's going to happen now.'

Rieckert glanced over the paper. 'She must have been worth millions. I'm surprised nobody bumped her off before.'

'It was a heart attack, she was over eighty and the size of an elephant.'

'They open tonight, will you be using your ticket?'

'Pardon?'

Rieckert tossed the paper on to Torsen's desk. 'The circus, they gave us free tickets, you going? They open the big show tonight.'

Torsen had forgotten about the free seats, and he chewed his lip, opened a drawer and took the tickets out. 'I'd forgotten . . . Yes, yes, I think I will use my two.'

Rieckert left for the kitchen and Torsen called the nursing home and asked to speak to Nurse Freda. 'I have two tickets for the circus . . . tonight, I'm sorry it's short notice, but I was wondering . . . if you aren't on duty, if you would care to . . .'

Freda shrieked that she would love it, and generated such excitement that Torsen went pink with embarrassment. They arranged to meet at seven.

He gave out his orders for the day, and said if he was required for anything urgent he would be at the records bureau. He left, taking one of the few patrol cars in good condition – to the aggravation of the *Polizei* instructed to check over the prostitutes.

Tommy Kellerman had been buried by a rabbi from the Oranienburger Tor area. His body was taken to the run-down quarter inhabited by the Eastern Jewish community. No one attended his burial. The plain black coffin was carried from the city mortuary before sundown, as Ruda Kellerman had requested. The costs for the burial were delivered to the station, and Torsen forwarded the receipt to Ruda Kellerman, care of the circus.

Vebekka had slept soundly and had eaten a little breakfast. She was in a small room, white-walled, with an old iron bed-frame painted white. There was a white chest of drawers, but a bowl of fresh flowers gave colour to the room. The door had a peephole, and no inside handle. A white-tiled bathroom cubicle, with bath and toilet, led off the room, without a door. The room was devoid of mirrors, of any adornment. There was no telephone.

Dr Franks drew up the only chair in the room. 'How are you?'

'I'm fine, do I have to stay in this room?'

'Only for a little while, then we'll go into my lounge. You remember you were there yesterday?'

She nodded, it seemed years ago. Franks told her that her husband had called and he would be in soon after he had breakfasted. If she felt like it she could have a bath and get dressed.

He asked if she needed anyone to help her, and she shook her head. He said all she had to do was ring the bell by her bedside, and Maja would be with her in moments.

She rested her head back and sighed. 'They should never have brought me here. It's very close here, I feel it . . .'

Franks cocked his head to one side, and held her hand. 'Feel what?'

'I don't know, a presence. I've felt it before, but not this close.'

Franks threaded his fingers through her long perfect slim hands, soft, beautiful skin, perfect nails. 'Maybe we will find out what this presence is, send it away from you . . .'

She gave him a sweet sad smile. 'They've sent me away this time, haven't they? Ah, well . . . I suppose it had to come.'

'You are not away anywhere, Vebekka, you are here, in my clinic, until we sort things out. You do want me to help you, don't you?'

Tears welled in her eyes, and she turned away. 'I don't think anyone can help, I hoped . . .'

He stood up and leaned across her. 'I want more than hope, my dear. I want everything you want, want you to get well, want you to help yourself, help me to help you. OK?'

He returned to his office and picked up his notes, carefully transcribed for him by his son. Two passages he had underlined:

(1) Get me to lie down and talk to me, so I would be calm.
(2) Put her in a cupboard and throw away the key.

Vebekka's own words, describing what her mother had done and had told her to do. Franks was sure that the key Vebekka's mother had said to throw away was at the root of her problems. He was so engrossed in thinking through his approach for the day's session that it was a moment before he realised his phone was blinking. Baron Maréchal had arrived, bringing with him the copies of the newspapers

Franks had requested. He told his receptionist to show the Baron in, a little irritated that he was so early.

Lena Klapps opened the front door while eating a slice of toast. Seeing Helen, she was about to slam the door shut in her face, but Helen put her foot across the threshold. 'I know this is an intrusion, but I had to speak to you. Please, I won't take more than a few moments.'

Lena turned and walked into the hall, pushing open the door. 'I have to leave in fifteen minutes. I have to get my bus.'

'I understand, but I can give you a lift to the records bureau in my taxi.'

Lena hesitated and walked out, calling to her husband to finish his breakfast. She returned carrying a cup of coffee, but did not offer Helen one. She stood with her back to the large bookshelf. 'I told you everything I know. I do not see how I can assist you any further.'

'You have worked at the records bureau for many years? Is that correct?'

Lena nodded; she picked at a food stain on her skirt with her fingernail, the same grey pleated skirt she had worn on Helen's last visit.

'I have checked the hospitals for any possible record of your sister. You said she worked at one of the main hospitals just after the war, after she returned to Berlin. Everyone I spoke to referred me to the main records bureau. You head the department, don't you?'

Lena nodded, and continued to sip her coffee. When Helen asked how long she had worked there, she swivelled slightly in the seat. 'You have no right to pry into my personal affairs, Miss Whatever-your-name-is. I have told you all I know. Now, please, I would like you to leave.'

'If you refuse to help me then you leave me and Baron

Maréchal no alternative but to make enquiries as high up as we need to go. I want to find out if your sister Rosa Muller adopted a child, I want to know the background of this child – I do not care, Lena, if the adoption was legal or illegal, all I am interested in is trying to help a woman who lives in a nightmare.'

Lena stared into her empty coffee cup. Two pink dots appeared in her cheeks, a small muscle twitched at the side of her mouth. 'We all have our nightmares.'

'No, no, we don't. But are you really telling me that a sister, a sister you grew up with, didn't make any contact with you when she returned to Berlin, didn't try to see you?'

Lena looked up, her eyes filled with hatred – whether for Helen or her sister, Helen couldn't tell. She banged the cup down on the table.

Helen was losing patience; she didn't mean her voice to rise but she couldn't help herself. 'All I want is to know more of Rebecca's background, I am not interested in yours.'

Lena whipped round. 'Please keep your voice down, I don't want my husband to hear you.'

She clasped her hands together. 'No one has ever been interested in me. When I was a child it was always Rosa this, Rosa that – she was always the beautiful one, always the clever one. She had everything, looks, brains . . . She had everything, and you know something else? She was always happy, always smiling, like she had some secret, something filling up her life. My father doted on her, he worshipped her. She broke his heart.' Lena pursed her lips. Helen said nothing. 'She refused to listen to him. He begged and pleaded with her to break off her relationship with David Goldberg. It was very embarrassing for him, for all of us. My father was a very well-respected scientist, with many connections, my brothers—' She wafted her hand, as if unable to continue, turned her back, facing the bookshelves. 'I cooked and cleaned and waited hand and foot on him when Mama died . . . but he wanted Rosa, always wanted Rosa. She made a fool of him, a fool of all of us, but she refused to listen . . . and then . . . then she became pregnant.'

Lena remained with her back to Helen, her arms wrapped around herself. Helen had to know more. 'You told me Rosa had an abortion, but I need to—'

'It was not an abortion.'

Helen half rose to her feet: Rebecca was their daughter after all?

'My father and my brothers locked her in the house, and my father . . . he performed the operation himself, he sterilised her.'

Helen sat back, shocked.

Lena's hand shook as she patted the coiled bun at the nape of her neck, but she looked defiantly at Helen. 'This Rebecca is not my sister's child.'

Helen showed not a flicker of what she felt, pressed her hands flat against her thighs.

Lena moved closer, until she stood in front of Helen. 'I did lie to you, I did see my sister again. She was working at the main refugee hospital with some of the children picked up from the streets, picked up from the camps, from everywhere. It was my job to try to keep a record of how many, if they knew their names. My father was dead, my brothers dead. I lived in the cellar, in the rubble of our old home, for years . . . and I hoped . . . hoped she would one day come back. I saw her, and she was smiling, she was still beautiful, still happy, she was playing with a group of Jewish children.' Lena repeated the same wave of her hand, a dismissive wave as if she was shooing away a fly. 'She smiled at me, and then . . . then she drew this child forwards, she said, "This is my daughter, Lena, this is Rebecca."'

Helen stood up. 'You have a record? The child's family name? The adoption papers?'

'There were no papers, no documents. The child couldn't even talk. She was from Birkenau.'

Helen closed her eyes, pressed her fingers to her eye sockets. Suddenly she heard a loud banging, and her eyes flew open. Lena was hurling books from the bookcase.

'She left me, she left her family, she left me, and all I have are these – these, and a broken-down man! Rosa was happy, she was always happy!'

Helen reached for her purse, picked up her coat. Lena began to weep uncontrollably. 'Why – why did you come here? Go away, leave me alone . . .'

Helen asked if she could take Lena to work, but she shook her head, wiping her face with her hands. 'No, just go away.'

One of the large medical books had fallen in front of the door. It was an old medical journal, and it was open to a picture of a man's head, his brain, with diagrams pointing to the front lobe. 'The World of Hypnosis'.

Helen picked up the book. 'Hypnosis? Lena, do you know if Rosa ever—' The book was snatched out of her hand before she could say another word. Lena held the book close to her chest, hugging it tightly. 'This was my father's – this was my father's book, go away . . . *go away*!'

Helen left, the door slamming shut behind her. She ran down the steps to the waiting taxi, eager to pass on her findings to Dr Franks.

Ruda was in high spirits, singing in the shower. She washed her hair and tied a big towel around it. She called out to

Luis that she would only be a moment longer. He shouted back that coffee was on the table, he was going over to check the meat delivery truck, it had just arrived.

Ruda whistled as she sat down to breakfast – fresh rolls and black coffee; the newspaper lay folded on the table with a large bunch of flowers. Luis had made a card with 'Congratulations!' scrawled across it. She smiled and poured herself coffee. She bit into the roll, opened the paper – then slammed it on to the table. 'MAMA MAGDA DEAD'.

She read the article and leaned on her elbows, staring at the fat woman's face. Then she laughed, it was very fortuitous. With Kellerman dead, it was as though fate had suddenly started to turn good for her. She had the promise of a contract with Ringling Brothers, the show opened that night, she was feeling good and even Luis had remained sober, had seemed as pleased for her success as she was.

Ruda finished her breakfast, then took a pair of scissors and cut out the article. Folding it neatly, she got up and went into her bedroom. She pulled the stool up, and stood on it to find her black box, felt around the cupboard and withdrew it, putting it down on her dressing-table. She reached down to fold back the carpet and get the tiny key, then straightened up, staring at the old tin box. She turned it round, saw the scratches on the hinges, the indentation where Grimaldi had tried to force it open. She had fitted a new lock after Tommy Kellerman had broken it open, now Luis had done the same. She knew it could be no one else. Luis.

She unlocked the box, knew by looking that the contents had been taken out. Her heart hammered inside her chest, she held up the small ribboned package of clippings. She slipped the new cutting about Magda under the ribbon, then relocked the box. She felt as if the contents were

406

burning into her hand . . . the memories began, like scars opening, bleeding . . .

Inspector Torsen checked his watch, it was after nine.

He asked the receptionist again if he could be allowed into the record room, and she apologised. Mrs Klapps had never been late since she had worked there, and she was sure she would have called in if she was not coming. She suggested Torsen have a cup of coffee somewhere. Torsen scribbled a note asking for both records to be ready for him, together with any record of a marriage licence between T. Kellerman and a woman of the same name, Ruda.

Torsen, having use of the patrol car, headed for Mama Magda's club; he wished to know who was taking over and if they could discuss the matter of the influx of prostitutes.

He pushed through the beaded curtain, getting one section caught in his lapel. Eric was checking over orders for flowers, and at the same time looking at coloured swatches of material for redecorating the club. Eric looked up fleetingly, then returned to his colour charts.

'I am Chief Inspector Torsen Heinz from the East Berlin sector.'

Eric turned and sighed. 'Not another one. The *Polizei* have been in and out of here all morning already, last night there were more *Polizei* than customers. What do you want?'

Torsen asked if they could talk in privacy. Eric led him into Magda's office. It smelled of stale tobacco, as did the entire club. He perched himself on Magda's cushions and Torsen sat on the chair opposite the untidy desk.

'I would like to talk to you, since you are taking over the clubs, and we have to try to stop the prostitution getting out of hand. I believe Magda controls the—'

407

'Did. I am her main beneficiary, Inspector, I was her husband, so let's get down to basics. How much do you want?'

Torsen frowned. 'I am giving you a warning, I am not here for money, bribes are against the law. You were not attempting to . . .'

Eric screwed up his face, trying to recollect if he had seen this one with his hand out. He sat back and listened as Torsen said that four of his officers had been attacked and chased. Eric interrupted him. 'I'm sorry, I don't follow, you say your men were chased?'

Torsen elaborated. His men had been chased by four men in a high-powered Mercedes, the number plate was being checked. He was there simply to warn the new establishment that he would not allow such things to continue.

Eric pretended great concern, agreed that he would personally look into what girls and their pimps were working over in the West.

Torsen was about to leave when he remembered to offer his condolences. Eric murmured his thanks with downcast eyes, and then regaled Torsen with the details – how he had just been sitting exactly where the inspector was when she just keeled over . . . 'It was a strange night, there was this woman Magda insisted she knew and the woman insisted she didn't know her. I think it was this woman's fault she had a heart attack. Magda really got agitated about her, screaming and carrying on, as only she could do.'

Torsen rose to his feet, hand outstretched. Eric jumped up.

'Ruda, that was her name, shot out of here, and Magda hit the roof, wanted her boys to get her, you know the way Magda was, but I'd never seen her before.'

Torsen hesitated. 'Ruda Kellerman?'

Eric shrugged. 'Don't ask me, but she put Magda in one hell of a mood. Eh, I should grumble, she's dead, and I don't mind telling you, telling anybody, I've waited a long time for that to happen.' Eric continued talking as he led Torsen out of the club. Torsen headed up the stairs and back to his patrol car.

Eric waited until he saw the inspector's shoes disappear up the staircase, and then returned to the bar, clicking his fingers at the barmaid. 'Can you get Klaus in? I need to know who we've got working over in the Eastern sector, how many girls, etc. Do you think this plum would look good on the wall?' He held it up. Not waiting for a reply, he returned to the office to order the fabric. It was a coincidence that Torsen had been sitting not two feet away from the carving knife which had sliced through Jeczawitz's arm . . .

Torsen waited as Lena put down the file discs for the rest of the Js. She then handed him two more files on males listed with the name Kellerman.

'Thank you, this is very kind of you.'

She nodded, but walked out without saying a word. Torsen looked after her, and then turned his attention to the files. Perhaps she had had a bad morning.

Two hours later, his back aching from straining forwards to see the screen, Torsen found what he was looking for. He found the registration of the marriage licence between Rudi Jeczawitz and a Ruda Braun. Stamped across Ruda's name was 'No documentation available'. She had signed her name with a strange childish scrawl.

He was even luckier with Thomas Kellerman and his wife, also Ruda Braun. He took copies of both licences and matched the handwriting. Ruda Braun's signature was identical to Ruda Jeczawitz's. His heart was thudding in his chest as he looked from one document to the other. He gathered up his papers to put them into his briefcase. As he did so, he realised his newspaper was tucked inside; he was about to throw it away, when he looked again at the 'MAMA MAGDA DEAD'. The first line of the article leapt out at him. 'Last night one of the most well-known women of West Berlin's red-light district, the infamous Magda Braun, known as Mama Magda . . .'

Torsen's head was spinning with coincidences as he made his way back to the station. He was sure he had enough evidence to interrupt his *Direktor*'s holiday, and ask for permission to arrange a warrant for the arrest of Ruda Kellerman.

As usual, the station was virtually empty, the main bulk of officers having taken off for their lunch. He had to wait five minutes before they opened the yard gates to let him drive in. Once in his office he began to lay out in front of him all the evidence he had accumulated. He had to make sure he made no mistakes. Ruda Kellerman was now an American citizen – and a famous performer. This would be his first murder arrest, he could not afford to be wrong. He ran his fingers through his hair, flicked through his notes, and then tapped with his pencil. He should have commandeered the boots. He still didn't know if they were Grimaldi's or Ruda's, or if they were in it together. He swore, checked his watch; it was almost one o'clock. He needed a search warrant – had to get a search warrant.

His desk phone jangled and he snatched it up. It was the manager of the Grand Hotel who wanted to discuss with someone the nightly invasion of prostitutes hanging around outside the hotel entrance; they were even walking audaciously into the foyer of the hotel itself. Torsen said he would send someone over straight away. He was then caught up in calls: there were more burglaries from tourists' cars than they could deal with, and the rabbi rang, asking when he would be paid for Kellerman's funeral. Torsen diverted the calls, then dialled the receptionist. 'I have to go to the circus.'

'Yes, I heard you and Rieckert have free tickets.'

'I'm going on business, I'll be using the same patrol car, contact me direct to it if I'm needed. And have you got another girl to take over from you?'

'We've got three applicants, but this is a very old board, you have to have experience with this one.'

'I want someone on that switchboard day and night, is that understood?'

The receiver was slammed down and Torsen stared at his phone; he hadn't had any lunch and it was already two o'clock. He picked up the rabbi's bill for Kellerman's funeral; he would use it as an excuse to talk to Ruda, and then ask if he could take the boots. If he waited around for a search warrant to be issued, it could take hours.

Grimaldi was looking for Ruda: he'd not seen her since breakfast. She was late for feeding time and, as she always fed the cats herself, he was worried that something had happened to her. When he saw the inspector easing his way round the puddles, he hurried towards him. 'Is something wrong?'

'No, no, I was just coming to see you, or your wife. I have the receipt for Kellerman's funeral costs. You recall she said she would pay for the funeral?'

Grimaldi shrugged. 'I don't know where she is, but come on inside.'

Torsen stepped into the plush trailer, wiping his feet on the grid and noticing that there were no boots. He sat on the cushioned bench turning his cap round and round, as

Grimaldi opened the envelope from the rabbi. He looked up after reading, and delved into his pockets. 'I'll pay you now, cash – that all right?'

Torsen nodded. Grimaldi counted out the notes, folded them and handed them over. 'Not much for a life, huh?'

Torsen opened his top pocket, asked if Grimaldi required a receipt. He shook his head, and then crossed to the window lifting up the blind. 'This isn't like her, she's never late for feeding, I wonder where the hell she has got to?'

Torsen tried to say it nonchalantly, but he flushed. 'Perhaps she has gone to Mama Magda's funeral?'

Grimaldi started. 'Who the fuck is she?'

Torsen explained, growing more embarrassed at his attempt to be a sly investigator. 'She was a famous West Berlin madame; she died last night at her club, Mama's. I believe your wife was there last night.'

'What are you talking about?'

'She was at the club, Mama Magda's, last night. I was told about nine, nine-thirty . . .'

'Bullshit! She was in the ring, we had a dress rehearsal last night, you got the wrong girl!'

Torsen pointed to the newspaper on the table. 'It was in the papers this morning, Mama Magda . . . photograph.'

Grimaldi snatched the paper and opened it. 'I've never heard of her, and why do you think Ruda was there?' He looked at the paper, could see where the article had been, but it had been cut out. He said nothing, tossed the paper back on to the table.

Torsen felt exceptionally nervous: the big man still scared the life out of him. 'Do you mind if I ask you a few questions? I'm sorry to inconvenience you.'

Grimaldi sniffed and rubbed his nose. 'She's never late.'

'Do you have a leather trilby, or a similar hat – a shiny black hat?'

Grimaldi turned. 'Do I have a what?'

Torsen stuttered slightly as he repeated his question. Grimaldi shook his head. 'No, I never wear a hat.'

'Does your wife?'

'What? Wear a hat? No, no.'

Torsen explained the reason why he had asked, that their suspect in the Kellerman murder investigation wore a black shiny hat, but it was possibly Kellerman's own hat, worn as a disguise.

Grimaldi sat on the opposite bunk, his legs so long they almost touched Torsen's feet. 'So you think I had something to do with Kellerman's death? Is that why you're here?'

Torsen swallowed, wishing he'd brought someone with him. 'I am just following a line of enquiry and elimination. An unidentified man was seen leaving Kellerman's hotel.'

Grimaldi nodded, his dark eyes boring into Torsen. 'So why do you want to know if Ruda's got a trilby?'

Torsen tugged at his tie. 'Perhaps our witness was mistaken, perhaps the person leaving, er, the man with the hat, was in fact a woman.'

Grimaldi leaned forward and reached out to hold Torsen's knee. His huge hand covered it, and he gripped tightly. 'You suspect Ruda? I told you, she was here with me all night, I told you that, and I don't like your insinuations.'

Torsen waited until Grimaldi released his kneecap. 'We also have a good impression of a boot, or the heel of a boot. Would it be possible for me to . . . to check the – if I could look at your boots, and your wife's boots . . . ?'

Grimaldi stood up, towering above Torsen. 'The only boot you will see is mine – as it kicks your ass out of my trailer, understand? Get out! *Out! Fuck off out of here!*'

Torsen stood up, folded his notebook and stuffed it into

his pocket. 'I just need to check your boots for elimination purposes. If I am required to return with a warrant, then I shall do so.'

Grimaldi loomed closer, his voice quiet. 'Get out. Come back with your warrant and you'll fucking eat it – get out.'

Torsen slipped down the steps as the door slammed shut so fast behind him it pushed him forwards. He returned to his patrol car, his legs like jelly. Next time he would get a warrant, but he'd send Rieckert in for the boots.

Grimaldi went over to the meat trailer. All the trays were ready, Mike and the other young hands finishing preparing the meat. Grimaldi leaned against the chopping board. 'She still not shown up?'

Mike said nobody had seen her, but the cats were getting hungry. Grimaldi checked the time, said to leave it another half-hour. Then he looked at Mike. 'Eh, where did you say you put my hat?'

Mike chopped away, not even looking up. 'Mrs Grimaldi took it from me, I dunno where it is.'

Grimaldi stood at the open door, cracked his knuckles. 'You ever meet that little dwarf, the one that got murdered?'

Mike flushed slightly, because he knew that Mrs Grimaldi had been married to that dwarf. He covered his embarrassment by carrying the trays out to the waiting trolley. 'No, I never saw him.'

'I think *I* did.'

Mike jumped down, not hearing the other young hand who was running water into buckets. Grimaldi turned, easing the door half closed. 'What did you say?'

The boy turned off the taps. 'Day we arrived, I think it was him, I dunno, but he came in here, well, came to the steps, asked for Ruda, she was out by the cages.'

Grimaldi nodded. 'You told anyone this?'

The boy started to fill another bucket. 'Nope. Nobody's

asked me.' He turned back to Grimaldi. 'I saw him later talking to Ruda so I presumed she must have said he was hanging around here. Have they caught the bloke that did it, then?'

Grimaldi rubbed the lad's shoulder with his hand. 'Yeah, they got the bloke, so don't open your mouth, we don't want those fuckers nosing around here any more than they need to. OK?'

The boy nodded, and Grimaldi strolled out. 'I'll just see if I can find that bloody woman.'

Grimaldi walked through the alley between the cages, and then stopped. She had lied, Kellerman had not only been to the circus, but he had talked to her! He shrugged it off. Maybe she just didn't want anyone to know she had been married to him. He walked on, worrying about the hat, and then his heart thudded. He remembered seeing her in the meat trailer, the night of Kellerman's murder. She had been covered in blood, it was over her shirt, her trousers. Shit! He remembered asking why she wasn't wearing one of the rubber aprons. He stopped again. Dear God, he had been so drunk that night he wouldn't have known if she was in the trailer or not.

Grimaldi ran back, slammed the door behind him, and went into Ruda's bedroom. He opened the wardrobe, searching for the shirt, trying to remember what clothes she had worn that night, but gave up, he couldn't remember. He rubbed his head. What did that little prick want to check their boots for?

The sound was half moan, half sob, but low, quiet, it unnerved him. He looked around, heard it again. He inched open the small shower door. She was naked, curled up in the corner of the shower, her arms covering her head, as if she was hiding or burying herself.

'Oh, sweetheart . . . baby . . .'

He had to prise her arms away from her head, her face

was stricken, terrified. She whispered, 'No, please . . . no more, please no more . . . red, blue, red, red, red . . . blue, green . . .'

Grimaldi was unsure what to do, she didn't seem to know him, see him, her body curled up so tightly. Her voice was like a child's. He couldn't understand what she was saying. Some sort of list of colours – the plinths? It didn't make sense. Then he heard distinctly: 'My sister, I want my sister, my sister, please . . . no more . . .'

He took a big bath towel, gently wrapped it around her, talked quietly, softly, but she refused to move. He tucked the towel around her and eased the door shut. The cats had to be fed if there was to be a show that night, they had to have their routine.

He went back to the meat trailer, and then, for the first time in years, fed the cats. They were very suspicious, snarling and swiping at him, but they were hungry and the food became their priority . . . except for Mamon. If Grimaldi even went near the bars, Mamon went crazy; he couldn't get within an arm's length of the cage to throw in the meat. Grimaldi swore and cursed him, then got a pitchfork and shoved the meat through the bars. Mamon clawed at the fork, his jaws opened in a rage of growls and he lashed out with his paws. He didn't want the meat, he never even went near it, but prowled up and down, up and down, until Grimaldi gave up trying and returned to the trailer.

She was in exactly the same position, curled up, hiding now beneath the bath towel. He knelt down, talked to her, keeping his voice low, encouraging her to come out. He was talking to her as if she was one of his cats. 'Come on out, that's a good girl, good girl, give me your hand . . . I'm not going to hurt you, that's a good girl.'

Slowly inch by inch she moved towards him, crawling, retracting, and he kept on talking, until she allowed him to put his arms around her. Then he carried her like a baby to the bed, held her in his arms and began to rock her gently backwards and forwards. 'It's all right, I'm here . . . everything's all right, I'm here.' He wanted to weep, he had never seen her like this.

'Sister, I want my sister . . .'

She felt heavy in his arms as he continued to rock her, and then he eased the towel from her face; she was sleeping. He was afraid to put her down in case he woke her; he held her as he would the child he had always wanted, sat with her in his arms, and said it over and over. 'I love you, I love you, love you . . .'

Then he saw the box on her dressing-table, saw beneath the old ribbon the newspaper clipping, 'Angel of Death' and he whispered, 'Dear God, what did they do to you? What did they do to you, my baby?'

CHAPTER SEVENTEEN

HELEN ARRIVED at Dr Franks's apartment just as he was leaving. He was on his way out to see a patient. Helen asked if he could direct her to his library. He gave her a quizzical look when she told him what books she wished to read. 'My housekeeper will make you comfortable, bring you some coffee.'

Helen was shown into Franks's drawing room. The comfortably furnished room was dominated by bookshelves on every wall. Helen began to look over the books, moving slowly along the ranks of books carefully listed in alphabetical order until she had a stack to take to the table.

She turned the pages slowly, very slowly, sickened by what she was reading. She didn't want to, but she had to go on reading about the experimentation carried out under the auspices of Joseph Mengele at Birkenau concentration camp. He had used shortwave rays, administered by placing the plate on his female victims' abdomens and backs, in determining the rapidity of cancer production cells. The electricity was directed towards their ovaries, the X-rays given in such huge doses that victims were seriously burned. Cancer invariably followed, and then the gas chamber. The women suffered unspeakable agony as the waves penetrated the lower abdomen. Women's and children's bellies were cut open, the uterus and ovaries removed to observe the lesions, and the victims left, with no medication or pain relief, to determine how long they could stay alive.

Mengele paid particular attention to women and young

girls, his experiments purporting to discover the fastest means of mass-sterilisation and, incongruously, to study fertility. Mengele attempted to produce an impressive report to send back to Berlin, his 'Special Mission' to reproduce a genetic master race, using his pitiful patients as guinea pigs. His experiments had no apparent order, no rules. So-called gynaecologists used an electrical apparatus to inject a thick whitish liquid into the genital organs, causing terrible burning sensations. This injection was repeated every four weeks, and was followed each time by a radioscopy.

Sometimes selected women and small female children were injected with 5 cc of a serum in the chest – no one has since discovered what the serum contained – at the rate of two to nine injections per session. These produced large swellings, the size of a fully grown man's fist. Certain Birkenau inmates received hundreds of these 'inoculations'. The children were often injected in their gums because Mengele wanted to speed up the reaction. Depending on his mood, he would change from one experiment to another, no one ever knowing what new, diabolical test he would demand that his nurses and physicians carry out next.

The Germans were experimenting with sterilisation in many other camps; it was a sickening race between mad men who believed they would win the war, and, once victorious, ensure they would never be threatened by a new generation of an inferior race.

Mengele raged when he discovered typhoid epidemics spreading through Birkenau. He ordered vast amounts of serum, directed the medical orderlies to begin vaccination, then demanded they vaccinate outside the hospital, not to bring the creatures inside for fear of contamination. He would scream abuse at his 'helpers', insinuating they were sabotaging his programmes. One day he would reproach the orderlies for not seeing enough patients, the next day he would be in a violent rage about their wasting time and precious medicines on the sick.

Typhoid was followed by malaria. Mengele decided that it was the Greeks and Italians who had been the carriers, and, on the pretext of curbing the disease, sent thousands to the gas chambers. Whatever concept lay behind Mengele's work in the camp, his experiments lacked any scientific value, all his actions full of contradictions. He would take every precaution during a childbirth, noting and observing that all aseptic principles were rigorously observed and that the umbilical cord was cut with care. Half an hour later mother and new-born infant would be sent to the gas chambers. He carried out serious health treatments on internees, whom he then immediately dispatched to the gas chambers. He would order phenol injections at random, to curb the fevers, and then, when supplies ran out, substituted petrol. To his actions there was a zealot's energy not for life, but for wretched, agonising death.

Helen had to stop reading, she simply could not take in any more. She checked her watch, it was almost ten, and she began to collect the books she had removed from the shelves. One book she had not had time to read was a small slim volume, written by an Auschwitz survivor; it chronicled specifically the work and brutality of Joseph Mengele, and Helen was about to replace it when she saw the words 'Angel of Death'. The nickname had, she read, been given to Mengele because he was always charming, always smiled as he sent thousands to their deaths. Mengele wore white gloves, his uniform was specially designed by his own tailors. He was a high-stepping peacock of a man, handsome, dark-eyed, high-cheekboned. The description surprised Helen – she had assumed the man would be as physically repellent as his crimes.

She stared at his photograph. It was unnerving: there was a similarity to Louis, the same haughty stare. But Mengele was a monster, a terrifying killing machine, a nightmare man with no morals, no feelings; he sent babies to their deaths as easily as he sent old men, young men, women, even pregnant women. No one escaped him . . . except twins – identical twins.

Helen looked at her watch again, knew she should leave, but now she could not stop reading. Mengele had one passion, the author wrote, one specific experiment that he first pursued in the privacy of his deathly hospital. Telepathy. He was determined to discover the powers of human telepathy, and he centred his experimentation on identical twins. Male and female twins were separated from their families, placed in a well-run camp hut, well fed and, according to the author, treated kindly. That word made Helen gasp: this monster sent thousands to their deaths, yet could still be described as 'kindly'. The author contended that many desperate mothers pretended that they had twins, lied that sisters and brothers were twins in a misguided attempt to 'save' them, unaware of the sickening experiments that were being prepared for those selected. Mengele became very particular, personally inspecting the children, rewarding a guard if he had 'salvaged' twins from the gas chamber. Soon, all the guards awaiting new arrivals would scream at the tragic passengers asking if there were any twins . . .

Mengele, it seems, became frantic if a twin died during his experiments; he would send the other to the gas chamber, but only after he dissected and matched the internal organs of the dead with the living twin. He operated on these children, sometimes without anaesthetic, on their eyes, their ears; he switched their organs, he starved one and overfed the other to watch their reactions.

He personally tortured and mutilated these children in the name of science. Eight thousand identical twins passed through the camp. Only seven hundred children survived.

Helen walked to the clinic, needing to breathe fresh air. But when she sat down with Franks in his office, she was close to tears. He listened, his hands forming a church tower, staring at the index fingers, until Helen calmed down.

'I'm sorry, perhaps everything I have told you, you know already. It's just – to see it written down in black and white, to read it, to know it happened, to read him described as "kindly" – it is beyond my conception of a human being. I'm sorry.'

Franks gave Helen a steady stare and, in a soft quiet voice, his eyes fixed to a point on the wall ahead, he said, 'People in the camps lived from day to day, their only concern to stay alive until the next day. But, Helen, in order to live through each day one needed such courage, such toughness and, perhaps most of all, luck. Anyone who collapsed physically would die quickly, or be finished off by the Kapos, block seniors and the SS men – all of them experts in brutality, it was their trade. The ones who stayed alive were, as a rule, young. Some of the older men grew used to camp conditions, managed as best they could. It was always worst for the new arrivals, they had no idea what a concentration camp meant. It was, Helen, a completely alien atmosphere. The key was to discover the art of staying alive, and it was an art, Helen, unless you were exceptionally lucky. The survivors were often men with no scruples – those men advanced rapidly inside the camp. They came to power, could not afford to be squeamish about the means they chose, the human suffering, even the loss of human life. The most important thing was to make sure of your position. You filled your stomach with stolen rations, you were forced to become criminally minded to survive. You had to become cruel and ruthless – if not, the hopelessness of your position gave you only one alternative, to run at the electrified barbed wire fences.

'I often thank God, Helen, that I was one of those whom fate spared. But it was many, many years before I came to terms with what I had been forced to become, simply to survive, many years before I was able to hold my head up high . . . many years.'

He sat back in his seat, his eyes met Helen's, a strange direct stare, before he looked away, clasping the wooden carved arms of the old desk chair. 'I think the worst thing is that we forget – Germany, every German, should carry the cross of what was done. But memories fade, scars heal, and now we have adolescents not even born when this took place. This city, this country is a monument to a savagery that still makes one weep with shame. But life goes on . . .' He hesitated a moment, as if about to continue, then decided against it, not wanting to discuss his own past any further. He motioned to the newspapers on his desk.

Franks told Helen that the Baron had brought them, spent time with Vebekka, and then gone for a bite to eat. He gave a half-smile, and a shrug of his solid shoulders. 'He is very confused, guilty, I think, and perhaps frightened. Perhaps you would like to see her before we start, it'll give me a few moments to get myself something to eat. Are you hungry?'

She shook her head and picked up her handbag. 'I'll see her, I'd like to.' She then reached over and touched his hand. Franks smiled.

'We all have our secrets, Helen, but, thankfully for me, they are no longer a nightmare, but a reality. Whatever is in Vebekka's past, must also become her own reality.'

It was a few moments after Helen had left the room

before Dr Franks looked at the old framed photograph of his parents and grandparents, his brothers and sisters. He was fourteen years old, it was his parents' wedding anniversary. There he was, leaning against his mother's chair, smiling to the camera and wearing plus-fours, a hand-knitted sweater and socks. He could even remember their colour, a mixture of brown and green wool, and his shoes, highly polished dark brown lace-ups. It was the only photograph that existed, just as he was the only member of the entire family who had survived the holocaust.

Vebekka was dressed, sitting on the edge of her bed staring out of the window. She didn't turn when Helen entered, but seemed to know it was her. 'I'm glad you came. Come and sit beside me.'

She seemed very calm, very rational. 'I asked Louis, I said to him, if things don't go well for me, I asked if he'd make sure I had some sleeping tablets. Of course he won't, he may think about it, but in the end he won't be able to help me, so, I'm asking you.'

'Please don't, because you know I couldn't do that.'

'I couldn't bear to be locked up in a little room like this for the rest of my life . . . and I know that is a possibility. I know, Helen.' She got up from the bed and walked around the small white-walled room. 'You know what is so awful? I never know – never know when it will take me over, and now I can't stand it any longer, to see the fear in that sweet-faced Hylda, the same fear in my children's eyes. I can't tell you what that does to me, to know I've hurt them, but not to know what I have done.'

Helen twisted her ring round her fingers. 'Do you know what you did last night?'

Vebekka giggled. 'Yes, I got very drunk, and I think I

got screwed in a toilet, but that often happens to sane people – they get drunk and screw, don't they?'

Helen laughed softly. 'Yes, I suppose they do.'

Vebekka was working her way gradually round the walls towards the door, to be directly behind Helen, and Helen suddenly felt wary. She turned quickly. Vebekka was leaning against the wall, her eyes on the ceiling.

'I met this big fat woman, and she kept on calling me by somebody else's name ... It was strange, frightening, because I knew I didn't know her, and yet I was sure I had been there before. Do you ever feel that way?'

'You mean *déjà vu?*'

'Yes, yes, that you are in a place that you have been to before, do you feel that way?'

Helen nodded, said she did sometimes, and Vebekka did a delighted quick twirl, like a dancer, ending up flopping on to the bed. 'I feel it all the time, all the time!'

She rolled on to her back, her arms spread out wide. 'You know, Louis loves me, he told me so, he's such a child, like a schoolboy. I think he's – he's afraid, Helen.'

She sat up and wrapped Helen in her arms. 'Take care of him, please, and Sasha, look after my baby for me.'

Helen hugged her tightly. 'Now, don't! You talk as if you were going away, but you're not.'

Vebekka rested her head on Helen's shoulder. 'I feel as if I am, Helen, I am so frightened. Please don't let him open the trunk, please tell him not to do that.'

Before Helen could answer, Dr Franks walked in. He made a mock bow and gave Vebekka his arm.

Torsen waited for the *Direktor* to come to the phone. He cleared his throat in preparation for his speech, but the rasping voice snapped out what the hell did Torsen want?

This was his holiday, the first he had taken in Switzerland since he had been married. Whatever it was had better warrant the interruption of his lunch. Torsen flicked a look at his watch, it was after three. Why on earth was he still eating lunch?

'Well, what do you want?'

Torsen began his laboured explanation of the investigation into the murder of Tommy Kellerman, his evidence and suspicions, constantly asking if the *Direktor* was still on the line, as he remained silent. At last he finished, turning to the last page of his copious notebook.

'And that's it? What's your most concrete piece of evidence? Sounds as if it's all supposition to me. The woman has an alibi, she has no motive, she's an American citizen. You need more, you need an eyewitness – the one you've got says he saw a man not a woman, you're going on a fucking imprint of a boot! That's your main evidence, isn't it? Have you got the boots? Do you know if they're hers?'

Torsen stuttered out that he required a search warrant to get the boots.

'So you haven't got the boots? As far as I can tell you've got fuck all – and you've seen too many American movies.'

Torsen asked his *Direktor* what he felt the next move should be. He was instructed brusquely to wait, told that the woman was not going anywhere, she was performing at the circus, so, until he had more concrete evidence, he should wait. The telephone was slammed down, and Torsen was about to replace his receiver when he heard the click from the switchboard and knew the operator had been listening. It infuriated him.

He tore out of his office and stormed into her booth. 'You were listening to a private call! Don't ever do that!'

She made a great show of removing the wires and plugs. 'I have a call for you, I was simply trying to put it through.

426

This exchange is antiquated, sir, and we need an extension buzzer. Would you like me to place the call through to you now, sir? It's the manager of the Grand Hotel.'

Torsen snapped at her to tell the man he was busy, and to call back. He burst into his office, kicked the door shut and swiped at his desk. His accumulated lists scattered, his notebook fell into the wastepaper basket, and his report sheets, neatly typed up for the *Direktor* to inspect on his return, received the dregs of his morning coffee. 'Shit! *Shit!*'

He sat in his chair, refusing to clean up the mess he had just created. He knew Ruda Kellerman was guilty of murder, knew it, and he should have taken the bloody boots. He dragged open his desk drawer, fished around for the envelope he had been given by the circus administrator containing his free tickets. At least he had got something out of all the hours he had put in. Attached to the tickets was an advertising leaflet, a coloured picture of Ruda Kellerman's face with the cats grouped behind her.

Torsen stared hard at her face, and then grabbed his coat. It was a chance, a long one, but if he could break Ruda Kellerman's alibi for the night of the murder, he knew he had enough to charge her, with or without the *Direktor*'s approval. His one hope was the bus conductor who had described the woman passenger the night Kellerman died; he might recognise her from the leaflet.

The Baron slipped into the viewing room, Helen turned and smiled, patting the seat next to her. They could see Vebekka lying on the sofa in the lounge area, eyes closed, a blanket covering her body.

'Rebecca, I want you to tell me about your mother, the way she used to say lie down, lie down and talk to me, so you would be calm, do you remember that?'

Franks waited, it had taken much longer this time to put

427

her under, but she was now deeply hypnotised. He waited, leaned forwards a fraction. 'Tell me about your mother, Rebecca, how she used to encourage you to—'

She interrupted him, lifting her hand lightly and then resting it on the blanket. Her voice sounded strangely tired, as if Rebecca the woman was formulating pictures, seeing herself as a child. 'Yes, it was in the study, in Papa's study, the big couch, he used to sleep on it, when he was working late.'

Franks waited again, then gently coaxed her to continue. 'What did she used to say to you?'

'Close your eyes, listen to my voice . . .'

'Do you know why she asked you to lie down?'

'Yes, because of my nightmares.'

'Did she take you from your bed to talk to you?'

'No, it was our name, we called them my nightmares, but I was not asleep, they happened in the day.'

'Can you tell me about one, about what happened?'

'Oh, Papa was playing his records, and . . . it started, I was very naughty, I broke Mama's china, all her precious china, every single piece. It was the music.'

'Why did you break your mama's china because of some music?'

'I remembered it.'

'What music was it? Do you know the name?'

'Wagner . . . he never played it again.'

'Why do you think Wagner upset you so much?'

She whispered, still speaking as the adult Rebecca, her voice conspiratorial. 'Uncle played it all the time, all the time.'

Franks frowned, looked to the glass and shrugged his shoulders, and then remembered. 'Your uncle Ulrich?'

'No, no. Uncle, uncle!' She plucked at the blanket, very distressed. Franks waited, and then softly told her to listen to her mama's voice, to stay calm, to be calm, and she sighed deeply.

Franks leaned forwards and checked her pulse. He frowned. 'Can you hear me, Rebecca?'

'Yes . . .' She sounded very distant, very quiet.

'What did your mama mean when she said put her in the cupboard and throw away the key?'

'Me.'

Franks asked if Rebecca was in the cupboard. She plucked at the blanket, seemed to be growing disturbed again. 'No, it was my other me.'

'You mean the one who broke your mama's china?'

'Yes, put her in the cupboard, lock away the key, forget her, forget the bad Rebecca, she was a naughty girl, she did bad things.'

'Is it Rebecca locked up? Is it Rebecca in the trunk with chains on?'

She started to struggle, very agitated. Again he told her to listen to her mama's voice, to stay calm. Again she calmed, and he checked her pulse, she was going deeper and deeper, breathing through her nose, making a pursed lip as she released the air.

'What is it in the trunk that frightens you so much?'

Her face pulled down like a child's as she started to cry; he let her cry for a while and asked again. She tossed and turned, and he repeated the question. She mumbled something and he didn't catch what she had said, he asked again, and this time the pitch of her voice was higher. 'My sister's in there.'

'Why is that so bad?'

'Because I ate her.'

'You hate your sister?'

'*No, no, I ate her.*' She twisted her body, squirming, her face distorted, and then she began to sob, and her words

429

tumbled out. She had eaten her sister, they told her she had eaten her, that was why she was fat, she had eaten her alive.

Franks had to tell her to calm again, to listen to the calming voice of her mama, and slowly she rested again, her head bending forwards.

'But you know that is impossible, people don't eat each other, so maybe that isn't true.'

Her voice was strong, it took him by surprise. '*Hah!* You don't know, you don't know . . . They stack the babies up, big pile of babies, and they put them in the ovens to eat them. *Hah!* See, you don't know!'

'Did you see that, Rebecca?'

'Yes.'

'And this person, this person inside you, did she see that?'

'Yes, we see it, we see it.'

Franks looked to the two-way mirror, gave a small shake of his head. 'Does this person—'

'Sister, she is my sister.'

'Ah, I see, your sister.'

'*Yes! Yes!*'

'And she is inside you because you think you have eaten her?'

'*Yes. Yes.*'

'Does she have a name?'

'*Yes. Yes!*'

'Will you tell me her name?'

Vebekka's face pulled down in a clown-like show of heartbreak. 'Ruda.'

Franks looked at the mirror. Both Helen and the Baron stared back at him. Then Helen jumped up and left the room. She called for Maja, asking her to pass a message to Franks. Maja asked her to write it down, and then she put her fingers to her lips, and entered the lounge area.

430

Helen returned to the viewing room and stared at the glass. Maja held up the note, he looked towards Helen and smiled. Maja crept out, closing the door behind her soundlessly.

'Is Ruda your twin?'

'*Yes! Yes, Ruda and me, me and Ruda!*'

'I see. I understand now, and Ruda is inside you?'

'*Yes! Yes!*' She pulled at the blanket, her brow furrowed. She twisted again, began the wringing motion.

'What are you doing? Rebecca? Can you hear my voice? Tell me if you can hear my voice. Rebecca?'

She was in the dark airless room. It was so cold outside but in this room it was always hot.

'Hot, I'm hot . . .'

'Where – can you tell me where you are?'

The reply was fast, as if an order had been given to her. The child's voice remained: 'Hospital, C 33 wing, hospital hut 42.'

Franks removed the blanket. She seemed not to notice.

She was seeing him, remembering him, watching the white gloves lay out the cards, one by one, she could hear that persuasive voice, she could smell him, he was telling her to concentrate on the cards, to look at the cards. 'Remember the cards, Rebecca, keep on looking at the cards, remember the cards . . .'

Franks asked Rebecca to listen only to his voice, whatever else she was seeing, but she sat up, bolt upright, and her head began to swivel, right left, right left. Franks asked what she was doing. She didn't answer. He told her to hear her mother's voice, to stay calm. She kept on flicking her head from side to side, a set expression on her face. She saw the white gloves move to the curtain, she wasn't ready, she wasn't ready, but the curtain began to move slowly, and then she saw Ruda, poor Ruda. She was held up by the woman; seeing Rebecca she gave a tiny wave of her

431

hand, but she was too weak to stand up, she was so thin, her body was covered with sores, and Rebecca had to remember.

Franks became concerned: Vebekka was dragging at her clothes, still sitting upright, dragging and pulling at her clothes. 'Rebecca, listen to me, can you hear me?'

Again she made no answer, she had to get the colours right, she had to get the colours right, she had to get the colours. The same soft persuasive voice was talking to her again. 'Feed your sister the colours, feed them to her, make her call out the colours and she will have sweeties, she will have toys . . . Come along, my pretty one, the curtain will be closing, I am closing the curtain.'

Vebekka was rigid. Franks checked her pulse, it was very fast, she was not responding to him, seemed not to hear him. 'Rebecca, listen to me, start to come through the years now, listen to my voice.'

She began to speak in German for the first time, still paying no attention to Franks, her words like small rapid bullets: 'RED, RED, BLUE, RED, GREEN, BLUE, RED, BLUE, RED, RED, RED, RED, RED, BLUE, GREEN . . .'

Franks pressed his emergency button for Maja to enter. Vebekka continued to call out the colours, as Maja moved to his side. She carried an electrode box.

The Baron looked to Helen. 'Dear God, what is happening in there?'

Helen, unsure herself, tried to calm him. 'It's all right, he knows what he is doing.'

'Red, blue, green, red, red, red, green, blue, red, green . . .' She suddenly grew quiet, her voice trailing away, her head slumped on to her chest.

'Rebecca, *Rebecca*, can you hear me?'

She murmured, and he signalled to Maja that he didn't need the electrode box. He moved close to the bed, held Vebekka's hand, and spoke softly to her, bringing her through the cycles. She seemed drugged, her voice slurred. 'Yes, I can hear you . . .'

Franks asked where she was. She made no answer, and he asked again, telling her to listen to his voice, her mama's voice was gone, just to hear his, he wanted her to remember what she had been telling him, it was important she remember . . . They watched her as she came closer and closer to the surface, and then he held her hand. 'Sleep for a little while now, sleep and when you wake you will feel well, you will feel able to discuss everything we have talked about, do you hear me?'

'Yes, I can hear you.'

'Who am I?'

'Dr Franks.'

'Who are you?'

'My real name is Rebecca, but I call myself Vebekka.'

Franks relaxed; he dabbed his head with his handkerchief. He ordered Maja to sit close to the bed, then he walked out.

Helen and the Baron joined Franks in his office where he was sipping a glass of water. 'Well, now we know. Your wife, Baron Maréchal, had been hypnotised by her mother to forget, possibly in an attempt to help her. But the outcome, as you know more than anyone else, has been catastrophic. She is deeply traumatised by her childhood. I will need many sessions, we have only just begun.'

Helen could not sit down and paced up and down. 'As you know, Mengele experimented with tiny children, in particular identical twins, more with the females than the males – he discovered females were more telepathic, but first he had to decipher which twin was the more adept at receiving.'

Franks took a number of books from his shelves. 'We will need to examine every possible record of Mengele's tests. I think Rebecca was repeating some kind of code – the colours were spoken not in French or English, but German. Yet she has always maintained she did not speak German, did not understand it.'

The Baron stepped between them. 'I don't think you have any idea what you are doing. I saw her in there – how can you allow this to continue, don't you think she has been used enough – experimented on as a child? Now as an adult you want to take it another step. I refuse to allow this, I refuse!'

Franks sat heavily in his chair. 'You cannot do this – you cannot leave her in limbo because that is where she will be. We have opened up the horrors inside her and she will need extensive therapy to be able to control them and come to terms with—'

'*No*, I refuse, I refuse!'

Franks looked at Helen. 'You had better discuss this in private.' He walked out, furious. The man was a fool – they had made incredible progress and he was sure, with therapy, Rebecca could come to terms with her past, face it head on.

He walked down the corridor, as Maja came out of the lounge area. 'Is she still sleeping?'

She nodded, and looked past him to his office. 'Trouble?'

He sighed, and gave an exasperated gesture. 'Isn't there always? He wants us to stop.'

'But you can't – doesn't he realise what you accomplished today?'

Franks smiled ruefully. 'I think Vebekka's mother accomplished a great deal today, tomorrow I will begin work, I hope. Go talk to him, persuade him for me.'

Franks let himself into the lounge area. Vebekka was already sitting up, her feet on the ground, but she looked tousled, her hair standing up on end, as if she had been deeply asleep.

'How is my sleeping beauty?' he asked gently.

434

'A bit bruised, shaky, but she's still here.'

She looked up to him and he opened his arms, she went to him and held him tightly. Her voice was muffled. 'I want my sister, I want my sister.'

He stroked her hair. 'I know, I know, and you've hidden her away for all these years, haven't you? But you know now you didn't hurt her, it wasn't you, Vebekka. It was not you.'

She gave a wobbly smile, and asked for a drink. He went to a side table, and poured some iced water. 'Your husband is very afraid, for you. He wants to end the sessions.'

She took a cigarette from a box provided and he lit it for her; she inhaled deeply, and then picked up the glass of water. 'Do you think this longing I have felt always . . . is it for Ruda?'

He nodded his head. 'Of course – she was part of you, she was your twin.'

She nodded as if trying to assimilate the fact, and then sat down on the sofa. 'I feel a terrible sense of loss.'

'That is only natural, you have lost your safety barrier, your trunk, the one with all the chains, the one you were so afraid to open, you've lost that.'

She stubbed out the cigarette. 'What did they do to me?'

He crouched down in front of her. 'We'll find out, we'll find it all out, my pretty one, and gradually you will understand. But it will be hard going, we have a long way to go.'

She nodded again. 'I don't remember . . . I don't remember.'

He touched her head, moving a strand of hair away from her brow – she felt hot. He stood up. 'Drink up, drink the water.'

'I'm tired.'

'Then sleep, you can sleep in here, no need to go back to your room, rest here.' Franks settled her down, tucked the blanket around her and waited as she lay with her eyes open. 'Don't try to remember, just rest. We will take it stage by stage, year by year until all the pieces are back in place. You have a lot to catch up on, your mama—'

'She wasn't my real mama, I know that.'

He smiled down at her. 'I think you will know everything, I sincerely believe it, and there will be no more rages, no more violence, it was, if you like, poor Ruda – you locked her away, but she wouldn't lie quiet. Now you will be able to give her peace.'

She frowned. 'Peace,' she repeated. Her eyes closed, and she seemed to have fallen asleep. Franks quietly let himself out and signalled to Maja to be close by. He felt tired himself.

Maja went to her office, the desk exactly opposite the lounge, giving her clear access to the door. She was just about to sit down when Helen called out to her. 'Do you have some aspirin? Baron Maréchal is feeling ill.'

Maja went into the medicine cabinet, took out a bottle of aspirins and fetched a glass of water. The Baron was very pale, and thanked her profusely, saying he had a bad headache. She smiled understandingly, and said it must have been a difficult afternoon for him. She had been gone from her desk no more than five or ten minutes at most. She returned to her desk, and looked around for her handbag. It had gone. She returned to the office, then looked into reception. She was sure she had left her handbag by her desk, but went and checked in the viewing room to make sure. She did not see her handbag, but that became of secondary importance because when she looked into the lounge area, Vebekka had gone.

Maja ran back to the office. She called for Helen, the panic rising. 'Is she with you?'

Helen joined her in the corridor. 'She's not in the lounge, I'll try Dr Franks's son's room.'

Helen walked into reception. 'Has the Baroness been through here?'

The young nurse looked up and smiled at Helen. 'Yes, about five minutes ago.'

'Did she leave the building?'

'Yes, yes, she said her taxi was waiting. Is something wrong?'

Dr Franks came into reception. 'I don't believe this. Helen has just told me – is it true? – Vebekka has gone, just walked out and nobody stopped her.'

Helen said that she could not get far. She had no handbag, no money on her, but Maja said she was wrong – her own handbag was gone.

Louis looked up, his head thudding, as Helen walked in. She held the door. 'We have to go, quickly. Vebekka just walked out, nobody knows where she has gone, she's taken Maja's handbag. We'll get a taxi and start searching the streets, Dr Franks will remain here. We have to find her.'

Vebekka sat in the back of the taxi, opened Maja's handbag, removed some money, and got out of the cab at the Grand Hotel. She handed Maja's handbag back to the driver. 'Would you return with this to the clinic – but in about an hour? They'll pay the fare for the delivery. Thank you.'

Vebekka strolled through reception, asked for the key to their suite, and then rang for the lift. She hurried to their suite, locked the door behind her, ran into the bedroom and began to pick out a few garments. She fetched a purse and rifled through Louis's bedside table to find some cash. She froze as there was a light tap on the main door to the suite. She crept towards it and the light knock was repeated.

'Who is it?' Vebekka whispered.

'Hylda, it's just Hylda, Baroness. I saw you down in reception and . . .'

Hylda stepped back as the door inched open. 'Hylda, I am afraid I can't see you. Wait, please, wait one moment.'

The door closed and was relocked. Hylda looked around. Had the Baron returned, too? She had not seen him. She tapped the door again. 'Are you all right? Baroness?'

The door was unlocked and Vebekka opened it, only a fraction. 'This is for you. I have no money. Please, please take this.'

The leather box was thrust into Hylda's hands, but she was not interested in the contents, more concerned for the Baroness. 'Where is your husband? And Dr Masters? Baroness?'

'They are due any moment. I must go. God bless you, dear Hylda, take care, goodbye.'

The door was shut and locked once again. Hylda hesitated, only now opening the gift. She gasped. The beautiful bluebird brooch nestled in the velvet lined box. She snapped it shut. She would return later, give it back, if not to the Baroness then to her husband. Hylda went slowly towards the staff staircase, opened the box again. It was, she knew, one of the Baroness's favourite pieces. So like her, the bird, as if in flight, so fragile, and she knew she would have to return it. What she did not know, could not have known, was that she would never see the Baroness again.

Vebekka slipped out of the suite fifteen minutes later. She was looking refreshed and elegant.

She went downstairs and asked the doorman to call her a taxi. One drew up at the red carpet within moments.

'The club, Magda's, Mama Magda's, quickly, please. I am in a great hurry.'

She sat well back in the seat and took out her dark glasses, afraid she would be seen. She knew they would be looking for her but she had to know why the big fat woman had called her Ruda. She knew now that Ruda was free – she had released her – and she felt a strange sensation inside her. The feeling of loss was disappearing because, she was sure, Ruda was alive.

CHAPTER EIGHTEEN

LUIS HAD let Ruda sleep, was sitting as if on guard in the trailer. He was very concerned, and kept an eye on the clock; she had already missed any chance of a pre-show rehearsal. He had explained her absence by saying she had a migraine. Would she be capable of doing the main show that evening? Her first spot was at eight forty-five, and he knew that if she was no better, he would have to withdraw the act.

'Luis? What time is it?' She stood in the doorway, her face very pale, and she was shaking badly.

He rushed to her and helped her sit down. 'You've missed the rehearsal, sweetheart, but don't worry.'

'Oh, God!'

She hung her head, and he slipped an arm around her shoulders. 'They've all been fed, and after last night they won't need a run this afternoon. You just rest, I've got you a hot chocolate.'

She closed her eyes, leaning on the bench cushions. He held out the mug of hot chocolate, a thick skin on top. She smiled, and pushed it aside with her finger. 'You always burn the milk.'

He crouched down in front of her. 'What happened?'

She sipped the chocolate, her hands cupped round the mug, and gave a wan smile. 'Ghosts . . .'

'You want to talk about it?'

She shook her head. He went and sat opposite her. 'Will you be fit enough for the show tonight?'

'Try and stop me!'

He chuckled, but he was very concerned; she seemed to have no energy, her body was listless, her eyes heavy as if weighed down.

'Is it about the box? The tin box? I wasn't prying, I was looking for my old albums, you know me, always looking to the past. I found it, I know maybe I shouldn't have opened it, but to be honest I didn't think you'd find out.'

'No, you shouldn't have opened it, but you did, so that's that.' She put the mug down. 'I'd better check on the cats.'

'No, I've done it, and the boys are there. You just rest, you'll need all your strength for the show.'

She nodded, and again he was deeply concerned; it was unlike her to agree to anything he suggested. He snatched a look at his watch: there was time. She stared through him, beyond him, her eyes vacant.

'Do you want me to tell you what you said?'

'What?' She seemed miles away.

'I found you all curled up in the shower, carried you in my arms like a baby – bet you haven't let anybody do that for a long time, huh?' He was trying to make light of it, attempting to draw her back.

'Nobody ever held me when I was a baby, Luis, nobody, only . . . only my . . .'

He waited but she bowed her head. 'Sister?' he interjected. 'You said you wanted your sister, I've never even heard you talk about a sister before, I mean, were you dreaming? You were freaked out!'

Her whole body shuddered and she clasped her arms around herself, staring at the floor, her voice so soft he had to strain to hear her. 'You know when we went to the Grand Hotel? After we'd been to the mortuary, something sort of happened inside me. I had a feeling . . . so many years, Luis, I've tried, tried to find her, but – she was called Rebecca, and I was called Ruda. We were taken in a train, hours and hours on a big dark train. Rebecca slept, but I kept guard over her, I watched out for her, she . . . she didn't talk too good, I used to talk for Rebecca.'

She leaned back with her eyes closed, remembering the noise of the iron wheels on the rails. She could remember someone, someone crying all the time, the rat-tat-tat of the wheels and the weeping, but everyone was crying, howling, screaming, rat-tat-tat . . . hand in hand they were crushed and pushed and trodden on as the big doors were inched back. Had it been days or hours? She lost count, but at last the rat-tat-tat had stopped. Rebecca was crying because she had messed her panties, done it in her panties, she cried for Mama, but they had no mama, she was gone, and then the voices, screaming, screaming voices.

'Women to the left, men to the right, women and children to the left, men to the right.' So tiny, so young they didn't know right from left.

'Any twins? Twins over here, twins here, dwarfs, giants . . . twins . . .'

Ruda was picked up and thrown to a group of screaming women. Rebecca fought and shouted to her sister, and the guard had picked Ruda up by her hair and tossed her across to another group. The screaming went on and on, and, pushed and kicked, they were herded towards a long, long path, at the end of which were gates, big high gates. Fences, with barbed wire as high as the sky, surrounded hundreds and hundreds of huts.

Ruda dodged between legs, squeezed under the marching, bedraggled, weeping women and screeching children. At the gates she caught up with Rebecca, holding a strange woman's hand, and the guard started shouting orders. Ruda tugged at his sleeve. 'My sister, my sister!'

The guard had looked into their identical faces, grabbed them and hauled them into the back of a truck, just inside the perimeter of the gates. '*Twins! Twins!*'

The truck rumbled and swayed over potholes and

ditches, a truck filled with children, clinging in pairs, identical faces clung in terror to each other – boys, girls, all shapes and sizes, but with one thing in common: they were twins.

Luis sat next to her; he wanted to hold her, comfort her, but she remained leaning back with her eyes closed. He heard only part of what she was saying; she lapsed into silences, and then odd words came out, disjointed words, some in Polish, Russian, Czech and German, but she remained motionless. Seeing with her adult's eyes what she had seen as a two-year-old – the carts of dead skeletons, the strange eerie women with their shaven skull-like heads . . . the screaming women giving birth on a stone slab, and the babies taken, still with the afterbirth covering their tiny bodies, and thrown on to a seething mass of babies, dying, taking their first breath with their last, and the weeping and wailing never stopped, and the cold icy wind never stopped, the snow and ice freezing, freezing the memories like crystals.

They clung together, slept together, and played together. No mother, no father, no brothers, no religion, no surname, all they knew was that they were sisters, Ruda and Rebecca, and, protected by being a pair, they fought when needed as one.

The normal ration for all prisoners was a bowl of soup, and anything could be found in this watery filthy liquid, tufts of hair, buttons, rags – even mice. The soup was their nourishment for the day. The evening meal was black bread, a ration of six and one half ounces, with more sawdust than dough. Hunger-ravaged faces, clawing hands begging, pleading for food.

In comparison with the other inmates, the twins were fed well. They were given not only clean clothes but toys, and their childish laughter tore into the tortured minds of the rest of the inmates, made them weep and scream for their lost babies. Men and women clung to the wire meshing that segregated these special children, clung and screamed abuse at them, hating them because they were playing. Some mothers clung on in desperation to see the faces of their children, and some crept out in the freezing night and twisted their rags to hang themselves.

But the twins who were old enough to understand knew it would be only a short time before the innocent laughter stopped. They knew what was to come, they had seen the twins carried back to their bunks in the dead of night from the hospital. Tiny, broken bodies lifted from the trolleys, minus limbs, blinded, bruised and disorientated by drugs and chemicals pumped into young veins . . . and those that knew wept in silence, because they knew that one day it would be their turn.

Gradually even the tiny ones, the new inmates, the fresh twins, the ones as young as Ruda and Rebecca, began to understand. When the nurse called out the numbers to go to the experiment wing, they trembled in fear . . . The fear made the children grow old fast – only the fit survived, only the strong survived the mutilations, the drugs. Hundreds came and went, but those who survived grew an inner strength, learning to interchange with each other to save the agony. They switched places, they stole to feed each other; they each became a single unit.

Papa Mengele had a particular liking for the two tiny girls; he had them called out regularly. To the jealousy of the other children they had sweets, and a very special treat – they had chocolate. Ruda and Rebecca began to trust the man who said they could call him 'Papa' or 'Uncle'. They liked him, and went to the experimental wing hand in hand.

Mengele was fascinated by the way they interacted. Rebecca, slow to talk, began a sentence and Ruda completed it. They were so close, they often spoke in unison, moved in unison. Their closeness absorbed him, and for many weeks he simply examined them, monitored them together.

Ruda reached out and held Luis's hand, she clenched it tightly now, as words and sentences seemed to be dragged painfully from her memory. At times her voice was so soft he had to bend close to her to hear. 'She was always smiling. He even let her play with his precious white gloves; she would sit on his knee and hug and kiss him, and he teased her, said she could call him "Papa", and she would put her arms around his neck and kiss him . . . But his eyes, Luis, his eyes were like the Devil's, and he would stare at me. I was afraid of him, I tried to warn her, he knew I didn't trust him, he knew it. I couldn't go near him, I was always afraid of him, but Rebecca had no fear, and then, one day, he said he was going to show her something pretty. I tried to stop her, and she slapped me, said to leave her alone, she was going with her papa to see something nice, and she held his hand, and she left me . . .'

Ruda got up, she went to the window and stared out, her hands hanging limply at her sides. 'She didn't come back for three days. For three days my body burned, my head ached, I screamed with the pain, cried out for them to stop. I knew . . . I felt every single injection, I knew they were hurting her. Then they brought her back, the nurse carried her in, pushed her on to the bunk bed. Her eyes were glazed, she was burning hot, and she just lay there. I didn't know what they had done to her – her face was bloated, her belly distended, her cheeks flushed bright rosy red. They didn't call us for a long time. I stole what food I could, slept with her in my arms, warmed her with my body . . . and just as she was better, able to get up, they came back for her. When they called her number, I took her place.

'But they knew who I was, and I was punished for trying

to fool them.' She covered her face with her hands. She couldn't tell him what they had done that had hurt . . . but what had been worse was not being with Rebecca, and each day they promised she would see her soon. They gave her no food, nothing, and every day came the interminable agonising X-rays, the electrodes to her head, the drugs. They burnt her insides, kept on asking her questions she didn't understand, asking the same question over and over, 'Tell us what your sister is doing, tell us. If you tell us you will be given sweeties.'

Ruda sobbed, wringing her hands. 'I didn't know what they wanted, I didn't understand. I hurt so much, I was in such terrible, terrible pain, all I did was cry. Luis, they hurt me so much, and then . . . then they took me to this little room, locked me inside, all alone, all by myself, nobody came to see me, nobody gave me any food. And then the new pains began, my head, my arms, my knees were on fire. I screamed, louder and louder, begging them to stop, to stop hurting her.'

Luis leaned closer. 'I don't understand.'

She almost screamed it, her face puce with rage: 'I felt what they were doing to her, I felt every pain. I knew what they were doing to her, because I felt it.' She gave a sobbing laugh, stood up to pace around the trailer. 'Papa was very pleased with me. They came to me then, and I was carried into another room. They gave me hot milk and cookies, kept on telling me what a good girl I was.'

Ruda stared from the trailer window, then pressed her head against the cold windowpane. 'They took care of me, bandaged my knees, put ointment on my legs and stomach, dressed me in clean clothes. Then they took me into his office, made me sit in front of him. He had . . . a – ' she turned back to Luis, 'telephone, and he was smiling at me. They were playing music on a gramophone, he spoke to someone, told them to begin. Oh, Luis, I screamed out –

446

my head, I said they were hurting my head, then my stomach. The more I cried out in agony, the more agitated he became, shouting into the phone, again . . . again, until I fell to the floor. Then he replaced the phone, picked me up and sat me on his knee, told me what a good girl I was. Then she came in.'

'Your sister?' asked Luis.

'No. Papa's assistant. She came in, and he said to her: "This is the strong one. Say hello, Ruda, say hello to—"'

She couldn't continue, slumped on to the bench. Luis reached out and drew her into his arms. 'Did you ever see her again?'

She whispered: 'Through the glass window . . . they used to show me her through the glass window. Her face was like a stranger's, she was fatter, more bloated, but she still tried to smile at me. Then they would draw the curtain, and she was gone. The nurses would tell me that if I was a good girl, if I could tell them what Rebecca was thinking, they wouldn't hurt her any more.'

He held her close, his cheek resting against hers. She kept on staring ahead, whispering, 'You remember the silk scarves? The old magician? That's where I learned it, Luis. They said they wouldn't hurt her if I could tell them the colours, and I used to try so hard, try to tell them what they wanted to know, but they still would never let me see her, touch her.'

'But why, what did any of it prove?'

'They wanted me to read her mind, they showed her all these colour charts, cards, and . . . and I failed, I couldn't get it right, so many, they wanted so many. I tried, I used to try very hard. When I failed they would burn me, make me try again, and I did, because then they didn't hurt her. If they had done, I would have known, but she wouldn't concentrate. I'd always been able to think for her, talk for her, but she . . . didn't concentrate hard enough. And then one day they came to me, clearly, one colour after another. Papa applauded and shouted, and they let me see her. They told me I was a good girl, that I had saved my sister and if I continued to be a good girl she would not be hurt.'

'Did they continue to torture you?'

She nodded. 'Not so much – but they would not let me hold her. I was kept all by myself, but you know, I knew she was being taken care of, so it was all right. But then, I got so tired I couldn't, I couldn't do it. They took her away, it was my fault.' Her voice was hardly audible, as she whispered, 'They hurt her . . . but all I could feel was her terror.'

Luis felt so inadequate. He held Ruda tightly. 'You listen to me. From now on, when something hurts you, when you remember, you tell me. Because no ghost is going to touch you, blame you. I love you, Ruda, do you hear me? You have done no wrong, you have done nothing wrong, you can't blame yourself, you were just a baby.'

She broke from him, and gave him a strange look. He could feel her mistrust.

'It's true, Ruda, you have done nothing wrong! You have to believe that!'

She reached the door leading to the small hallway. 'I had better rest before tonight.'

'You sure you will be all right to do the show?'

She nodded. 'I do care for you, Luis, you know that. I think I always have. Maybe, in my own way, I—' She couldn't say the word.

'Ruda, maybe it's taken me a long time to realise just how much I need you, that I'm nothing without you . . . but I understand that you need me, you need me, Ruda, and it makes me feel good.'

'Don't tell anyone what I have told you.'

'As if I would . . . but, remember, you have nothing to be ashamed of.'

She gave him that look, her eyes slightly downcast. 'I didn't tell you all of it, some things you can never tell anybody, you know why? Because nobody could really believe it ever happened.'

'Can I ask you something?'

She looked at him impatiently.

'Did you know Kellerman at the camp? Was he at the same place?'

'Yes, Kellerman was at Birkenau with us. I didn't know him there . . . He had it bad, they made him fuck dogs for their entertainment – and you thought it was funny to make jokes about the size of his dick, didn't you? See, look at you, you don't really believe it, do you? Kellerman the clown, *haw haw*! They degraded him, defiled him, and treated him like an animal, *haw haw*. Kellerman was not a clown, not in his heart.'

'You did see him, here in Berlin. You saw him, didn't you?'

She stared at him directly, not a flicker of an indication she was lying. 'No. I suppose he came to try to squeeze money out of me, but I didn't see him. Look, I'd better go and rest, then I'll check on the animals.'

She closed the door of her bedroom. Grimaldi cleared away her half-finished mug of hot chocolate. He ran the water into the sink and turned off the taps, then strode across the trailer, rapped on her door. She pulled it open. 'What?'

'The *Polizei*, that little prick of an inspector was here. He wanted to know about the night Kellerman died, something about a pair of boots, the ones he'd seen outside.'

She shrugged, gestured to her closet. 'He can take whichever ones he likes. Is that all you wanted to say to me? I got a lot to do.'

He looked at her and started to walk out. 'I'll go and check over the props – and, Ruda, if you still have

449

Kellerman's hat, get rid of it, they asked about that, a leather trilby. Mike borrowed it, he said that you had said it was mine. Get rid of it, Ruda.' Grimaldi slammed out of the trailer.

Ruda kicked her door shut. 'Shit! Shit!'

She paced up and down. She had got rid of everything, she was safe, they couldn't connect her to Kellerman's murder. Then she realised that maybe the *Polizei* had not made any connection, but Grimaldi had. She stood, hands clenched at her sides. 'Shit!' She talked herself through, making herself calm. Well, she could handle him . . .

Torsen hovered around the bus station, checking his watch. He had been there over an hour and he was getting edgy. He had to get back to his apartment, bath, change and collect Freda; he wouldn't make it if the bus didn't come soon. There was a loud bang as a car backfired, and Torsen looked out. His man had arrived in a cloud of exhaust fumes. Torsen hurried towards the conductor as he slammed the door shut. 'Eh, you'd better be careful, slam it too hard and the engine'll fall out.'

Torsen smiled. 'Could I have just a word?'

The conductor nodded, said he would have to make it quick as he was due out of the depot ten minutes ago. Torsen produced the leaflet showing Ruda Kellerman's face, having carefully cut around the circus name and cut out the lion's head. 'Can you look at this? It's not a proper photograph, but it's a very good likeness of someone we think may have been the passenger on your bus the night the dwarf was murdered. You remember we spoke about it?'

The conductor nodded again, clocking in with his card, and collecting his money bag from the office. Torsen trailed after him, back to the waiting bus. 'Would you have a look, please?'

'You know, it's a while back now, I dunno if I can remember her, let me see . . .' He squinted at the picture of Ruda, tipped his hat up. He held it this way and that. 'I'm sure I've seen this before . . .'

'But is it the woman on your bus that night?'

'I have definitely seen this woman's face before, but whether it was her or not, I couldn't honestly say. I just took her fare, I didn't even have a conversation with her . . . It could be, but I wouldn't say it was.'

Torsen slipped the picture back into his wallet. 'Thanks for your time. Have a good night!'

Torsen returned to his car and was unlocking it as the bus rumbled past. Displayed on the side of the bus not seen by Torsen was a large poster – of Ruda Kellerman's face about a *foot high*. Torsen threw up his hands. So much for a valued eye witness. He drove back to his apartment. On the way he radioed in to see if there were any messages, and said he would be requiring the patrol car for some work that evening. Everybody in the station knew he was going to the circus and using the patrol car in off-duty periods was against the regulations. Rieckert called back to Torsen asking if he could pick him up. There was just his girlfriend and himself. Torsen snapped that he thought he was giving the tickets to his wife and kids. Rieckert laughed. 'Nah, they hate the circus. See you about seven, over and out!'

Mama Magda's was empty when Vebekka pushed open the door. She called out and, receiving no reply, crept down the dark unlit staircase to the basement club. She passed through the arch with the beaded curtains and called out

451

again. The office – the room where she had sat with Magda – had a light on. Eric opened the door.

'Could I see Magda, the woman who owns this club?'

Eric squinted in the darkness, unable to see her face clearly.

'I just want to talk to her.'

'That would be very difficult. Who are you?'

Vebekka said who she was, and Eric opened the door wider. 'Please, it is very important I speak to her.'

Eric gestured for her to come into the office. She stood in the doorway. 'You're twenty-four hours too late, she died last night.'

Vebekka sighed and leaned on the door frame. 'Oh, no, no, please, no!'

Eric offered her a chair, but she refused. 'Can I help in any way? I've taken over the club. Sit, please sit.'

'She called me Ruda . . .'

Eric remarked that Magda called a lot of people names, and then he saw how distressed Vebekka was. 'Look, I'm sorry, I can't help you.'

Vebekka walked out, Eric watched her leave, then remembered the handbag he still had. If she was who she said she was maybe she could cause trouble. He opened the drawer, picked up the bag and scuttled after her. He could see her up ahead of him on the pavement and he called out. She stopped and turned back. 'You left this last night, your handbag. No money, there was no money in it, OK?'

She stared at the bag, uninterested. Eric thrust it towards her. 'It's yours. Eh, are you OK?'

She took it and tucked it under her arm. She seemed close to tears. 'It was perhaps just a coincidence, you see . . . Ruda – Ruda was my sister. The big woman called me Ruda, kept on calling me Ruda.'

'I can ask around for you. What's her surname?'

'I don't know.'

452

Eric backed away. She was a fruitcake. 'Well, I can't help you then, goodbye. Any time you're passing, drop in.'

He made his way back, and heard a screech of tyres. She had walked out into the street and a car had narrowly missed her, but she kept on walking, not even turning to the shocked driver.

Helen hurried to the Baron; she was out of breath, having run from the hotel forecourt and back to reception. 'She came to the hotel, she went up to the suite, and then took a taxi. The manager spoke to her, the driver has just got back. He said Vebekka went to a club, "Mama Magda's", he's waiting to take us there now.'

When they reached Magda's club, Eric explained that the Baroness had been there, but swore he had returned her handbag left from the previous evening.

'We are not interested in that, we simply want to know where she went. Do you know?'

Eric explained she was looking for her sister, someone called Ruda, and the next minute she almost got herself killed, walking across the central road, straight into the traffic. He followed them out to the pavement, and watched them virtually get knocked over as well as they ran across the road, car horns tooting at them. He shook his head. Crazy foreigners, all of them crazy.

Vebekka walked on, bumped into passersby, kept on walking, walking . . . she turned into a churchyard, unaware of where she was, where she was going. Pictures kept cutting across her mind, fragments, disjointed memories. She walked into the church and sat in a pew at the back. Rosa used to take her to church on Sundays; her adopted father never accompanied them. Vebekka closed her eyes, bowing

453

her head. She used to call Rosa 'the woman', she had not known who she was, but the woman worked at the hospital where they had taken her after the camp was liberated, when she had been very ill.

The woman had been so kind, the way she had explained she was just examining her, trying to see if she needed any medication. She was so kind, gently touching her arms, asking what her name was, asking if she remembered her name, but Rebecca was too terrified to talk. Any moment she expected the needle, any moment they were going to stick needles into her arms. When the needles didn't come, she was in terror they would bring the electric pads, and she hid beneath the sheets, but after a few weeks, maybe even months – she knew only night and day, not weeks or months, she lived only for each day – eventually, she had begun to believe she was safe; then they had taken her to an X-ray department, and she had screamed and screamed.

The woman used to come every day with little presents, and Rebecca would refuse to take them: she knew it was a trick. She had been in the hospital for six months before she was transferred to an orphanage; she had still not spoken, and she had begun to get used to the nice woman's visits. She had explained to Rebecca that she was in Berlin with her husband, that she was not a qualified doctor, just helping in any way she could. She had held the frightened girl's hand, saying she just wanted to help her, she must not be afraid, and she would keep on coming to see her, if Rebecca wished. She had asked Rebecca if that was what she wanted and Rebecca had slowly nodded . . .

The older children used to tell terrible stories, steal her things, pinch her; she was so fat – they called her a pig, she was a fat pig. They were too young, too bruised themselves to know she had been injected and tortured, they had all suffered, but for Rebecca – who looked fit and healthy – the teasing and jokes ostracised her. She rarely spoke, she

454

mourned her sister, cried for her every night. Then the nice lady arrived with her husband. She asked if Rebecca would like to come away with them, if she would like to live with them.

Rosa and David Goldberg had many children to choose from, but Rebecca had touched Rosa deeply; she was also the most outwardly healthy of the children, and Rosa was sure that, in time, she would overcome her terror, and they knew she was not dumb.

They had attempted to trace Rebecca's family but to no avail; she could not remember her surname, they only knew her first name because one of the children told them. Rebecca left with the Goldbergs a year and a half after her release from Birkenau, but it was months before she began to believe they were not going to hurt her.

Rosa made the decision never to speak of Birkenau. What she had so far learned of it was too much for her to accept and she felt it was better for Rebecca to forget, never to speak of the past. They had a plastic surgeon remove her tattoo, and although the operation had distressed her, the doctors and nurses terrifying to her, she recovered remarkably quickly.

Nevertheless, three years after the adoption, Rosa was beginning to despair. Rebecca still hid food, urinated on the floor, wet her bed every night. She remained suspicious and uncommunicative, retreating into sulking silences for so long that Rosa began to think she would never settle down. And she had nightmares: virtually every night she woke screaming hysterically and would let no one near her. At school she disrupted the class. She had no friends, she fought and spat and kicked at other children. She stole the children's toys and their luncheon boxes.

Her eating habits varied from refusing food for days on end to eating binges; Rosa would find her sitting on the

455

floor by the fridge eating everything she could find – mustard and jam, raw eggs, anything her hands could reach for, she would stuff into her mouth.

Rebecca was sly, she lied, she would fly into terrifying, uncontrollable rages, and she wore Rosa Goldberg down. No care, no love seemed to break through her resistance. She was as cruel and vicious to pets as to the smaller children at the school. The Goldbergs began to feel they had adopted a monster.

Therapy sessions followed, and in some way helped; through the therapy her adoptive parents discovered she had a twin sister. Rosa had tried to trace Ruda in a desperate bid to help Rebecca, but it was a long, fruitless search, financially exhausting as well. Ruda, it was presumed, had died in the camp. There was no record of her leaving Birkenau, no record in any orphanage; she had, like thousands of others, disappeared; no grave, no name, no number was ever traced.

David Goldberg was at his wits' end; under the strain of caring for Rebecca his wife was becoming a nervous wreck, obsessed with helping the child. As a last resort, when they arrived in Philadelphia Rosa arranged a session with a hypnotherapist. For the first time Rebecca calmed, and then Rosa read every book she could find on the subject. She trained at a local clinic until she could give Rebecca sessions at home, and gradually she began to blank out from the child's mind the memory of her past.

Rebecca did not transform overnight. There were setbacks when Ruda was remembered. So Rosa found the solution. She talked Rebecca into locking her sister away, so she would not come out, would not make her do bad things. She would lock her away and lose the key. It was, in some ways, justified, because from then on Rebecca was able to study at school and she caught up well . . .

Vebekka sat back, staring at the altar. She understood

now why she had been so afraid for her babies, afraid they would be born with two heads, born twisted, with ropes. She had been too young to understand what an umbilical cord was. She had seen the skeleton-headed women cut at the twisting baby rope with a rusty knife; she had seen and looked with the curious fascination of a young child at all the babies she'd seen the skeleton women deliver, and at the rows of deformed, tragic foetuses held in the hundreds of jars in the hospital.

In the silence of the church Rebecca let the past play out its grotesque dance, the darkness passing into the lightness of her moments of happiness – the relief and joy she had felt holding her newborn, touching their fresh perfect bodies. She whispered, her voice echoed softly round the dark empty church, 'I'm so sorry . . .' She had never meant to hurt them, it was beyond her control. She thought of Sasha, and for a moment felt panic-stricken: sweet innocent Sasha. She had wanted Sasha to see the burning babies in the hidden secret compartments she had stored in her mind. She had wanted Sasha to understand. Rebecca moaned, remembering how she had frightened her daughter, frightened Louis, poor dear Louis. He was such an innocent. How could a man with such a pampered, charmed existence be expected to understand? He had only wanted her to love him, but Ruda demanded her love, ached inside her. The powerful longing to be reunited had dominated everything in her life, but it had been locked away, Rosa had locked Ruda away.

She sat back, feeling the hard bench of the church pew against her. The colours of the stained-glass window drew her attention, the red, green, blue glass sparkled in front of her. She lay her hands flat against the prayer shelf and kept on staring at the colours. She heard his voice, that soft persuasive voice, she heard the music . . . He played the same Wagnerian recording over and over, he even whistled it as he walked through the camp, he used to hum it to her when he laid out the cards . . .

'Clear your mind of everything, look at the cards, red, green . . . look at the cards, there's a good girl, now more cards . . .'

The white gloves snapped down the coloured cards. At first she had liked the game – it was fun, and Papa Mengele had kissed and cuddled her when she remembered each one, and when she could pass the exact colours to Ruda he rewarded her with chocolate, breaking off pieces, popping them into her mouth.

Then the games had become frightening. She was forced to pass more and more colours. It had begun with just three cards, then next day it had been six. She found it hard to concentrate, she was hungry. Once she had complained, said she couldn't remember them because she was hungry, and she had been force-fed until she was bloated. Now, he had told her, you are full. Now show me how clever you are. This time there were twenty cards; she had concentrated as hard as possible. The card sessions went on every day and gradually Rebecca was able to pass telepathically up to twenty-five colours, in correct order, primal red, blue and green, to her sister.

If Ruda made a mistake, if Ruda could not repeat the exact order of the colours, she would be punished. They told Rebecca that was her fault, she was hurting her sister. Papa displayed fifty cards, and Rebecca started to cry. That day Papa had withdrawn the curtain and made her see what she had done to Ruda.

Ruda sat on a high chair with things clipped to her head. They could see each other, but they couldn't touch, they couldn't hear. Poor, sick Ruda held up by nurses. When the curtain was drawn again, she concentrated even harder and was duly rewarded, told that as she had been such a good girl, Ruda would also be rewarded.

Rebecca rubbed her temples, staring at the coloured glass. It began to blur, her head throbbed. She was trying to reach Ruda, just as she had as a child. Rebecca began to weep. She could not hope to reach out to her, it was too late. She held her hands to her face, could not help but feel embittered by her mama's foolishness. If only Rosa had understood, had not been afraid, if only she had allowed Rebecca to open up her past, then she might have been able to find Ruda. Instead, Rosa had buried Ruda alive inside Rebecca's mind.

Ruda looked over the props, even though Grimaldi had done so already. Next she went to the meat trailer, asked if all the cats had eaten. She was on her way to Mamon's cage, when she remembered the time, and checked her watch. The crowds would soon be starting to line up. She was heading back to the trailer when, suddenly, her head felt as if it was bursting open. She gasped with the pain and leaned against the side of a trailer. A young girl jumped down, asked if she was all right. Ruda nodded, and pushed herself to carry on, telling herself it was because of all those old memories of her past. She was tired, she had to lie down again, rest again, she hadn't eaten – that's what it was, she had to have something to eat.

Torsen arrived at Freda's apartment building and, giving a quick brush of his hair with his fingers, rang the bell. She opened the door before he had time to take his finger off the buzzer. She had her coat over her arm, and her handbag in her hand. Freda remarked on the patrol car. She asked if it meant he was on duty, and he shook his head. They drove off as he explained they were to pick up his sergeant and then his girlfriend.

The two couples talked animatedly, looking forward to the

show. Rieckert kept taking out his free tickets, showing the price, and replacing them in his wallet. Torsen kept giving Freda small sidelong glances. 'How was my father today?'

'Well, he was fine at breakfast, but then it was snowflake time again.'

Rieckert asked what she meant, and Freda explained, pulling a little bit of tissue from her purse, licking it and sticking it on the end of her nose, then blowing it off. 'He does it for hours until the bedcover and the floor look like there's been a snowstorm.'

Rieckert laughed and nudged Torsen, said he would keep his eye on him, it could be hereditary. Torsen seethed. He would have to speak to Freda about this snowflake business, it wasn't funny. As Rieckert started to do it in the back seat, making his girlfriend shriek with laughter, Torsen got more and more uptight. 'If it was your father, you wouldn't think it was funny! It is *not* funny!'

Rieckert blew a fragment of tissue off his nose. 'I agree! But it's one hell of a hobby!'

As the Baron and Helen continued walking, they passed one of the circus advertisements. Helen stopped, looked at the face surrounded by lions. She hesitated . . . Louis turned back to her and she pointed to Ruda Kellerman's name. 'Ruda,' she repeated, and then stepped out to hail a passing taxi.

Louis joined her. 'Why a taxi? He said she was walking.'

Helen bent down to the driver. 'The circus, please take us to the circus!'

The circus car park was filling up, crowds began walking from the train stations, the coaches deposited parties near the fenced perimeter. The main ticket office was crowded with lines of people waiting to buy their tickets. Children waited impatiently to have their photograph taken on top of the elephant's back. Clowns passed leaflets, sold balloons, the speakers roared music, and two drum majorettes paraded up and down banging their drums, their red costumes covered in sequins.

Ruda sat in the bedroom of her trailer. She wore her boots and white trousers; she did not have her jacket on, there was plenty of time for that and she didn't want to crease it. She was shaking, her body wouldn't stop trembling. She pressed her hands together, they were wet with sweat, she had never felt this way before. She didn't know what the matter was, she was beginning to get frightened. Luis hurtled into the trailer.

'Standing room only, they're going to have to turn away hundreds, it's pandemonium out there. Have you taken a look? Come on, come and see the crowds, they're going to let go with the laser beams, it's one hell of a sight! Come and see!'

'Luis, something's wrong with me, look, I'm shaking, I don't know what's the matter with me!'

He caught her in his arms. 'It's just nerves, because they are coming to see you, Ruda. Look – see, it's your face on every poster, your face, your act . . .'

Ruda heard the roar of the crowds as Luis opened the trailer door.

'*Jesus Christ* . . . Ruda! Look at the laser beams. My God, I've never seen a show like this, that old bastard knows how to draw the crowds!'

High in the sky, in brilliant colours, the lasers wrote:

RUDA KELLERMAN, THE MOST FAMOUS FEMALE WILD
ANIMAL TRAINER IN THE WORLD . . . RUDA KELLERMAN,
RUDA KELLERMAN, RUDA KELLERMAN!

*

Rebecca quickened her pace; she seemed buffeted along by the crowds heading towards the massive circus. She could feel the urgency of the crowd following behind her, see more people way ahead. Even if she wanted to turn back she would find it difficult, but she was not attempting to turn away, she was frantically pushing her way forwards, as if someone was calling out to her, someone was telling her to hurry. She had an overpowering urge to run, to push with all her strength. Suddenly the stream of people ahead stopped, they began pointing upwards to the laser beams in the sky. They gasped and called out, still surging forwards, but now with faces tilted skywards, but all Rebecca saw, all her mind focused on, was the name 'Ruda'. She could hear a child's voice calling out, screaming, 'I'm here, I'm here . . . I'm over here.' Lost in the milling people a little girl screamed for her mama, but to Rebecca it was a sign, a signal, and she had to get to the front of the crowd. 'Let me through, please, please let me pass!'

Ruda stood in the open door of her trailer, staring at the sky. Slowly she looked back to the crowds. Thousands of people were milling around, eating candyfloss, carrying balloons, surging toward the massive triple-ringed tent . . .

But there was someone else, she could feel it with every nerve in her body.

Rebecca stood with her face tilted to the sky, her head spinning at the blazing name. 'RUDA KELLERMAN!' She began desperately heading towards the trailer park. A steward at the gate was about to stop her, then waved her through with an apology – he thought she was Ruda Grimaldi.

Luis was like a kid, clapping and shouting. He turned to Ruda. She stood motionless in the open doorway.

'Are you OK, honey? Ruda?'

She stared ahead. He asked again if she was all right, but she didn't answer, she couldn't. She didn't even hear him, she didn't hear the crowds, the band, anything, because standing within yards of her was Rebecca.

Rebecca could not move, she could hear nothing, no sound, no voices. All she could do was look at Ruda, framed in the doorway, standing as motionless as she was. The sisters had not seen each other since before the liberation of the camp, and yet they knew without question, without hesitation, that they were confronting each other, were within yards of each other, both hearing in their frozen minds the other's childish voice, screaming as, hand in hand, they entered the nightmare of Birkenau.

'She is *my sister*. *She is my sister*.'

Luis was not sure what was happening. He saw the tall elegant woman, but so far away he couldn't see her features clearly. 'Who is it?' he asked, but Ruda stepped down from the trailer. He watched as she moved, step by step, closer and closer. She moved into the lights from the trailer windows, and still he did not connect, but she continued to move, step by step, closer and closer. 'Oh, Mother of God!'

Shadows played across her face, but he saw her eyes. They were Ruda's eyes, and he knew then . . . but he was immobilised, unable to move. All he could do was stand and look on . . . look as Ruda and the woman came steadily closer, oblivious to everything that surrounded them.

There was one pace, one step between them. They stood, the exact same height, but Ruda was more powerful, her

463

body blocked Rebecca entirely from Luis. It was as if he saw only Ruda, as if the other woman did not exist. He moved sideways, trying to see, but he could only see Ruda's back shielding, hiding, as if protecting her other self.

They did not speak as their hands moved in unison to touch each other's face. But they spoke each other's name in their minds, in unison, as they melted into each other's arms, every touch like a mirror image.

Way past their heads, past the car park, out in the road leading to a circus entrance, Luis saw the ominous blue flashing light of a patrol car. 'Please, dear God, no. Please don't let them have come for Ruda, not now, not tonight.'

CHAPTER NINETEEN

THEY LAY together like long-lost lovers, devouring with their identical eyes the physical changes in their faces.

They felt the rapid beating of their hearts. They had so much to impart to each other, to ask of each other and yet they could not break from the embrace. It had to be broken, and by Ruda. Inch by inch she released her hold, then rolled over to lie on her back. She felt Rebecca shudder.

'No, don't . . . don't cry, please don't.'

It took all Ruda's willpower to move away from the bed. She reached for one of the posters pinned to the wall, and turned back to Rebecca, holding the poster up for her to see. 'I am Ruda Kellerman.'

'I am . . .' Rebecca's lips trembled, she couldn't say her name.

Ruda held out her hand. 'Come. Come with me!'

Hand in hand, side by side, they looked at the photographs framed on the walls. Ruda pointed, speaking softly, odd descriptive sentences, and then their mind communication began.

'Chicago, London, Florida . . .'

Rebecca made soft, hardly audible 'Mmm' sounds, nodding her head, and their interchanges became repetitive. Ruda would begin a sentence, and Rebecca would finish it.

'This was taken in . . .'

'Summer, taken in . . .'

'Yes, Mexico, this was the old . . .'

'Trailer. Who is . . . ?'

'That's Luis, he is . . .'
'Your husband, yes . . .'
'Yes, husband, you . . .'
'Yes, I married too . . .'
'Your husband?'

They both spoke at the same time, as they repeated their husbands' names – different spellings but the same sound. Then they giggled, at exactly the same time. As if they were regressing back to their only memories of each other, their voices took on a childish intonation, and their words were no longer spoken in English but in disjointed mixtures of made-up languages; sometimes a word in German, or Polish, even Czech, their own language began to emerge. Every move was mirrored by the other. When Rebecca put her hand to her cheek, Ruda automatically touched hers. They were held in a world of their own.

But the outside world was closing in. The entire showground was a heaving mass of bodies. The car park was jammed to bursting point. Lines of people were waiting to buy ice creams and circus memorabilia; more lines formed by the ladies' and men's toilets, and the mass of ticket holders surging towards the big tent entrance was four to five abreast.

In all the mayhem some children were lost, a few screaming for their parents. Meanwhile the announcements continued, describing the biggest circus acts ever to come to Berlin, while lasers lit up the sky.

Luis was pushing and shoving his way towards the stream of waiting cars. He could still see, about half a mile ahead, the *Polizei* car with its blue light flashing. He had made up his mind what he had to do and say. He began to run as best he could towards Inspector Torsen's patrol car.

Torsen was red-faced. Twice he had turned off the

flashing light, but Rieckert had shouted that unless they used it, they would not make it in time for the opening parade. Rieckert was as excited as a child, urging Torsen on, digging him in the shoulderblade. 'Go on, put the siren on, make them pull over for you.'

Torsen banged the steering wheel. 'Look, there's hundreds ahead of us. They won't start the show, it's not due to begin for another three-quarters of an hour. We just have to wait like everyone else!'

Freda turned angrily to the back seat. 'He's right – we'll get there. They won't start the show before everyone's seated. Look up ahead, you think they won't let everyone inside first? Just sit back and enjoy the fireworks!'

Their car inched forwards, now minus the flashing light. It was frustrating to see passersby hurrying past on foot. Then the line came to a complete standstill. A car up ahead had overheated, and there were roars of laughter and calls of abuse as four young boys tried to push it over to one side.

Far back in the long line of cars was a taxi. Louis and Helen began to think they should turn back; after all, it seemed so far-fetched. Yet Vebekka was looking for a sister named Ruda, and one Ruda Kellerman was starring in the circus. There was, at least, a chance . . .

Helen suggested they get out and walk, they would certainly move a lot faster. Louis agreed, but the driver argued, as he could not turn back. Louis paid him more than the fare would have come to, and the well-dressed couple began to hurry alongside the cars.

The rain started, lightly at first, but after a while it began to come down steadily, so now there were umbrellas adding to the crush. Torsen could see Luis Grimaldi coming towards him, and he lowered his window. Luis was soaked, his hair wringing wet, and he was out of breath as he called out, 'Inspector . . . Inspector . . .'

467

Torsen smiled, and turned to Freda. 'This is my friend, Freda, I think you know Sergeant Rieckert . . .'

Rieckert leaned forward to shake Grimaldi's hand. 'I keep telling him to put his siren on, just to get us through the crowds. Will they start on time?'

Grimaldi looked puzzled, but then Torsen waved his tickets. 'We have complimentary seats, Mr Grimaldi, front row. Will everyone get in, do you think?'

Grimaldi walked alongside the car. 'Yes, yes. There are always enough seats or, if not, there's standing room. The show can be held maybe ten, fifteen minutes – but it's not usual. So, you are just here for the show?'

Torsen nodded, slamming his foot on the brake as they almost ran into the back of the vehicle in front. 'I am greatly looking forward to seeing your wife's act.'

Grimaldi walked away, relieved, but turned back again as Torsen called to him through the window. 'Mr Grimaldi . . . *Grimaldi*! You are welcome to ride with us. I don't suppose you could have a word on our behalf? It looks as if the car park's full,' Torsen said.

Grimaldi hesitated, then suggested that when they got to the barrier they ask to use the staff parking area. He would talk to the gatekeeper.

'Satisfied now?' Torsen said rather smugly to Rieckert.

The Baron and Helen held up their collars as they pressed on, surrounded by cars and people, many in such good spirits that they shared raincoats and umbrellas.

Grimaldi did not speak to the gatekeeper, but hurried back to his trailer. He passed Mike and two of the boys and asked why they were not in the animal tent.

'We've got to pull the barriers back to make more room for the crowds.'

Grimaldi nodded, and kept going. His mind churned over how narrowly he had come to making what could have been a disastrous mistake: the inspector wasn't coming for

Ruda, just for the show. He gave a mirthless laugh, told himself he was a foolish old bastard. As he scraped the mud from his boots, he remembered again the query regarding Ruda's old boots. He sighed. Best just to ignore it, he told himself, forget it.

Luis banged on the door and let himself in.

The women turned towards him in unison. Ruda smiled. 'This is my . . .'

'Sister,' said Rebecca.

Ruda's cheeks were flushed, her eyes brilliant. Her mouth was tremulous, quivering; torn between smiling and crying.

They spoke as one: 'We are sisters – sisters . . . She is my sister, sister!'

Luis found it unnerving, the way they moved together, spoke in the same high-pitched singsong voice.

'We are twins.'

'Twins,' repeated Rebecca. They both lifted their right hand, touched their right cheek, and laughed. They laughed as one, and it was exactly the same pitch.

Luis looked from one to the other. 'But – you're not identical.'

They sat down at the same time. Crossed their left legs over the right. Ruda leaned forwards, Rebecca leaned forwards. 'We were, we were, we were, but Rebecca . . .'

'I had my nose altered.'

'Plastic . . .'

'Surgery.'

'Yes.'

'Yes.'

Luis poured himself a brandy. When he offered them a drink, they both shook their heads and said, 'No,' at the same time. For a moment he wondered if they were playing some kind of game with him.

'Just remember, Ruda, you've got a show to do!'

They talked together, heads very close. They made soft shushing sounds and there were jumbled words. Then they both looked towards him.

'Rebecca want to see . . .'

'Show, yes.'

'Yes!' They said, in unison.

Their eyes were identical in colour. So were their lips, their cheeks.

Luis felt uneasy. 'I see it now . . . the likeness. I see it.'

They nodded, smiling as if very pleased that he could see they were twins.

Luis looked at Rebecca. 'How did you find Ruda?'

Ruda answered, 'She went to the church in the city.'

'The lights . . .'

'Yes.'

There followed a conversation that Luis could not make head nor tail of. He just heard the name Magda repeated, then watched as they both put their hands over their faces and laughed.

Luis leaned forward. 'Ruda, keep an eye on the time.' She ignored him. He got up and looked out of the window. 'The lines are thinning out.'

Their eyes seemed to follow him around the trailer. He sat down again, then half rose. 'Do you want to be alone? Left together?'

He saw the way they pressed closer, and he sighed, looking at Rebecca.

'She must start to get ready. Do you understand?'

They stared back, with their identical wide eyes. He sipped his brandy. 'Where are you from? I mean, do you live in Berlin?'

Ruda answered saying that Rebecca was staying in a hotel. 'Her husband is called . . .'

They both said, 'Louis!' and then giggled, bending their heads.

Their interaction began to irritate Luis. He drained his glass, putting it down. 'I'll go and check on the boys.'

As he opened the door, he asked, almost as an afterthought, 'Do you work in a circus, Rebecca?'

'No,' said Ruda. They both said the one word, 'Mother.'

'I'm sorry?' Luis didn't understand.

Ruda said her sister was a mother. Rebecca nodded, and shrugged her shoulders. Ruda gave the same shrug, but Rebecca answered. 'I am just a mother.'

'Mother,' said Ruda.

Luis had his hand on the door handle. He wanted to leave them, and yet there were so many questions he wanted to ask. 'Does she know where your parents are? I mean, if they're alive?'

They both looked at him, turned to each other, then back to him.

'For God's sake, stop this! You're acting crazy, Ruda. I mean, can't she speak for herself?'

'Yes,' they both said, and Luis yanked open the door.

Then Ruda answered solo. 'She was adopted.'

'Adopted, yes,' chimed in Rebecca.

'After the war,' said Ruda, firmly.

'After the . . .' Rebecca's voice trailed off.

Luis sighed, it was too much for him to handle. 'Well, I'm glad – glad you've found each other.' He didn't mean it to sound so hollow, so lacking in warmth, as if they had been apart for only a few hours, days, weeks – not a lifetime. He felt guilty, forced a smile. 'You two have a lot to catch up on, but don't delay too long, Ruda.'

They stood up, hands still held tightly. 'Nothing will ever separate us again.' They spoke as one, turned and held each other, lifting their arms, so synchronised it was like a slow dance.

Luis closed the trailer door behind him, rested his back against it, not sure what he should do. A feeling of dread swamped him and his hands were shaking. Seeing the sisters together upset him. In some ways he was angry with himself, knew he should have stayed to make sure Ruda got herself ready.

The rain was bucketing down and Luis had no coat. He muttered to himself. It was stupid, all he had to do was turn around, walk inside the trailer to fetch one. But he didn't want to see them again, not just at this moment. He looked at his watch and knew Ruda should be getting ready. Then he looked over towards the main tent. Just a few stragglers stood at the box office now, and the last cars to be parked were being directed towards the car park, the gatekeeper in his bright yellow cape making authoritative, sweeping gestures.

Luis passed by the lighted window of his trailer. He peered into it, but the blinds were down, he could see nothing. The laser beams continued to spell out the acts, and he looked up, waiting for Ruda's name. Suddenly the sky blazed with the looped, magical writing: RUDA KELL-ERMAN. He said a silent prayer that being united with her sister would not distract Ruda. He, more than anyone else, knew just how important it was for Ruda to have all her wits about her. He plodded heavy-footed through the sodden ground and made up his mind that, just in case, he would be more diligent outside the performance ring tonight, would carry a loaded rifle. He stopped, unconcerned that he was getting soaked to the skin.

'I love her.' He said it out loud, helplessly, to no one. The dawning of how little he really knew about Ruda and her past shamed him. 'I love her.' Of course he did. Hadn't he been prepared to tell that strait-laced inspector that he had killed Kellerman himself? He, Luis, could have been in handcuffs by now. It was just sad that after all the years they had been together, it was only now that he realised

472

just how much he loved Ruda. He shook his head, smiling to himself, and then chuckled.

They would be on the move soon, out of the country. She would be safe, he had time to make up for the bad years. Luis hesitated again, wondering if Rebecca would be coming with them . . .

'I love my wife . . .' he said again, out loud. Anyone who had witnessed his slow stop-start progress from the trailer would have concluded he was drunk, talking away to himself in the pouring rain, without a coat on.

Helen and the Baron reached the barrier and asked the way to the administration offices, sure they would be able to gain their information there. The ground was slippery; Louis held Helen's elbow tightly to ensure she did not fall. They stepped on to duckboards leading to the offices.

Their arrival was not welcome. At first the secretary believed the Baron was simply trying to get tickets in the main guest arena, to be invited to the small champagne party the owners had organised. She politely asked if they would wait while she tried to reach one of the administrators, inferring that it was an inopportune moment for anyone to request a private meeting.

The Baron, charming as always, gave a winning smile and said that rather than wishing to interrupt anyone, and far from wanting tickets to see the show, he simply wished to speak to Ruda Kellerman.

The girl beckoned the Baron over to a layout map of the trailer park. 'Ruda Kellerman is Luis Grimaldi's wife, but whether or not she will agree to see you, sir, I can't say. She will be getting ready for the show.'

The Baron smiled gratefully, and ushered Helen out, back down the slippery boards. They stood trying to remember which direction they should take. 'Perhaps, Helen, this was not such a good idea.'

Helen tucked her arm in his and said that as they had come this far they might as well try to speak to Ruda Kellerman.

Mike showed off the meat trailer, the freezers and the massive carcasses to Torsen and his party. He had been the one Torsen had approached to enquire whether Grimaldi had mentioned they could park in the artists' private parking area. Mike had signalled them through. 'I work for the Grimaldis,' he had told Torsen, and had been flattered at their interest. As they began to head towards the main entrance, Mike had offered to show them a short-cut. He had led them behind the trailers, pointing out the ones owned by the big acts, and then offered to show them the meat trailer. Until the show started he had nothing else to do.

Torsen checked his watch, worried he would miss the opening parade, but Mike had assured him there was plenty of time. He told them that the 'Big Boss' would make sure every single ticket was sold, every seat taken, before the parade began. 'You think they'll never get everyone seated in time, but they always do. Maybe five, ten minutes late – never more. Besides, I'll show you the artists' entrance – if your tickets are for the front row, it'll be much easier.'

As they peered into the freezers and looked over the cleavers and hammers, Vernon came in, already in costume. Mike made the introductions, and was about to suggest they follow him to the big top when Torsen asked nonchalantly if Mike had ever met Tommy Kellerman. Mike said he had seen him the day he was murdered – briefly, up by the lions' cages. Torsen turned to Vernon

474

and repeated his question. Vernon flushed, shrugged his shoulders, muttered he was not too sure whether he had seen him or not.

'You know he was brutally murdered?' said Torsen.

Freda looked at Torsen, and he could see that she was impressed. He decided to elaborate. 'Yes, Kellerman was brutally murdered. So if you saw him, anything you can tell me could be of great importance. I am heading the homicide investigation.'

Mike gave Vernon a warning glance, then checked his watch. 'Look, I'd better go and change!'

Vernon suggested that, since he was already dressed, he could show Torsen to the big tent, and Mike, after another warning look at him, skipped off. As they hurried across the muddy ground towards the big tent, Torsen asked again about Kellerman. Vernon said nothing, holding open the tent flap and instructing them to turn right through the main arena entrance. 'I hope you enjoy the show.'

Torsen smiled and was about to step inside, when the boy called out to him. He turned. The boy held the umbrella down, the rain glanced off the black-soaked canvas. 'I did see Kellerman, sir, but only for a brief moment. He was standing talking to Mrs Grimaldi, up by Mamon's cage. It was early afternoon the day I think he was killed.'

Torsen stepped closer. 'Were they having a friendly chat?' He felt water trickle down his neck, and inched beneath the umbrella.

'I don't know, I couldn't hear, sir. In fact I thought, at first, that he was one of the kids, you know, from the school parties. They take them around the cages. She looked as if she was telling him off. She had been in one of her moods – Grimaldi had been hitting the bottle a bit, on one of his binges, so he was pretty useless and she'd had to do everything . . . and the plinths, the new pedestals were wrong. She's got a right temper, has Mrs Grimaldi, and she's always telling the kids off for getting too near the cages, but then – I noticed his hat.'

Torsen stepped further under the umbrella. 'His hat?'

'Yes, sir, it was a trilby, black leather trilby.'

'How did you know it was leather?'

'Oh, well, I saw it again, in the meat trailer. Well, I think it was his hat – Mike was wearing it.'

'Mike?'

'Yes, sir, the other helper, sir. He was wearing it. He said he'd found it in the trailer, but Mrs Grimaldi took it off him, she said it was her husband's, but it looked like the same hat I saw Kellerman wearing. Dunno why I remembered it, but then everyone around here's been talking about the murder, so it sort of stuck in my mind, you know, wondering if it was him I had seen.'

'But you said you did see him?'

'Well, I don't know for sure if it was Kellerman, sir. Just, well, he wasn't with this circus – I know that. He wasn't with any of the acts, or I would have recognised him.'

They heard a loud fanfare, and Torsen looked at the big tent.

'That's the parade starting, sir, you'd best hurry or they won't let you get to your seat this way.'

Grimaldi had seen them all leaving the meat trailer, had followed Vernon and Torsen towards the big tent, had watched them huddled beneath the umbrella together. As Vernon hurried away, he stepped out and caught the boy by his coat.

'I want to know what he asked you. What did he want sniffing round the freezer truck like a stray dog?'

Vernon backed off, terrified of Grimaldi. 'He said you'd told him he could park in the artists' car park, then he asked about the cats. Mike brought him in, he offered to show him the trailer. That was all, sir.'

Grimaldi patted Vernon's shoulder. 'I'm sorry, son, just that I'm a bit on edge tonight, it's a big occasion. Have you seen Ruda?'

Vernon said that he had not, and was relieved when Grimaldi started to walk away.

'Oh, Vernon, tell Mike I'll be watching the cages tonight.'

'Yes, sir.'

Grimaldi looked back, his eyes narrowed. 'You sure that prick wasn't asking questions about Tommy Kellerman?'

'Yes, sir.'

'Cats all lined up ready, are they?'

'Yes, sir, I'll double check them before we go in.'

Grimaldi nodded and waved his big hand to indicate that Vernon could carry on with his business. In truth, he was not sure what he should do himself. He looked at his watch; there was still a good three-quarters of an hour before Ruda went on with the act, but she had to be dressed ready for the parade. He didn't want to go back to the trailer, not yet, so he meandered around, making his way towards the line-up of cages. He heard his name called, turned and saw Mike waving to him.

'Boss, there's a bloke and a blonde woman. They've been asking the way to your trailer. They went towards it about two minutes ago.'

Grimaldi hurried to Mike. 'They say who they were?'

'Yeah, I think the guy was a baron, maybe one of the celebrity guests. There's a bit of a bash in the main conference room over in the administration block.'

Grimaldi pulled a face. There were always the stars, the rent-a-celebrity, at these big opening shows. He ran his hands through his soaking hair. 'Sod 'em. Oh! Mike, in future you want to show any bloody people around the freezer and meat trailers, you get permission, OK, son?'

'Yes, sir.'

477

They walked on to the covered tent attached to the big tent housing the animals.

'What did he want to go in there for, anyway?'

Mike was uneasy, he knew he should have got permission, so he lied. 'Oh, he asked us a few questions, you know, if we'd seen Kellerman, Mrs Grimaldi's ex—'

'I know who he was!' snapped Grimaldi.

'As it was raining, we took cover in the trailer.'

'What did you tell him?'

Mike wiped his face. 'Nothing, sir. I'd better check the props.' He tried to move away, but Grimaldi held onto his arm.

'The cats all settled and in order?' Grimaldi asked.

'Yes, sir, everything's in order.'

Grimaldi walked from one cage to the next. As always, the cats touched him with wonder; their wild beauty, their menace, affected him deeply. The big cats had been part of his entire life, he truly loved them. He checked each cage, and then he heard the low heavy growl, like a dull rumble.

Grimaldi stood about two feet away from Mamon. Even waiting for the act, he was solo. Grimaldi paused.

Mamon's eyes glinted, his head hung low, feet splayed out, sensing the man's fear, enjoying the domination.

Their voices spoke together. 'Sasha! Sophia! Jason, Luis . . .' Four of Ruda's cats had the names of Rebecca's children. They hugged and laughed at the coincidences. Grimaldi hid behind Mamon's cage, watching them. They walked in step. But from a distance, Grimaldi could detect that Rebecca was just a fraction behind Ruda, as if the movement was not instinctive, but copied. She was like Ruda's shadow, and because she was so slender – willowy almost – the shadow effect, in the low lights of the animal arena, made them appear even more like one being.

They had not caught up the lost separation years, they could not in so short a time. Only disjointed sections of each other's lives had been snatched and clutched at. Ruda knew Rebecca was married with four children, Rebecca knew Ruda was married and trained big cats. The scars held firm, but a thin layer had already slipped from them both . . . There were many layers to uncover, many questions to ask, but all they wanted now was this closeness. They constantly studied each other, touched each other, to make sure they really were reunited.

Rebecca showed no fear of the cats, only an extraordinary excitement. She wanted to touch them, put her hands through the bars, and Ruda had to hold her back, whispering that it was too soon.

'Too soon, yes, yes, too soon . . .' repeated Rebecca.

Ruda's physical strength made Rebecca weak with adoration, to feel the powerful body, the rough hands, made her want to be constantly wrapped in Ruda's arms. Ruda felt the dependency of her sister, it awoke in her a gentleness, a protectiveness that made her body tingle. She showed off her life with pride, wanting Rebecca more than anyone else to see her loved ones, to see her perform.

'This is everything I dreamed . . .'

'Yes, you dreamed this, and I want . . .'

'You to see me, with my children.'

'Yes, they are my children,' Ruda paused, realisation dawning, and gave a strange half laugh. 'Sasha, your last daughter, she is twelve, yes?'

Rebecca nodded. Ruda recalled the pains she had felt at the time of each birth, each child. Sasha's birth pains she remembered most clearly, they coincided with the time she had been told she could never carry a child herself. As if she knew this, Rebecca clasped her sister's hand in comfort. In some ways it was as if they had never been apart. Rebecca accepted Ruda without question. She had reverted, unknowingly, in that one hour to the way the relationship had always been. Ruda was dominant, Rebecca passive. Ruda had been born first, by two minutes.

The fanfares grew louder, and Grimaldi watched Ruda lead Rebecca towards the artists' entrance. By now he was soaked, and knowing the trailer would be empty he made his way back to change for the show.

The fanfare was deafening. Torsen couldn't see Freda or Rieckert and his girlfriend anywhere. Apologetically, he edged his way through a group of jugglers waiting to enter. The waiting performers stared suspiciously at him, and he mumbled his reason for being there. A painted clown gestured to him to go through the entrance flap quickly. 'You shouldn't be here, hurry.'

Torsen moved cautiously along the sides of the tiers of seats. He stood at the edge of the ring and looked around the audience. He could see walls of lights, tiers and tiers, thousands of seats. He didn't have his seat number – all he knew was that they had front-row seats – and he squinted through the semi-darkness, searching the sea of faces. Beyond the small ring was the vast central main ring, beyond that the third ring. Dear God, he thought, I'll never find them. Suddenly the huge big top was in complete darkness. The crowd murmured, sensing the show was about to begin. The fanfares blared, once, twice: 'LADIES AND GENTLEMEN, SCHMIDT'S WORLD FAMOUS CIRCUS WELCOMES YOU! THREE RINGS, HUNDREDS OF ARTISTS. WE WELCOME YOU TO A NIGHT OF UNPARALLELED EXTRA-VAGANZA! FROM ARGENTINA, THE WORLD FAMOUS BARE-BACK RIDERS – THE COMANCHEROS . . .'

Torsen, his eyes at last accustomed to the darkness, made out his companions' faces. They were seated at the side of the main ring's entrance. He bent low and scurried along the narrow alley between the front-row seats and the ring itself; he tripped and stumbled so he stepped on to the rim of the ring and ran the last few yards, to fall into his vacant seat just as the horses thundered into the ring.

Freda clasped his arm. 'Isn't this exciting? You know, I have never been to a circus before!'

Torsen inched off his wet coat, and wriggled it down beneath his seat. Freda moved away to give him room and then as he sat up, rested close to him, slipping her hand through the crook of his arm. Torsen touched her fingers. 'I am glad I asked you to come with me, Freda.'

She looked in awe at the massive ring as the Argentinian riders screamed and called out at the top of their voices. Twenty-five horses, groomed and gleaming, galloped around carrying a sparkling banner. The bareback girls whooped and yelled as they bounced and bobbed, leaping in one fluid move to stand upright on the horses' backs with nothing more than a glittering red ribbon for a rein. The smell of the horses, the sawdust, the resin added to the excitement.

Torsen felt happy. His father had been right: Freda was lovely.

Grimaldi had pulled on his clean shirt, was buttoning the high collar, listening to the fanfares. He knew exactly how many there would be before the parade ended, and he quickly tucked his shirt into his trousers. Then he opened the bunk seat, and looked over the rifles, searched around for ammunition . . .

The Baron and Helen approached one of the car-park stewards, and the Baron asked which was the Grimaldi trailer. He was taken aback when the man turned on them. 'Where's your pass?'

'I don't have one, I am Baron—'

'You don't have a pass, then please leave the artists' section.'

'No, I wish to speak with Mr Grimaldi – his wife Ruda Kellerman. It's very important.'

'No way. See the big tent – they'll be in there. I'm sorry, please leave. I can't let you wander around here. Go on, through the barrier.'

The Baron was about to argue some more when Helen suggested that perhaps they should wait; it was obvious they would not be able to speak to either Grimaldi or Ruda Kellerman now.

'Sir! Mr Grimaldi!'

Luis turned, quickly hiding the rifle beneath his rain cape.

The steward ran to Grimaldi. They conferred, then the steward pointed back to the Baron and Helen. 'I told them to wait, sir. They got no pass, but they said it was important.'

Grimaldi walked up to the Baron. 'What do you want?'

The Baron asked if they could talk somewhere in private, but Grimaldi shook his head. 'Not before the show. What do you want?'

'It is very important. I need to speak to you about my wife.'

'Your wife?' Grimaldi held his hand up to enable him to see better as the rain lashed at his face.

'Yes. This is Dr Helen Masters. My wife is her patient. Have you met Baroness Vebekka Maréchal? We think there may be some connection between her and Ruda Kellerman.'

Grimaldi hesitated.

Helen moved closer. 'Please help us, she is very sick. We think she may have tried to see Ruda Kellerman.'

'Is the woman called Rebecca?'

'*Yes!* Yes.' The Baron stepped closer, but Grimaldi moved back sharply. 'Is she here? Have you seen her?'

Grimaldi had to shout above the noise of the circus orchestra, the rain. 'She came here. She was with Ruda, but I don't know where she is now. Come to the trailer after the show.'

'Did you speak to her?' asked Helen.

'Yes, yes, I did. She's sick, you say?'

The Baron gripped his hands tightly. 'This is very important. Please, we must talk to her.'

Grimaldi looked back to the tent. 'I can't talk to you now, the show's starting. Your wife, she says she is Ruda's sister; they were together earlier, they said they're twins.'

Helen grabbed hold of Grimaldi's rain cape. 'Is Ruda Kellerman here?'

'She is about to go into the ring. Look, I don't know what you can do now. I'll try to find her, tell her you're here. Wait at the trailer, the big silver one over there – but after the show. I have to go!'

'Please, please, wait – your wife, Ruda—'

Grimaldi backed away, pointed again to his trailer. 'Meet me here, after the show.'

The Baron and Helen watched him hurry away, then stop and turn back. He shouted for them to mention his name at the box office, to go into the big tent.

Helen and the Baron crossed towards the box office. All the tickets were sold, but there was still standing room left. The Baron was soaked, his shoes muddy, and he was about to insist they return to the Grimaldi trailer, but Helen ignored him and opened her handbag. 'Louis, we'll do as he said, just wait until the end of the show. We'll take two standing-room tickets, please.'

'You will have a very good view, it'll be worth it,' said the cashier, and pointed towards the tent. 'I'd hurry, the parade's already started.'

483

The artists were lined up, waiting at the edge of the entrance to the rings, watching for their lights: red for stand-by, green for go. The music blared from massive speakers as the live orchestra, its conductor in a tuxedo, gave each act in the parade its set piece of music as the ringmaster introduced it, his red frock coat, his black silk top hat and whip caught in the spotlight.

'FROM RUSSIA – THE GREATEST HIGH-WIRE ACT IN THE WORLD . . . THE STRAVINSKY FAMILY!'

Ten men and four women in crimson robes ran into the ring, bodies fit and muscular. They paraded with a marvellous arrogance, strutting and twirling their cloaks, eyes flashing.

Ruda Kellerman never did the parade with her cats, but she walked it. Now she waited her turn to enter. The hectic swirling events buffeted and frightened Rebecca, but also exhilarated her, made her whole body tremble. Ruda kept tight hold of her twin's hand, describing some of the acts. Anyone close was proudly introduced. 'This is my sister!'

Ruda had dressed for the parade in a tailored black evening suit, a white silk shirt with heavy ruffles at her neck, and a flowing black cloak with white satin lining. The trousers were skin tight, and she wore black polished high Russian riding boots. She held a pair of white gloves and a top hat, and smiled broadly, joking with friends as they passed her to enter the ring. Her red warning light flicked. The Tannoy warned: 'Stand by, Ruda Kellerman.'

She whispered to Rebecca that any moment it would be her cue. But when she released her hand, Rebecca clung to her. Ruda cupped Rebecca's face in her strong hands. 'Just for a moment. Watch me!'

'LADIES AND GENTLEMEN, THE MOST DARING, THE MOST FAMOUS, THE MOST AUDACIOUS, FEARLESS, FEMALE, WILD ANIMAL TRAINER IN THE WORLD . . . PLEASE WEL-

COME TO BERLIN THE STAR OF OUR SHOW. WELCOME TO BERLIN, RUDA KELLERMAN! RUDA KELLERMAN, LADIES AND GENTLEMEN!'

The spotlight hit Ruda who stood with arms raised above her head, the cloak swirling around her. She stood motionless, held in the brilliant beam of light, then strode to the centre of the ring. She turned to the right, to the left, bowing low, taking her applause. She continued across the ring. The cheers and applause had never felt so sweet.

Torsen stared at the confident figure, leaning forwards slightly. Having met Ruda, to see her now was fascinating. Rieckert turned to Torsen. 'Eh, she's something else isn't she? I can't wait to see her with the big cats.'

Helen and the Baron were five rows behind, in the standing-room section. Helen could not even see the ring. Louis looked at her.

'I told you. This is a waste of time, we can't see.'

Helen beckoned to Louis to follow, as she pushed and shoved her way through the section. 'Look, Louis, there's four seats vacant in the second row. Why don't we just take a seat? If the ticket holders arrive, then we'll move. Come on.'

'FROM FLORIDA, AMERICA'S ARABIAN NIGHTS – THE FINEST ARAB HORSES IN THE WORLD . . . THE FINEST HORSEMEN . . . THE FRANKLYNN BROTHERS!'

No one stopped them. Louis and Helen now had a perfect view of the centre ring. They took their seats as Ruda Kellerman left the ring. Helen leaned across to the couple sitting next to them and asked if she could borrow their programme. Louis was astonished at her audacity. Helen looked down at i. and passed it to Louis.

'Ruda Kellerman is on last, just before the intermission.'

Louis looked over the programme, holding it at a slight angle to enable him to read in the semi-darkness. His handsome face was caught in the half light, his high cheekbones accentuated. He leaned across Helen to thank the owner of the programme. Helen saw his charming smile, saw the woman blush as she said, 'Any time!'

'THE BELLINIS! PLEASE WELCOME – FROM ITALY – WELCOME DIDI AND BARBARA BELLINI . . . AND THEIR TEAM OF DOGS!'

Ruda was hurrying round the back of the tent when she saw Luis. She called out to him, with a broad smile, 'What a house, can you hear them?'

He nodded. As they drew close, he could see her eyes were shining. 'I can't wait . . . *I can't wait, Luis! Tonight, I will be the most magnificent, the best . . .*'

She was walking so fast he almost had to jog to keep by her side. She drew off her white gloves and flicked them at him. 'You know what it means for me to have her here? For her to see me? You know, Luis, we used to make up stories and always, always, Luis, I would say: I am the lion tamer!'

She hurried back to the artists' enclosure, talking nineteen to the dozen, unbuttoning her cuffs and the buttons on her shirt. Then she stopped and turned to him. 'You made my dreams come true, Luis. Did you know that?'

He had never seen her so happy, so relaxed. She seemed to dance, light quick steps as she hurried on, tossing the cloak to him. 'You made my dream come true. *I am here, Luis*, and . . . and my sister is here. My heart, Luis, my heart is breaking open!'

'I love you, Ruda.'

But she had moved on. With his arms full of the heavy cloak, her hat and gloves, he couldn't keep up with her. He trailed behind like a lackey, tripping, stumbling and then he watched as Rebecca ran to Ruda. They embraced, Rebecca giving Ruda frantic childish kisses.

'Rebecca! Wait! Your husband was here looking for you with a woman, a doctor!'

Rebecca stared wide-eyed at Grimaldi. She seemed terrified, but Ruda, impatient to change for her act, drew Rebecca towards the exit.

'Did you hear what I said? I told them to meet us at the trailer. Ruda?'

They ignored Grimaldi and ran out, step for step. He saw Ruda stopped by the steward, saw him point at Rebecca, and Ruda fling a protective arm around her shoulders. No one was allowed guests at the back of the arena unless with a special pass. Ruda pushed the steward roughly out of her way, holding the flap open for Rebecca. 'She is not anybody, she is my sister!'

Torsen flicked through the programme and turned to Rieckert, pointing out when Ruda Kellerman was on. He then put his arm around Freda's shoulders. She was laughing at the clowns who rushed around with a bucket filled with soap suds. Torsen's initial genuine enjoyment suddenly palled. The small clown, with his short legs and funny bowler hat, was the same size as Kellerman. It could have been Kellerman – except he was dead and buried. Torsen watched the diminutive figure hurl himself around the ring. Everything he had been told began to niggle and eat away at his pleasure. Seeing Ruda in the black suit had not really meant anything, but now he felt sure it was she who had walked away from the murdered Kellerman's hotel, who had worn the dead man's hat to disguise herself. He knew she had lied to him, not once but many times. She was strong enough to have killed Kellerman, he knew that. The question was, how in God's name could he prove it?

Everything going on in the ring blurred as Torsen concentrated on piecing together what little evidence he had accumulated against Ruda Kellerman. All three rings

487

were bursting with activity, chimpanzees, clowns, acrobats . . .

'THE WONDERS OF THE ANIMAL KINGDOM . . . RAHJI THE ELEPHANT MAN!'

Grimaldi had given her an alibi, but the young boy, Vernon, had said Grimaldi had been on one of his binges. What if he was drunk on the evening of the murder? Would he have known what time she came or went? Had Grimaldi lied? And where were the boots?

'It's the elephants next!' Rieckert shouted, his tie loose, his face flushed pink.

Torsen pursed his lips. They did not sleep in the same room. How could Grimaldi give his wife an alibi if he was drunk? Torsen remembered Ruda saying Grimaldi was snoring, that he had kept her awake. So obviously he had been sleeping. Could she – did she – leave the trailer, return . . . while Grimaldi slept through?

Freda clutched his arm as the elephants started to enter the ring. They came so close, they were within touching distance. Rieckert shouted excitedly to Torsen, 'I hope they don't let the lions this close, eh?'

An elephant's trunk swung dangerously close to Torsen, and he pressed back in his seat – much to the delight of Rieckert who shrieked with laughter. The giant animal gently placed his front feet on the ring rim: giant feet, carefully, delicately placed down, then the massive trunk swirled above their heads. They screeched and cowered as the elephant slowly turned back, and all eight elephants began to waltz.

Freda suddenly sighed.

'You OK? You weren't afraid, were you?' Torsen asked.

'It's sad in a way, isn't it? They are so wonderfully huge, and I don't like to see them looking foolish, dancing. It's not right.'

At that moment a baby elephant began to perform what

488

could possibly have been termed a pirouette. The crowd roared its delight. But Freda obviously did not approve. Torsen began to like her more and more. He leaned in closer. 'If I get rid of Rieckert, would you have dinner with me? Tonight, after the show?'

She nodded her head, and his grip tightened. She rested her head on his shoulder and he wasn't thinking of Ruda any more.

Helen was laughing, amused by the antics of the baby elephant. Louis turned to watch her. She had such a lovely face, such neat features, she was a very attractive woman. It was as if he had never really noticed her before this evening. He reached over and held her hand. 'You know, I don't think I have ever really said how much I appreciate your kindness, your care of Vebekka. You must think me a very—'

Helen withdrew her hand. 'I think you have been under tremendous stress. I understand, and I hope—'

'I love her, Helen, I always have . . . I always will.'

'Yes, I know.' Helen knew no one could take Vebekka's place. He was a weak, delightful man. A charming man who had always found solace in women. Louis had turned to other women to survive – that was all his infidelities were, substitutions. His weakness was his inability to face reality; instead of seriously trying to help Vebekka, he had others take that responsibility for him.

'THE FEARLESS, DARE-DEVIL DUPRÉS – FROM PARIS, FRANCE . . . NO SAFETY NET, LADIES AND GENTLEMEN! THE FLYING DUPRÉS DEFY DEATH!'

The main ring darkened as slim, white-clad figures climbed the ropes to the roof of the big tent. Louis looked up, watched the young beautiful boy expertly swing the trapeze backwards and forwards, his eyes on the catcher who dropped down, his arms free, his legs hooked over the bar of the swing. The swing picked up momentum, the boy continued to push out the free swing, and then sprang forwards, flying through the air. The swings passed each other, high above the audience's heads, and the crowds gasped, 'Ohhh!' and 'Ahhh!' as the young boy flew from his swing and performed a perfect triple somersault, the catcher reaching out with split-second timing to clasp his hands.

Louis looked at Helen. 'You know, that is how she makes me feel – like I am supposed to catch her. I almost touch her hands, almost get to hold her, save her, but she slips away, she falls. Helen?'

She patted his hand. 'We'll find her. You'll hold her, and maybe next time she won't fall, if she feels you are strong enough, but—'

'But?' he queried.

Helen smiled. 'But maybe we will need Dr Franks as a safety net.'

Louis nodded. 'Do you think this Ruda Kellerman really is her sister? It would be an extraordinary coincidence, wouldn't it? That she should be here in Berlin? And my wife may be here somewhere in the circus with her?'

Helen edged closer, whispering, 'You know, Vebekka, I mean Rebecca, kept on saying, "It's close, it's very close." What if "it" meant her sister was close? I mean, if they were twins, then ... like it was some kind of telepathy between them. She knew her sister was close, but because of what had been done to her, she didn't, or couldn't remember she had a sister, or one that was alive.'

Louis gasped as, way above him, a trapeze artist slipped. The crowd gasped too. But it was a very carefully rehearsed mistake, one designed to make the audience afraid. The tent was silent as the artists prepared for a dangerous jump: springing from the swing on to a high wire in the darkness, not even seen by the audience. He seemed to fly downwards and then swung his body over and over the taut high wire, twelve feet below.

Helen stared high into the roof of the tent, trying to recall everything Rebecca had said. She felt her palms begin to sweat. She recalled the incident at the circus in Monaco. Rebecca had attempted to get into the ring. Could it have been instinctive, telepathic connection to her sister? Helen leaned against Louis. 'Louis, the time Rebecca attacked the circus clown. Do you know if Ruda Kellerman was also with the circus then? Louis?'

He did not hear the question. 'I wasn't there for her, Helen. I should have found out more about her past, cared more. Now I feel as if I have a second chance, and I intend to be there for her from now on. All I hope is that I am not too late.'

Rebecca helped Ruda into her costume, and then delightedly agreed to change into trousers and boots herself, and wear one of the boys' red jackets.

'Good, it looks good. Now you don't have to stay by the entrance, you can come right into the ring! Stand outside the cages. Luis will look after you, won't you?'

Luis was not happy about it, said that Rebecca would only get in the way and besides it was too dangerous, she might distract Ruda or make her concentration waver. Ruda dismissed his fears with a sweep of her hand. 'Rubbish. You take her in, she can stand by you and then you take care of her, yes?'

Rebecca repeated, 'Yes?' and when he shrugged his compliance, they both gave an identical gleeful giggle.

'But you must go now, Ruda. I'll bring Rebecca. Please – you haven't been near the cages.'

Ruda nodded, then took Rebecca's hand. 'We're ready!'

Grimaldi stood beside Rebecca as Ruda went over to the boys. At last she seemed to be concentrating, checking the props and cages as usual. Then she gave a signal for the boys to start stacking the tunnel sections to the entrance. Two more acts and they were on.

Ruda went from cage to cage. She had changed into tight white trousers tucked into her black shiny boots, and a white frilled Russian-styled shirt. The simplicity of her costume made her appear smaller, slimmer, more vulnerable. She carried only a short stick. Rebecca stepped forward as if she wanted to follow Ruda, but Grimaldi held her arm firmly. 'No, no, you must leave her alone now. This is very important, she must pace herself now, get herself ready.'

'Yes, yes, I understand. Get herself ready, she must be ready.'

Ruda was starting her pacing, up and down, up and down. Twice she stopped and looked over at Rebecca. She smiled, then returned to walking up and down, asking the boys if the fire hoop was set up, the pedestals stacked. Like her old self, she went over every detail. Grimaldi felt relieved as he saw the transformation, saw her twisting her head from side to side to relax her neck muscles, clenching and unclenching her hands over her stick. Then her pacing began in earnest, and as sharp as ever she pointed out to Vernon that one button was undone on his tunic.

Mike stood by the mass of stacked railings; four circus hands waited for the signal to move into the main ring. There would be two sets of clowns and jugglers covering the mounting of the cages in the central ring. The main ring would be in darkness as the safety barrier was erected; the boys waited for their standby light.

Red light on. Mike looked to Vernon. 'Stand by. OK, boys, stand by, we got the red light. Red light, Mr Grimaldi.'

'Two minutes for Kellerman's act. Stand by, you have red light . . . *go green, Miss Kellerman, please stand by.*'

Luis looked at Rebecca. She was shaking; he patted her shoulder. 'When the red light comes on over there, that is our cue to go into the ring. We go in first, then Ruda will get her own red and green light.'

In the darkened ring, the cages were brought into position, the tunnel erected. The first cage was positioned at the trapdoor of the tunnel.

Mike checked the trapdoor and used his walkie-talkie. 'Cages in position for tunnel over . . .'

'LADIES AND GENTLEMEN! SCHMIDT'S ARE PROUD TO ANNOUNCE FOR YOUR ENTERTAINMENT TONIGHT, THE MOST FAMOUS, THE MOST DARING WILD ANIMAL ACT IN THE WORLD. PLEASE REMAIN IN YOUR SEATS. DO NOT ATTEMPT TO MOVE FROM THE RINGSIDE ANYWHERE NEAR THE BARRIERS. PLEASE DO NOT MOVE DOWN THE AISLES DURING THIS ACT. ANY ONE OF THESE WILD ANIMALS CAN KILL, PLEASE REMAIN SEATED . . . ANY MOVEMENT OUT-SIDE THE BARRIERS CAN DISTRACT THE ANIMALS, CAN ENDANGER THEIR TRAINER.'

The crowds murmured, excitement increasing as the orchestra now began a slow drum beat.

Grimaldi got his green light to enter the ring. He picked up his rifle and beckoned for Rebecca to follow him. She kept close as he entered the darkened arena, making his way carefully to the far edge of the barrier to take up his watching position.

Vernon was already in his watcher's position opposite Grimaldi, and he lifted his radio. 'In position, Grimaldi on the far side with the woman. Eh! Looks like he's got a bloody rifle!'

Mike kept his eyes on Ruda as she paced up and down. He lifted the radio. 'He's just showing off, Vern. OK, we got the red! Stand by for green!'

Ruda pulled on her leather gloves. She seemed to make small jumps on the spot.

'LADIES AND GENTLEMEN . . . RUDA KELLERMAN!'

Green go! Green go!

Vernon heard the command and withdrew the bolts from the trapdoor leading from the tunnel into the ring. The entire ring was still in total darkness. Ruda entered from the side trapdoor, and made her way in the gloom towards the open trap from ring to tunnel. She backed into the tunnel ten paces, exactly ten paces.

'She's in position, over!'

Vernon heard Mike tell him the cats were released. *Bang!* Up came the central spotlight, pinpointing Ruda Kellerman running from the tunnel into the centre of the ring while close on her heels came Roja, her lead tiger. Packed behind him came fifteen more tigers. The crowd murmured. It looked, as it was supposed to, as if the tigers were chasing Ruda into the ring.

The act began. Rieckert gasped, 'Holy shit!'

Helen gripped hold of Louis's arm. 'My God, look at her, look at her face! Can you see, Louis?'

Louis half rose out of his seat. From where they were sitting, Ruda could have been Rebecca. Totally, utterly stunned, he couldn't get his breath. Helen pulled on his arm. 'I know, I know. I can see. My God, they're almost identical!'

Torsen released his arm from around Freda, and stared at the ring in astonishment, awe. There she was, surrounded by a mass of terrifying cats, running around her like sheep, their bodies so close they seemed to brush against her legs.

Ruda was in perfect control as she gave her commands. In perfect co-ordination they kept up the tight, circular move; tightening, faster and faster.

'Good, Roja . . . Roja, good . . . *Roja, break!*'

The massive tiger broke to his right. Now the sixteen tigers formed two circles as Ruda backed to the barrier and picked up the reinforced ladder. The spotlight spilled over to the barrier, picking out Grimaldi and Rebecca. It was only a split second, but it was enough for Helen to stand up. 'She's at the side of the ring, Louis. I saw her!'

Helen's jacket was pulled by the man behind her and she was sharply told to sit down. But Louis had seen too. White-faced, he turned to Helen. 'I saw her, I saw Vebekka. She's with Grimaldi.'

Torsen was on the edge of his seat. He leaned across to Rieckert. 'Did you see her? The woman across the ring, on the opposite side?'

Freda turned to Torsen. 'What did you say?'

Torsen stared into the ring, and then gasped. 'My God! Look what she's doing!'

Ruda was backing up the ladder now. Roja turned inwards, the circle getting closer, tighter round the ladder. The ladder rocked dangerously – assisted by Ruda.

'Roja! Move move . . . *right* . . . *right! Sasha! Sasha, down!'*

This was the most dangerous part of the sequence. Ruda poised and ready to make her famous flying leap, the cats forming the tight group in front of her. Grimaldi moved closer to the bars, Rebecca pressed her face against them.

'Sasha, *down.*'

Grimaldi looked at Rebecca. She was repeating word for word: 'Sasha . . . Sasha . . . Sasha!'

Grimaldi looked back to the ring. Sasha was playing up. '*Down!* Sasha. Down, down!'

At exactly the same time Ruda gave the command to Sasha, Rebecca repeated it. Grimaldi grabbed her arm. 'Shut up! Shut up!' he hissed.

Rebecca turned to him, seemingly unaware of who he was.

'*Down! Down!'*

495

Grimaldi kept his grip, then sighed with relief. The sound was lost in the roar from the crowd as Ruda sprang forward and lay across the cats' backs. The cartwheel turn, then Ruda jumped back on to her feet. She gave the command to spread out. The applause was deafening. Now the cats were running like a wild pack. Ruda bowed, gave the animals the command for them to form the chorus dance line . . .

Sasha played up again. This time she refused to back up on to her hind legs, swiping at Ruda, snarling and growling. Then she started after the tiger next to her. They swiped and snarled at each other, and Ruda crossed over. '*Sasha, no . . . up, up, up!*'

Rebecca was shaking, repeating over and over, 'Sasha, Sasha . . .'

Vernon became very tense. The cats were refusing the commands repeatedly. Fights were breaking out, instigated by Sasha. Then Sophia, the big female at the end of the line, broke out of her place and joined in. Sweat streamed off Ruda's face.

Ruda pushed, Ruda cajoled, she shouted and ordered. At one point she cuffed Sasha's nose – hard. Sasha lashed out, but at last they were in line, behaving. They began to form the pyramid, then the roll-over, as Ruda moved one of the pedestals into the centre of the arena. It was a bright red pedestal, with a gold fringe. As rehearsed, Roja broke from the row and nudged Ruda from behind. She turned round to face him, shaking her finger, then returned to setting up the next pedestal.

Vernon kept his eyes glued to the waiting tigers. At a command, they all sat back on their haunches, paws waving in the air. Ruda looked as if she was gesturing to each to keep in the sit-up position, but she moved in and out of their territory, giving small hand signals for one or other to try to get off their pedestal. They swiped at the air with their paws, as if refusing. Ruda put her hands on hips in mock frustration.

Vernon got the radio message from Mike. 'Mamon's on his way down.'

With her back to the tunnel, still pretending to admonish the tigers, Ruda got a large bottle of milk and fed Roja, then looked back as if pleading for him to sit on the pedestal. The children in the audience shrieked with laughter, unaware just how dangerous it was not only to feed the big cat, but to take the bottle away.

A small spotlight spilled out to hit mid-centre of the tunnel. Now Mamon crept slowly down the tunnel, as if sneaking up behind Ruda. When she turned, she appeared not to see him, but actually gave Mamon the command to move behind her, while still pretending to encourage Roja to sit on the pedestal.

Roja refused. Ruda pretended to get angry. The children, as expected, began to shout, 'He's behind you!'

As trained, Mamon kept moving stealthily behind Ruda. Every time she turned she gave the command for a tiger to head back down the tunnel. Each time she turned back to her row of tigers, there was always one missing. Ruda made an elaborate show of counting tigers, looking puzzled, but she knew exactly where each cat was. Roja feigned an attack, Ruda sidestepped him, and the audience hushed as Roja made another run at her. This time she crouched down and he jumped over her head and ran into the tunnel. Ruda took out a bright red handkerchief and wiped her forehead. When she turned back, she stared in astonishment – all the pedestals were empty! All the tigers had gone down the tunnel!

Vernon whispered into his microphone. 'All clear . . . all clear. Bolt on, wait for Roja, over. OK, he's clear, he's out.'

The children screamed once more. 'He's behind you!'

Mamon roared. Their screams went silent. Ruda turned

in mock fear to face the big lion. Vernon got the radio message. 'All back. Trapdoor down.'

Ruda was now left with Mamon, who was supposed to go and sit on the red pedestal all by himself, as if that had been his intention all the time, to clear away all the other cats and be the star.

Ruda gave Mamon his command, using the single word: 'Red!' and continued to play-act, bending to the empty tunnel, puzzled that the others had all disappeared.

Grimaldi tensed up, Vernon moved closer. Mamon was behind Ruda, but he was nowhere near where he should be, nowhere near the pedestal. His head hung low, he was moving stealthily forwards.

'Red . . . Ma' angel . . . Ma' angel . . . !'

Grimaldi heard Rebecca gasp. She broke free of him, clung to the bars. Her face was rigid. '*Red . . . red . . . red!*'

The sawdust churned up behind Mamon as he made a fast U-turn, and at a terrifying full gallop careered across the ring, flinging himself at the railings, at Rebecca. He seemed crazed, swiping at the bars . . . snarling, pushing forwards.

The audience went silent. Ruda moved to the centre of the ring. Only the ring was lit, not the barrier, so the audience could hardly see Grimaldi or Rebecca. But Rebecca fell back, terrified.

Ruda kept the pedestal between herself and Mamon. '*Yuppp Mamon . . . up up . . . red red . . . Ma' Aangelll!*' He was too far across the ring to force back to the tunnel again. He began a crazed run around the barrier, teeth bared, his eyes crazy . . .

'Red, *good boy* . . . ma' angel . . . red!'

Rebecca was scratching at Grimaldi, saying over and over, 'Red, red, red . . .'

Vernon snapped an order for someone to get over to

498

Grimaldi, get ready to let Ruda out of the trapdoor on that side. Mamon was going crazy.

Torsen bit his knuckles, his face white. 'It's out of control . . . look at it, it's going for her!'

Rieckert was pressed back in his seat. 'Bloody hell . . . she must be crazy! It's going to attack her—'

Mike sent one of the boys to stand by the trapdoor. Grimaldi signalled for him to get to his side. He pushed Rebecca forward. 'Take her out, just get her out of the way. I'll handle it, I'll see to the trapdoor.'

Rebecca called out to Ruda, but the orchestra was playing at full volume. Only the few rows close to Grimaldi could hear, could sense something was very wrong.

Rebecca was dragged out, her eyes turned back to the ring. Grimaldi cocked the rifle. There was a gasp from the rows and banks of seats close by. They could see him aiming it into the cage. The whispers spread, the fear was picked up around the vast tiers and tiers of seats.

Helen gripped the Baron's hand. 'Can you see him? He's got a rifle, but I can't see Rebecca. I think something is wrong. Do you think this could be part of the act?'

Mike listened as Vernon repeated into the radio that Mamon was going crazy, Ruda couldn't control him . . .

'He's acting up! No . . . no . . . hold the panic.'

They faced each other. Without Rebecca's presence Mamon seemed calmer. He still wavered, but Ruda moved in closer. She felt her whole body sweating, tingling, the adrenaline pumping through every vein. She faced him out, dared him. 'Come on . . . come on, ma' angel. Up red . . . red *up*! *Mamon*.'

She moved closer, closer. His massive jaws were open and drooling as he tossed his head from side to side. There was silence now. The orchestra had quietened, not because there was panic, but because towards the end of the act they played a soft, gentle piece of Wagner's *The Ring*, the moment when Siegfried discovers his beloved . . .

Ruda knelt on one knee and bowed her head. There was a gasp as Mamon sprang as if to attack her, but leaped over her head and landed perfectly on the pedestal. He eased his paws around to gain his balance, then sat, in a comfortable position, and slowly lifted his front paws up in the air. Ruda crossed to the pedestal and stood in front of him. Directly beneath him, she opened her arms to accept the applause, facing him.

'Mamon . . . good, good. Gently now, good boy.' Ruda turned, giving Mamon her back, and slowly he lowered his massive front paws to rest on her shoulders. The spotlight shrank . . . shrank until it shone on the great animal's head above Ruda's. Then she turned again to face him. The position was lethal, his paws on her shoulders. She could smell his breath, hear his heart pumping.

'Good boy . . . good, *kiss*!'

Ruda stepped quickly away. On command he was off the pedestal and running for the tunnel. She was left alone to bow, to take the thunderous applause. Many in the audience gave her a standing ovation.

'LADIES AND GENTLEMEN WE NOW HAVE AN INTERMISSION . . . BUT HURRY BACK TO SEE THE SECOND HALF OF THE FEARLESS, THE EXTRAORDINARILY DARING RUDA KELLERMAN'S ACT. MEET WANTON, THE PANTHER. MEET MORE OF RUDA KELLERMAN'S AMAZING FAMILY OF WILD BEASTS.'

The lights came on as the ice-cream girls streamed down the aisles. Many of the audience remained in their seats dazed, unsure of what they had just seen, uncertain whether they had really been afraid or not.

Ruda was panting, patting her face dry with a towel as she ran across to her trailer to change in readiness for the second half of her act. Grimaldi was waiting. 'Don't take him into the second half, he's crazy. He refused time and time again.'

She turned on Grimaldi. 'I can control him, *I did.* Now back off from me, I know what I'm doing.'

Only then did she stop, look around. 'Where is she? *Luis, where is she?*'

Grimaldi snapped back that she was by the cages with Mike and Vernon. He continued to follow. 'She became as crazy as the bloody animals. Ruda – *Ruda, will you listen to me!*'

Ruda was splashing through the mud towards the trailer. 'I hear you, Luis. But please don't ask me to *listen to you!*' She exploded into fury. 'I saw the rifle, Luis! I don't want you in or near the ring for the second half, hear me? You are pitiful, *pitiful! So desperate to be part of the act you have to stand there like something out of a Wild West show!*'

She ran on. The sweat she had worked up in the ring now mingled with the cold rain, making her shiver. She entered the trailer leaving the door open for Luis. 'I'm cold. *I'm cold. Run the shower.*'

Rebecca was not with Mike, as Grimaldi had believed, but on her way back to the trailer. She was about to open the door when she heard Ruda's angry voice. She stood motionless as Grimaldi shouted, 'You don't give me orders like I was a dog!'

'Then what are you? What possessed you to stand like a prick with that bloody rifle?'

'Maybe, just maybe I was worried about you – you hadn't rehearsed, you were all uptight because of this Rebecca business.'

'She is my sister, *my sister, Luis!* You know what that means to me? Can you even contemplate what it means to have found her? She came to me, *she came to me, Luis!*'

Grimaldi sat heavily on the bunk bed, wiping his hair with the towel Ruda had tossed aside. She was pulling off her boots as she talked. Outside, Rebecca was frozen, unable to move from the trailer steps, huddled in Vernon's rain cape.

'Boots, help me with my boots.'

He held the toe and heel and jerked hard. 'She took a long time finding you. Why has she never appeared before?'

The boot came away in his hand and Ruda fell back. She pushed her other foot out to him, and he began to pull off the boot. 'She didn't know I was alive.'

'She tell you she looked for you?' he asked.

Ruda pushed against him. 'I looked for her, she looked for me. *Yes, yes, yes!* Oh, come on, pull, Luis, I've got to change.'

'There's something wrong with her, Ruda. I tried to tell you earlier. There was a man, said he was her husband, he was with a woman, a doctor. They said she was sick. I think they meant crazy sick, you know!' He pulled hard at the boot-heel. The boot came away and Ruda fell backwards again.

'What did they tell you?'

'Nothing much. I just felt it from the way they were so desperate to find her. They knew about you, came looking for you. I said they'd best come to the trailer after the show.'

'Why did you do that?'

'What else was I supposed to say? I knew she'd been here – Christ! They wanted to try to find you there and then. If it wasn't for me they'd have been wandering around—'

'You should have just minded your own business.'

'You are my business.'

'Since when?'

Luis hesitated. 'Since . . . since you killed Kellerman.'

502

She stared at him and he sighed. 'I know, Ruda, so don't deny it. I know you killed him.'

Ruda unbuttoned her shirt. 'Ah, I see. You're going to blackmail me, is that it?' She pulled her sweat-soaked shirt off. 'Try it and I'll get your bloody rifle and I'll shoot your fucking head off . . .'

Luis grabbed hold of her. 'You know what I was prepared to do for you? That inspector – when I saw them arrive, you know what I wanted to do? Say it was me, say I killed Kellerman! I was going to do that for you, Ruda, because—'

Ruda let the shirt drop. 'Oh, God, what did you tell him, you fool?'

'I told him nothing. They were just coming to see the show, they had free tickets. I said nothing.'

She seemed almost amused. 'You were really going to do that for me?'

He pointed to the clock. 'You got ten minutes. I'll get the boys ready.'

She unzipped her pants slowly, never taking her eyes off his face. 'He took a long time to die. I never meant to kill him – but he threatened me and . . . there was this big ashtray, green, very heavy. I kept on hitting him and his teeth fell out. I remember seeing his teeth, on the carpet. It sort of made me real angry, funny. He was always so proud of his white teeth, but they were as false, as fake as he was.' She took a strange hard intake of breath, blinking rapidly. 'Oh, God, Luis. He took such a long time to die.'

Ruda drew down her trousers and kicked them off. The terrible jagged scars were heightened by the sweat and the tightness of her clothes. She looked up at him, held out her arms to him, and he hugged her tightly. 'Nobody will hurt you. I won't let them.'

She stroked his face. 'So if they come for me, you'll say you did it? You'd really do that for me?'

Luis kissed her forehead; the vicious burn scars at the

side of her head were shiny red with perspiration. He touched them. 'Yes, yes, I'll say it was me. Nobody will ever hurt you again, I promise you.'

She cupped his face in her hands, and kissed his lips. Her eyes searched his face, her expression unfathomable, and he flushed like a boy, covering his embarrassment, his love. She traced his lips with her fingers. 'Be nice to her, Luis, she was always the weak one.'

'Yes, I can tell that.'

She gave a strange smile. 'Can you now? I have under-estimated you.'

Luis tapped his wrist to indicate the time, started to fetch her costume. He heard the shower being turned on, and eased off the plastic cover from the white jacket, glad to be needed.

Outside, Rebecca sat hunched on the steps. When she heard Ruda call out for her costume, she moved away, afraid to be seen. She lost her footing, falling in the thick mud. She crawled along then tried to stand, but she had slithered half beneath the trailer. The door opened. She could see the polished boots, hear Ruda telling Grimaldi to bring her to the ring.

'And, Luis, no gun! Promise me?'

As Ruda hurried away, Rebecca could see Grimaldi's feet. She crawled a few inches, called out after him. The mud oozed beneath her, she could smell it, smell the wet earth, and she was lost. The dank stinking tunnel, the stench of the sewers, the scurrying rats. Two tiny girls forced to stay silent. They clung to each other, could hear above them the heavy feet, the clank of the steel-edged boot-heels against the rim of the manhole cover. They were waist-deep in the filthy water. The water pulled at their coats and scarves. Rats swam around them. They heard the echoes of boots, screaming voices.

The darkness began to swallow her. Rebecca's heart beat

rapidly as she tried to force the smells, the memories, away. She tried to concentrate on where she was, to get herself out from beneath the trailer, but the fragmented memories were stronger than the present.

Ruda snapped at Vernon that she could handle Mamon, all they had to do was their job, she would do hers. Vernon backed off and looked at Mike. They were radioed up to the main soundboard, ready to start the second half of the show. Ruda looked at Mike. 'Where is she?'

Mike was so concerned about Mamon that for a moment he looked blank.

'My sister. She was with you, wasn't she?'

Mike shook his head. 'She went back to the trailer.'

'Go and get someone to fetch her, she might have got lost. Tell her to stand by Grimaldi.'

Ruda was pacing up and down as the orchestra started the introduction to the second half. 'Mike! I don't want him with that bloody rifle. If he comes in with it, get it off him. Don't let him go in the ring with that goddamned thing.'

Mike nodded. He didn't even know where Grimaldi was, and he would not risk looking for him now. He signalled to one of the helpers to go and search for both Grimaldi and Rebecca.

Ruda edged closer to the entrance. She stamped her feet. She was wearing her second costume, a white jacket, black trousers and black boots, with black leather gloves. The white shoulders of the jacket were padded as she would be working with Wanton. He was very unpredictable and could give a nasty scratch. She was, in fact, always more worried about Wanton, though he was only a quarter of the weight of Mamon. Panthers were more difficult to train by far.

The release cages, used for the cats ready to enter the ring, were lined up. Three fully grown male lions paced up and down, as eager to get into the ring as Ruda. Behind the lions came the lionesses, behind them the tigers. The last two smaller cages held Wanton and Mamon.

'LADIES AND GENTLEMEN – PLEASE TAKE YOUR SEATS FOR THE SECOND PART OF THE SHOW. TAKE YOUR SEATS, PLEASE . . .'

Ruda peeked through the small aperture. The audience was still settling down, the orchestra ready to switch to her intro music. She turned to the standby board. The red and green lights were not on. She looked back to the ring, it was growing darker.

Ruda eased her head from side to side. Her neck was tensing badly. 'Come on, come on,' she murmured, her hands clenching and unclenching.

Mike received the radio control signal that Grimaldi was in position on the far side of the ring. Alone.

Vernon came to Ruda. He pressed his earpiece. 'Bit of a delay with a big party on the left bank of seats.'

Ruda clenched her hands. 'Shit! Any money it'll be the bastards that haven't paid to get in anyway.' She eased her weight from one foot to the next. She sighed impatiently, then gave a fleeting look around for Rebecca and asked again if Mike had located her. He smiled, gave the thumbs up. Ruda nodded. 'Make sure she's OK, will you?' Again he nodded, and Ruda breathed in deeply, exhaling on a low hiss. She looked again to the lights, then over to Vernon. He shrugged.

She closed her eyes trying to concentrate on the act, but she couldn't stop thinking of Rebecca. Her clothes . . . when she'd helped her change, she'd noticed they were of the finest quality, even her underwear. She had worn a big diamond ring! Ruda tapped her stick against her leg. Rebecca had four children, a rich husband. Her life must have been very different from her own. She wondered if Rebecca *had* tried to find her, tried as hard ... Ruda opened her eyes, forcing herself to concentrate.

'Are the pedestals set up?' Ruda asked no one in particular, as if she were on automatic pilot. Vernon replied that they were. Ruda looked again to the lights. 'What the bloody hell's going on? Come on, light up! Red, come on red ... green, red, green!'

Rebecca curled her body into a tight ball, hemmed in beneath the trailer. The colours came in rapid succession. She had to catch them, remember them. She had to remember each colour, she had to give them to Ruda. If she didn't give them to her sister, Ruda would be given no food, they would hurt her. She heard Papa's voice, saw the cards being laid out, red, green, blue ...

The red light flickered. 'Stand by, Miss Kellerman.'

Ruda stood rigid. She didn't see the draped entrance to the main ring, but instead the dark green curtain. The hand that drew the curtain open was always clean, nails painted red; manicured oval nails, and the beautiful blonde hair swept in a perfect coil. Her face with the painted eyelids, cheeks rouged and powdered as if she were an actress. The dark red lips were often parted in a half-smile. Ruda could see him behind the glass, he used to stand just a fraction to the right of Red Lips, one of his gloved hands resting against the high dentist's chair. They made a handsome couple. His oiled, slicked-back, ebony black hair, his chiselled features and immaculate uniform. When he smiled his teeth were even, white. As white as Red Lips's large, square teeth.

Rebecca looked like a doll: frilly dress, white socks and little black patent shoes. Once, when the curtain was drawn back Ruda saw that she had been holding a doll, and she had held it up for Ruda to see. A doll with orange hair and a china face, pink-cheeked, pink-lipped, with delicate china hands. Ruda had pretended that when they drew the curtain back she was looking into a mirror, seeing herself. It had calmed her, made the pain go away.

He made the unwrapping of a toffee like a gift from God, holding each end of the wrapper delicately between finger and thumb, as if afraid to get so much as a trace of toffee on his white gloves. Ruda's mouth was always dry, rancid, tasting of metal. She longed for the sweet, watched the elaborate unwrapping of the treat with wide desperate eyes. When he smiled, when he touched Rebecca's chin to indicate she should open her mouth, when he looked through the glass to Ruda and smiled that smile as he popped the sweet into Rebecca's mouth, Ruda could taste the sweet, soft caramel. The green film over her tiny baby teeth became sweet and delicious.

Days, weeks later when Red Lips drew back the curtain, Ruda could see Rebecca changing. The frilly white dress was dirty. What were they doing to her that made her mouth gape open? She could see the tears, see her fighting and scratching and sobbing, but she couldn't hear because the curtain draped a soundproofed cage. She was desperate to get to her sister, desperate to know what frightened her so much, what terrible things they were doing to her. She, too, would scream and scream, but Rebecca couldn't hear. No one could hear on the other side of the curtain.

What Ruda could not have guessed was that Rebecca's hysterical outbursts, her screaming, was because they were showing her what they had done to Ruda.

Vernon shook Ruda's shoulder, once, twice. She turned, startled. 'My God! Hurry, you've had the green light twice! Are you OK?'

Ruda took a moment to get herself focused, then she

nodded, licked her lips. They were repeating her intro music. She waited a beat, then walked into the ring. Cheers and loud applause greeted her entrance.

'LADIES AND GENTLEMEN – RUDA KELLERMAN!'

CHAPTER TWENTY

REBECCA REMAINED hunched beneath the trailer. Her head started to throb and she whimpered, prayed for it not to happen, not here. Someone was squeezing her brain. Then through the throbbing pain she heard his voice. He was saying over and over that she had been a bad girl, she had not tried hard enough, now she would see what she had done. They tied her to the chair. She was rigid with terror, screaming for them not to draw back the curtain. But back it moved, slowly, inch by inch. And there was Ruda.

Ruda's body was covered in weeping sores. They had cut off her hair. Rebecca could see the sores on her scalp, the wires attached to her head. She could see Ruda through the glass panel, see them propping her up – she was too weak to walk, too weak to stand up.

The little girl, unable even to hold up her head, smiled through the glass. The effort of lifting her hand drained her, but she gave a tiny, pitiful wave as if to say, 'I am still here. I'm still here, Rebecca.'

The pain was excruciating. Rebecca sobbed, buried her face in the mud. All she could see was Ruda's tiny wretched face. Was this the memory she had blotted out of her mind? The more she held on to the picture of Ruda, the more agitated she became, scratching the muddy ground with her fingers. She wanted the pain to stop, wanted the memories to stop – but they squeezed through, kept on coming. 'Please help me, somebody help me . . .'

But no one could hear, everyone was at the big top. She

couldn't stop them coming, another memory squeezing out. Rebecca could see herself in the frilly white dress, feel her bladder empty, urine trickle down her legs. She was afraid they would open the curtain, afraid to see what she had done to Ruda, and she tried desperately to remember what Papa wanted. Her face pressed into the ground as she sobbed. What was it he wanted? What *was* it?

Red – red – green – blue, red – red . . . roses are red, violets are blue, pass the colours from me to you . . .

Sixteen tigers, three lions and the black panther. The massive ring seemed to seethe with cats. Twice Ruda attempted to give the command for Roja to move to the red pedestal. Instead she repeated four colours rapidly. It was as if her mind was locked. Command after command was confused and the cats started to veer away from the pedestals and meander around the ring.

Vernon moved close to the bars and whispered urgently into his microphone. 'Hold back Mamon. Is he in the tunnel yet? Shit! Don't open the trapdoor yet, keep him in the tunnel. Repeat. Don't release Mamon, don't let him through. Get Grimaldi.'

Mamon moved stealthily down the tunnel and reached the midway gate just as it clanged shut in his face. He backed, ran at it again, angrily this time. Vernon used one of the long sticks, prodding him backwards. Mamon growled and swiped at the stick, but they got him moving back down the tunnel to the safety of his cage.

Ruda remained motionless, the pain across her eyes blinded her. The massive spotlights began to haze and stream out brilliant colours. Her voice was hardly audible as she began to repeat in a monotone: 'Red red green blue red red green.'

The cats became seriously disorientated. Almost in slow

motion the tigers, led by Roja, reverted in their confusion to the first part of the act, moving from the arena bars closer to Ruda, forming a circle around her motionless body. The audience was mesmerised, silent. No one knew anything was wrong. The orchestra played on; the conductor, who took his music changes with the act as it progressed, repeated the same music used for the pedestal pyramid. He turned, baton up, and seeing the cats forming a circle cut the music to a low drum beat . . .

Grimaldi opened the side trapdoor leading into the arena. He carried a long whip stick and the cats immediately turned their attention towards him.

'Roja, *up* . . . *red up* . . . *Sonia*, green, *Sophia*, blue . . . *up!*'

Ruda stared ahead, still mumbling colours as if unaware Grimaldi was in the arena. He came quietly, authoritatively to her side and took her left hand, smiling – but his eyes were focused on the cats.

'Jason . . . green. Good boy . . . *up, up!*'

The cats seemed relieved that order had returned. They began to return to the pyramid formation, Grimaldi all the while drawing Ruda gently back from the centre of the ring. He felt her hand tighten in his, but he kept his attention on the cats . . .

'You OK?'

Ruda gasped. She had completely blanked out and the realisation of what was happening made her freak for a second. Then she was back in control. They worked together, like a team, and the audience applauded as the cats sat poised on their pedestals. Grimaldi slowly handed more and more of the commands back to Ruda, standing a few feet behind her just in case he was needed.

Wanton began to leap from one high pedestal to the next, and the audience cheered. Grimaldi saw Ruda turn towards the trapdoor, expecting Mamon.

From behind her he said softly, 'No Mamon, Ruda. Finish the act on Wanton.'

Ruda was startled, confused again. Then she looked to Luis and gave a brief nod. As Wanton made his final leap to the top rung, Vernon passed the hoop of fire between the bars. Ruda took the flame torch and showed the audience the massive hoop. The orchestra picked up again. Ruda fixed the hoop to its stand, then stood back as she touched the cloth to set it alight. The entire hoop blazed, spotlights pinpointed the cats who held their position, waiting for the commands. The trapdoor to the tunnel was slid back in readiness.

Back at the cages the helpers, under Mike's supervision, cajoled and pushed Mamon back into his small cage. They had to move fast, push the cage out of the way in readiness for the cats coming back down the tunnel from the ring. The men were sweating with the exertion. Mamon was frantic, lunging at the bars, trying to swipe through his cage.

'Don't even try to put him back in his main cage, let him calm down. Get him out of the way. Come on, move it!'

The tractor was hooked up to Mamon's lightweight cage and wheeled out of the clearing. In the ring, Roja led off from his pedestal. He jumped through the hoop and ran straight to the tunnel. One by one the cats followed, leaping through the flames as the lights flickered and spun, their massive bodies moving with grace and agility, herding back down the tunnel to their cages, on command and in perfect formation.

Last to leap came Wanton. From forty feet in the air the cat sprang and for a moment the spotlight caught him in midair. He sprang from the lowest pedestal and upwards through the hoop in one fluid move, his sleek black body bursting through the blazing hoop, as if leaping into darkness.

The ring went black, and came up with Wanton draped over Ruda's shoulders. He remained relaxed, resting across her, impervious to the wild cheers. Ruda slowly bent on one knee, dropped her head down and Wanton sprang off and returned down the tunnel.

Ruda took Grimaldi's hand and they bowed together. As she leaned forwards she felt the ground give way beneath her feet. Grimaldi swept her into his arms, and smiling, waving, he carried Ruda from the ring, acknowledging the rapturous applause.

The safety barriers were dismantled fast and as the helpers carried out the gates, they saw Ruda assisted to a chair by Grimaldi. Water was brought and she drank thirstily, resting against her husband. She covered her face with her hands. 'Oh, God. Oh, God . . .'

She rocked backwards and forwards on the chair. Grimaldi angrily waved away Vernon as he came near. 'No. Leave us alone. Leave us alone, she's OK.' He didn't want anyone to see her this way, he knew how gossip ran wild and he didn't want anyone saying Ruda Kellerman was sick. They had six more weeks, the chance of going back to the States. Grimaldi lifted Ruda to her feet. 'Right, we'll go and get changed for the final parade, OK, Ruda? All right, lads, everything's under control, no problems. All the cats back in their cages?'

The tractor was drawing all the cages into their covered tent to be put back into their regular heavier cages. Mamon growled and hissed, swiping and butting the bars. Grimaldi assisted Ruda from the arena, then gestured for Mike. 'Be careful with that bastard, he looks mean,' he whispered. 'Don't move him if you're worried, we'll deal with him when he's calmed down.'

Mike nodded, murmured that he'd get the feeds ready, then looked back as Mamon roared out his fury. Mamon's cage rocked dangerously as it disappeared. Grimaldi didn't have to repeat his order: no one would go near him.

The cold air made Ruda gasp. Grimaldi put a protective arm around her shoulders. She took in gulps of air, her chest heaving. 'You were right, Luis. I should have listened to you. Seeing Rebecca again my mind went, but I'll be OK . . . maybe need to lie down for a while. I'll be OK.'

As Grimaldi walked her to the trailer he stepped on Vernon's yellow rain cape, left by the side of the steps. He chucked it aside and helped Ruda in. She sat down on the bunk, her head between her knees. Grimaldi poured a brandy and held it out for her. Ruda took the glass, cupping it in both hands. 'You did OK out there, you old bastard.'

He grinned and fetched himself a drink. 'Well, you know me, always did like a challenge.' He caught his reflection in the mirror, gave a chuckle. 'I felt good. It was good. It's been too long. Maybe if we did the first half we could work something up together. But I won't work with Mamon, he's your baby. If you look at the show tonight, you don't need him. You know what, we could maybe try and get another panther. Wanton's a great crowd-puller, they loved him. Did you hear that applause?'

Ruda inched off her leather gloves. Grimaldi was staring at himself in the mirror. 'I'll start working out, get this fat off me.' Grimaldi slapped his belly.

Ruda sipped her brandy, turned her face away. 'Where's Rebecca?'

He sat opposite her, the way they used to in the old days, his long legs propped up beside her. She didn't even notice his muddy boots on the cushions.

'Vernon's taking care of her, you just relax now.' Grimaldi cocked his head to one side. 'So, you want to tell me what happened? I mean, you blanked out, Ruda. In the middle of a bloody big act! It made the old ticker jump.'

He smiled, but Ruda paid him no attention, rested back against the cushions. 'You sure she's with Vernon?'

'Yes, just relax. Eh! Did you see how fast I shot through that trapdoor? They were going into the first part of the act again, Ruda. Ruda?'

She frowned, turned her head as if listening. 'You sure she's with Vernon? I feel her. God, it's hot, I'm so hot.'

Rebecca felt so cold. Her head ached and she didn't know how long she had been there. Had she fainted? She sighed, this had happened before so many times – hours blanked out, even days. She tried to clean her face, afraid if Ruda knew she was sick she wouldn't want her. She was about to crawl out from beneath the trailer when she heard Ruda's voice and the darker, heavier tones of Grimaldi. They were directly above her.

Ruda pushed open the trailer window. 'She has no memory of what happened. Strange, she remembers nothing. But she is to blame for what happened tonight, I know it.'

'Oh, come on. I don't think you realised the emotional impact it had on you to see her. I told you, I warned you.'

'You don't understand,' Ruda snapped.

'Well, why don't you help me understand, Ruda? I want to.'

She laughed. 'Oh, aren't you Mr Wonderful all of a sudden! You think I don't know why? Got your balls back tonight, did you? I may have fouled up, but you'll never replace me. It's my act, Luis, it's mine.'

'How the hell do you think you'd have got out of there tonight without me? Maybe I did get my balls back, but it's good I still had them! I admit I've been scared, Ruda, but tonight I faced it, didn't even think about it. The fear went, I had no fear, Ruda!'

'What the fuck do you want me to say? You did great, you did good. Now leave me alone. I need to think about something. Just leave me alone.'

'One of these days, Ruda, I might do just that.' He patted his pockets for a cigar. Finding one on the coffee table, he glanced around for some matches, and found some in the ashtray. He puffed the cigar alight, then turned back to her, prepared for a fight. He was surprised by the soft tone of her voice.

'I kept on seeing colours. I couldn't give the right commands – the pedestals, the colours of the pedestals.'

Luis looked at the burning tip of his cigar. He drew the ashtray closer and was about to interrupt when she continued. 'We were so young, they could only do the tests with colour cards . . .'

'You told me.'

'No, you don't understand. We could transmit coded colours – don't you realise how our minds are linked? That's what was wrong tonight. It was me, Rebecca—' She suddenly stood up. 'Oh, my God, where is she?'

'Look, just forget her for a second, OK? Sit down.' He poured another brandy, but Ruda was edgy, she knew Rebecca needed her – she could feel it.

Grimaldi handed her the brandy, stood over her. She stared into the glass. 'What was any of it for, Luis? We were just another one of his insane experiments. He tried with other twins, used to be able to discover which one could receive – it was always the stronger of the two, the weaker one was the transmitter.' She stared at the brandy, then passed him the glass. 'I don't want this. Here, you have it.' She breathed in heavily. There was a slight tremor to her entire body. She began to rub the scars at the side of her temples. 'The pain in my head. They clamped these wires to my head, they used to burn me, hurt my head. I didn't understand what they wanted. When I finally did, it was easy, I always knew what she was thinking. If she bruised a knee I felt it, could soothe her. I always knew, Luis, as if she was inside my head, you know?'

He said nothing, simply watched her.

'After – years after – I sometimes felt she was close. It was strange. You ever had the feeling? Like you know you are about to meet someone, see someone, and you do. Well, I would often have a strange feeling she was close by. It would just be a feeling, and I would concentrate on her, as I had at the camp, picture her face. But then the feeling would go away and we'd travel on . . . But so many times I was sure I had her. I remember once in New York, I was so sure she was close, and then here – remember me saying I had this feeling? Well, she's staying at the Grand Hotel. So close . . .' He saw her hand tighten into a fist. 'I knew, always knew she was alive.'

'Why did you never tell me about her? If you knew she was alive, we could have searched for her together, put ads in the papers, there's even organisations that—'

She interrupted him. 'I searched, I never gave up hope, that's why I started all my astrology letters, remember them? I was always thinking about her. You know, hoping maybe one letter would be from her. Everywhere I went I'd put ads in the papers, things that only she would understand, and I thought about her, concentrated on her.'

He sipped his brandy and waited, then encouraged her to continue. 'Go on, you concentrated on her and . . . ?'

'Oh, I would think about what she owed me, what I had done for her. Then I would become angry, so angry because I knew she had to feel me too, had to know I was alive, and I would curse her, hate her for not coming to me. I wanted her to come to me, I wanted to put my hands round her throat and squeeze her to death.'

'What?'

'She left me . . . she left me, Luis, she left me.' Her voice was hardly audible. He poured himself another measure of brandy, uncertain if what he was hearing made any sense. Ruda was silent, staring from the window.

When she continued her voice was stronger, but her hands still clenched and unclenched. 'I kept her alive. But when the Russians liberated the camp, I saw her from the hospital window hand in hand with a soldier. She was able to walk. Then the soldier lifted her up on to his shoulders. I saw him give her chocolate. And she never turned back, never came back for me . . .'

She began to bite her fingernails. 'She never tried to find me, Luis, I could have forgiven everything, if she'd just tried to find me. With her rich husband, her children, she had money, she could have found me. I know that now.'

'It was a long time ago, she was just a child. Maybe you . . .'

'Maybe I nothing, Luis. Everything with you is always maybe this or maybe that. I know she knew what they were doing to me, she knew because she could *see*. They starved me and fed her like a pig. They put these things on my brain, and they gave her dolls. She knew what they were doing to me.'

He wanted to comfort her, to put his arm around her, but she shrugged him away.

'Ruda, what difference does it make now? She's here, you're reunited. Now you can make up for all the—'

She screamed at him, '*You don't understand!*'

Luis put his hands up. 'Jesus Christ – I am trying, Ruda! I wasn't there, Ruda. All I know is what I hear, what you tell me.'

Ruda kicked out at the table. 'Shut up! You don't know. You weren't there.'

'I know that, sweetheart, of course I don't know.'

'No, you don't know. How could you? Nobody can even imagine what happened there. The longing, Luis, I longed for her so much, like a well inside me, that filled up and drowned me. I drowned with longing for her to come to me, to . . . make what had happened real.'

'Who told you? I can't follow what you're saying. Who are they?'

She sighed. 'The doctors, the nurses, the stupid fat-faced nurses in the asylum, they put me in with crazy people because there was nowhere else. Just forget, just forget. Take this, swallow this, this'll make you sleep. Nothing happened, it's all over. Forget? How could I forget when every white coat made me remember, every needle, every whispered voice terrified me.'

Her mouth was trembling. 'Forget? Tell me how? There were all these babies, newborn babies. But not one was alive, they were blue from the freezing cold. Some were bloody, some still had their cords dangling out of their bellies. Rebecca thought they were dolls. She asked if she could have one. But I knew, I knew they were dead babies. I knew, because from my window, where they kept me, I would see them being born, outside on the slabs in the snow. Don't touch them, Becca, they're not to play with. Don't touch them. But she had one, Luis, she had one in her arms.'

Her face twisted into a silent scream. She covered her mouth as if she couldn't stop opening the wounds which had been locked up inside for so many years. 'Every time I see a baby I remember. Papa told me it was all right, he used to stand with me and watch the babies coming. He was holding my hand, and I didn't think anything was wrong because he whistled. He whistled. He was always whistling.'

Luis felt sick. The image of the dead infants already haunted him. Ruda's hands plucked at her jacket. 'He liked me to call him Papa.'

She tried to say the name of the man whose face was buried inside her mind, the man who had tortured and tormented her and instigated an anguish that was indescribable. Deep beneath her scarred body, beneath her entire adult existence lay a consuming, confused and heartbreaking guilt. Slowly it began to surface. She was the little girl sitting on his knee, hands clasped round the sweet he had given her. The little girl who said, 'It's mine!' He had kissed her cheek, pinched her chin, teased her. She could hear his voice.

'Open it, you can open it!'

'No.'

'Don't you want it?'

'My sister, want it for my sister.'

He had laughed, jumped his knee hard so that she fell to the floor. 'What is your sister's name, I forget?'

'Rebecca.'

'Ah, yes. Is she well?'

Ruda nodded, and he crouched low, resting on the heels of his polished boots. He traced her cheek with his white-gloved hand. 'Tell me, do you feel pain when your sister is hurt?'

'Yes.'

He seemed delighted. He brought out a box of sugared almonds with a pink ribbon, gave a small bow, clicking his heels. 'These are for you and your sister.'

She reached out, but he withdrew the box. 'I want a kiss.' She stood on tiptoes, slipped her arms around his neck and kissed first his right, then his left cheek. He smelt of limes. With the box of almonds tucked under one arm, her hand in his, they walked into the hospital wing.

'Bring her sister. I want her sister! These are going to be my special twins.'

Grimaldi had said nothing, simply sat watching her, her

head bowed. She stared unseeing as the face of the monster emerged. The face of the man who had embraced the child with love, and yet committed heinous crimes against her tiny body. The being who had distorted and twisted her mind for some foolish experiment that meant nothing, benefited no one. Why had he never stood trial? Why had he never been punished? He had been free, the Dark Angel's wing had overshadowed her life. Alive, he had been living proof that no one cared, it had not happened. But it had. And the rage against him began to unleash.

Rebecca pressed her body against the side of the trailer. She could feel the rage rising inside her. For the first time she felt apart from it, as if watching it manifest itself. She could see her hands clenching and unclenching. When this had happened before, she had always lost control, had no memory of what occurred. But now she knew the rage was not hers, but Ruda's. Now their minds entwined, like an electric circuit fusing, ready to ignite . . .

Rebecca fought against its taking over, tried to reach for the trailer door, to call out that she was there, that she had not tried to find Ruda because she didn't know she existed, she had been forced to forget. Now the memories opened in a blinding, red-hot blaze.

Luis saw it happen and was helpless to stop it. He saw the rage explode from Ruda. Every muscle in her body tensed, the veins in her neck throbbed, her hands flayed the air, her mouth drew back in a terrible silent scream. But, above all, it was the madness in her eyes which made him freeze.

The rage she had held inside for so long, and the fury of her torment, made her blind to the fact it was Luis she attacked – she believed him to be the Papa, and she had to destroy him.

Mamon lay with his massive head resting on his paws. Mike, easing open the trapdoor, pushed the feed tray inside. Vernon was carrying bales of clean straw. He called across to Mike. 'Eh! I wouldn't try that, Mike. Leave it for Mrs Grimaldi. She's not in the arena, they'll be going into the parade any minute.'

Mike half turned, his hand still on the bolt of the trapdoor. At that moment Mamon lunged forwards, his whole weight hitting the side of the cage: the trapdoor flew open, knocking Mike off his feet, and Mamon was out.

Vernon dropped the bale of straw and threw himself out of the way, but Mamon wasn't interested in either of them; he was loping towards the open tent flap, churning up the sawdust. His roar of rage was terrifying in its volume and intensity.

'Oh, shit! Oh, my God! *Get the nets – fucking get the nets!*'

Word spread fast; within minutes the area was cordoned off and gatekeepers and parking attendants warned that no one was to be allowed beyond the barriers. The helpers ran towards the trailer park, their flashlights flickering as they questioned anyone who might have seen where Mamon had run.

As the panic spread the security men were alerted.

The grand parade was just drawing to a close, the audience cheering, flowers tumbling from the very top of the massive tents, balloons cascading down.

Thousands of chattering, laughing people streamed from the big tent exits. They gathered alongside coaches, or made their way on foot back down the road. Some ran to their parked cars. Children were carried in arms, overwhelmed by the excitement and now fast asleep, others ran whooping and screaming, carrying circus maps, toys and balloons.

The sky opened again with a heavy roll of thunder and more rain came lashing down.

Mike, in a state of nervous hysteria, made his way to the Grimaldi trailer. At the same time Torsen and his group headed back to their car, via the trailer park and inside the barriers.

Helen and the Baron were pushed and buffeted along by the crowd at the main circus entrance. They fought their way against the crowds to head for the trailer park barriers.

Inside his trailer Grimaldi tried desperately to control Ruda. She had overturned the table, ripped at the cushions. It was difficult to move out of her reach in the confined space. Twice he had caught her arms, but she had forced herself free. She scratched, kicked and tore at him. She herself heard nothing, the violent rage consuming her. She was biting, her jaws snapping like an animal's, her fury giving her an even more terrifying strength.

Grimaldi had hold of her by the hair. Ruda twisted, punched her elbow into his stomach and, as he released his hold and buckled over, dragged his head up, forcing him back. Her hands gripped his throat.

Rebecca banged and pushed at the door, hit it with the flat of her hand and then ran to a window, screaming to be let in. Ruda turned to the window. For a moment she was frozen, then she picked up a chair and hurled it at Rebecca's face. It shattered the window. Grimaldi got to his feet, but Ruda was going for him again. And Rebecca now punched at the glass, trying to heave her body through it into the trailer. A jagged slice of glass cut into her cheek, blood mingling with the mud. It made her look as crazed as Ruda. Her hand flew up to her face.

Ruda backed away, held her hand to her cheek as if she had cut herself. Then she reached out and hauled Rebecca inside, crushing her in her arms, holding her so tightly Rebecca couldn't breathe. It was a killing embrace, a furious protection. They were locked into each other, totally one.

Grimaldi grabbed hold of Ruda from behind, wrenched her away, but Rebecca screamed, making no effort to fend for herself, to escape. She felt as if she was being plucked out of her own body.

Grimaldi slapped Ruda's face hard, jerking her head from side to side.

'*You're killing her! Ruda! Ruda!*'

She seemed to deflate. He gripped her face in his hands. 'Ruda, it's me, *it's me*!'

Running towards the trailer, Mike screamed out, '*Ruda! Ruda!*' He appeared at the shattered window. 'He's loose, Mamon's loose! Nobody can find him, we've got the nets standing by.'

Ruda's punch sent Grimaldi crashing into the wall, banging against Rebecca. They fell in a tangled heap as Ruda ran out.

Rebecca started to scream and he crouched down beside her. 'Listen to me, stay here. Do you understand? Don't leave the trailer, I'll get someone here to help you, but stay inside.'

'Ruda, I want Ruda. Ruda, *Ruda*!'

Grimaldi lifted her off her feet, sat her down. 'Just do as I say. Don't leave the trailer. We'll sort everything out.'

Rebecca was shaking with terror as he threw the bench cushions aside, searched for his gun. In her confusion she believed he was going to shoot Ruda. She lurched towards him, clinging to his arm. '*No!* Please – please don't hurt her!'

Grimaldi pushed her roughly away. 'The hurting's been done. Just stay inside, *stay inside*!'

'She needs me. I have to go to her.'

He turned on her in a fury, wanting to slap her face. '*You are too late. Stay in the goddamned trailer!*'

Grimaldi slammed the door shut and ran towards the torchlights and shouting voices. Every available man formed a human wall cutting off the trailer area from the crowds. A disembodied voice shouted that Mamon had been spotted. He was behind the animal tents. Hand in hand the men walked forward, step by step, alert and watchful, drawing the chain of arms tighter as the helpers with the big nets ran to the clearing by the tents.

Ruda was running ahead of Mike, repeating over and over, 'Don't hurt him. Don't let them hurt him.'

Helen and the Baron were confronted by two parking stewards. The men pulled a barrier across the opening. 'Stay outside the barrier. No one is allowed inside.'

The Baron demanded to be let through.

'I'm sorry. No one can come into this area until we have clearance. Please wait!'

Helen tried unsuccessfully to explain they were to meet Grimaldi at his trailer. She was brusquely informed that no one was allowed beyond the barrier. The Baron stepped back and took Helen's elbow, pulling her away.

'But this is ridiculous, Louis, we've been told we can meet him.'

'Look over there. Can you see?' Louis pointed to the lights. Helen looked across the barriers. She could see the human chain of men, some still in costume, linked hand in hand, moving closer and closer.

'What's going on?'

The lights of the disappearing cars, the noise of tooting horns, car doors slamming, people shouting, all added to the confusion. The Baron and Helen saw a group being ushered by two gatekeepers.

'It's the inspector, Louis. Maybe he can help us.'

They hurried to Torsen, but he was unable to help them, as he too had been asked to leave. They all stared across at the lights. Two men ran into view carrying a large net. They shouted to the gatekeeper. 'They got him cornered on the open ground over by the rubbish bins. We're getting the nets around the back, just in case!'

Torsen stepped forward. 'I am a police officer. What's happened?'

The gatekeeper waved his hand to indicate they should all stay behind the barriers. 'Everything's under control now, sir. Just keep moving, please leave this area.'

Torsen looked to Rieckert, then to the Baron. 'What do you think's wrong?'

Again the Baron approached the gatekeeper. 'My wife is with the Grimaldis. Has something happened?'

The irate man banged the top of the barrier. 'Please. Just stay out until I've got clearance. It'll soon be all over.'

'What will, for God's sake?' Louis was furious. He looked back to the lights, and caught sight of Rebecca. He shouted, called to her but she disappeared out of sight. 'That was my wife. Please, please let me through!'

'No, sir. I'm sorry, this is for your own safety.'

'WOULD ALL CUSTOMERS PLEASE LEAVE THE PREMISES AS QUICKLY AS POSSIBLE. NO ONE IS ALLOWED NEAR THE ARTISTS' TRAILER ENCLOSURE. FOR YOUR OWN SAFETY, PLEASE REMAIN OUTSIDE THE BARRIERS.'

The Baron and Helen waited impatiently. Torsen and his group began to make their way back to the patrol car. The loudspeakers repeated the warnings. The barrier was now heavily guarded. A group of boys in jeans and T-shirts soaked from the rain tried to climb over. The gatekeepers ran to throw them out. Over-excited and unaware of the dangers, the boys dodged the gatekeepers, as if it were all a game.

Helen and the Baron eased back the barrier and made a

run for it, just as Torsen returned to assist the gatekeepers in ejecting the boys. They made their way towards where they had seen Rebecca. They could now see clearly the human chain edging closer. They went towards it.

Torsen and Rieckert found themselves in an ugly scuffle as the boys fought back. One boy threw a wild punch which caught Torsen on the nose and knocked him to the ground. He shot to his feet and gave the boy a good belting. 'I am a police officer. Now, do as you're told or I'll arrest you for disturbing the peace. Go on – out, get *out*!'

The boys trudged away. The gatekeeper thanked Torsen. 'There's a big cat loose, sir. That's what all the panic is about. Obviously I can't tell the kids, it'll cause mayhem, and then that kind will think themselves tough, try to get back in. But they've got it under control now. He's over on the open ground by the rubbish bins, that's what the nets were for.'

Torsen wiped his bloody nose. 'You sure they don't need a couple of extra hands?'

'Thank you, sir, but for your own safety just stay back there. It's all under control now. He's probably in the nets already!'

One of the clowns, his make-up still on, ran past shouting that they needed more men over on the far side. Torsen called Rieckert over. 'Come on, let's give them a hand.'

Rieckert and his girlfriend clung to the barrier. 'Maybe I should stay with the girls. No need for both of us to go!'

'Fine. You do that. Get them into the car. I'll see if I can help.'

He smiled at Freda. She told him to take care, and he kissed her. 'I will.'

*

Mamon had moved out in the open, then eased back, weaving in and out beneath the big trailers, his body low to the ground. They kept the burning torches stuck in the ground as the nets were set up. As long as they could see him, there was no panic. They preferred to wait until all the crowds had gone.

The human chain remained, the torches lighting the area reasonably well, and the nets began to be linked up, cornering Mamon.

Ruda pulled on a pair of heavy gloves and picked up a long pole, Mike following with a bucket of meat, as she pushed her way through. 'Thank you. Thank you everybody. But please stay back, please stay back! And keep quiet. Thank you.'

'He's under the big trailer with the red shutters, been there a good five minutes.' The trapeze artist was still in his tights and T-shirt. Ruda smiled her thanks and continued on. She entered the circle, two men breaking their hands apart, rejoining them as soon as she was through.

Ruda looked around at the strained, fearful faces. 'OK, everybody. I want to see if I can encourage him back out into the open. Those with the loose nets get in closer, but everybody stay back until I give the word. Please stay well back, he's probably panicky, but I can control him. Just stay back . . . and please keep silent.'

They did not need to be told twice: no one wanted to get in close. The boys began to bring out the barriers used in the act, to make an open-air caged arena. A tractor towed Mamon's main cage in close. When everything was quiet, Ruda moved further and further into the clearing.

The back wall of the tent cut off one route and now the barriers were cutting and hemming Mamon in on all sides. He eased between the trailer wheels, his fur flattened, his paws muddy. He squeezed out and darted under the second trailer, but the lights picked him out clearly, and the trailer was low. He struggled and began to swing his head, easing out backwards.

'Ruda, he's between the two trailers,' Mike called, then turned as Grimaldi moved behind him. Mike saw the gun, but said nothing, looking back at Ruda. 'They've got him trapped, sir. He's between the trailers on the far side.'

The cage was drawn closer, the trapdoor open. Mamon could see it directly ahead of him. He was fifty to sixty feet away from the clearing, standing in an alley and hemmed in by the trailers on either side. Behind him were the nets. The only clear route was ahead. He began a very slow walk, his front paws crossing over each other as he moved closer and closer to the arena. He paused, sniffing the air. He could smell Ruda.

'Good boy! Come on, come on, ma' angel . . . Good boy. Come to Mama, come on . . .'

Mamon was approaching her slowly, his eyes like glittering amber lights, his teeth gleaming. Panic made his chest heave, saliva dribbled from his open jaw. He was coming to her, she knew it and smiled encouragement. Ruda bent down slightly, whispered to him. He kept on coming, her voice quietening, soothing him. 'Come on, good boy. Come to Mama! He's coming, please keep silent. Don't unnerve him.'

Rebecca slipped under the linked arms of two men. They were confused for a brief moment, thinking she was Ruda. When they realised their mistake, it was too late to stop her – she was already hurrying between the trailers.

Rebecca saw the torches, saw the nets, but they meant nothing to her. She wanted to get to Ruda and she could see her, standing in the clearing.

Helen and Louis, now aware that the panic was because of an escaped lion, stood outside the ring of men. They watched, unable to see Mamon, but they could feel the electrifying tension.

Torsen joined them. Helen pointed across the ground,

told him they were still trying to get the lion back in his cage, but she hadn't seen him, just knew he was still loose. Louis tried to make out Rebecca in the flickering lights, but he couldn't see her, and looked back at Ruda. He was struck by the eerie likeness, her shadow streaming behind her, making her seem like a giant . . .

Mamon made his slow journey down the aisle between the trailers. Rebecca ran the last few yards between the trailers adjacent to Mamon and burst into the clearing.

'Ruda! *Ruda!*'

She was caught between Ruda and Mamon, unaware that the big cat was no more than twenty feet behind her. Mamon froze. Poised, head up, he sniffed the air, then swung his head low and growled, darting back fast. He ran crazily to the nets, turned again snarling with anger, wheeled around, ready to charge back into the clearing.

The men held the big nets in readiness: fifteen feet wide, six feet high, heavy poles linking the nets. If Mamon came close they could release the poles to drop the nets over his entire body . . . but he was wily, keeping his distance, moving further into the clearing. Now there was nothing – no men, no nets – between him and Rebecca. He snarled, lashed out with his paw.

Rebecca turned, saw Mamon, and looked back to Ruda in terror. Ruda's voice was soft, persuasive, cajoling and calm. 'Don't move. Stay perfectly still. Don't move, keep your hands at your side.'

She inched forward, moving a fraction to her right, keeping Mamon directly in her line of vision. Mamon tilted his head to the right, to the left. He stepped forwards, stopped. Crouched. He was ready to spring.

'Move to me, one step at a time . . .'

Grimaldi knew the cat was enraged enough to attack. He was sure of it and his face went rigid. He swore to himself at the stupid bitch, his heart thudding, but he knew that if he were to make a single move now it could be fatal for both women. So, like everyone else, he remained totally still, his hand gripping the rifle.

Rebecca took one step forward, her back still to Mamon. He was watching her. She moved forwards again, and he followed, still low on his haunches . . .

Grimaldi lifted the rifle, trying to release the safety catch silently, but the click made Mamon lift his head.

Ruda heard the slight noise, but did not take her eyes off Mamon. Her voice remained soft, calm.

'Don't touch me, just move very slowly behind me. You can do it, nobody will hurt you, Becca. Come on, I'm here. Ruda's here.'

Slowly Rebecca moved behind Ruda, becoming part of the giant shadow streaming behind her. 'Good, Becca, good. Now, when I step forward, you step back. But slowly, very slowly. Wait!'

Mamon hurtled from the aisle, his outline clear to everyone. He seemed to begin a lunge and then stop, his chest heaving as he glared around. The sisters remained together.

'Back! Mamon, back . . . *Ma' angellll!*'

The Baron tried to break through the human chain, but he was pushed back, forced to watch with everyone else the way Ruda slowly but surely moved closer to Mamon, placing herself in danger as, step for step, Rebecca eased away to safety.

Louis pushed forward and grabbed hold of Rebecca.

'Is she safe?' Ruda kept her voice calm, never taking her eyes off Mamon. 'Is she safe?' she repeated.

Grimaldi eased a step into the arena. 'I've got her, Ruda. Now back up to me, I'm about four feet behind you, just start backing towards me, sweetheart, I'm here . . . Ruda?'

Luis thought she was going to do as he asked. First Ruda

slowly lifted her right arm, let the whip drop, but remained in the same position. She lifted her left arm, both arms open wide, and there was a moment of total silence. No one moved, no one spoke. Luis, expecting Ruda to go back, stepped a fraction to his right, aiming the rifle and it happened in a split second.

Afterwards, everybody had a different version. Ruda did not move back, she stepped forwards. Mamon and Ruda seemed to move in unison towards each other, but he reared up on to his hind legs, then sat back on his haunches. His front paws seemed to embrace Ruda. Perhaps he was simply obeying a command, a command he was used to being given in the ring . . . *kiss*, and Ruda was in exactly the same position that she took in the ring when Mamon laid his paws on her shoulders, but now she was facing him and he was not on his pedestal. His massive paws enveloped her head and shoulders in what appeared to be a terrifying embrace. Did she give him the command? Nobody heard it, but she did say something. They clearly heard her say, 'Ma'angel.' Then the shots rang out.

The first bullet hit him in his right shoulder. He keeled forwards, and she was wrapped in him, his black mane hiding her face. His jaws screamed open as the second bullet hit him just above his right ear. The third bullet – all three in rapid succession – entered his right side, just below the elbow of his right paw. It struck his heart, but he was already dead. The big animal crashed forward still holding her, his weight crushing her, snapping her neck. She made no sound, no cry.

Four men had to ease him away from her. Both her hands held tightly to his fur, his blood covering her shirt. At first they thought one of the bullets must have hit her. Only when Grimaldi lifted her in his arms did they realise her neck had been broken. The big man held his wife, rocking her gently, sobbing. The men moved in closer, as if protecting him, shielding him. They formed a circle around him, and they bowed their heads.

Mamon's carcass was dragged away in the nets. In death he seemed pitiful, all power gone. His limp body was sodden from the rain, his claws and feet caked in mud. The three bullet wounds were hidden beneath his thick fur, but the dark blood matted his coat.

Helen and Louis Maréchal helped Rebecca to the first-aid room. She said nothing, seemed dazed, robot-like. By the time the doctor came to see her, she was in a complete catatonic state. She did not understand where she was, did not recognise Louis or Helen. When Dr Franks arrived an hour later, they arranged for her to be taken to his clinic.

Torsen sat in the patrol car, his face so pale it seemed almost blue. 'She's dead. The lion attacked her, she's dead . . .'

Rieckert swore. 'Shit! What a thing to miss. Wish I'd been there.'

Torsen shook his head. 'No. No, I don't think so. It was one of the saddest, most horrifying things I have ever seen. I don't think I can drive home. Will you drive us back?'

Rieckert drove and Torsen sat in the back seat, Freda holding his hand. She knew he was crying, but that made her feel even closer to him.

'She seemed to give herself to the animal. She had no fear, she seemed to embrace death. From where I was standing I could see her face . . . and she smiled, I am sure of it. She smiled, as if she knew she was going to die.'

Freda snuggled against his arm. 'I see it every day. I see those who are afraid to let go, and those who welcome the end. It's strange, when it's over for them all the pain in their faces is gone.'

He was quiet for a moment, rubbing his chin against her hair. 'I know she killed once, maybe twice. No one will ever

534

know exactly what happened and I doubt if I would ever have been able to prove it.'

Luis Grimaldi, wearing a big overcoat, stood by the stonecutter, whose overalls were white with dust. Even his face was ingrained with a fine film. The man's large, gnarled hands held the sheet of paper, the wind tearing at it, and the rain that had not stopped for days made the ink drawing run.

'Can you do it?'

'Yes. It'll take a while, and I'll need a very large block. It will cost – black marble is the most expensive. I have to have it shipped in from Italy.'

'That's immaterial. I'll pay whatever it costs. I've brought you photographs. If there's anything else you need, you know where to contact me.'

The stonecutter watched the big broad-shouldered man walk out of his yard. He carefully folded the damp sheet of paper. He had received a few strange requests for headstones in the past, but never one like this.

When the marble was chosen he set to work, taking great care. In truth, he relished the challenge and, as the massive head began to take shape, it seemed to take on a life of its own. He buffed and polished, then stood back to gaze in admiration at his finished work. He felt an enormous sense of achievement. This work surpassed any of the other angels who rested over the dead.

Grimaldi negotiated for all the cats to be bought by the Russian trainer. At first he had considered taking over the act, but every animal reminded him of her, and Mamon's empty cage broke him. It was over, there could be no going

535

back. He arranged for the trailer to be sold and when that, too, was bought by the circus management, there was nothing left to keep him in Berlin. He made no attempt to find Rebecca, but wrote a brief note, care of the Grand Hotel, giving details of Ruda's burial. He also sent Ruda's small black tin box, feeling that perhaps the contents would mean something to her sister. But he did not want to see her. He blamed her for the end.

Luis had no thought of what he would do next, where he would go. Having had his mind occupied for the weeks after Ruda's death, he suddenly found himself at a loss. Without Ruda he didn't seem able to function in the world to which he had introduced her.

He knew just one thing. He had to wait until the headstone was ready.

The sky was clear and cloudless the day he went to say his last goodbye. Grimaldi could see him immediately, towering above the other tombstones, and his breath caught in his throat. He had done something right. Immediately after Ruda's death, when he had been inconsolable, blaming himself, the tears he had shed had broken from him in gasping sobs. Now he wept gently, tears welling up and spilling down his cheeks.

He towered above her, his wonderful head resting on his paws, his black mane, his wide black eyes. His jaw was open in warning not to touch or trespass upon the grave. Carved in gold was his name. MAMON.

RUDA GRIMALDI

Died February 1992

A Wild Animal Trainer

May she rest in fearless peace

CHAPTER TWENTY-ONE

REBECCA HAD remained catatonic after the tragedy, and had no memory of Ruda's death. She was kept heavily sedated until Dr Franks felt she was mentally and physically strong enough to face the ordeal ahead of her.

Helen Masters had returned to France, but wrote regularly to and received detailed letters from the Baron. He explained Rebecca's sessions, as if writing the letters was in some way therapeutic for him. These sessions continued every other day, and gave time for Rebecca to accept and understand each new development. Under deep hypnosis she was able to recall the incidents that her adopted mother had sought to cover over. The pattern of breakdowns linked directly to the close proximity of Ruda. Whenever Ruda tried to contact her, be it out of hatred or love, the communication became distorted. Rebecca's rages, the self-abuse, even the attacks on her family were carefully listed and dated. Louis Maréchal worked diligently, checking each date against circus schedules. He determined that, in each case, even though she didn't know it, Ruda had been within a short distance of his wife.

Rebecca's later mental breakdowns had coincided with the arrival of Mamon in Ruda's life. Mamon's strong will, his aggression and wildness had forced Ruda to use all her willpower to train him. Reverting to the colours of the pedestals, she had reached Rebecca's subconscious. The result, when Rebecca was in close proximity, were the violent brainstorms.

Gradually, the jigsaw became complete. Rebecca was

taken back again to Birkenau. She gave horrifying pictures, but the descriptions were always from the eyes of a child. At times she seemed quite cheerful. She told them about all the babies, how she had wanted one as a doll. She chattered on, unconcerned, about the funny thin people, the wires, the other children. Then at one session she stunned Dr Franks by laughing.

'What is so funny?'

She described one of the young guards who used to play with the children. He used to rip up little bits of paper, put them on the end of his nose and blow them away like snowflakes. 'We called him the Snowman!' she said.

'Was this man kind to you?'

She fell silent, and Franks repeated the question. She whispered that he was not very nice, not all the time. Franks tried to find out why the 'Snowman' was not nice, but she was unsure, saying he would take them away across the wire fences, take them to the grey hot place where they baked bread. Whoever he took away never returned.

She talked for a long time about what her papa gave her, the white frilly dress, the white socks and patent leather shoes, and she said that she loved him.

She giggled a high-pitched giggle. 'I got a dolly with yellow hair. He said it was as yellow as the dirty Jews' stars.'

Often the sessions disturbed Louis. He felt a hopelessness, as if his Rebecca would never be returned to him. He had to walk out of the viewing room, but he always went back.

Six months after Ruda's death, Franks felt Rebecca was strong enough to delve more deeply, at times without hypnosis. She talked of the woman nicknamed Red Lips by Ruda. Franks surmised that the woman was the notorious SS woman Irma Griese, known for her beauty – and

538

remembered for her cruelty to the inmates at Auschwitz. Rebecca said she always smelt of flowers.

'Ruda said she wanted to be like her when she grew up. Red Lips used to wear her whip tucked into her boots, like a lion tamer, and when she was near, we didn't smell the bread. They made bread every day, every night in the big ovens. Papa told us that was why the flames were red, the ovens had to be hot for the sweet bread.'

The next session, Franks noticed a physical change begin. The child in Rebecca had gone, she was subdued. When he asked if she was feeling unwell her voice took on a strange dullness.

'My frock is dirty.'

Franks waited but she said nothing more. He reinstigated the hypnosis and, deeply under, she sat for this session, her head remaining bowed. She didn't smile, not any more.

'Where are you, Rebecca? Where are you?'

She slowly lifted her head. Her eyes were dead, her mouth gaped open. 'Ruda's gone with the Snowman.'

'Where are you?'

She spoke in a dull, almost drugged monotone as she began to describe the glass booth with the dark green curtain, the dentist's chair where she was lifted to sit down and face the curtain. Dr Franks could feel the child had gone; she seemed old now and wizened, yet she could have been no more than four. She described seeing what they had done to Ruda, how they would force her to look at her through the glass window.

'Papa took out her insides to show me. He said it was because I was naughty. Papa cut off her hair. Papa put something in her belly. Papa said it was a baby like me. Papa said I was a bad girl because I couldn't remember. I try, I try hard to remember! Try to feed her . . .'

*

After that particular session, she refused her sleeping tablets. She rang her bell, kept on ringing it. She didn't want Maja the nurse, she didn't want her husband, she wanted Franks. By the time he had been brought from his home she was hysterical, pacing up and down her room. When he let himself in, she turned on him.

'Why are you doing this to me? Why? Why are you making me remember these things? *Why?* You are killing me!'

'No, no, I'm not. I am helping you. These things happened to you, they are real events. You have to face them, go through them.'

'Why?'

'So that you can leave here, leave with your husband, to be with your children. These events happened. You have been denied the memory, and all I am doing now is opening your memory. If you wish it I can stop. It is entirely up to you.'

She went quiet and sat on the edge of the bed. 'I want to tell you something . . . about Ruda.'

Franks rested his chin on his hands, waiting. Rebecca plucked at her blanket as she explained how she had seen Ruda, seen her through the glass. Then she looked up. 'It was a mirror. I didn't see Ruda, it was a mirror.'

'I don't understand, what mirror?'

'He cheated me, he lied to me.' She twisted the blanket harder, round and round in her hands in a wringing motion. Franks quietly asked who had lied to her and she spat it out.

'Papa – lied! Don't you understand? It could not have been Ruda I saw.' Rebecca became greatly distressed, and Franks suggested that she rest. She wafted her hands. 'No, no, listen to me. You see I understand now. I mean, it wasn't logical, how could her hair have grown overnight? He didn't show me Ruda. It was me, in a mirror.'

She stood up and crossed to the window. She held the white-painted bars. 'I saw myself in the mirror. Not Ruda, but me, and then they gave me cakes, sweets, milk – and I ate everything, I saved nothing for her.'

Franks moved to her and held her shoulders. 'But you were a baby then. You cannot blame yourself, there is no guilt.'

'There is. She hates me. I ate and ate, and she went hungry.'

'Nobody hates you, and you should rest. Get some sleep before tomorrow. Rebecca?'

She sighed and turned, flopping down on to the bed. 'Rest? You open my mind all day and expect me to sleep at night? I am beginning to detest you, Dr Franks.'

She closed her eyes. 'They start now, even when I'm alone, without you. It's as if I cannot stop the past.'

'That's good. So, what have you remembered?'

'A soldier, the one who took me away from the camp. I remember . . . he took my hand, asked if I wanted some chocolate and I demanded another piece for Ruda because she was inside me, she needed a piece of chocolate, but . . . Please, please don't leave me alone.'

She became very upset again, and Franks assured her he would stay. He watched in silence as she stared at her own face in a small mirror, repeating over and over, 'It was a mirror . . .'

Franks stayed the entire night and was able gradually to piece together what it was she was desperately trying to release.

When the telepathy began to work beyond his first expectations, Mengele could not let Rebecca see that her sister had not been rewarded or fed as promised and instead attempted to trick her by simply placing a mirror across the booth's window. So, Rebecca did not see Ruda in the white dress, but herself . . . And the adult Rebecca was now able to realise the trickery. She was, however, consumed by guilt because she had not understood then.

Franks saw her wrestle with her conscience. 'How could I know? And Papa was very pleased with me, he kissed and cuddled me and one of the *Schutzhaftlings* took me over to the warehouse to choose a new frock. We passed the latrine cleaning group – they spat at me! One woman hurled mud at me, I remember . . . I remember the way they shouted after me. The children hit me, kicked me and I cried and cried. I said that when Ruda came back she would make them cry, too. I only wanted to show off my new dress – and they told me she'd gone with the Snowman. That she would never come back for me.'

Two days after Rebecca had been given her new frock, the camp was liberated. In the mayhem that followed the liberation, Rebecca and a number of other children from her ward ran into the main hospital wing. There she went from bed to bed, each one filled with dying children. She was trying to find Ruda, looking for Ruda, calling out for her.

Ruda was skin and bone. The lice crawled like black ants over her shaven head. Her skin was tissue thin, a deathly bluish white, and protruding from her stomach were tubes, tubes with dark congealed blood, left hanging. A filthy plaster only partially covered a jagged open wound in her distended belly. Rebecca saw the pitiful bundle of rags, and ran screaming from the sight into the arms of the young soldier. He had crushed her to him, he was crying. He carried her from the ward, not wanting her to see the corpses, the dying . . . Not knowing, unable to comprehend, that the child in his arms had lived and played among them.

The soldier carried her past the glass partition and, unwittingly, past the mirror . . . and Rebecca at last found Ruda – she was with her, in the soldier's arms. It was at this moment that Rebecca began totally and utterly to believe that Ruda and she were one being.

Franks, aware that the adult woman at last had emerged, discussed the last events of the liberation. He knew that when Mengele received news that the Russians were advancing he had determined to get rid of the evidence. He had commenced with manic energy to clear the camp of the dying; thousands lost their lives in the gas chambers only days away from liberation. Mengele himself had run, after destroying his experimental documents; they were burnt along with the corpses. As if he had wings, the Dark Angel had remained a shadowy nightmare for those who survived. Never brought to justice, never paying for his crimes against humanity, he subsequently haunted the living. The young survivors whose minds he had twisted, whose bodies he had tormented and crippled, were taken to hospitals and institutions. Many were separated, in a desperate bid to give them the medical care they needed so badly. Ruda and Rebecca were just two of the tragic children.

Rebecca was given many books from Franks's personal library, books carefully chosen by him, for her as an adult to accept and understand more fully those nightmare years. She was calm, often discussing what she had read. Then, late one afternoon, Maja sent an urgent call to Franks's home that he should return to the clinic immediately. There had been a development: Rebecca had become destructive, abusive and violent, not to herself or any of the nurses but, in a rage, she had systematically wrecked her room. As Franks hurried along the corridor, he heard her angry, hoarse screams, heard the terrible banging and thudding of furniture being hurled against the walls. He looked through the peephole in Rebecca's door, then instructed Maja to bring him a seat. He remained sitting outside the room until the banging and the screams subsided. It took another hour, and not until there was silence did he enter the room.

Rebecca stood by the barred window, her exhaustion evident as she turned to face him. She seemed utterly drained, her eyes red-rimmed from weeping, and he knew intuitively that this was not Ruda's rage – it was not Ruda rising to the surface again – but it was Rebecca's, her own unleashed blazing fury at what had been done to her. At long last it was out, and she had bravely faced it alone, she had embraced it like a primal scream, and she was cleansed.

After almost a year of treatment, Franks determined that Rebecca was now ready to be told the truth about Ruda. There was no hypnosis, they sat together in his lounge at the clinic. Even Louis was not allowed to be there, but he was waiting, as he had been throughout the entire year. Sasha had stayed with him at the hotel during her school holidays. Louis had taken care of her himself: no nanny, just father and daughter, and in the time they had spent together he had attempted to explain in simple terms her mother's illness. When Sasha asked if her mother was well again, Louis had hesitated, knowing his wife was at a critical stage. Franks had told him that being made aware of Ruda's death might mean a major setback for Rebecca, and to be prepared for it. Considering the mental anguish she had been subjected to, the impact of knowing that Ruda had been alive and now had died could possibly send her over the edge. An edge on which she had balanced precariously for years . . . Louis told Sasha only that they would know very soon.

He had been warned not to expect too much, even with the best results, that it could still be a long time before Rebecca was adjusted and able to return to Paris. He was

glad his daughter was with him at the clinic, he needed
her.

Franks began in a soft gentle voice, asking her first if she
could recall arriving at the circus. Rebecca surprised him,
looking at him with a tranquil, gentle expression on her
face.

'I know. I was wondering when you would tell me, but I
know. And I know her last words were to ask if I was safe
... I remembered days ago, but I didn't want to tell you, I
wanted to face it by myself. I needed time alone. She was,
you see, always the stronger ...'

'Do you blame yourself in any way?'

'Yes, of course. I endangered her, I ran into the clearing,
I was stupid, but ... I think she could have got him back
in his cage, she was very calm.'

She gave Franks a strange, direct stare. 'She was also
very disturbed, very confused. I wish, I wish we had found
you together, but ...'

Franks leaned forwards. 'But?'

'But we didn't. I think, throughout my entire adult life, I
have somehow been searching for a mother figure. I have
expected too much, loved too much – and given so much
pain to those I have loved. Now at last I have found her. She
lies within myself. Having mothered my sons, my daughters
– albeit at times distressed them, terribly – I think I have
found my first good, mothering experience ... with you.'

She smiled at him. 'You, doctor, have given me the
unconditional, loving acceptance I have always sought, the
support I have always needed, the understanding I have
craved. You have given me back my childhood, but most
important, through my relationship with you, I have
learned to accept and love myself, to give myself the kind
of caring that will heal me, heal from the inside out. I am

going to get stronger. I know that, because I want to live – for my children, for my husband, most of all, I want to do something with my life. My experience must be used, you must use me, reach out for others like me, Dr Franks, because I am strong now and I want to do this for me and for Ruda, who was the only mother I ever really knew.'

'But you are not Ruda.'

'No, my dear friend. I am Rebecca, just Rebecca, and I am whole – thanks to you.'

Franks couldn't help himself. He suddenly leaped from his chair and wrapped his arms around Rebecca. 'I love you, Baroness! You know what you are? A fighter. God bless you!'

Louis knew by the wonderful expression on Franks's face that they had at last broken through. Dr Franks held Sasha's hand, smiling warmly. 'You stay with me a few moments, Sasha.' He looked at Louis. 'Go and kiss your beautiful wife, Baron.'

She was leaning against the chair. Louis was unable to contain himself: he sobbed as he lifted his arms to her. There was no space, no void – he clasped her to him, as if afraid ever to let her go. They kissed, clung to each other.

'I'm coming home, Louis. I want to come home.'

Dr Franks tapped on the door, peered round, asked if another visitor could be made welcome. Opening the door wider, he ushered in Sasha. The child hung back a moment, then ran into her mother's open arms, and Rebecca swung her round and round, bent down on her knees, cupping the girl's face in her hands. 'What a wonderful surprise! Sasha!

My beautiful Sasha. I am your mama, and she's coming home! Kiss your mama hello!'

Snow was falling as the Mercedes made its slow progress through the snowbound streets. Rebecca sat between Louis and Sasha; on her knees was Ruda's black treasure box. She opened it, and Sasha looked inquisitively inside.

'Do you know what this is?' Rebecca held up a small hard object. 'It's a potato!'

'But it looks like a stone, Mama.'

'When we were in the camp they were prizes worth keeping, and my sister, Ruda, kept this potato, oh, for so long, and then when we came to eat it . . . it was hard, like a small rock. It became her talisman, this funny little hard potato.'

The car drew to a halt outside the clinic, and Dr Franks hurried from the doorway, woolly hat pulled down and a big scarf wrapped around his neck. The Baron opened the door for him and, squashing himself into the back seat, Franks let Sasha sit on his knee, as the chauffeur drove away.

'Give this to your mama, Sasha.' Franks passed over a small square leather box.

Sasha gave it to her mother, and watched as Rebecca lifted the lid. It was a gold Star of David. Rebecca bent her head and kissed it, then rested against Franks's shoulder.

'Thank you,' she whispered, then gave a soft laugh. 'You know, Dr Franks, I think you have telepathic powers! This morning, before these two were even awake, you know what I did? I went to a synagogue to pray for Ruda. I have never been in one before. It felt . . .'

Dr Franks had to look away, out of the window to the snow-laden streets. He felt very emotional. 'It will feel better. Go again, go for the faith denied you, denied Ruda!'

They fell silent, a comfortable warmth between them. Only when they were within half a mile of the cemetery did Rebecca straighten. She lifted her head, still resting against Franks's shoulder, as if sensing a presence. She knew Ruda was close by.

The car stopped and Franks opened his door. Sasha bounded out, but he caught her hand, held it tightly. 'Just wait a moment, Sasha.'

The Baron took his daughter's other hand, about to offer his arm to Rebecca, but Franks gave him a small wink, an indication to let her walk alone.

'But she won't know where the grave is.'

Franks smiled. 'She will.'

Rebecca walked on ahead, at first unhurried, then quickened her pace. Hand in hand, Dr Franks, Sasha and Louis looked on as Rebecca suddenly began to run. She didn't pause, knew intuitively where she would find her. Threading her way between the big dark tombstones, across the narrow, snow-filled lanes, her feet left an impression with every step.

Grimaldi had chosen not just the headstone, but the plot where Ruda lay. It was separated from the other graves by a semi-circle of high trees. The sun broke through the grey sky, streaking brilliant shafts of light which glanced off the trees above her tomb, making a delicate white crystal cradle over the wondrous black marble head of Mamon. He roared in icy silence, protecting his beloved beneath him.

Rebecca stood staring at Mamon, then slowly she knelt down and placed the treasured potato stone between his paws. She let her hand rest a moment, and closed her eyes. She didn't weep, but drew from the cold, hard black marble a soothing calm. 'Goodbye, Ruda, I'll come back to you every year,' she whispered.

*

Dr Franks followed, watching Rebecca, now hand in hand with her husband and daughter. He felt a great sense of achievement and a fatherly pride.

The snow had melted in the wintry sun, it trickled in tears from Mamon's sightless eyes. Franks knew there were tears still to be shed, lost souls to be reunited. Memories that must not be forgotten, or hidden, but kept alive so that the living will never forget. Must never forget.

Lynda La Plante
The Legacy £5.99

'A saga to end all sagas, a blockbuster of a novel'
SUNDAY EXPRESS

1905–1945

THE LEGACY

was a curse . . .

For Hugh – the hard-drinking, two-fisted lion of the Welsh valleys. For his loyal daughter Evelyne – who lost her heart and her father's trust to the charm of a travelling gypsy. And for handsome prizefighter Freedom – saved from the gallows to do battle for the heavyweight championship of the world . . .

From the poverty of the Welsh pit valleys to the glories of the prize ring, from the dangers of Prohibition America to the terrors of Britain at war, Lynda La Plante begins the bestselling saga of their lives and their fortunes . . . and the curse that made their name . . .

'A torrid tale of love, intrigue and passion . . . packed with glamour, big business and big, big money'
DAILY EXPRESS

This Pan edition contains Books 1-5 of *The Legacy*, first published in hardback by Sidgwick & Jackson. Books 6-14 of *The Legacy* appear in *The Talisman*, also available in Pan Books

Lynda La Plante
The Talisman £6.99

1945–1980

THE TALISMAN

is the key to a fortune . . .

For Edward – the brilliant scholar who inherited his father's looks . . .
and his father's curse. For Alex, his brother, whose quest for revenge
fuelled an empire built on corruption. And for Evelyne and Juliana, the
fourth generation, still haunted by the secrets of their family's past.

From the gold mines of South Africa to the boardrooms of the City of
London, from the risks of the casinos to the heady glamour of the
London fashion, Lynda La Plante continues the bestselling saga of a
family's lives and fortunes . . . and the curse that made their name . . .

'A torrid tale of love, intrigue and passion . . . packed with glamour
and set against the London world of big business and big, big money'
DAILY EXPRESS

All Pan Books are available at your local bookshop or newsagent, or can be ordered direct from the publisher. Indicate the number of copies required and fill in the form below.

Send to: Macmillan General Books C.S.
               Book Service By Post
               PO Box 29, Douglas I-O-M
               IM99 1BQ

or phone: 01624 675137, quoting title, author and credit card number.

or fax: 01624 670923, quoting title, author, and credit card number.

or Internet: http://www.bookpost.co.uk

Please enclose a remittance* to the value of the cover price plus 75 pence per book for post and packing. Overseas customers please allow £1.00 per copy for post and packing.

*Payment may be made in sterling by UK personal cheque, Eurocheque, postal order, sterling draft or international money order, made payable to Book Service By Post.

Alternatively by Access/Visa/MasterCard

Card No. ☐☐☐☐☐☐☐☐☐☐☐☐☐☐☐☐☐☐

Expiry Date ☐☐☐☐☐☐☐☐☐☐☐☐☐☐☐☐☐☐

Signature _____

Applicable only in the UK and BFPO addresses.

While every effort is made to keep prices low, it is sometimes necessary to increase prices at short notice. Pan Books reserve the right to show on covers and charge new retail prices which may differ from those advertised in the text or elsewhere.

NAME AND ADDRESS IN BLOCK CAPITAL LETTERS PLEASE

Name _____

Address _____

_____

_____

_____

8/95

Please allow 28 days for delivery.
Please tick box if you do not wish to receive any additional information. ☐